T0246290

THE ICARUS CHANGELING

BAEN BOOKS by TIMOTHY ZAHN

THE ICARUS SAGA
The Icarus Plot
The Icarus Twin
The Icarus Job
The Icarus Changeling
The Icarus Needle (forthcoming)

Battle Luna (with Travis S. Taylor,
Michael Z. Williamson, Kacey Ezell & Josh Hayes)

Blackcollar: The Judas Solution
Blackcollar (contains *The Blackcollar*
and *Blackcollar: The Backlash Mission*)

The Cobra Trilogy (contains *Cobra,
Cobra Strike,* and *Cobra Bargain*)

COBRA WAR
Cobra Alliance
Cobra Guardian
Cobra Gamble

COBRA REBELLION
Cobra Slave
Cobra Outlaw
Cobra Traitor

MANTICORE ASCENDANT
A Call to Duty by David Weber & Timothy Zahn
A Call to Arms by David Weber &
Timothy Zahn with Thomas Pope
A Call to Vengeance by David Weber &
Timothy Zahn with Thomas Pope
A Call to Insurrection by David Weber &
Timothy Zahn with Thomas Pope

For a complete listing of Baen titles by Timothy Zahn,
and to purchase any of these titles in e-book form,
please go to www.baen.com.

THE ICARUS CHANGELING

TIMOTHY ZAHN

BAEN

THE ICARUS CHANGELING

A Baen Books Original

Baen Publishing Enterprises
P.O. Box 1403
Riverdale, NY 10471
www.baen.com

ISBN: 978-1-9821-9348-5

Cover art by Dave Seeley

First printing, July 2024

Distributed by Simon & Schuster
1230 Avenue of the Americas
New York, NY 10020

Library of Congress Cataloging-in-Publication Data

Names: Zahn, Timothy, author.
Title: The Icarus changeling / Timothy Zahn.
Description: Riverdale, NY : Baen Books, 2024. | Series: The Icarus Saga ; 4
Identifiers: LCCN 2024005427 (print) | LCCN 2024005428 (ebook) | ISBN 9781982193485 (hardcover) | ISBN 9781625799678 (ebook)
Subjects: LCGFT: Science fiction. | Novels.
Classification: LCC PS3576.A33 I26 2024 (print) | LCC PS3576.A33 (ebook) | DDC 813/.54—dc23/eng/20240207
LC record available at https://lccn.loc.gov/2024005427
LC ebook record available at https://lccn.loc.gov/2024005428

Printed in the United States of America

10 9 8 7 6 5 4 3 2 1

THE
ICARUS
CHANGELING

CHAPTER ONE

As my father used to say, *When you find yourself in the middle of nowhere, odds are you're hunting someone, being hunted by someone, or been ordered there by someone. The first two someones probably aren't any happier to be there than you are; the third someone probably doesn't care.*

Alainn wasn't exactly the middle of nowhere. I could grant it that much. Actually, the planet as a whole was a reasonably well-respected regional hub, with a couple of Spiral-1 Class landing fields in each hemisphere that ran a brisk traffic in transshipped goods from the planets around the system. When Selene and I had first been ordered there, I'd had visions of decent barbeque and better-than-decent Dewar's scotch.

Unfortunately, even the most advanced planet had patches of nowhere. On Alainn, that nowhere included the town of Bilswift.

And like my father's saying went, I was pretty sure Admiral Sir Graym-Barker had the third category pretty well covered.

"Interesting," Selene murmured as we walked down the zigzag ramp configuration from the *Ruth*'s entryway. The Spiral-1 Class fields had landing cradles that would let us reconfigure the zig-zag into a ramp that much more conveniently led straight across to the edge of the cradle. The Bilswift field, unfortunately, was limited to four flat pads, which meant a lot more climbing if we wanted to get into or out of our ship.

Still, I supposed I should be grateful that Bilswift had even that much. The nearest alternative was a good eight hundred kilometers away, with the nearest fancy Spiral-1 field five thousand kilometers farther than that, on the edge of the regional capital of Tranlisoa. Aside from the daily suborbital shuttle from Tranlisoa to Bilswift I had no idea what kind of long-range transport options the region had. Anyway, the thought of leaving our ship that far out of reach would have made me twitchy even at the best of times.

Which, naturally, this wasn't.

"What's interesting?" I asked, looking around as we continued downward. If the spaceport was no great shakes, the town stretching beyond it didn't look a whole lot better. Bilswift's collection of low, unimpressive buildings were laid out along a mix of wide and narrow streets, with patches of trees or other greenery popping up at seemingly random locations. It was hard to make definitive judgments from a distance, but it looked like the larger buildings—businesses and some light industry, the data files said—were concentrated along the wider streets while the smaller ones were private homes or small apartment complexes filling in the space along the narrower ones.

"The mix of aromas," Selene said. "I smell a lot of different cooking styles."

"Human or other?"

"Mostly human."

"Reasonable," I said, nodding. The Narchners and Ulkomaals had been putting colonies on Alainn for two hundred years, starting near the equator and spreading out in both directions, but other species hadn't really gotten into the game until sixty years ago, with humans bringing up the rear ten years after that.

But unlike most of the others, who were looking for comfortable living space, the human entrepreneurs had targeted locales with a mix of economic expansion possibilities. The Bilswift area had caught their eye, offering lumber, exotic seafood, and possible tourism. The tourism angle hadn't worked out as well as the developers had hoped, but the other two were keeping the community's financial head above water.

Still, the city's history meant it had remained very much dominated by humans, which fit with Selene's analysis.

Not that I could smell much of anything except the salty

ocean air around us. But I didn't doubt her analysis for a second. The breeze was light, but it was coming from the east, which meant it was carrying traces of the entire spectrum of Bilswift's aromas toward us.

I was used to Selene's magic myself, of course. She and I had been together for many years, first as bounty hunters, then as crocketts, then as whatever the hell our official position was these days with the Icarus Group. But Kadolians were extremely rare in the Spiral, and their hypersensitive sense of smell was guaranteed to surprise the socks off most of the rest of the population.

More than once I'd considered parlaying Selene's talents into bar bets and free drinks. So far I'd resisted that temptation.

"It's the two unfamiliar ones that concern me," she continued, an unhappy look in her deep-set gray cat's-eye pupils. "One of them seems to be Patth."

"*Seems* to be Patth?" I echoed, frowning. It wasn't like Selene hadn't had plenty of experience smelling Patth cuisine, after all. Way more experience, really, than either of us had ever wanted.

"Yes, seems to be," she confirmed. "There are distinct Patth elements, but there are … variations from the ones I'm familiar with."

"Maybe it's their version of gourmet cooking," I said, feeling my stomach tighten as I eyed the low, tree-covered foothills to the east that ran between the higher mountains in the near distance right down to the edge of town. Add in the ocean to the west, a wide river bordering the city to the north, and more encroaching forest to the south, and Bilswift took on a definite sense of claustrophobia.

I'd hoped we could finish the job the admiral had sent us here for and get out of town before the Patth arrived in force. Clearly, we were too late.

Unless …

"Any way to tell from the strength of the aroma how many Patth are chowing down?" I asked. "I'm wondering if what you're smelling is just the advance team."

"You mean it might be an upper-class variant?" she suggested.

"Exactly," I said. "If we're talking an organizer or conciliator, maybe even a sub-director if Nask has sent someone ahead, then the archeologists and diggers the admiral said were on their way might not have arrived yet."

"That's possible," Selene said, her eyelashes fluttering as she tried to sift the more elusive aromas from the air. "Either way, there's no way to tell the number of Patth by the strength of the aroma."

"Either way, the clock's ticking," I said. "I'm thinking maybe we should hit the ground running. A quick drive up into the mountains as soon as we can grab a runaround and see if we can at least figure out whether there's anything up there that was worth burning through hyperspace at plus-thirty for."

I peered off to the west. "In fact, with a good four hours of daylight left, we might even be able to finish off the whole thing."

"We can try," Selene said, more cautiously. "Uh-oh."

I followed her pointing finger. A middle-aged and decidedly overweight Ihmisit was trundling toward us at a speed usually reserved for younger members of her species. She was carrying an info pad, and as her arms pumped up and down I spotted the spaceport logo on the back of the pad.

I winced. So something both official and urgent.

Terrific.

We reached the bottom of the zigzag about three steps before the Ihmisit reached us. "Stop," she puffed as she came to a halt. "No farther. You are"—she paused to look at her info pad—"Gregory Roarke?"

"I am," I confirmed, focusing briefly on the shiny PERRIFIL nameplate on her collar. "Is there a problem?"

"Yes," she said, gesturing up toward the *Ruth*. "You must vacate this spot immediately. It has been reserved."

"Absolutely," I said firmly. "It's been reserved by *me*. Six days ago, and I have all the proper paperwork."

"The promise of the paperwork has changed," Perrifil said, her attitude starting to come back in proportion with her breath. As my father used to say, *Never be out of breath if you're trying to pull rank, especially if you're a mid-level bureaucrat. It just makes people laugh.* "A Patthaaunuth representative has requisitioned this spot for an incoming ship, which may be here at any time. Furthermore, a Ylpea ship is due in three days' time. You must therefore depart immediately."

"I see," I said. So whether the Patth cooking Selene smelled was just the advance team or the team plus some diggers, they had another batch of the latter on the way. I had no idea what the Ylps could possibly want in Bilswift, but unless the Patth had hired them for some reason they weren't likely to be a problem.

What *was* going to be a problem, as Perrifil had already pointed out, was that the *Ruth* was currently occupying the fourth of the spaceport's four landing pads. If we got chased off, even if the Ylps took the slot away from the incoming Patth, the fact that the Patth were already here meant that us getting knocked that far out of position would likely lose us the race to the pot of gold.

And that could be disastrous. Admiral Graym-Barker and his Icarus Group were currently locked in a quiet but furious race with the Patth to locate and grab more of the portals that had been left behind by a mysterious and long-vanished species Selene and I had dubbed the Icari.

As far as anyone knew, the Icarus Group was currently ahead of the game. They had three full-range Icarus portals in their possession, huge double-sphere devices that could be set to instantly send a traveler to any of potentially thousands of other portals like it. They also had a pair of what we called Geminis, portals that were exclusively dyad-linked to each other. The Patth, in contrast, had only a single Gemini pair.

The big caveat here was that those two Geminis were all we *knew* they had. There were indications that the mahogany-skinned little rotters had known about the portals and been hunting them a lot longer than the seven years or so since Jordan McKell and his band of misfits had stumbled across the *Icarus* and subsequently put humanity onto what had once been the Patth's private playing field.

But one way or the other, that score was likely to change in the next few days. Graym-Barker had intel that strongly suggested there was a new portal half buried in the forests east of Bilswift. The Patth had a team in place and more on the way.

The Icarus Group, in contrast, had Selene and me. And as with any game, sheer weight of numbers would eventually win the day.

But as my father used to say, *If you can't beat 'em at their game, change the game.*

Perrifil was still standing there, presumably waiting for me to apologize for inconveniencing her and the entire Bilswift Spaceport operations department and promise to get the *Ruth* out of there as soon as humanly possible. "I see," I said again. "I presume both groups want the pad undamaged?"

Perrifil's insectoid antennae twitched at the odd question. "What? Yes, yes, of course they will. Why such a question?"

"Because if I lift now, it won't be," I said. "Our portside

thruster is on its way to losing a couple of collimator vents. If even one of them goes, so does this pad. *And* probably a couple of the others along with it. Not to mention the ships currently occupying them."

Perrifil looked up at the *Ruth.* "Why didn't you report this before you landed?"

"Because it didn't flag until we were already on the ground and powering down."

"You did not report it then, either."

"Because I need to do a complete diagnostic before I can tell the mechanics what I need them to do," I said, putting as much strained patience into my voice as I could manage. Ihmisits were better than the average alien at reading human vocal nuances, and I needed to impress on her the seriousness of the situation. "The diagnostic is running now. As soon as I get the full report I'll go to the maintenance office and see what they can do for me."

She looked up at the *Ruth* again, probably wondering how she was going to explain this to whichever high-level Patth had ordered us kicked out. "Perhaps we could carry it elsewhere?" she suggested.

"That might work," I agreed, sifting rapidly through my options. If the supposed damage to the collimator vents had also run fracture damage to the longitudinal modulator feed line . . . "I assume Bilswift Spaceport has insurance that will cover any additional damage that might ensue?"

Her antennae twitched again. "*Additional* damage?"

"As in what lifting the *Ruth* could do to the longitudinal modulator feed line," I elaborated. "And of course, if the portside thruster has a problem, chances are the starboard thruster has one, too, in which case *that* modulator line could also be damaged. Still, a lift and move would probably only run you seventy or eighty thousand commarks. I just want to make sure you've got that possibility properly covered before I sign off on it."

"Yes," Perrifil muttered. Mid-level bureaucrat, all right, with enough rank to deliver messages and threats but not enough to handle major policy decisions. "If I order expedited repairs, how soon can you leave?"

"Depends on how much is wrong," I said. "As I said, I won't know that until the diagnostic is finished."

"When will that be?"

"I was going to check on it after I touched base with you in the operations office," I said. "Now that you've saved me that trip, I can go do that right now. Unless you have more you'd like to chat about?"

"No," she said. "Go. Report your damage and repair needs as soon as you can."

"Absolutely," I promised, giving Selene a nudge. "Okay, Selene. Back we go."

Selene waited until the hatch was sealed and we were heading to the bridge before she spoke. "I think she was convinced," she said. "But it's difficult to separate suspicion from anxiety."

"I'm guessing it was probably some of both," I said as I sat down at the helm. Fortunately, I'd started a diagnostic as a matter of course as soon as I'd powered down the ship, so I wasn't going to be suspiciously late with my report. Even more fortunately, way back in our bounty hunter days I'd added the capability for planting false readings for alibi purposes and never gotten around to removing that programming. "Whoever the Patth is who's having dinner out there, I'd hate to be the one to tell him he's going to have to go to Plan B."

"I would guess Plan B involves chasing off one of the other three ships," Selene warned. "If so, that won't take very long."

"I know," I said, scowling at the data scrolling across the display as I considered which set of semi-catastrophic failures I wanted to add in. "And it gets worse. The only way to maintain this bluff is to let the mechanics tear off the collimator vents or something else equally vital. Once they start, we may be stuck here."

"With a Patth ship on the way."

"With *another* Patth ship on the way," I corrected her grimly. "At least one of our three neighbors has to belong to our gourmet diner across town." I frowned, throwing her a look. "It's not Nask, is it?"

Selene's pupils indicated a negative. "I didn't smell him."

"Yeah," I said, turning back to my board. "Okay."

Which struck me as odd, because if there was one place Sub-Director Nask ought to be it was here. He held the Patth mandate for portals and portal retrieval, and he was not the kind of person it was safe to lock horns with.

In the old dramas I used to watch as a kid, this would be

the point where the hero confidently proclaimed that he and his partner had the enemy outnumbered. But as my father used to say, *Don't pattern your life after media heroes. They always have better writers than you do.*

"Maybe he's on the incoming ship," Selene offered into my thoughts.

"Or won't bother landing but will just park the *Odinn* in orbit and direct the operation from there," I said. "Or will stay home and recuperate like his doctors probably keep begging him to do."

"I don't see Nask as being the sit-around type."

"You also didn't see how badly he was injured," I pointed out.

"No," Selene said quietly, a quick mix of revulsion and compassion flicking across her pupils. "I wonder if they've taken the mandate away from him."

I shrugged. "After Kanaloa they'd be crazy to do that," I said. "Still, we've seen Patth do stupid things before." I gestured at the display. "In the meantime, let's see what we can do to create the maximum repair time from the minimum of damage."

"And the maximum cost, too?"

I sighed. "Unfortunately, those two factors do often seem to coincide."

In the end we came up with a package of one collimator vent, a backscatter sensor cluster, and two modulator feed-line joints. Long on repair time, short on repair parts, and we could probably safely blast our way off Alainn if we absolutely had to. Estimated completion time: three and a half days.

"Five days," the mechanic foreman said flatly. "*If* you're lucky and we can find the parts we need."

"If we're not and you can't?"

"Six days. Maybe seven."

I made a show of scowling out the office window. In theory, Selene and I should be able to get through Graym-Barker's job in a day or two at the most. But an additional three to five days' worth of excuse to stay put might not be a bad thing. Especially since we *could* get out of here sooner if we absolutely had to. "Fine," I said, with an equally showy sigh. "Just get the ship working properly again."

The expression on his face suggested that *working properly* was a goal the *Ruth* probably hadn't achieved in years. But he just nodded and tapped the spot on the info pad where I needed to sign. I did so, handed over the five-hundred commark deposit, and ushered Selene out of the office.

Next door was the operations office, where Perrifil was back at her desk. On a hunch, I opened the door and stepped inside. "Excuse me?"

She looked up, and from the annoyed twitch of her antennae I could tell she remembered me. "Did you get your repairs set up?" she asked.

"Yes, thanks," I said. "Unfortunately, it's going to take several days. I'm sorry about the inconvenience to your Patth friend's incoming ship. If you could tell me where to find him, I'd be more than happy to explain the situation and apologize to him in person."

"He is not my friend, and I don't know where to find him," she said, a bit frostily. "Perhaps the Panza can tell you."

"Thank you," I said. "Where do I find the Panza?"

"At his café, of course," Perrifil said shortly. "Good day."

Clearly, she was ready to be done with me. "Thank you," I said again, and beat a quick but dignified retreat.

Selene was waiting outside where I'd left her, working her info pad. "You heard?" I asked.

She nodded, her pupils showing concentration. "Panza's Café is about three kilometers across town, on the dividing line between the Grymary and Wellington districts."

"Of course it is," I growled, looking around. The data files on Bilswift had said there were vehicles available for rent, but the runaround stand at the edge of the spaceport was devoid of vehicles. As we came closer I saw that the price board under the wide overhang carried a CLOSED UNTIL FURTHER NOTICE sign that was dated nearly four years ago. I'd spotted a couple of cabs in the distance as we walked to the repair office, but none of them had gotten close enough for me to flag down and there were no cab companies listed in the directory. Apparently, Bilswift's internal transportation was handled entirely by independent contractors, none of whom we had contact information for. "Were you able to get through to that vehicle rental place?"

"Yes, and I reserved us a ground car," Selene said.

"No aircars available?"

"No aircars at all," she said. "He told me the people who rent here mostly want vehicles that can handle mountains and off-road trails. Too many trees up there for aircars to land."

"Point," I conceded. Actually, given the admiral's tentative location for the portal, off-road and mountain was probably exactly what we wanted. "Good enough," I said. "Better than good enough, really. That's the rental place in Wellington, right?"

She nodded. "Three blocks past Panza's."

I looked behind me at the western sky. Earlier, I'd thought we might get this whole thing finished today. Probably not now. "Let's get started," I said, starting down the walkway. "And keep an eye out for a cab."

There were no cabs, or at least none that came near us. We were about twenty minutes into our trip, and somewhere inside the Grymary district, when Selene abruptly jerked to a halt. "What is it?" I asked softly, dropping my hand to my holstered plasmic as I ran a quick visual three-sixty. No threats, or at least nothing I could see. "Selene?" I asked, looking at her but keeping a grip on my weapon.

I felt that grip tighten. Her pupils were ablaze with shock, disbelief, anticipation, and horror. "Selene?" I repeated.

She took a deep, shuddering breath. "This way," she said, angling off north toward the river and picking up her pace. "Come. Now."

We hurried down the street, passing humans and a mix of other species, the general cut of their clothing marking them as working class. Most of them flicked a glance or two at the strangers walking their district's streets, but it seemed more idle curiosity than anything else. Certainly there was no suspicion or hostility I could detect. A couple of them gave Selene lingering looks, but given that they'd probably never seen a Kadolian before that was to be expected.

Finally, a tense five-minute walk later, we reached a storefront with a heavy aroma and a stock of fish and other seafood in open trays at the counter. A freshly painted sign over the counter identified the place as JAVERSIN BROTHERS SEAFOOD. "There," Selene breathed. "In there."

"Got it," I said, touching her arm reassuringly as I moved ahead to take point. Standing at the counter were two burly humans, chatting with the customers as they industriously scooped up fish from the various trays and stuffed them into travel containers.

A few meters back from the counter, in a preparation area with long tables, trash bins, and filleting knives, was something I wasn't expecting: a Patth in the unmarked gray robe of a commoner, industriously chopping heads and tails off more of the product. Beside him, his back to us, was a shorter figure with a bit of pure white hair peeking out from beneath his knit cap. He was walking slowly past a set of trays with some kind of purplish squid-like stuff in them, his head held low. The Patth said something inaudible, and his companion half turned toward us as he picked up a scoop and handed it to him.

And I felt the same kaleidoscope of reactions flash through me that I'd just seen in Selene's pupils.

It was a young male, small and thin, probably no more than ten or eleven years old. He was dressed in the same working-class style as most of the rest of people we'd passed on Grymary's streets.

Only he wasn't human, or Patth, or Ihmisit, or any of the other species I typically ran into on the streets of the Spiral.

He was a Kadolian.

CHAPTER TWO

I gave him a good, long look, half convinced that the raw fish fumes had somehow scrambled my eyesight. But as my father used to say, *Seeing is believing, unless an illusionist or con man is involved.*

I turned back to Selene. Her pupils had settled down a bit, but there was still a mass of confusion swirling around as she gazed at the boy. "Friend of yours?" I asked as casually as I could manage.

"No," she said, still staring at him. "No, I've never seen him before. Gregory, what is he *doing* here?"

"No idea," I said, studying the boy. He'd turned away from us again, and for a moment I wondered why he hadn't smelled Selene the same way she'd smelled him. But the wind was now coming directly toward us, and he was surrounded by odoriferous fish, and maybe he was just too young and inexperienced to properly sort through all the scents around him.

All of which was speculation. With him standing twenty meters away from us, there was a much more straightforward approach to getting information. "Let's just ask him," I suggested.

"Do you think we should?" Selene asked hesitantly. "What if he has family? No, he can't—I'd have smelled them. But—"

"It's okay," I said, taking her arm in what I hoped was a

calming grip and backing us away from the storefront. Between the fish shop and the woodworking studio beside it was a narrow lane where she would be mostly concealed. "Stay here. I'll bring him to you."

"All right," she said, still sounding a little lost. "Gregory—"

"It's okay," I said. "I'll be right back." I gestured to her own flow of white hair. "You'd better put on your scarf, too. We're conspicuous enough as strangers as it is."

She nodded mechanically and pulled her scarf from a pocket. I gave her hand a reassuring squeeze, then headed back to the storefront.

The crowd had gone down somewhat while I'd been getting Selene settled; clearly, the two fishmongers had their sales and packaging routine down to a science. I joined the end of the queue, studying the place as I waited. I'd already noted that the prep area where the Patth and the Kadolian boy were working was mostly a single open space, with storage and washing areas as well as the cutting tables. But from my new perspective I could also see that there was another room tucked away at one side, probably an office. The left end of the serving counter had a drop-leaf section the owners could use to move in and out of the shop, and there was a metal roll-down that would presumably be lowered over the serving area when the shop closed for the day. I could see no actual door into the shop; either it was blocked from my view by one of the storage racks in the prep room or else opened directly into the office.

The Saffi female in front of me got her order, grunted her thanks as she handed over payment, and it was now my turn. "Evening," one of the men said as I stepped up to the counter, running a quick evaluating look over me. "What can I get you?"

"Evening," I greeted him in return. "Those purple things back there, the ones the boy's working on? I'll take one of those."

"Maybe," the man said, turning toward the boy. "Tirano?" he called.

The Kadolian boy turned around. "Yes, Mr. Bicks?" he called.

"How's the mari-mari doing?" Bicks called back.

"Not yet," the boy said. He turned back for a quick sniff. "Twenty-three hours."

"Got it." Bicks turned back to me. "It's still ripening," he said. "You can have some tomorrow. Anything I can get for you now?"

"Wait a second," I said, frowning. "Since when does fish need to ripen? That *is* fish back there, isn't it?"

"Yeah," he said, giving me another once-over. "You're new here, aren't you?"

"Just got in today," I confirmed. "So what's with this mari-mari? Does it really ripen like some kind of fruit?"

He shrugged. "*We* call it ripening. Don't know what the ivy-tower types call it. Point is that mari-mari is best if it's eaten within two or three hours of that one best minute. That's why we won't sell it until tomorrow."

"Never heard of anything like that," I said, and for once I didn't have to fake interest. I really hadn't ever heard of any non-plant that behaved that way. "So what does the boy back there do, use some kind of sonic probe on it?"

"The boy has his ways," Bicks said, suspicion creeping into his voice. "So you want any fish, or don't you?"

"Not today," I said, nodding back toward the Kadolian. "I'll come back tomorrow and give that mari-mari a try. Thanks."

I smiled and stepped out of line and headed back toward where I'd left Selene. I waited until I judged Bicks's attention would be fully engaged with his new customer, then ducked into the narrow lane.

Selene was standing about halfway back, her scarf now covering her hair, and as I got closer I could see the tension still rippling across her pupils. "Did you talk to him?"

I shook my head. "I get the feeling Mr. Bicks has him on a tight leash," I said. "Or maybe considers him less of an employee and more of a trade secret. His name is Tirano, by the way."

A wince flicked across her pupils. "We need to talk to him, Gregory," she said earnestly. "As soon as possible."

"I agree," I said, turning and looking down the alley at the western sky. So much for grabbing our rental and at least having time to take a drive up into the hills. "But there's too much going on there right now. We'll have to try again later. So are we talking a lost colony of Kadolians or something?"

"No, that's impossible," she said. "But if he was part of a family, I'd have smelled them."

"Maybe they live out in the forest and he just comes into town to work," I suggested. "That might explain why some of the people we passed on the way here seemed to recognize you. Or at least knew what you were."

"Maybe," she said. "Could you tell if Tirano is his full name, or if it's a partial?"

"No idea. Why?"

Another wince. "It's not important. What are we going to do?"

"The plan is to come back later and talk to him," I said. "This seems to be the leading edge of local dinnertime, which is probably why everyone in town is out buying fish. But their sign says they're open another three hours, so we'll try again later after the big rush has settled down a little."

"What if Bicks still won't let you talk to him?"

"He will," I promised grimly. I knew a lot of ways to convince people to do what I wanted, and not all of them were painless. "In the meantime, let's head over to the Wellington rental place and get our car."

"All right," Selene said reluctantly. Reluctantly, and more than a little fearfully. Clearly, she wasn't happy about leaving the boy here alone.

"And don't worry about him," I soothed as I took her arm and continued us toward the far end of the alley. "He's clearly been here awhile. He should be able to handle another three hours."

The rental place was another fifteen-minute walk toward the east. Along the way we passed Panza's Café, a nice-looking place with at least a surface layer of sophistication and an aromatic hint of expensive alcohol.

After all we'd been through with Perrifil and Bicks, I was sorely tempted to at least go in for a quick drink and a preliminary assessment. But for the moment, tracking down high-ranking Patth would have to wait.

The vehicle rental procedure might have been reasonably quick by Bilswift standards, but by the runaround street-rental standards I was used to it was glacial. I'd assumed the owner would have filled out the paperwork in the time that had elapsed between Selene's call and our arrival, but it turned out he hadn't even started the forms yet. The fact that we'd come in on our own ship instead of arriving on Alainn aboard a liner or commercial vessel seemed to complicate matters even further.

Fortunately, it seemed to be more a matter of inexperience and incompetence than one of deliberate obstruction, which meant I didn't get to trot out any of my persuasion techniques.

Just the same, we had to stand around doing nothing for a good half hour while he got it all done.

But the vehicle we finally got was everything we could have asked for: impressively big, with large wheels and high clearance and a generous helping of power and traction. Whatever uncivilized terrain we ended up in, the thing should be up to the job.

It turned out I'd been mostly right about dinner-buying time in Bilswift. There was still a line at the counter when we arrived back at the Javersins' shop, but it was much shorter than it had been earlier. We found a place to park our new car, then went over and watched from an inconspicuous spot until the last customer trotted off with his package. Then, as the two countermen began moving the empty trays back into the prep area, Selene and I headed over.

The man I'd talked to earlier, Bicks, spotted us as we approached the counter. "The mari-mari's still not ripe," he said.

"We're not here for fish," I said, doing a quick check behind him. The Kadolian boy and the Patth had moved back to the deep washtubs at the rear of the prep area and were busily cleaning the bins and utensils. "We need a word with your Kadolian."

I'd expected the name would get a reaction, and I wasn't disappointed. Bicks's eyes widened, and he twitched back a little. "I—what are you talking about?"

I rolled my eyes. Denial and lies were right up there with twitching as part of the standard reactionary package. "You want to waste your own time, fine," I said. "But kindly don't waste mine." I gestured to Selene, standing a couple of paces behind me.

And as she stepped to my side she slipped back her scarf.

Bicks's reaction to her white hair and alien face was even better than his first one. But I hardly noticed. My full attention was on the Kadolian boy in the prep room, who'd paused in his work and turned to face us. Now, as Selene revealed herself in all her own alien glory—

Nothing. No surprise, no flicker of recognition, no fear, no nothing. The boy showed no reaction whatsoever.

Which suggested that maybe he *had* spotted Selene on our earlier visit, but simply hadn't cared enough to say or do anything about it.

Meanwhile, Bicks had recovered enough to get his nerve back. "Who are you?" he demanded. "Never mind—I don't care. Darnell?"

"What is it?" the other counterman asked, setting down the tray he'd been carrying and striding over. His eyes flicked across us as he walked, lingering on Selene's face. "What do they want?"

"I don't know," Bicks growled. "They're asking about Tirano."

"You can't have him," Darnell said firmly as he came to a stop beside Bicks. His hand moved across the counter, closed on the handle of one of the big spatulas he'd been using to load fish into its packaging. "He's ours."

"We're not looking to hire him away from you," I assured him. "All we want is to talk to him."

"We have papers," Darnell insisted. "They're right back there in the safe. Lukki's sig and the right endorsements and everything. He's *ours.*"

"So I've heard," I said. "That's a really nice spatula, Darnell. How many men have you killed with it?"

He blinked. "What?"

"I'm sure it's great against dead fish," I continued. "Probably not so much against something that might fight back."

Bicks took half a step forward and picked up a spatula of his own. "Are you threatening us?" he demanded.

"All I want is a word with your employee," I said mildly. "I'm just pointing out that you two are the ones holding weapons."

For a long moment I thought they were actually going to be stupid enough to take things to the next level. I stood without moving, making sure my plasmic was visible to them but making no move toward it. A couple of passersby had stopped to watch, but no one seemed inclined to join the conversation.

Finally, Darnell set down his spatula. "Tirano?" he called, his eyes still on me. "Some people here to see you."

I inclined my head to him and shifted my attention to the boy. He was still standing by the washtubs, but now his Patth workmate had also paused to watch our little drama. The boy hesitated a couple of seconds, then pulled a towel from the dispenser over the tub and started across toward us, wiping his hands as he walked.

"You've got one minute," Darnell warned. "He's still got work to do."

"One minute it is," I agreed. As my father used to say, *Agree to whatever they want, then do whatever you need to.* "A little privacy, if we may?"

Glowering, Darnell took a couple of steps back from the counter, gesturing Bicks to do likewise. I made a little shooing motion with my fingertips, and they reluctantly backed up the rest of the way to the long prep table. The boy glanced at Bicks as he passed him, but continued on to the counter. "What?" he asked in a flat voice.

Selene launched into a flurry of her own language. The boy hesitated, then replied with a few syllables of his own. She spoke again, got another terse reply. I tried to read the boy's pupils, but he kept his eyelids half closed and I couldn't get a clear enough view. He and Selene had one more exchange—

"Don't mind me," I put in. "I'll just stand here."

Selene turned to me, her pupils troubled and a little embarrassed. "I'm sorry, Gregory," she said, shifting to English. "This is Tirano, he's ten years old, and he's been"—she hesitated briefly—"indentured to Darnell and Bicks Javersin."

"Ah," I said, a shiver running up my back as I studied the boy. *Indentured*—a nice, antiseptic word that was often a stand-in for *enslaved*.

But I still wasn't getting anything from Tirano's pupils. Did his emotions run a different pattern than Selene's? "What happened to his family? I assume he had a family once."

"My family is dead," Tirano said, switching to English. "I am content here. Please leave."

I looked at Selene. Her pupils were still troubled, but there wasn't anything else I could get from them. "Glad to hear it," I said. "Who's this Lukki person Darnell mentioned?"

"She's a broker," Darnell called from the prep table. So much for giving us privacy.

"Where do I find her?" I called back.

"You can't have him," Bicks bit out.

"Who says I want him?" I countered. "Maybe I just want to hire a Kadolian of my own."

Bicks pointed at Selene. "You already have one."

"It's sometimes good to have a spare," I said. "Where do I find her?"

Bicks looked at Darnell, got a shrug and a reluctant nod in return. "I don't know where she lives," he growled. "We did our business with her at Panza's Café."

"Really," I said thoughtfully. So Lukki and our gourmet Patth both hung out at Panza's? Suspiciously convenient.

Or maybe not as much of a coincidence as it looked. The Patth back there who'd returned to his scrubbing work had to be from somewhere. Maybe Lukki had a whole stable of slaves for sale.

I'd never heard of Patth selling each other into slavery. But there was a lot about the Patth that no one had the first clue about. For all the economic dominance they and their high-speed Talariac Drive had achieved throughout the Spiral, they were remarkably restrained on both the bragging and promotional fronts.

My personal theory was that their carefully constructed public image of a stable, monolithic culture wasn't even close to the truth. But given their collective secrecy, I wasn't expecting to have that assumption confirmed anytime soon.

Meanwhile, we had more pressing business on our plate. "Let's go see if she's in tonight," I said. "Tirano, you can come with us—"

"Whoa," Darnell cut in, starting back toward me. "He's not going anywhere. He has work to do."

"What if we rented him for a couple of hours?" I suggested. "That way—"

"I have work to do," Tirano said. "Thank you for your concern. Good-bye."

Without waiting for a response, he turned his back on us and headed across the prep area toward the washtubs. I started to call to him, felt Selene's warning touch on my arm, and instead just nodded. "Thanks for your time," I said to no one in particular. Taking Selene's arm, I headed us toward our car, noting that the passersby who'd been watching the drama had also resumed their own various travels. If they'd been hoping for violence, they were disappointed.

Still, given Tirano's status and the Javersin brothers' apparent disinclination to let that status change, the onlookers might get another chance.

"We can't let him stay there," Selene said tautly as we reached our car. "We have to get him out."

"I agree," I said, glancing around casually as I unlocked the car door. Pedestrians moving along the walkways, vehicles driving placidly along, stores open with customers visible through the windows—it all looked fine and normal.

But something out there didn't feel quite right.

I climbed into the driver's seat as Selene got in beside me. "What if we go to Lukki and buy him back?" she asked.

"Not sure how that'll play with the admiral's budget," I said, looking around again. "Did you smell anything odd out there?"

"Not really," she said, her thoughts still clearly on Tirano. "Gregory, we need to—"

"Try again," I said, rolling down the car's windows. "Take a good sniff."

Her pupils flashed annoyance that I was sidetracking the more important issue of Tirano this way. But she obediently leaned out her window, her nostrils and eyelashes working. "Humans," she said. "Some Narchners, Saffi, Drilies—all the species you saw buying fish earlier."

"Cooking odors?"

"The same ones I smelled earlier," she said. "Including the Patth and the one I couldn't identify."

"So there's Patth food here," I said. "What about Patth themselves?"

"The one at the shop," she said, her pupils starting to look a little cross. "Possibly there's one eating at Panza's. The—"

She broke off, her eyelashes fluttering a little harder. "There are more," she said, her voice and pupils going subdued. "One more. Maybe two."

"Nearby?"

"Yes," she said slowly. "Yes, I think so."

I looked out around us again, a fresh knot forming in my stomach. I hadn't actually seen them, but old bounty hunter observational reflexes had picked up on the subtle offness of normal citizens reacting to something unexpected that they could see but I couldn't. "Any Iykams?"

"No," she said, her pupils frowning as she looked at me. "Is there a problem?"

"I don't know yet," I said, trying to think. "Let's think this through. The admiral thinks we've got a portal out there. The fact that there are at least a couple of Patth on the ground, with more on the way, is a vote in his favor."

I waved out at the city. "Having our gourmet and presumably head honcho headquartered here in town makes sense. He's a supervisor and probably not interested in getting his shoes dirty until there's something solid for him to look at."

"I'm just wondering why these other Patth are here in town," Selene said slowly. "Shouldn't they be out looking for the portal? It's still a couple of hours to sunset."

"That's certainly where *I'd* have my minions during working hours," I agreed. "Especially since they almost certainly know by now that you and I are here."

"Maybe the ones I'm smelling aren't with the portal group," Selene suggested. "There's that Patth at the fish shop. Maybe the others I'm smelling are his family."

"Yeah, I don't think that works," I said. "They're Patth, presumably under the authority of anyone higher on the pecking order than they are. You think a sub-director or even a conciliator would hesitate half a second before walking him out of the fish shop—him *and* his family—handing them shovels and weed cutters, and tossing them out into the field with everyone else?"

"Maybe they're trying to keep a low profile," Selene said. "Just because you and I are here doesn't mean we know anything important."

"Okay, fair point," I agreed. "But if that's what they're hoping, maybe we can pull a little sleight of hand on them."

Selene peered off toward the western sky. While we'd been talking to Tirano and the Javersin brothers the sun had disappeared behind a layer of dark clouds, the kind that promised late afternoon or early evening rains. "We take a drive into the mountains?"

"*You* take a drive into the mountains," I corrected her. "Nothing fancy or dangerous—you're not going to try anything or even get out of the car. All you're going to do is drive along the road, do some judicious sniffing, and see if you can narrow the playing field a little."

"All right," she said, a hint of suspicion in her pupils. "What are *you* going to do?"

"I'm going to find this Lukki and see what she has to say for herself."

"Yes, I thought that was what you were going to say," Selene murmured, the suspicion shifting to concern. "Are you sure you want to face her alone?"

"I'll be fine," I assured her. "Nice friendly conversation, nice public place with lots of witnesses. Besides, she's a businesswoman. As long as I don't make trouble, neither will she."

"Maybe," Selene said, her pupils not necessarily buying that argument.

But she recognized that our primary job was to hunt down the portal, and adding Tirano to the list was going to require some juggling of our schedule. "I suppose that makes sense. Do you want me to drop you off at Panza's on my way out of town?"

"Yes, please," I said, starting the car. "You have your plasmic?"

She nodded, patting her jacket over the spot where the weapon was holstered. Selene usually preferred to keep a lower profile than I did on such things. "I suppose you'll want me to leave my phone with you, too."

I grimaced. I didn't like the idea of being out of touch with her when she was heading out on her own. Actually, I actively hated it.

But phones could be tracked, and even though ours had been specially programmed to give false locations, all the gimmicking in the Spiral would be of limited use out in the middle of nowhere. A false location mark that nevertheless showed her traveling through dense forest or across a river at highway speeds would quickly unravel the trick. Out in the forest east of Bilswift, with only one or two roads available, it would be child's play to take the phone's theoretical location and recalibrate it back to reality.

Selene out on her own was bad enough. Selene out on her own with bad people knowing exactly where she was was an order of magnitude worse. "I suppose that's a good idea," I conceded. "The car probably has its own tracker—rentals usually do. I'll make sure to disable it before you leave Panza's."

"All right," she said. "Gregory...are you sure you want to do this? It doesn't have anything to do with the job."

"No, but it has a lot to do with you," I said firmly. "Last I checked, you were my partner, not Admiral Sir Graym-Barker. So, yes, I'm sure." I turned on the engine and pulled out onto the street. The rain I'd anticipated was starting to come down, and I sent up a silent hope that I could get the car's tracker disabled fast enough to avoid getting soaked. "And who knows? Maybe Panza's will have some decent barbeque."

CHAPTER THREE

It took me nearly fifteen minutes to find and disable the car's tracker in a way that wouldn't send up any red flags. Fortunately, the rain stayed mostly moderate, which meant I got wet but avoided the drenching I'd been concerned about. I stepped through the door to Panza's Café, shook the water off my jacket, and looked around.

I'd already concluded from the activity around the fish shop that Bilswift was in the middle of its usual dinnertime. The crowd packing Panza's was just an extra underscoring to that inference.

In cold-approach situations like this, I'd found that the bar was usually the best place to start. I worked my way through the maze of tables and chairs toward the waist-high wooden structure at the back, avoiding hurrying servers and strolling patrons, and doing a quick scan of the tables and booths for anything that looked like a Patth robe.

Nothing. Apparently, our gourmet Patth was eating in tonight.

The place was busy enough to need four bartenders: one Saffi, one Drilie, and two humans. I headed toward one of the latter, still dodging people and catching snatches of conversation as I walked.

Like most professional bartenders I'd encountered over the years, the one I was aiming for had already tagged me as a newcomer to his establishment. By the time I sidled my way between a pair of unoccupied stools he was waiting for me with a smile and a look of polite anticipation. "Evening, bud," he greeted me, just loudly enough to be audible over the buzz of general conversation. "What can I get you?"

"Large Dewar's," I said, pulling out a fifty-commark bill and laying it on the counter. "And an introduction."

His smile didn't disappear, but it took on a decidedly knowing edge. "Anyone in particular?"

"I'm told her name's Lukki," I said.

"Lukki," he repeated as if pondering the name. "Don't know. That's a pretty common nickname around here."

"I'm sure you know the one I'm talking about," I said, laying down another fifty. "Does a brisk indenture business."

"Ah," he said, giving the two bills an evaluating look. "Yes, I know her. Not sure she's in tonight."

"Too bad," I said, scooping up the bills. "On second thought, I can probably find a Dewar's somewhere else." I paused, my eyebrows raised in silent question.

His lips puckered. "Third booth clockwise from the door," he said.

"Thanks," I said, putting the two fifties back on the bar and adding a third. "You can send the Dewar's to her table, along with another of whatever she's drinking."

"Sure," he said, picking up the money. "Tell her Lefty sent you."

I nodded and headed back across the room. The woman in the third booth was younger than I'd expected, wearing an expensive form-fitting black suit topped by a loose burgundy half cloak that covered her left arm and shoulder. Even from across the room I could see the sheen of moisture on it; apparently, she'd come in through the same rainstorm I had.

Cloaks were great for keeping out the weather. They were also a favorite of people who wanted to carry weapons without anyone seeing them but didn't want to bother with the kind of expert tailoring that could achieve the same result with more subtlety. Like the bartender, she'd already noticed me and was watching as I made my way to her booth. "Evening," I said politely as I reached her. "I'm looking for a lady named Lukki. I'm told that's you?"

"Could be," she said. Her voice was a pleasant alto, but I'd met too many nasty people with lovely singing voices to make any assumptions about her character either way. "You have a name?"

"Roarke," I said. "I was hoping we could talk a little business."

"Could be," she said again, gesturing to the seat across from her. "What sort of business?"

"The kind of business you're in," I said. I sat down, folding my hands together on top of the table. "Incidentally, the bartender said to tell you Lefty sent me, by which I assume he wanted to warn you I was an armed stranger not necessarily to be trusted but not showing any obvious threat."

Her eyebrows went up a millimeter. "You got all that from his nickname?"

"He's not left-handed," I said. "And, of course, you're currently holding a gun in your left hand and pointing it at me under the table. Not a very inventive password; but then, it doesn't have to be."

"No, it doesn't," she agreed, frowning at my face. "And for the record, I'm not holding a gun on you. Never carry them myself—I've got people for that."

"Ah," I said. She was lying about that last part, of course. The cut of her cloak and the subtle tug on the fabric of her shirt showed she was carrying *something* out of sight down there. But people lied about weapons so often that I was more surprised when they didn't.

And given that shirt tug, she probably did indeed still have it holstered.

"*Roarke,*" she said, frowning. "Why does that name sound familiar?"

"I used to be a bounty hunter, if that helps," I said. "Mostly retired now."

A sudden knowing look flicked across her face. "*Gregory Roarke.* Yes, I remember now. You and your—" Another flash of understanding. "Your *Kadolian.* I'll be damned. You're here to talk about Tirano, aren't you?"

"Very good," I said, impressed in spite of myself. Of course, as my father used to say, *Always assume the mind reader has a plant in the audience.* It would be easy for Lukki to jump to the right conclusion if one of the Javersin brothers had already called to warn her I was on my way. "Now that we've established who we are, let's get down to business. How much to buy the boy away from the fish shop?"

She shook her head. "Sorry. Not how it works."

"Why not?" I asked. "You sold him to the Javersins. Buy him back and sell him to me instead."

Her eyes narrowed a little. "No one's been *sold*, Roarke. Selling people is illegal, remember? No, this is a purely aboveboard indenture. I match workers with employers, a contract is drawn up, and they all go on their merry way."

"Right," I said, nodding sagely. "Because you can't spin in a circle without hitting a Kadolian wandering the streets looking for work. All of them need someone to set them up with a job."

She shrugged. "What can I say? I'm a dealer in exotics—everyone knows that. The point is that once the deal is made, I'm out. Whatever the Javersins and Tirano have going, it has nothing to do with me."

"Of course not," I said, trying hard not to be too sarcastic. Just because slavery was illegal on all Commonwealth worlds didn't mean there weren't loopholes people like Lukki had learned how to find and exploit. "So what are the terms?"

"You'd have to ask the Javersins about—"

"What are the terms?"

She regarded me coolly. "Let's cut through the fog here, shall we?" she said, her voice changed to something considerably less pleasant. "You want to know how long before Tirano's out of his indenture and a free man. Free Kadolian. Whatever. Right?"

"That's a good place to start," I agreed. "So?"

She gave a small shrug. "Like I said, you'll have to ask the Javersin brothers. All of that is up to the employer."

"You said there was a contract."

"Certain details are, shall we say, a little squishy."

I took a calming breath. "So speculate a little," I said. "How long?"

Her eyes flicked over my shoulder toward the bar. "I've been by the Javersins' place a few times," she said. "Purely out of curiosity, you understand, to check on how it's working out. Given how vital a part of the business Tirano is, what with the mari-mari and their other time-critical products, I'd guess it'll be awhile."

"As in probably never?"

"As in *possibly* never."

"So it *is* slavery."

Lukki's face hardened. "You said you're not so much a bounty hunter anymore. So what *are* you?"

"Selene and I are crocketts," I said, the back of my neck tingling. That look over my shoulder had likely been a signal to however many goons she had sprinkled around the bar. "We hunt for useful planets—"

"Yeah, I know what crocketts are," she said, her suspicious look still in place. "You wouldn't by any chance be working for the Commonwealth government on the side, would you? Maybe teamed up with some politician who's gotten it into his head to harass honest businesses with completely unfounded accusations of slave-trading?"

"If I was working for the Commonwealth don't you think I'd have brought at least a little backup with me?" I countered, trying to sound both sincere and irritated by her question. Technically speaking, I *was* working for the Commonwealth, or at least whatever corner of it was funding the Icarus Group.

Which had nothing to do with Lukki and her borderline illegal activities, of course. But even if that was a topic I could talk about, I doubted she would appreciate the subtleties involved.

"Wouldn't have done you any good if you did," Lukki said, looking casually around the room. "Say hello to Willie and Braun."

Right on cue, there they were: one thug detaching himself from the general crowd of passersby and taking up position beside her seat, the other one coming up from behind me and settling into a similar spot at my side. Their clothing was bone dry, which meant they'd been here and in position before Lukki herself slogged in. Not the ideal bodyguard technique, but good if you liked springing ambushes. "Hello," I said calmly. "Which is which?"

"Willie," Lukki said, gesturing up at the man beside her. "Braun." She pointed at the one beside me. "They'll see you out."

"Fine," I said, starting to sidle out of my seat. Braun caught my left arm as I did so, hauling me out from behind the table and into an upright position without giving me the opportunity to do the job myself. "I was leaving anyway."

"Of course you were," Lukki said in the patronizing tone I'd always hated. "One more thing. If you ever want to sell your Kadolian, let me know. I'd give you a very good price for her."

Patronizing, insulting, and exactly the opening I'd hoped for. I let my eyes narrow, my face tighten, and my hands bunch into fists. "Don't you *ever* say something like that to me again," I snarled. Shaking off Braun's loose grip on my upper arm, I took a long step forward toward her as if planning words or actions that would underline that warning.

Willie was far too experienced to be taken by surprise at such an obvious and predictable threat. He took half a step into my path, put both palms against my chest, and gave me a hard shove that would have sent me sprawling onto the floor if Braun hadn't been there to catch me.

It was a move I'd seen a hundred times, and experienced personally more times than I cared to remember. Human pinball, someone had once dubbed it, a back-and-forth between thugs designed to both humiliate the victim and take the fight out of him without inflicting any injuries he could take to the nearest badgeman. From the smug smile on Willie's face, I guessed he and Braun had the technique down to a science.

But as my father used to say, *Whenever you think you've got something down to a science, remember there's always more science out there.* As I staggered backward from the force of Willie's shove, I raised my arms to chest height, flailing them as if I was trying to maintain my balance. The kind of movement that attracted attention, especially if you had concerns about a palmed weapon.

Which meant neither of the thugs was looking the right direction as I lifted my right leg, set my heel against the corner of the table, and shoved backward with all my strength.

Braun was ready for the human pinball Willie had sent. He wasn't nearly ready enough for the human cannonball I'd suddenly become. I slammed hard into him, the impact breaking his own balance and sending both of us falling backward onto the floor.

Luckily for me, I was the one on top. Unluckily for him, he wasn't. I caught the look of surprise and consternation on Willie's face as he grabbed for the weapon belted at his side—

And then Willie, Lukki, and the whole damn bar went totally still and totally silent at the sight of my plasmic pointed at Willie's face.

I let the tension play out for a couple of heartbeats. Then, keeping my plasmic trained on Willie, I shifted my attention to Lukki and raised my eyebrows. "Are we done with this silliness yet?" I asked conversationally.

For another moment she just sat there watching me. Then, a lopsided smile touched her lips, and she made a small gesture to Willie. "I think the word is *touché*," she said as Willie reluctantly let go of his weapon. "Yes, we're done. Enjoy your stay in Bilswift, Mr. Roarke."

"Thank you, I will." I rolled off Braun and got to my feet, keeping my plasmic in hand but no longer pointing it at anyone in particular. "Fair warning: I *am* going to get the boy back. If I were you I'd check the fine print and see if there's a way for you to make some money from the transaction."

"I'll do that," Lukki promised. "Don't be a stranger."

"Wouldn't think of it," I assured her. "Enjoy the drink I ordered for you if the bartender ever gets around to delivering it. Willie and Braun can flip a coin for my Dewar's."

Sidling past Willie, I made my way to the door, keeping half an eye on them over my shoulder as I walked. Some of the people I'd dealt with over the years would try to take one last shot at me at this point.

But Lukki was apparently a classier act than that, or else just didn't want to have to talk to any badgemen tonight. As I closed the door behind me Willie was helping Braun up from the floor and the overall conversational buzz was starting to come back.

The intensity of the rain had increased somewhat since I arrived, the dark clouds blocking what was left of the lingering daylight. Holstering my plasmic, I stood under the doorway overhang for a moment while I looked around for a cab. But none of them were in sight. Turning up my collar, thinking unkind thoughts about a town that apparently didn't care enough about visitors to keep up a runaround rental service, I headed west toward the spaceport. Next time, I told myself firmly, I'd make sure we rented *two* cars.

I was a block away before it occurred to me that I'd never found out if Panza's had any barbeque.

I was three blocks from the spaceport, soaked to the skin, and thinking longingly about how a hot shower would feel, when everything went straight to hell.

My only warning was a small but sharp jab in my upper right back. Reflexively, I reached over my shoulder to that spot—

And even as I pulled out the tiny dart the world turned sideways under my feet and I found myself staggering in a supreme effort to keep my balance.

It was a losing battle. The vertigo drug the dart had injected into my blood was way stronger than anything my inner ear could counter. One single effort, and I saw the wet ground rushing up at me as I toppled over onto my chest.

Unfortunately, this time I didn't have a nice soft thug to cushion my fall. I managed to get my hands under me, but I still hit the ground hard. My left arm collapsed with the impact and I fell over onto my back, the impact sending a fresh splash of cold water onto the nape of my neck. I'd slowed myself enough not to have the air knocked out of me, but the spinning world kept me from bouncing back up onto my feet again.

And then, as I clenched my teeth against the waves of nausea, a brilliant light suddenly blazed into my eyes.

Blind, woozy, and queasy was the absolute worst combination for accurate shooting. But I didn't care. Squeezing my eyes shut against the light, I snatched out my plasmic and tried to line it up on the spot where I remembered seeing the light first appear.

Not surprisingly, I didn't really have a clue where my assailant was or where he might have moved to. Also not surprisingly, I barely had the weapon settled when it was plucked neatly from my grip. "Who are you?" I demanded, using up most of that breath's collection of air in the process.

My answer was to have my jacket opened and my wallet pulled from its pocket. The light seemed to shift slightly, perhaps indicating my assailant was looking through the various cards or, more likely, relieving me of the weight of my cash. There was a thud against my chest, a small splash beside my head—

The light winked out, I heard hurried splashing footsteps, and it was over.

I blinked my eyes open, wincing as the rain pelted into them, trying to see through the big purple afterimage floating where the blaze of light had been. But it was no use. By the time I could see again my assailant was gone, leaving me dizzy and wet but otherwise none the worse for wear.

I fumbled a hand to my chest and found that the bump I'd felt had been the thug thoughtfully returning my plasmic. The splash I'd felt near my head turned out to be my wallet, not so courteously dropped into a puddle.

Under other circumstances I'd probably have grabbed both of them and charged off to find my attacker. But with the vertigo drug still kaleidoscoping the universe there was no chance of that. Returning my plasmic to its holster, I retrieved my wallet, shook off the extra water, and slid it back into its pocket. Then, moving carefully, I rolled up onto my right side. The holstered plasmic was uncomfortable to lie on, but there was nothing I could do about that.

Closing my eyes again, thinking even more yearningly about that hot shower, I settled down to wait.

Typical vertigo dart loads could leave the victim helpless for up to an hour. This one wore off after only twenty minutes. As I got warily to my feet, I supposed I should be grateful for that.

I slogged the remaining three blocks to the port, then walked the additional half kilometer to the *Ruth*'s pad. At least my attacker had waited until I was close to home before jumping me. I didn't see anyone along the way; evidently the fine citizens of Bilswift knew enough to come in out of the rain.

Given how the rest of the day had gone, I half expected to find that Perrifil had called in a heavy lifter and sent the *Ruth* way the hell off to parts unknown. But no, the ship was right where we'd left it, glistening in the rain and the port's woefully substandard lighting. There was no sign of our rental car, and I wondered uneasily if Selene had run into a hornet's nest of her own out in the mountains.

But she could take care of herself, and anyway there wasn't anything to be gained by worrying. Wearily, I headed up the zigzag.

I was nearly to the top when I saw the figure huddled unmoving against the entryway hatch.

I stopped short, my hand darting beneath my jacket to where I was hiding my plasmic. The visitor was wrapped in a Patth robe, I saw now, the same plain gray commoner type I'd seen being worn by the employee at the fish shop. The hood was twisted sideways to cover his face, protecting it from the rain.

Or else what was lying there was a dead body my new playmates had dropped on my doorstep as their final contribution to the day's festivities, and the hood was arranged that way in order to preserve the fun surprise of who it turned out to be.

If it was Selene...

I forced that thought out of my head. A quick look around

me—the port appeared to be as deserted as the city streets had been—and I resumed my cautious climb up the zigzag. I reached the top, and was steeling myself to pull back the hood when it moved of its own accord.

It wasn't Selene. It wasn't the Patth from the fish shop. It wasn't Lukki or anyone else I'd seen at Panza's place.

"Hello," Tirano said, his white Kadolian hair matted against his head, small rivulets of water trickling down into his face. "I think I'm in trouble. May I come in?"

CHAPTER FOUR

I got him inside and sealed the hatch, making sure to engage the mechanical deadbolt I'd added after learning that the Patth had built secret back doors into most standard lock protocols.

The deadbolt could only be worked when there was someone inside, of course, so my next move upon returning to the *Ruth* would normally be to give a quick search of the ship to make sure no one had sneaked aboard in our absence. But in this case, I first had to take Tirano to the bathroom, point him to the shower and a towel, grab a towel for myself, then head to my cabin to strip down, dry off, and change out of my own soaked clothing. I grabbed my knee-length white nightshirt, set it just inside the bathroom for Tirano, and told him to meet me in the dayroom when he was done.

And after *that* I made a quick but careful search of the ship.

I was waiting in the dayroom, a couple mugs of hot tea and a selection of Selene's favorite snacks ready to hand, when he emerged from the bathroom. "How do you feel?" I asked, running a critical eye over him as I offered him one of the mugs and waved him toward the array of snacks. His hair was still damp and clinging to his head, but he looked a thousand percent better than he had huddled outside the *Ruth*'s entryway.

"I'm well, thank you," he said. He accepted the tea, frowned uncertainly at the snacks, then sat down on the foldout couch. "I'm sorry to have intruded on you this way."

"Selene and I get intruded on all the time," I assured him. "So what's this all about?"

He paused to take a cautious sip of the tea. "I'm not sure," he said. "This evening—"

"Hold that thought," I cut him off, heading toward the hatchway. I'd heard a syncopated quadruple thud on the entryway hatch, today's signal for whichever of us had gotten back to the *Ruth* first to unlock the deadbolt for the other one. "Be right back."

I confirmed via the external display that it was Selene, and that she was alone, before I unlocked the hatch and swung it open. "Sorry I'm late," she huffed as she stepped inside. The brief run through the rain from the car up the zigzag had left her far less sodden than my own hike across town, but she still looked pretty uncomfortable. "I had to drive—"

She broke off, her pupils showing a mix of astonishment and disbelief as she caught Tirano's scent. "Gregory?"

"And it only gets worse," I told her, closing and locking the hatch behind her. "First things first."

I pulled out my plasmic. "Had a little incident on the way back," I said, turning the weapon sideways and offering it to her. "I couldn't see whoever it was who jumped me, but I persuaded him to grab my plasmic by the barrel. Afraid it's been rained on, but I did what I could to keep it as dry as possible."

"Are you all right?" she asked, her eyes on me as she carefully took the weapon by its grip and sniffed at the barrel.

"I'm fine," I assured her. "Vertigo dart with a light load, and he didn't even rob me. Best guess is he wanted to look at my ID and find out who I was."

"He could have just asked," she murmured. "It's faint, but... yes. He was a Patth, Gregory."

"A *Patth*?" I echoed, frowning. "Since when do Patth do their own dirty work?"

"Maybe there weren't any Iykams around he could call on," she suggested. "Though that seems a little odd."

"Maybe not," I said. "We typically travel in upscale Patth circles, where there's always an Iykam or two to call on. I assume the more plebian sorts have to do everything themselves."

"I suppose that makes sense," she said, handing the plasmic

back to me. "I never heard of a Patth being violent, though. Oh, and your attacker was one of the ones I smelled earlier outside the fish shop."

"Explains how he knew who to jump," I said, taking the weapon and dropping it into its holster. I'd have bet a stack of money my attacker had been Willie or Braun or some other thug on Lukki's payroll.

Unless the Patth who'd attacked me *was* one of Lukki's people. The Patth at the fish shop might have been sold to the Javersins the same way Tirano had been.

"Or he could have picked up you at Panza's," Selene suggested. "Did you find Lukki?"

"Oh, I found her, all right," I said ruefully. "Officially, Tirano's been indentured to the Javersin brothers. Unofficially, he's a slave."

Selene's pupils flashed revulsion. "We're going to get him out, though, aren't we?"

"We're certainly going to try," I said. "Let's go hear what Tirano has to say for himself."

The Kadolian boy was standing by the snack selection when we arrived in the dayroom, his eyes turned toward the hatchway. "Hello, Selene," he said, his voice sounding a little cautious as he went back to the foldout and sat down. "I'm sorry to have intruded on you this way."

"It's all right," she assured him. "Are you hurt?"

"No, I'm unharmed."

"Good," I said. "Let's start with how you ended up outside the *Ruth*'s entryway wrapped in a Patth robe."

Out of the corner of my eye I saw Selene's pupils flash a fresh jolt of surprise at my comment, and caught the subsequent twitch as Tirano caught the shift in her scent. For a moment they just looked at each other, and then Selene gestured to him. "Go ahead," she said.

"It was closing time," Tirano said, speaking slowly as if choosing his words carefully. "It was raining. I had cleaned my hands and face when Galfvi came to me holding his robe."

"Galfvi's the Patth worker at the fish shop?" I asked.

"Yes," Tirano said, his eyes still on Selene. "He told me I was in danger and that I needed to run to my friends right away."

"What kind of danger?" Selene asked.

"He didn't say." Tirano winced. "But he was afraid. I know him well enough. He was afraid."

I nodded to myself. Selene was adept at reading a change in someone's emotions by the subtle shifting of their scent, especially when it was someone she knew or at least had a reasonable baseline for. Tirano presumably had the same ability, though he probably didn't have Selene's more extensive skill and experience. "And then, what, he gave you his robe?"

"Yes," Tirano said, his eyes briefly flicking to me before returning to Selene. "He said the spaceport was a long ways away and that I needed something to protect me from the rain."

"He wasn't concerned about the rain himself?" Selene asked.

"He didn't say," Tirano said. "He said he'd come back to me for the robe later. I was confused, but he was afraid, so I took his robe and left."

"And came here," Selene said.

Tirano held his hands out in a sort of helpless gesture. "He said to go to my friends."

"And that's us?" I asked.

The boy lowered his hands. "I have no friends," he said quietly. "But you came to see me. I thought he must mean you."

For a moment no one spoke. "Do you know where Galfvi lives?" I asked into the silence.

"Why?" Tirano asked, sounding puzzled.

"So we can return his robe," I said. "Do you?"

"No," Tirano said. "I think he lives in a house near the shop—not mine, but one of his own. But I don't know where."

"Can you maybe call him?" I suggested.

Tirano shook his head. "I lost my phone."

"You can use mine."

"I don't remember his number."

"What about the Javersin brothers?"

"I don't remember theirs, either."

"Ah," I said. No numbers, no trackable phone, and someone else's outerwear. If Tirano hadn't already looked like someone on the run, all of that heaped together would definitely have done it.

"Maybe there's some ID in the robe itself," Selene offered.

"I'll check," I said, heading for the dayroom hatchway. "Be right back."

Tirano had left the robe in a small puddle in a corner of the bathroom. I picked it up, wincing at the unpleasant cold wetness, and wrung it out as best I could into the shower stall. At least the boy had known enough to hang up his towel. Pulling it off the rack, I kneaded the robe with it, trying to wick out a little more of the water. I got to the lower hem.

And frowned. There was an unusual stiffness at the bottom of the robe. Not all of it, but in several sections. I flipped the robe open, trying to figure what might be in there.

I felt my throat tighten. There was a sealing strip all around the inner edge, disguised as a normal hemline, that created a long and inconspicuous pocket.

I thought about prying it open and seeing what was inside. But whatever it was, it deserved a bigger audience than just me. Wrapping the robe in the towel, I headed back to the dayroom.

I found Tirano back at the snack selection, looking over the assortment but not touching any of them. Selene was standing at his side, murmuring brief descriptions of each of them. Apparently, he wasn't as familiar with such things as Selene was. Or possibly wasn't familiar with them at all.

They both turned to face me as I came into view, though both had surely already smelled that I was on my way. "Here we go," I said, stepping over to one of the fold-down seats and sitting down. I laid the towel on the deck and picked up the robe. "Let's see what we can find in here—an ID, or address, or anything else that might be of interest."

I bent over the robe and started unfolding it, not bothering to look at Selene, knowing she'd picked up on my comment. I got my fingers on the edge of the sealing strip and started working them beneath it.

It turned out to be harder than I expected. The strip was a very good, very stiff seal, the sort that a casual investigator might easily pass over. But I knew better, and after a few seconds I managed to get a fingertip through the seam. I pried it far enough to get another finger in beside it, and then just worked my way along it in both directions until the opening was wide enough for me to get my hand in there.

One touch was all I needed to know what I'd found. "Well, well," I said conversationally. Prying the seam open a little farther, I pulled out the flat pack of commark bills that had been hidden there. "The Javersin brothers have an interesting bonus policy," I added, holding the stack up for them to see.

Tirano seemed to shrink back from the bills. "That's not mine," he insisted.

"Well, it seems to be yours now," I said, flipping through the stack. There were tens and twenties there, with a couple of fives at one end. "As my father used to say, *Possession is nine points of the law unless someone else's name is already on it.*"

"How much is there?" Selene asked, her pupils grim as she stared at the bills.

"I'd say four or five hundred," I told her. "And there are"—I felt around the edge of the hem—"probably ten more stacks in there. Depending on the mix of bills, it could be as low as a couple of thousand or as high as twenty."

"It's not mine," Tirano said again.

"And," I added, ignoring his comment and bringing my stack back for a sniff, "it smells a lot like fish. Any thoughts as to how this largesse came to be in your possession, Tirano?"

"I already told you," the boy said, his eyes and face looking haunted. "Galfvi gave me the robe to keep the rain off."

"He *did* say Galfvi said he'd be back for it," Selene reminded me.

"And now we know why," I agreed, setting the bills on the deck beside the towel. "Well. It's been a long day, we're all tired, and whatever's going on here it's not going to get settled tonight. Tirano, you'll have to sleep in here—that foldout converts to a bed—"

"He can sleep in my cabin," Selene put in.

I frowned at her. Her pupils had an unyielding look about them, the kind of expression that said she'd made up her mind and there wasn't a chance in hell I could talk her out of it.

I tried anyway. "You don't have to do that," I said. "The foldout's comfortable enough—"

"He's staying in my cabin."

"—or I could put him up in mine—"

"He's staying in my cabin."

As my father used to say, *Arguing with a brick wall almost never gets you anywhere, and people give you funny looks when you do.* "Fine," I said, giving up. "You want me to go make it up for him while you two figure out what we've got that he'll eat?"

"I can go," she said, moving toward the hatchway. "The Dungeness crab chowder should be fine."

"Okay." And if it wasn't, we'd eventually find something the kid liked.

And if I wound up eating the chowder myself, it would hardly be the worst thing that had happened to me today.

As it turned out, Tirano was more than happy to eat the chowder.

But only if he could eat it alone.

"Can I not eat in my room?" he asked, some pleading in his voice. "I don't—I'm not used to eating with others."

"Maybe it's time you expanded your horizons a little," I told him shortly. I already wasn't happy with him taking over Selene's cabin, and this just added an extra layer to my discomfort.

Which was silly, if I was being totally honest with myself. There wasn't anything the boy could do in there while eating that he couldn't do once he settled down for the night.

But I'd been attacked twice today, and been soaked to the skin, and I still hadn't had my hot shower. I wasn't in the most accommodating of moods.

Unfortunately for me, and fortunately for Tirano, Selene was.

"I really don't see why you gave in," I growled as I spooned some chowder into my own bowl.

"I'm sorry I upset you," Selene said. She was gazing down into her chowder, her pupils hooded and unreadable. "But he's been frightened and cold and hungry. I thought it would be for the best if we could avoid adding more stress to the day."

"Yeah, well, he's not a child, you know," I said impatiently. "And as for being cold and wet and hungry, so am I. Plus I was attacked. Twice."

She looked up at me, surprise and a hint of guilt in her pupils. *"Twice?"*

"I also had a short run-in with Lukki's thugs at Panza's," I told her. "Actually, I figured it was one of them who fed me that vertigo dart until you said it was a Patth."

"Yes." She hesitated. "But you said Tirano wasn't a child. In many ways, he truly is."

I snorted. "Because he doesn't know what kind of snacks Kadolians like?"

"That's just a symptom," Selene said, her pupils going a shade darker. "It's...I'm not sure how to explain it, Gregory. I'm not sure I *should* explain it."

I waited, my general irritation at the way the day had gone

fading into anticipation. Selene didn't talk about herself very much, and she talked about the Kadolian people and culture even less. "I'm listening," I said encouragingly.

She again lowered her eyes to her bowl. "Are you familiar with the term *changeling*?" she asked after a moment.

"I know the human folklore version," I said, frowning. "It was a fairy or troll secretly substituted for a human baby and left to be raised by the baby's parents. You're not saying that Tirano...?"

"No, not like that," Selene said. "But it's... similar."

She took a deep breath. "Our children are not like humans," she said. "They must be nurtured by their parents or another Kadolian adult, guided and disciplined, until they are six to nine years old. Without that ethical framework in place, they are unlikely to become properly functioning adults."

"Actually, that's not too far off from how humans are socialized," I said. "Though I don't know if there's a specific age we need to be taught by. Tirano said he was ten. Is that true?"

"I don't know for certain," Selene said. "He does have the usual physiological markers for that age. But the crucial question is how old he was when he lost his parents."

"Any idea what happened to them?"

Selene nodded. "We talked a little while you were getting Galfvi's robe from the bathroom. He says they died in an accident a few years ago, and that he was basically on his own until Lukki found him and took him in."

"Yeah, like a fox takes in a chicken," I growled. "So how long has it been since then?"

"He doesn't remember," she said. "But typically Kadolian children have a new syllable added to their names every two years until they reach youthage. If Tirano is his full name, as he says it is, that means he was between six to eight when he was orphaned."

"Terrific," I muttered. "So right in the middle of the crucial timeline."

"Yes," Selene confirmed. "But there are some other indicators. I presume you've had trouble reading his pupils as well as you read mine?"

"I can hardly read his pupils at all," I admitted. "I assumed it was just his age or the different environment he's in."

"No, that's part of our training," Selene said. "On the other hand, you can see how he's much better with gestures and facial expressions than I am."

"*Trying* to be better, anyway," I said. "So mimicking the non-verbal cues of all the other species around him?"

"Something like that," she said. "Though our faces aren't nearly as amenable to that kind of expression as human ones."

"Let's cut to the chase," I said. "Aside from trying to play human, are there any other consequences to this lack of proper training?"

"Yes, and they can be very serious ones," she said, her pupils going grim. "Kadolian changelings can drift ethically into crime, psychopathy, or sociopathy."

"Like he could steal some money or someone's robe?" I suggested. "And then lie about how he wound up with them?"

"Exactly," Selene said. "But it's worse. You know how I can read lies through a shift in the person's scent. But that assumes the liar knows he's telling a lie and feels some remorse or discomfort about it."

"Oh, lovely," I muttered as the full impact of that hit me. "So if Tirano doesn't realize he's lying, or doesn't think lying is wrong...?"

"Then his scent wouldn't change."

"And you wouldn't be able to tell," I said, nodding. "So how do we—?"

I broke off as the triple tone from the entryway announced a visitor.

"Great," I growled as I stood up. "Probably our unhelpful Ihmisit bureaucrat trying to kick us out again."

"Or else Galfvi's here for his robe," Selene warned as she also stood.

"Well, if it is, he's not getting it," I said as we stepped through the dayroom hatchway and headed aft. "Not until we sort all this out and figure out where all that cash came from."

The triple tone sounded twice more before we reached the entryway. Dropping my hand to my plasmic, I turned on the outside display.

And felt my stomach tighten. It wasn't Perrifil standing out there in the rain, or Galfvi, or even my Patth attacker here for round two. Giving Selene a quick look, I keyed open the hatch.

"Mr. Gregory Roarke?" the uniformed woman outside asked in a formal tone.

"Yes," I confirmed cautiously. The last time a badgeman had showed up at the *Ruth*'s entryway I'd been subsequently hauled off on suspicion of murder. "You?"

She held out her ID, just in case the badge on her chest wasn't clear enough. "Detective-Sergeant Tandra Kreega," she said, her eyes shifting to Selene. "You're Mr. Roarke's partner, I assume?"

"Yes, this is Selene," I said before Selene could answer. "What can we do for you?"

"There've been a couple of incidents this evening I need to talk to you about," Kreega said. "May I come in?"

"What kind of incidents?" I asked, staying exactly where I was.

Her lips compressed briefly. "Two disappearances," she said. "One of them was a boy named Tirano. One of your people, I believe," she added, looking at Selene. "The other was a Patth named Galfvi who works with Tirano at Javersin Brothers Seafood."

"You say they work together?" I said, resisting the reflexive impulse to express surprise over there having been a second disappearance. A response like that—commenting on one bit of news while ignoring the bit of news you already knew—was the kind of unthinking mistake badgemen were always watching for. "Okay, so maybe they're just out on the town together or something. You said they were boys, right?"

"The *Kadolian* is a boy," Kreega corrected. "The Patth is a young adult. It's very wet out here, Mr. Roarke. May I come in?"

Technically, I knew, I could refuse. Without a warrant or probable cause she had no right of entry. But upright citizens with nothing to hide usually didn't object to taking a wet badgeman in out of the rain.

More to the point, with a couple of Bilswift's citizens having apparently dropped off the edge of the planet, I didn't want Kreega suspicious enough to try to get official permission to search the ship.

Not to mention that if I didn't let her in, her Plan B for getting out of the rain would probably be to invite us to the station for whatever conversation she wanted with us.

I already had one stack of wet clothing in my cabin. I didn't really want to add a second to the pile.

"Of course, of course," I said, backing into the corridor to let her enter. "Sorry. Come in."

"Thank you," she said, shaking the water off her hat outside as she stepped over the threshold. "Afraid you're going to have to get used to this weather as long as you're here. Afternoon and early evening rains are typical of Bilswift this time of year."

"A little rain never hurt anyone," I said. "The dayroom will be more comfortable than standing here in the corridor."

"Sounds good to me," Kreega said, gesturing me to lead the way. "Oh, and there was one more incident this evening I didn't mention."

"A mugging?" I suggested as I headed down the corridor, wondering if someone had witnessed my attack. "Theft? Pillage?"

"Oh, nothing so pedestrian," Kreega said as she fell into step beside me. "Seems we've had ourselves a murder."

CHAPTER FIVE

"And I see I've interrupted your dinner," Kreega went on as we stepped into the dayroom and she saw the table and half-eaten chowder. "My apologies. Please; continue."

"Yes," I murmured, my head still spinning from her deliberately casual revelation. A *murder*? *Here*? "Ah...the foldout's there. If you want to sit."

"Thank you," she said, moving toward the couch.

But still keeping me at the corner of her eye. The folksy, off-handed manner was just an act, I realized now. Everything she'd said and done had been carefully planned to elicit a response from me, an attempt to see what I knew and whether or not I was trying to hide any such knowledge.

Fortunately, the very unexpectedness of her verbal gut-punch had overwhelmed any guilty reactions she might have been hoping for.

"Yes, it's the first murder we've had in Bilswift for over ten years," Kreega went on as she settled onto the couch. "Actually, there may have been *two* murders. We're not sure. But please; continue with your meal."

I looked at Selene, only then noticing that we were both still standing. "That's all right," I said to Kreega. "I think I've lost my appetite. You said *two* murders?"

"At least sit down," Kreega pressed. "This could take a while. Yes, it could be two, though we only have one body. The other is suggested by the Path blood we found at the Javersin brothers' fish shop."

I felt a fresh shiver run up my back as Selene and I resumed our seats at the table. Selene's earlier warning flashed across my mind: *Kadolian changelings can drift ethically into crime, psychopathy, or sociopathy.* "You're sure it's Galfvi's blood?"

"They're checking it now," Kreega said. "But there are only a few other Path in town, and as far as I know none of them patronizes the Javersin brothers' place."

"We've been told at least one of them sometimes goes to Panza's Café," Selene offered. "That's not too far from the fish shop."

"You've been both places, then?" Kreega asked. "I mean, to know where they are relative to each other."

"There are these things called *maps* that also do that job," I said, letting my tone go a little testy. It was time I got over my shock and started feeling a little righteously indignant. "But yes, we've been both places. If this is a formal interrogation, can we get on with it?"

"Nothing formal about it, Mr. Roarke," Kreega assured me, pulling out her info pad. "We're just trying to collect information, and you're two of the people we're hoping to collect it from. So. Darnell Javersin says you talked for a while with his Kadolian employee, Tirano. What exactly did you talk about?"

"I'm sure Mr. Javersin could tell you that," I said. "He made sure he was close enough to eavesdrop."

"Oh, he did tell us," Kreega said calmly. "I just want to hear your version."

"Not going to be any different from his," I said. "Tirano told us his age and that his parents were dead. Darnell said he'd been indentured to them by a broker named Lukki, told us we could find her at Panza's, and then Tirano went back to work. End of conversation."

"What about Galfvi?"

"What about him?" I asked. "We didn't talk to him at all. We didn't even know his name until you mentioned it a couple of minutes ago."

"And did you then go to Panza's to confront Ms. Parsons?"

From across the table I caught the subtle catch in Selene's breath. Kreega's scent had shifted, which meant her emotions had changed, which meant she'd just sidled casually up on one of the truly critical questions. "If by Ms. Parsons you mean Lukki, yes, But I went there to *talk* to her, nothing more."

"I'm told you pulled a weapon on her."

We'd reached the crucial question list, all right. "To be precise, I pulled a weapon on one of the men who attacked me."

"*Attacked* you?" Kreega echoed, her eyebrows rising. "I'm told it was a simple shoving match."

"I suppose that's fair."

"And you were the one who escalated it?"

I shrugged. "I just shoved harder than they did."

"Mm." Kreega peered at her pad. "Tell me, what kind of terms did you and Ms. Parsons separate on?"

"They were mostly cordial on my part," I said. "You'd have to ask her for her take on it."

"That would be a bit difficult," Kreega said, "given that Ms. Parsons is the one who was murdered."

I felt my lip twitch. So we'd finally gotten where I'd figured we were going. I *really* needed to stop opening the *Ruth*'s entryway to badgemen. "I suppose this is where I'm supposed to trot out my alibi?"

"If you have one, yes, this would be the time."

"I'm sure it would," I said. "Unfortunately, I don't. I headed straight back here from Panza's on foot. I got mugged about three blocks from—"

"*Mugged?*" Kreega cut me off, frowning. "Why didn't you mention that before?"

"Because it wasn't a big deal," I said. "Someone shot me with a vertigo dart, rifled through my wallet without taking anything, and left me in the rain to recover."

"I don't suppose you kept the dart."

I shook my head. "Sorry, but I assume it's still lying around the street somewhere. You want to see where it hit me?"

"Yes, please," she said, standing up.

I took off my jacket and shrugged my shirt off my right shoulder. "Somewhere there," I said, pointing to my upper back.

"Okay, I see the puncture mark," Kreega confirmed, taking a couple of quick pictures of the spot. "I'll have a couple of my guys look for the dart in the morning. I don't suppose you'd like to give me a blood sample to confirm it was a vertigo drug?"

"Is that an official request?" I asked, pulling my shirt back into place.

"If you mean do I have a warrant, no," she said, returning to her seat on the foldout. "But most people with nothing to hide are happy to cooperate with badgemen."

"Maybe so," I said. "But as my father used to say, *Everyone has something they'd prefer to keep to themselves, and you might as well put bodily fluids at the top of that list.* Besides, the drug's been metabolized and out of my system for at least the last half hour."

"Maybe," Kreega said, still not looking happy. "A sample still might help support your story."

"I doubt it," I said. "Anything else?"

"Yes." Abruptly, Kreega shifted her eyes to Selene. "What about *you*, Ms. Selene? You want to tell me where you've been this afternoon and evening?"

"Whoa," I protested. "What are you asking *her* for? *I'm* the one who had the run-in with Lukki and her thugs, remember?"

"And *she's* the one with blood ties to our missing Kadolian," Kreega countered. "The missing Kadolian, moreover, who was indentured to the Javersin brothers by the late Ms. Parsons."

I looked at Selene. There was quiet turmoil in her pupils, and a simmering anger.

She'd killed before, of course, back in our bounty hunter days. That was the price of the job: eventually you took someone's life, or someone took yours.

But those deaths had always been last-ditch decisions, and always done in self-defense. I'd never thought of Selene as someone who could kill in cold blood.

Now, gazing into those pupils, I wondered if maybe she could.

"I drove up into the mountains," she said. Her voice and face were their usual inexpressive calmness, and it occurred to me that if Detective-Sergeant Kreega was hoping to read guilt or innocence there she was going to be seriously disappointed. "Highway 306, the main road that leads up and around the mountains toward Cavindoss."

"Yes, I know it," Kreega said.

"I went as far as I could before sunset, then started back," Selene continued. "I drove through Bilswift and arrived at the *Ruth* about an hour ago."

"You came straight back from 306 to the ship?"

Selene's pupils went a little uneasy. "No," she said. "I first drove past the Javersin brothers' seafood shop, then past Panza's Café."

"Why?"

"The first because I wanted to see if Tirano was still there," Selene said. "The shop's shutters were in place and there were no lights showing, so I assumed he was gone. The second because I thought Gregory might have only recently left and that if I could catch up to him along the way I could give him a ride back."

"You didn't go into either place?"

"No."

For a moment the two women stared at each other, Kreega trying her best to read Selene's mind, Selene just being Selene. "So straight down the mountain, past the scene of two disappearances and a murder, then back to your ship."

"Or straight down the mountain, past two business establishments, then back to the ship," I growled. "If you're going to slant the evidence, at least wait until you're on the witness stand. And if you're going to formally charge us, let's get on with it."

"No one's charging anyone yet," Kreega said, standing up. "Right now, we're still just investigating. Thanks for your hospitality. We'll be in touch."

"I'm sure you will," I said, standing up as well. "By the way, may I ask how and where Lukki was killed?"

Kreega regarded me coolly. "Not that it's any of your business, but she took a single plasmic shot to the chest outside her apartment house."

"Range?" I asked. "Angle?"

"Point-blank," Kreega said. "One to three meters. Straight in."

"Lighting?"

"You saw what the streetlights are like out there," Kreega said. "Adequate, but nothing more. You always this nosy on matters that don't concern you?"

"You're on the edge of accusing Selene and me of murder," I reminded her. "I think that gives us a claim to it being our business. More than that, as a former bounty hunter I've had a certain amount of experience with such things."

"I'll just bet you have," she said darkly. "Oh, and don't try to leave the planet. We'll know if you do. Good night. Sleep well."

❖   ❖   ❖

Selene was still seated at the table, staring into her bowl, when I returned from seeing Kreega out and locking the entryway behind her. "You all right?" I asked as I sat down across from her.

"I'm fine," she said, still keeping her pupils out of my view. "I reheated the chowder a little."

"Thanks," I said. I'd already noticed the heightened aroma. "She's a real peach, isn't she?"

"She's worried."

"I'm not surprised," I said. "This might be the first murder she's ever had to deal with. Not to mention all the political repercussions."

Selene raised her eyes to me, her pupils frowning. "Political repercussions?"

"Our Lukki Parsons wasn't just your normal working-class citizen," I pointed out. "She's a self-styled dealer in exotics."

"And?"

"And look where we are," I said, waving a hand around me. "Bilswift doesn't exactly have the population density to support a brisk trade in exotic alien slavery or even exotic alien indenture. She set up shop here in this out-of-the-way place where all the major Alainn authorities are either oblivious to her business or winking at it in exchange for nice monthly payments."

"She might just use this as her base while she travels around," Selene pointed out. "She could have her own aircar, and there's a daily shuttle to Tranlisoa."

"True," I conceded. "Plus there's the StarrComm center there, so she might be able to do some of her business long-distance. Regardless, she must have had protectors, and whoever they were I suspect they're sweating ten-millimeter slugs right now that it wasn't *just* about Lukki."

"Yes, I see." Selene looked up, her pupils earnest and a little fearful. "Gregory...you believe me, don't you? That I didn't kill her?"

"Of course," I said with more conviction than I really felt. There were few enough Kadolians in the Spiral as it was, and to find one of them in slavery would surely have dug deeply into Selene's heart and soul. And I had no idea what her species' view was on retribution.

And lurking in the back of my mind was her reluctant admission a few months back that some of her people had once been hired as assassins, and that many of them had apparently taken to the job. "Look, there's nothing we can do about all that right now," I continued before she could respond. "Kreega and the other badgemen are on it, and we need more information before we can take our own look at it. So let's focus on the reason we came to Bilswift in the first place. Did you get anything from your drive up the mountain?"

"Yes, a little," she said, her pupils changing as she shifted mental gears. "There's definitely a major archeological site up there, with everything fenced off."

"How much everything?"

"A lot," Selene said. "The fencing starts at the edge of the forest about three kilometers outside of town, then runs along the road for at least fifteen kilometers before it curves back away again. A little ways north of the enclosure I found a jeep trail and followed that five kilometers to the river. From what I could see, it looked like the fence went all the way west again, paralleling the river's southern bank."

"Terrific," I growled. So the Patth had cordoned off an area of around seventy-five square kilometers. That was a lot of territory to search for even the twenty- to forty-meter diameter sphere of a typical Icarus-style portal. "What kind of fence was it?"

"A quick-set," she said. "Depending on how many Patth are in there, it could have been put up in two or three days."

"So how many *are* in there?"

"I couldn't get close enough for accurate numbers," she said. "There are a large number of plants and animals I'm not familiar with that confuse the scents. But I'm fairly certain it's just Patth."

"What, no Drilies?" I asked. With their squat builds and gorilla-length arms, Drilies were one of the chief go-to species for excavation work when bringing in digging machines wasn't practical.

"None that I could smell." Her pupils shifted to wry humor. "I know: Patth doing their own heavy labor. I'm as surprised as you are."

"Well, we *are* dealing with a portal," I pointed out. "As my father used to say, *If it's a choice between secrecy and sweat, choose the sweat.* How tall is the fence?"

"Only about two meters," she said. "But it has a series of sensor buds along the top."

I scowled. "So we can forget climbing or cutting through it. Any dips or pits in the ground beneath it that we might be able to squeeze through?"

"I didn't see any," Selene said. "But I only drove past it. We can take a closer look tomorrow."

"Sounds good." I hesitated. But it had to be asked. "Selene, you said changelings like Tirano could drift into sociopathy. Is it possible he could have killed Lukki without you being able to tell?"

"*If* he's a changeling," Selene corrected me firmly. "We still don't know that for sure."

"Granted," I said. "But if he is?"

She closed her eyes. "Yes," she said quietly. "If he felt it was necessary... yes, he could."

"And could he kill *us* if he thought it necessary?"

Her eyes snapped open, angry denial in her pupils. "No," she said firmly. "He wouldn't do that."

"But he *could*?"

She lowered her gaze, the denial fading. "I don't know," she said. "I really don't."

"Okay," I said. At this point, that was all I needed to hear. "Back to Plan A: You take back your cabin, and he sleeps in the dayroom."

"Gregory, we can't move him," Selene protested. "Not tonight. He's already asleep."

"So we wake him up."

"We can't do that."

"Why not?"

"Because I set up the cabin to..." She hesitated. "*Acclimate* isn't the right word. But it's all I can come up with. He's... it's like he doesn't really know how to be a Kadolian."

"I thought you said he had his parents until he was six," I said, frowning. "What part of being Kadolian didn't they get around to teaching him?"

"It's not really *teaching*," she said, still clearly struggling to find the right words. "It's a sort of immersion. He needs the sounds, the scents, the touch of the proper weave of linens, the warmth." She held her hands up helplessly. "I don't know how to explain it."

"He needs a sense of home and security?" I suggested. "Like a baby?"

"Like a *human* baby," Selene corrected. "Or like a Kadolian baby and child. It takes longer with us."

"Is that why you wanted to put him in your cabin? So you could rig all that up for him?"

"Yes," she said, quiet relief in her pupils that we were finally on the same page. "Maybe we can move him in a few days. But not tonight."

"I understand," I said. "Okay. But in that case, you're sleeping in my cabin tonight with the door locked. No argument," I added as she opened her mouth to protest. "I'm taking the foldout."

"Gregory, he won't hurt me," she insisted. "I'm one of his people. Besides, he's being acclimated. He won't leave the cabin during the night."

"That's a great theory, and I wish I could believe it," I said. "But as my father used to say, *When a theory runs into reality, it's the theory that breaks first.*"

"Gregory—"

"We agreed when we started this whole thing that I'm the *Ruth*'s captain," I said, trying to get this over with. The thought of sleeping in an unlockable dayroom with a possible killer able to roam free was creeping me out. But I sure as hell wasn't going to put Selene in that position, soothing baby-crib sounds or no soothing baby-crib sounds. "We also agreed that if we ever came to an impasse with no chance of compromise, I would have the final say."

A maelstrom of unhappy emotions whipped their way across her pupils. "All right," she said. "If you insist, I'll sleep in your cabin." She drew herself up in her chair, her pupils going defiant. "So will you."

I sighed. "Selene, there's not enough open floor space in there for a second person."

"I know," she said. "We'll both have to use the bed."

I stared, stunned speechless for one of the few times in my life. "You know that won't work," I said carefully. "Your sense of smell—you can't be that close to me for that long without it being a problem."

"I also can't let you sleep out here alone until we're sure about Tirano," she said. "As to the other part . . . I'll just have to make do."

I let out a hissing sigh. We'd had a brief time of closeness once before, which was how we'd found out that a couple of hours at a stretch was about all she could take. "All right," I said. "But you have to promise—*really* promise—that when it gets to be too much you'll wake me up and let me know. Deal?"

She hesitated, then nodded. "Deal."

"Okay." I scooped up a spoonful of chowder, only to discover that while we'd been talking it had gone cold again. "So," I continued, standing up and picking up both of our bowls. "I'm going to heat this up again, we're going to eat it, and then we're going to get to sleep. It's been a long day, tomorrow's going to be even longer, and I don't want either of us dozing off in the middle of it."

The *Ruth*'s beds weren't designed for more than one person, and fitting both of us into mine was something of a challenge. But eventually we sorted it out, with Selene on the wall side and me on the edge. She argued briefly about that, pointing out that if she was at the edge she could leave if she needed to without waking me up. I argued in return that if she tried to ease away from me while she was asleep she was going to drop right off the bed onto a very hard deck. In the end, she gave in.

I'd been asleep about an hour and a half when I woke to find her lying on her side, her back to me, her face and torso pressed against the wall as hard as she could, making quiet little noises in her sleep. Taking the cue, I rolled out of bed, picked up my plasmic, and left the cabin.

Unfortunately, there was no way for me to lock up behind me after I left. I could only hope she'd been right about Tirano staying in his cabin and out of mischief.

If she'd been wrong about that, my next best hope was that he would come for me first. At least I wouldn't have any familial-based qualms about shooting him.

I'd slept on the dayroom foldout far more often than I'd ever expected to and knew how to angle myself to take advantage of the most comfortable part of the mattress. I tucked my plasmic under my pillow, then dimmed the lights but didn't entirely extinguish them.

My last thought before drifting off to an uneasy sleep was that the first thing I was going to do when Tirano got up was reverse the lock on his cabin door so that we could make sure he stayed put during the night.

Assuming, of course, Selene and I were still alive.

CHAPTER SIX

Six hours later, I awoke to the pleasant and mildly surprising discovery that I had not, in fact, been murdered in my sleep. I got up, took a quick shower, made myself some breakfast, and got to work.

I was still at it when Selene joined me. "Good morning, Gregory," she said, her pupils looking a little uncertain as she sat down across the table from me. "Did I wake you?"

"No, I woke up on my own," I assured her. It was mostly true, hopefully true enough that it wouldn't trigger a change in my scent that she could pick up on. "Slept a little in here, then figured as long as the ship was quiet I might as well hit the day running."

She craned her neck to look at the Bilswift city map I'd opened on my info pad. "We're not going into the mountains?"

"Maybe later," I said. "Right now, I think we should look into Lukki's murder and Galfvi's disappearance before those trails go any colder than they already have."

"I don't think Detective-Sergeant Kreega wants our help," Selene warned.

"I wasn't planning to offer her a choice," I said. "The fact that she got here last night as quickly as she did tells me she's already leaning toward pinning everything on outsiders, which at the moment are you and me."

"And Tirano," Selene murmured. "All right. Where do we start?"

"The fish market," I said, tapping a spot on my pad. "Right now, both Tirano and Galfvi are effectively ciphers. We need to get to know them: how long they've worked at the fish market, how well they got along with each other and the bosses, what their usual routine was, where they lived, who else they hung out with, and all the rest of it."

"So we're treating Galfvi like a bounty target?"

"Exactly," I said. "After that, I want to go see where Lukki was gunned down. I have some questions that only a good look at the landscape can answer."

"Such as why the shooter was able to get to point-blank range?"

"*And* why he was at street level in the first place instead of sniping from a rooftop," I said. "*And* why her thugs didn't do a better job of protecting her. And if there aren't any badgemen around, maybe we'll see if there's anything of interest inside her apartment."

"I'm sure Kreega would want that sort of help even less."

"We'll try not to trouble her with such details," I said. "Regardless, we need to get a handle on both incidents. If we can find a common denominator, we may be able to connect the dots."

Selene suddenly stiffened. "Tirano," she said softly.

I was about to say that, yes, Tirano was definitely one of those common denominators when the boy appeared in the dayroom hatchway. "Hello," he said, a little uncertainly. "Am I interrupting?"

"No, not at all," Selene said, standing up and turning to face him. "Are you hungry? Can I make you something to eat?"

"I don't think I have time," Tirano said. "I need to get to work."

"Afraid you're not going to work today," I told him. "We need to keep you here."

"But I have work to do," he said.

"Tirano, Galfvi is missing," Selene put in gently.

"Missing?" Tirano said, giving her a sort of half frown. Kadolian physiology didn't lend itself to that sort of facial expression, but he was trying mightily to make it work. "He was there yesterday. How can he be missing today?"

"We don't know," I said. "But until we figure out what happened to him, we think it'll be better for you to stay here."

"And to stay here *quietly*," Selene added. "That means you can't leave or let anyone know where you are."

"Did something happen to him?" he asked, his eyes flicking back and forth between us, his pupils still unreadable to me. "Was he hurt? Was he stolen?"

"Was he *kidnapped*," I corrected. "Sapient beings like Galfvi are kidnapped, not stolen."

"Mr. Darnell says Galfvi and I are his property," Tirano said. "Like the seafood shop and the fish."

I looked at Selene, caught the sudden flash of anger in her pupils. "Mr. Darnell is mistaken," I said. "Whatever he told you, or whatever Lukki told you, you're a person, with all the rights and privileges as laid out in Commonwealth law."

"I understand," Tirano said, though I was pretty sure he didn't. "But Mr. Darnell will be angry if I don't come do my work."

"Don't worry about it," I soothed. "We're going to go talk to him this morning. We'll let him know what's happened."

"All right." Tirano looked back at Selene. "So then I *do* have time to eat?"

Selene had come up with several food suggestions, no doubt with Tirano's ongoing Kadolian acclimation in mind. But the boy asked for more of the crab chowder, so she heated up another bowl of it for him. Reminding him again not to leave the ship, call anyone, or let anyone in, Selene and I collected our gear and headed out.

Once again, mindful of our phones' tracking capabilities, we left them in our cabins.

"Were you going to tell him how to use the deadbolt?" she asked as we made our way down the zigzag.

"No, and I'm hoping he doesn't figure it out on his own," I told her. "The last thing I want is to get locked out of my own ship because our houseguest is sleeping deeply amid a potpourri of Kadolian spices or something."

"That's not really how it works," Selene corrected, her pupils looking a little cross. "Besides, there's always the back door."

"Theoretically," I cautioned. The *Ruth*'s secret back door was through the Number Two equipment bay, which held equipment normally accessible only from the outside of the ship. Our bay, however, was gimmicked with a removeable back panel that would allow us to get into or out of the ship without anyone who might be waiting by the entryway being the wiser.

Unfortunately, in this case, Bilswift spaceport's compact size and sparseness of standing monitors and fueling equipment worked against that kind of inconspicuousness. At most ports there was enough clutter and associated visual cover to let us slip into and out of the Number Two bay without being seen. Here, without enough of that to shield us from view, pulling that off without being spotted would take careful timing.

"But as a practical matter, I wouldn't want to try it until after dark," I added. "You'd be pretty exposed if you tried it in broad daylight. Where'd you park, by the way?"

"Under the runaround stand overhang," she said. "There'd been a little hail earlier during the rainstorm, and I thought the car would be better protected there."

"Good idea," I said. "Of course it meant a longer walk in the rain for you but...uh-oh."

"What?" she asked.

"That dark blue ground car," I said, giving a small nod toward a vehicle parked twenty meters behind the runaround stand. "Odds are that's a badgeman in an unmarked car."

"You think Kreega sent him here to watch us?"

"Unless he moonlights as the town greeter," I said with a sigh. "Might as well go see what he wants."

We reached the bottom of the zigzag and headed toward the two parked cars. We passed ours without stopping and continued on. The driver of the blue car slid down his side window as we approached. "Morning, Officer," I said as we came to a stop. "Out enjoying the morning air?"

"Good morning, Mr. Roarke," he said in a neutral tone as he held up a badge for my inspection. Apparently, Kreega's pretend folksy casualness wasn't official policy for the rest of Bilswift's badgemen. "May I ask where you're going?"

"To the Javersin brothers' fish shop," I said, eyeing the badge. It was Bilswift issue, all right, with the name ZILOR along the bottom. "We're interested in trying some of your local mari-mari, and Bicks Javersin told me yesterday that it would be ripe today."

"I've heard it's very good," Zilor said. "I'll give you a ride."

"Ah...thanks," I said, frowning. That was unexpected. "But we have our own car."

"I'll be happy to bring you back after you do your shopping."

"We may want to do more touristing after we get our fish," I said.

"As I said, I'll bring you back."

This was starting to get awkward. "I doubt Detective-Sergeant Kreega will want you playing chauffer to a couple of visitors," I warned.

"Actually, Detective-Sergeant Kreega has already instructed me to bring you to the seafood shop." Zilor touched a control, and I heard the back door locks disengage. "Please don't make me insist."

I huffed out a breath. "Wouldn't think of it," I muttered, opening the door and ushering Selene into the sealed rear compartment. "Especially since you ask so nicely."

"Bilswift is known all over Alainn for its politeness," Zilor said. "Oh, and just leave your weapons back there on the seat when we reach the seafood shop, okay?"

"We still have our bounty hunter licenses," I told him. "That entitles us to carry weapons."

"I know," Zilor said agreeably. "That's why I'm asking you to leave them back there instead of confiscating them right now and keeping them up here with me."

"Ah," I said. I wasn't entirely sure that was what the law said, but it wasn't a hill I was willing to fight over. "Again, since you're so polite about it. Can we assume this won't take very long?"

"You can assume anything you want," Zilor said as he started the car. "Doesn't necessarily make it so."

We arrived at the Javersin brothers' shop to find the place still shuttered as Selene had seen it when she drove past the previous night. There were two other badgeman cars parked along the street, this pair fully marked as such. One of them was an aircar, and as Zilor walked us past I noted it was marked as Cavindoss Law Enforcement. Either Kreega had elected to call in help from the much bigger city beyond the mountains or else someone had made that decision for her.

Which was probably not a move that would tilt things in our favor. Outside pressure tended to make officials grumpy and goad them toward impulsive and not necessarily well-thought-out verdicts. With Selene and me at the top of Kreega's suspect list, hasty moves were not what we were looking for.

Kreega and two other badgemen were waiting in the back of the shop near the interior door I'd noticed the previous day, conversing in low tones, as we were ushered in. One of them was considerably older than Kreega and the other uniformed badgeman and dressed in plainclothes, and I tentatively identified him as the out-of-towner. Darnell and Bicks Javersin were off by themselves in the prep area, also talking together and working anxiously at an info pad. No one in either group was smiling.

As my father used to say, *Watch out for people who look like they're going to a funeral when there's no obvious guest of honor. They could be holding that spot open for you.*

"Mr. Roarke," Kreega greeted me with a perfunctory nod as Zilor took us over to her group. "Thank you for joining us."

"Glad to oblige," I said. "As Badgeman Zilor probably told you, we were on our way over anyway. How can we be of service?"

"That's one of them?" the plainclothes badgeman interjected, nodding at Selene.

"Yes, she's a Kadolian," Kreega confirmed, the temperature of her voice dropping a couple of degrees. So much for his presence at her crime scene being her idea.

"And you wanted her here *why*?"

"To test a theory," Kreega said, beckoning to Selene. "If you'll follow me, Ms. Selene?"

Kreega led the way through the door into a small office with a pair of desks, a large file cabinet, a set of shelves with the usual random detritus of every normal office, and a waist-high Poconos Barline safe tucked into the back corner.

A waist-high safe whose door was swung all the way open.

"That's how the Javersin brothers found their safe this morning," Kreega said, waving toward it. "They say there were sixteen thousand commarks in there when they left last night."

"Ouch," I said sympathetically. Sixteen thousand: comfortably within the range I'd estimated for the stash hidden in Galfvi's robe. "Was it forced?"

Kreega shook her head. "Opened with the combination."

"Ah." I gestured toward the safe. "May I?"

"Go ahead," she said. "We've already pulled off everything we could."

I nodded and walked around the desks to the safe. The door was equipped with a standard keypad, the manufacturer plate identifying the lock as relatively low-end but still perfectly respectable. As Kreega had said, there were no indications the safe had been forced. "Who had the combination?" I asked.

"We did," Darnell Javersin said.

I looked back to find that he and Bicks had joined us and were standing nervously in the doorway. "Anyone else?" I asked. "Tirano or Galfvi never went into it?"

"No," Darnell said.

"No, no—remember?" Bicks said. "Couple of weeks ago. You had Tirano put some money in there."

"Yeah, but the safe door was already open," Darnell said.

"You're sure the money was there when you left last night?" I asked. "That was a lot of cash to leave lying around."

"It was, but we needed it," Darnell said. "We have a shipment coming in today, and we needed it on hand to pay for the goods. And yes, it was in there and the door was locked."

"But Tirano and Galfvi were still finishing up when we left," Bicks added.

"If you're quite finished, Mr. Roarke," the plainclothesman said impatiently, "we've already been through this."

"*We* haven't been through it," I pointed out. "Detective . . . ?"

He glowered at me. "Detective-Lieutenant Sovelli. And we didn't bring you here to play badgemen."

I raised my eyebrows politely. "No?"

"Detective-*Sergeant* Kreega," Sovelli said, leaning just a little too hard on Kreega's lower rank, "thinks the Kadolian who worked here might have been able to crack the combination. She thinks your Kadolian can prove that."

"Okay, let's start over," I suggested, raising a halting hand toward Selene as she started forward. "I'm Gregory Roarke, former bounty hunter, current crockett. This is my partner—not my possession, my *partner*—Selene. We're here because you have at least one murder on your hands, maybe two, and at least one disappearance, maybe two. You think we might be able to help sort through the ground clutter and help you find some answers, and you're very aware that we're under no legal obligation to do so. So let's have a little less hostility and a little more respect, okay? Because whoever foisted you on Detective-Sergeant Kreega is expecting results, and I don't think you want to disappoint them. Did I miss anything?"

Sovelli's face had gone through a whole range of expressions during my little speech, starting with disbelief, shifting to outrage, and ending up in cold loathing. For a couple of seconds he just stood there, and then he took a deep breath. "Fine," he said. "My turn. You have no standing, no authority, and no allies here. Furthermore, you and your *partner* are also prime suspects in this case. I don't need you here, I don't particularly want you here, and I'd just as soon toss you into one of the Bilswift cells to rot. You so much as lean over the line and I'll have you there so fast your ears will fall off. Did *I* miss anything?"

"No, I think you got it covered," I assured him calmly. Kreega, standing beside him, had a pinched sort of expression. Possibly trying to figure out which side of this she was on. "Just wanted to make sure we both knew where we stood. Now, what exactly do you want Selene to do?"

"I want to see if she can crack the safe," Sovelli said. "I'm told Kadolians have a good sense of smell, maybe good enough to pick up the Javersins' scent from the buttons. I want to see if that's possible."

"Fair enough," I said. Actually, that was one of the tests I'd been planning for Selene anyway. "Selene?"

Silently, she moved past me to the safe and knelt down beside it. Leaning close to the door and the keypad, she began sniffing.

I looked back at the Javersin brothers. "How long have Tirano and Galfvi worked for you?" I asked.

"Galfvi's been with us for nearly eight months," Darnell said. "Tirano for about a year."

"How have they been as employees?" I asked, frowning slightly. So if Tirano had been orphaned at six and was now ten, we were looking at a three-year gap. What had he been doing during that time? Wandering around on his own until Lukki ran into him?

"Decent enough, I suppose," Darnell said.

"What was their attitude like?" Sovelli asked. "Were either of them mouthy or argumentative?"

"No, neither of them," Darnell said. "Tirano was especially cooperative."

"Which he *shouldn't* have been, if you ask me," Bicks growled. "I mean, a fish-shop cutter after having once been a tracker? Doesn't take a genius to see that's a big step down."

"What kind of tracker?" I asked. "He track anything in particular?"

The two brothers exchanged a quick look. "No, no, not really," Darnell said. "There used to be some natives living up in the mountains—"

"The Loporri," Bicks put in.

"Yeah, the Loporri," Darnell said. "There used to be a village of them up the mountain near a place called Seven Strands. All gone now, but people still sometimes go up there looking for artifacts."

"Tirano used to sometimes go with groups to help sniff them out," Bicks added.

"Ah." The missing three years from his timeline? "Still, there's a lot to be said for a job where you're out of the weather and don't have to tramp up and down mountains all day. What about Galfvi?"

"He was fine," Darnell said. "Though I sometimes got the feeling he thought we were beneath him."

"Like Tirano *ought* to have thought," Bicks muttered.

"Did Galfvi come from Lukki, too?" I asked.

"No, he just showed up one day looking for a job," Darnell said.

"It was really kind of weird," Bicks said. "He just sort of popped up, said he liked fish, and asked if he could work here."

"Anything else odd happen that day?" Kreega asked.

"No, nothing," Darnell said. "Though—" He frowned at his brother. "Didn't we decide he must have come in on the Tranlisoa shuttle?"

"Yeah, because he wasn't local and didn't have a car or any way to have come from Cavindoss or anywhere else," Bicks agreed. "Yeah, I remember wondering why someone would leave a major place like Tranlisoa and come to the middle of nowhere without a plan."

"Maybe he had a plan and it fell through," Kreega said.

"Speaking of plans," Sovelli said, turning to Selene. "How is that going? You got anything?"

I turned back. Selene had finished her analysis and was waiting quietly for a break in the conversation. "Yes," she said. "It would take me a little time, but I could open it."

Sovelli threw me a significant look. "How?"

Selene looked at the brothers. "Is it all right if I tell the others the numbers?" she asked. "I don't know how many of each was used, or the order."

Darnell and Bicks exchanged looks. "I suppose that'll be okay," Darnell said cautiously.

Selene nodded. "The numbers are two, four, seven, and nine," she said. "As I said, that's all I know. But that knowledge would limit the possibilities to something a thief might find manageable."

"How do you know those are the numbers?" Darnell asked.

"They're the ones you and your brother touched."

"Did you smell either Tirano or Galfvi on them?" I asked.

"Not on the keypad," Selene said. "But there's the scent of the same plastic as is in the clean-up gloves out in the prep room."

"So the perp wore gloves," Kreega said, nodding. "Not surprising. Also nonconclusive."

"Sounds pretty conclusive to me," Sovelli said, a note of satisfaction in his voice. "Ms. Selene just proved Tirano's the only one who could get the safe open. He popped the lock, took the money, and ran."

"Maybe," Kreega said. "But Galfvi had access to the office, too. Didn't he?"

"I can smell traces of both of them in here," Selene confirmed.

"So he was here," Sovelli growled. "So what? Patth can't do what Selene just did. Either Tirano did it on his own, or he and Galfvi did it together. It's the only way it works."

Darnell's face screwed up. "I don't know," he muttered. "I can't help wondering why either of them would do it *now*. We've had more money than that in the safe before. Sometimes a lot more."

"Like with the Nellingham deal," Bicks said.

"Exactly," Darnell said. "We had nearly thirty thousand in the safe then. So why now, when all they could get was sixteen?"

"Maybe Tirano decided to run, and he took what he could get," Sovelli suggested.

"Or maybe he *needed* to run," Bicks said, his tone going dark. "If Tirano and Galfvi were working together...You said some of Galfvi's blood was in here, Detective-Sergeant?"

"There was some Patth blood, yes," Kreega confirmed. "But we're still analyzing it to see if it's Galfvi's."

"It is," Selene told her. "I smelled it when we came in."

"Or you just smelled *him*," Sovelli countered. "You already said his scent was all over the place."

Selene shook her head. "The scent of a person's blood is different from the scent of the person."

Sovelli grunted. "Whatever," he said reluctantly. "Anyway, it already seemed pretty straightforward. Tirano opened the safe and took the money. Galfvi caught him at it, they argued, Tirano cut him and they both ran off."

"And Galfvi didn't go straight to the badgemen?" I asked. "Or even just call them?"

"Maybe he couldn't," Sovelli said. "Maybe he's lying dead behind a house somewhere."

"No," Selene said. "The blood loss was very small, not enough to incapacitate him."

"Maybe Tirano dragged him out of here and he bled out somewhere else," Sovelli countered.

"There's no blood trail through the shop," Selene said.

"Did you find the weapon he was cut with?" I asked.

"It was one of the shop's cutting knives," Kreega said. "We've got it bagged back at the station."

"Could I examine it?" Selene asked. "I might be able to tell who was holding it when Galfvi was cut."

Sovelli snorted. "Like maybe space pixies? Come on. I know you want to protect a fellow Kadolian, but this has gotten ridiculous."

"Right," I said. "Because it saves so much time to come to a conclusion without having to wait for that pesky evidence stuff."

"And if I were you, I'd watch your own mouth, bounty hunter," Sovelli warned. "You carry a plasmic. Lukki Parsons was killed with a plasmic. You were seen fighting with her at Panza's Café. More of that pesky evidence?"

"Connecting dots isn't the same as evidence," I reminded him.

"It's usually a good start." Sovelli looked at Kreega. "I don't mean to tell you how to run your town, Detective-Sergeant, but I'd like to point out that you've got two prime suspects working your crime scene."

"They're helping collect evidence," Kreega countered. "There's nothing either of them is saying that won't be checked via other sources or other means."

"Well, then, try this one." Sovelli jabbed a finger at Selene. "She's already said she could open the safe. If that means Tirano could have done it, it also means she could have."

"Absolutely," I said sarcastically. "Because the first thing everyone does when they roll into a new town is pick a shop at random and rob it."

"Maybe you're all working together," he shot back. "Tirano does the recon and prep work, you swoop in and grab the goods." He turned again to Kreega. "I'd recommend you get a warrant to search their ship. I'd lay you odds that Tirano *and* the money are both there."

"Hey!" Zilor's voice came from the main part of the shop. "Come back here!"

I looked at the Javersin brothers, caught their sudden surprise and disquiet as they looked out the office door behind them. Reflexively, I dropped my hand to my holster before remembering my plasmic was tucked away out of sight in the back seat of Zilor's car. I glanced around, spotted a decorative paperweight in relatively easy reach on one of the desks that would do as a makeshift throwing weapon in a pinch. The Javersins stepped quickly out of the doorway—

As a pair of gray-robed Patth stormed into the office, a flustered Zilor trailing behind them. "Detective-Sergeant—" he began.

"Where is he?" the Patth in the lead demanded harshly. He twitched aside the right flap of his robe, revealing a holstered plasmic. "Where is he?

"Where is the person who murdered our kinsman?"

CHAPTER SEVEN

"Let's dial it back a quarter turn," Kreega said, the full weight of her authority in her voice. I glanced over, saw she and the other badgemen had their hands on their GovSev 6mm slug guns. "Leave that weapon in its holster, drop the robe flap, and just calm down."

I felt my lip twist with the subtle politics of the situation. With anyone else, flashing a holstered weapon in an aggressive way would have had the badgemen's guns instantly out and pointed. But with a pair of Patth, even completely nonofficial civilian types, restraint was the watchword of the day.

At least the second Patth had enough sense to know when he was teetering on the line. "Venikel, please," he said nervously, clutching at the other's gun arm. "These humans are badgemen. You cannot simply make demands of them."

"Our kinsman has been murdered, Kiolven," Venikel snarled back. "Vengeance is our goal. Vengeance is the only choice."

"You want choices?" Kreega countered. "Fine—here they are. Choice one: you drop the robe flap, calm down, and we talk. Choice two: you keep it up and you get shot. Pick one."

For a long, icy silence no one moved. Then Kiolven plucked again at Venikel's sleeve. "Please, Venikel," he pleaded quietly. "Needless violence will not gain Galfvi anything."

Venikel muttered something vile-sounding in the Patth language. But he opened his hand, letting the robe flap drop back to cover his weapon. "I am Venikel," he proclaimed, his tone marginally less confrontative. "I seek the murderer of my kinsman Galfvi."

"Detective-Sergeant Kreega, Bilswift badgeman," Kreega identified herself, easing her own hand off her weapon. "These are Badgeman Grazimink and Detective-Lieutenant Sovelli from Cavindoss. That's Badgeman Zilor behind you."

"Kiolven," Venikel said, gesturing dismissively toward his colleague. "We were told our kinsman Galfvi has been murdered."

"You were told wrong," Kreega said. "All we know for sure is that Galfvi has disappeared."

Venikel gave a wet-sounding snort. "There is no reason a Patthaaunuth would ever need to run or hide," he bit out. "If he is not here, he has been murdered." He sent a quick glare at Selene and me, and then turned to face the Javersin brothers, who seemed to be trying mightily to become statues of themselves. "Which one of you was Galfvi's employer?"

"We both were," Darnell said carefully. "I'm Darnell Javersin; this is my brother, Bicks."

"What do you have to say for yourselves?" Venikel demanded.

"Right now, they have nothing to say," Kreega put in. "They're witnesses in my investigation. *My* investigation, not yours."

Venikel spun to face her. "You dare—?"

"Venikel, *please,*" Kiolven said, starting to sound exasperated.

Venikel glared briefly at him, then turned to me. "And this one?" he demanded. "Is this one also a witness?"

"This one is an innocent visitor to Detective-Sergeant Kreega's lovely city," I said, "who would like to just get back to his own business. Who exactly told you Galfvi had been murdered?"

"We heard the news of his disappearance," Kiolven said. "There is no reason a Patthaaunuth would ever—"

"Yes, yes, we got it the first time," I cut him off, watching the two Patth closely. "So how did you get here so quickly? All of this only went down yesterday evening."

"When murder and vengeance are involved—" Venikel began.

He stopped as Kiolven again touched his arm. "We were in Tranlisoa on business when the news arrived," Kiolven explained. "We contacted his family and were asked to look into the matter."

"We then flew through the night to reach here," Venikel added.

"I see," I said. "Awfully handy that some of Galfvi's family were already on Alainn."

"We aren't his family," Venikel said, sounding slightly scandalized. "I merely said we'd talked to them. Whatever gave you the idea we were among them?"

"Because you're getting pretty emotional about someone you're not related to," I said. "You don't see that very often."

"All Patthaaunuth are kin to all others," Kiolven said. "As you kill or hurt or betray one, all the rest also suffer."

"Of course," I said. "Silly of me. Stimulating though this conversation is, Detective-Sergeant, if you want Selene to check out that knife, can we get to it? We have a full day's schedule ahead of us, and we're burning daylight."

"Certainly," Kreega said, still eyeing the Patth. "Badgeman Zilor will drive you."

"Thank you," I said, reaching an inviting hand toward Selene. Silently, she moved away from the desk and came over to me. "Oh, and is that mari-mari ripe yet?"

"What?" Darnell asked, sounding confused.

"Your brother said the mari-mari would be ripe today," I said. "We were hoping we could pick some up."

"I don't know," Darnell said. "Bicks?"

Bicks visibly shifted mental gears. "It's, uh, it'll be another five or six hours. Late afternoon. That's what Tirano said."

"Great," I said. "We'll come back then." I took Selene's arm and sidled us past the two Patth. "We're ready whenever you are, Badgeman Zilor. Masters Venikel and Kiolven, I'm sure we'll see you again."

"That does appear likely," Venikel agreed, eyeing me closely as we passed him. "May your tasks of the day be fully resolved."

We were halfway across the main shop when Selene finally leaned in toward me. "Venikel," she murmured.

I nodded acknowledgment. So Venikel, the hot-headed Patth, was the one who'd nailed me with that vertigo dart and left his scent on the barrel of my plasmic. So much for them flying in overnight. "Well, he's right about one thing," I muttered back.

"That Galfvi was murdered?"

I shook my head. "That he and I would be seeing each other again."

❖   ❖   ❖

Given that the knife that had cut Galfvi had been in the prep area where both Tirano and Galfvi worked, it wasn't surprising that it had both their scents on it.

Unfortunately, there was also glove scent on it, which meant whoever had cut Galfvi had worn gloves, which meant there was no way for Selene to figure out which one of the two had held it last.

Kreega was annoyed by Selene's failure, and didn't make much effort to conceal it. Sovelli was smugly condescending, and made even less of an effort.

Still, as far as I was concerned the side trip had been worthwhile. I'd now visited the Bilswift badgeman station, seen what their security was like, and marked where they locked up their evidence. If Selene and I needed to take a closer look at any of it, I knew how and where to start.

"What do you think of them?" Zilor asked as we got back in his car. "The Patth?"

"You mean Venikel and Kiolven?" I shrugged. "I don't buy their whole we're-all-kinsman speech, if that's what you're asking. I get the feeling there's something more personal going on under the surface."

"Yeah." Zilor was silent a moment. "I grew up near one of the Narchner areas of Porsto. I remember hearing one of them sing a song about how ancient Patth families dealt with internal trouble."

"Sounds like a rousing ballad," I commented. "Sorry I missed it."

"How they dealt with trouble," Zilor continued doggedly, "was that if someone shamed or embarrassed his family, he could be taken back to them, bounty-hunter style, and put on trial. If he lost, he'd be erased from all family records and banished to an island somewhere."

"That's all?" I asked, feeling a little disappointed. "Deleted from the record books and then banished? Narchner songs about other species usually come a lot bloodier than that."

"Indeed," Selene confirmed. "I once heard a Narchner song about Kalixiri who sent outriders off on hunts. If the outrider didn't bring back game, the Kalix would eat the outrider instead."

"They have a lot of songs about human torture methods and genocide, too," I said. "Stuff that we stopped doing four or five centuries ago. And there was a particularly catchy one about a

Ylpea dynasty that slaughtered surrendering enemies and then skinned the bodies for book bindings."

"Did the Ylps really do that?" Selene asked, a horrified look in her pupils.

"Maybe it was only that one dynasty," I said. "Or maybe it was all of them. Near as I can tell, Narchners just like singing about other species' darkest historical moments, the bloodier and more sordid the better. Simple boring banishment doesn't really sound like their style."

"I might have missed something in that one," Zilor conceded. "He was still going on as I left, and those upper harmonics they hit make my teeth hurt. But just because the songs are bloody doesn't mean they're wrong. Like you said about human genocide, a lot of legends and stories have a grain of truth in them."

"I concede the point about legends," I said. "Songs, not necessarily. What's your point?"

"My point is that we're badgemen," Zilor said. "We can't do anything to interfere with a potential crime until we have evidence or probable cause."

"Any particular crime you have in mind?" I asked.

"Kidnapping," he said bluntly. "Specifically, I'm worried about Kiolven and Venikel snatching Galfvi."

"I thought Galfvi was dead."

Zilor snorted. "You don't seriously think that, do you?"

"What about the blood?"

"Self-inflicted," Zilor said, as if that should be obvious. "A pathetic attempt to sidetrack our investigation."

"Kiolven and Venikel seem to believe otherwise."

"Kiolven and Venikel are family lackeys, not trained professionals," Zilor growled. "There was no blood trail, no other marks or droplets anywhere else, and none of the splatter that always happens when someone tries to jerk away from a knife that's cutting into him."

I looked at Selene, saw some grudging respect in her pupils. Small-city badgemen usually weren't great shakes in the detection department—probably why Detective-Lieutenant Sovelli had been called in—but so far Zilor was showing an aptitude for such things. Granted, his observations weren't quite solid enough to support his conclusions, but they were close enough.

Though my approval might be a bit colored by the fact that

I'd already come to those same conclusions. "Let's say for argument's sake you're right," I said. "Why are you telling us this?"

"Detective-Sergeant Kreega says you're bounty hunters," he said. "Like I said, we can't move without evidence. You have more freedom of action."

"*Retired* bounty hunters," I said automatically. "And that freedom of action only comes when the target's been registered with an official bounty."

"Okay," he said. "How do I post one?"

I frowned. The guy was more serious about this than I'd realized. "Why?" I asked.

"Why do I want you picking up Galfvi?" Zilor huffed out a frustrated breath. "I've been watching him for a long time, Roarke. He's shifty, too smooth a talker by half, and way too smart to be cutting up fish in a Bilswift fish shop."

"So you think he's up to something?"

"I *know* he's up to something," Zilor said. "He's either running a scam, planning a major theft, or something worse. The point is that I don't want a pair of Patth Johnny-come-dawnings sneaking him off Alainn and out of our jurisdiction before I get a solid crack at him."

"Understood," I said. *Way* more serious than I'd realized. "Okay. First, you need to go to the nearest StarrComm center and register the target with Bounty Hunter Central. That includes escrowing a sizeable monetary deposit. Second—"

"How sizeable?"

"Depends on how badly you want the target," I said. "Prices usually start around twenty thousand commarks and go up from there."

He threw me a stunned look over the back seat. "Twenty *thousand*?"

"You're inviting in hunters from all over the Spiral," I reminded him. "You have to make it worth their time or they won't bother."

"But I don't *want* anyone else," he protested. "I just want to hire you."

"You have to make it worth *our* time, too," I said. "But seriously, any bounty under twenty thousand is going to attract the monitors' attention and make them wonder what you're up to."

"I gather that's not a good thing?"

"Not if you're a badgeman," I said. "You really think you're the first to come up with the brilliant idea of bypassing Commonwealth law by hiring hunters to bring in a suspect you can't officially charge?"

"I suppose not," he muttered. "Yeah. Sorry to have wasted your time."

"Well, it's not like we had anything else to do right now," I said, looking at Selene and noting the prodding in her pupils. If Galfvi was found dead or injured, unless the badgemen could prove it was by his own hand the next logical suspect in line would be Tirano. "Tell you what," I continued reluctantly. "Selene and I will keep our eyes open. If we spot anything odd or suspicious, you'll get it first."

"Thanks," he said.

We continued on to the spaceport in silence. Zilor dropped us beside the runaround stand where our rental was parked, we said good-bye to him, and with Selene at the wheel, we headed out.

"It looks bad for Tirano, doesn't it?" she said quietly as she maneuvered us through the Bilswift traffic.

"Bad, yes," I conceded. "But hardly conclusive. There were at least three spots in that office where someone could set up a hidden camera to record the safe being opened."

"Why didn't you tell Kreega that?"

"I was going to," I said, scowling at the memory, "but right then the Patth made their dramatic entrance and I didn't feel like handing out any more free information. I'll tell her later. What did you think of their hot badge/cold badge routine, by the way?"

"It was good enough, I suppose," Selene said, her pupils going thoughtful. "Not sure why they thought it necessary, though."

"They were probably expecting to get a private meeting with the Javersin brothers and had to tweak the script a little when they got inside and realized they had a roomful of official witnesses. For some people, bluster is the go-to fallback position."

"Maybe," Selene murmured. "They didn't seem all that surprised, though."

I eyed her. I'd been reading what facial and body language cues I could, but of course Selene's analysis of these things went a layer deeper. "I was pretty sure Venikel wasn't the angry justice-seeker he was playing. But you say they weren't surprised, either?"

"I don't think so," she said. "But that's just from what I know about Patth in general. I don't have a baseline for these two in particular."

"Yeah," I said. Which unfortunately lowered her emotional reading accuracy from ninety-plus percent to probably somewhere in the midtwenties. "Well, we can take another run at them later. We've already agreed that's going to happen."

Selene was silent another block. "Do you still want to look at the place where Lukki was killed?"

"Very much so," I said. "And while I hate to put it off any longer than I have to, I think we should steer clear for another few hours at least. Even if Kreega is done with the crime scene, our pompous Detective-Lieutenant Sovelli may want to take a look for himself. I'd just as soon not cross paths with him again right away."

"And besides, this isn't our job?"

I winced at the anxiety in her pupils. "If Tirano's innocent, Selene, we'll find a way to prove that," I promised. "But yes, our first priority is to check out that portal."

I could see the question *And if he's not innocent?* hovering in her pupils. But she didn't say anything more.

Neither did I. As my father used to say, *Crossing bridges before you come to them doesn't gain you anything and puts a lot of extra off-road wear on your tires.*

Given the talk I'd heard from our car rental guy about tourists driving cheerfully up into the mountains, I'd expected the road would be wide, nicely paved, and conducive to a pleasant day's journey.

It wasn't any of those things. It was narrow, pocked with pits and bumps, had occasional drop-offs that would scare a mountain goat, and in general provided a real challenge to a tourist's determination and driving skills.

I'd wondered why Selene had taken so long to get up the road and back. Now I knew.

I also knew why Detective-Lieutenant Sovelli had opted for an aircar for his trip over the mountains from Cavindoss.

The fence Selene had told me about also wasn't as obvious as I'd expected. Instead of running right alongside the road it paralleled it about twenty meters away to the north, most of it nestled inconspicuously inside the first line of trees. For a while I hoped that might be our way in, that we could climb one of the outer trees, cross some convenient branches to one of the inner trees, and climb back down.

But the Patth who'd set up the barrier had known what

they were doing. The sensor buds, while primarily guarding the ground-level approaches, also had up-angle modules that would have a range of two or three meters. There were plenty of trees that were taller than that, but all the branches thick enough to hold our weight were well below that critical level.

We drove slowly the entire length of the fence, Selene battling the road, me watching for anything that looked like a gap or depression in the ground we might be able to wriggle through. But there was nothing.

The main road was challenging enough. The jeep trail she'd told me about, the one that angled off and headed north to the river, was even worse.

"So that's it?" I asked as we walked the last ten meters to the dilapidated boat dock at the end of the jeep trail.

"That's it," Selene confirmed. She stopped a meter from the gently rippling water and pointed. "You can see the fence—there and there—weaving in and out of the trees. But there are also a couple of places, one of them just past the big mottled brown tree, where you can see a feeder creek flowing into the river."

"So you're suggesting the creek may have cut a deep enough gap under the fence that we can crawl through the water to the other side?" I asked doubtfully.

"I know it would be uncomfortable," she said, her pupils going a little defensive. "But it might get us in."

"That it might," I agreed, leaning over a little more in hopes of getting a better look. "Certainly worth checking out. Problem is, we'd have to be in the river to stay clear of those sensors. I wonder if Bilswift has any places that rent out boats."

"I would think there would be at least one," she said, pulling out her info pad.

"Don't bother," I said, peering at the western sky. From my current vantage point I had a perfect view of the rain clouds rolling in toward us. "You can look it up when we get back. I'd like to try to get back to town before that road turns to mud."

We almost made it.

The rain held off until the last kilometer or two, where the mountain road was a little wider and almost worthy of the name. "We heading straight back to the ship?" Selene asked as we made our way along the city street grid.

"Let's stop by the fish shop first," I said, looking out at the pedestrians as they strode along, their feet making little splashes on the wet walkways as they dodged the larger ones created by the vehicles rumbling by. At least today we'd been smart enough to wear long all-weather coats and bring fold-up rain hats. "That mari-mari ought to be ripe by now."

"Actually, it should be a little past," Selene murmured.

"Yeah, maybe a little," I conceded. "But they *did* say there was a window of an hour or two when it's at its best."

"They should certainly know," she said. "That's odd."

"What is?"

"The shop seems to be closed."

I frowned. She was right: the shutters that had been covering the counter and windows were still in place. "I wonder if Kreega found some new evidence to examine," Selene said.

"More likely Sovelli decided to have her go over everything again for him," I growled. So much for having mari-mari for dinner. "Fine. Plan B. Swing around to Panza's Café and drop me off."

She looked across at me, surprise and concern in her pupils. "You going there *again*?"

"I still haven't tagged our gourmet Patth," I reminded her. "Unless you think Venikel or Kiolven fits the bill."

"I don't think so," she said. "The food aromas from their robes were fancy enough, but it wasn't what I smelled when we first arrived."

"So Panza's it is," I said. "While I do that, you can head back to the *Ruth*, check on Tirano, and maybe look into that boat rental if you have time."

"Don't you think I should come with you?"

I shook my head. "It might be handy, but it's been a long day, and if this becomes a waste of my time there's no point wasting yours, too. Just go back to the ship and get some rest. I've got my hat—I can walk back when I'm finished."

"That's what you thought last night," she reminded me, the tension level in her pupils amping up a bit. "Maybe we should go back to the *Ruth* first so you can at least get your phone."

"It's not worth the extra trip," I said. "Besides, Kiolven and Venikel found out last night who I am. There's no reason for them to take another shot at me now."

The look in her pupils told me exactly what she thought of

that logic. But she just nodded. "All right. But if you're not back in three hours I'm going to come and look for you."

"Make it four and you've got a deal," I said. "I'm still hoping Panza's has some decent barbeque."

Yesterday, the café had been comfortably full. Today, with my arrival closer to regular dinnertime, it was packed. All the booths were full, as were most of the tables and the line of stools at the bar. I had to go loiter by the stools for a few minutes until a pair of Saffi finished their drinks and I was able to grab their table.

Last night's bartender, the one who'd pointed me to Lukki, was back, this time serving as a waiter. I could tell he recognized me, but he merely took my drink order, assured me that, yes, Panza's had the best Earth-Kansas-style barbeque on Alainn, and took that order, too.

After that, all I had to do was sit back, sip at my Dewar's, and observe the rest of the clientele.

I'd been a bounty hunter a long time, first alone and then with Selene, and I'd learned how to read the sense of a room and the people in it. Here, the general mood was one of calmness mixed with the typical tired relaxation that came from the successful completion of yet another day's work.

But there were also a few small pockets that held a more serious undertone. Tirano and Galfvi hadn't been big names in Bilswift, but they were known well enough in the fish lovers' community that their disappearance had been noted. There were also one or two even darker moods that I tentatively tagged as reactions to Lukki's murder. Whether those people were friends, associates, or enemies, though, I hadn't a clue.

As my father used to say, *From the outside, dark fears of the future and dark plans for the future look a lot alike.*

Given Panza's status as a modest establishment in a minor town on a middling planet, I hadn't expected much from the cuisine. I was therefore pleasantly surprised when my rack of ribs arrived with extra sauce, side orders of garlic bread and local greens, and even a fashionable finger bowl with two lemon wedges poised on the edges ready to add extra cleaning power to the water. Keeping one eye on the crowd and the other on the main door across the room, I dug in.

They weren't the best ribs I'd ever had, but they were easily in the top twenty. If there was indeed an Icarus portal inside the fenced-off wilderness up there, and if we could get to it first, I would have to make sure Selene and I got assigned to the team tasked with digging it out.

I'd finished the first half rack and was starting on the second when the door opened and Venikel and Kiolven walked in.

I raised my hands and one of the ribs to my mouth, a pleasant meal turned instantly into face-obscuring camouflage. I tensed as the two Patth looked around, but I saw no indication in their body language that they'd spotted me. A moment later, they headed at an angle across the room to a booth on the other side and sat down across from a figure in a dark raincoat and hat.

I scowled. I'd done a quick visual of the room when I first came in, and remembered seeing the solitary occupant of that booth nursing a dark beer and an appetizer plate. But muffled in all that rain gear I hadn't been able to even identify his species, let alone get a good look at his face or build.

And just because Patth nearly always appeared in public in those hooded robes of theirs it didn't mean they couldn't branch out into something else if the occasion called for it.

Selene would have been able to tell me instantly if the cuisine she'd smelled yesterday was on tonight's menu. Without her, I'd just have to do this the hard way. A drunken walk-by, a brush of my hand against plate or glass or cutlery, and I should be able to pick up enough of his scent for Selene to analyze once I was back aboard the *Ruth*.

Alternatively, I could keep my distance, activate my artificial left arm's mirrored thumbnail, and use it to try to get a surreptitious look at our mystery guest as I headed for the door. That one had the virtue of possibly allowing me to pass them without being spotted in return, but the downside of offering only a glimpse and no way to tell in advance whether that one shot would gain me anything.

Or if I *really* wanted to shake up the evening, I could always go with the straight-up direct approach. In the secret wrist compartment of that same artificial arm were six quick-acting knockout pills that could be surreptitiously dropped into a target's drink and send him into peaceful oblivion for a few hours.

But one way or another, this was my chance to add another puzzle piece to my small but growing collection. I took a last bite from my rib, set it down on my plate—

"Well, well," a familiar voice said quietly from behind me. "You've got a nerve coming back here."

I swallowed a curse. At least I'd now eliminated one possibility as to who the two Patth were meeting. "Hello, Willie," I said, making sure to keep my hands visible. He wasn't pressing a gun to my head, but I didn't doubt he was quite ready to do so if he decided the situation called for it. "How are Braun's ribs doing?"

"Hilarious," Willie growled. "You'll have to tell him that one. On your feet. We've got places to go."

"Can I finish my meal first?" I asked, looking casually around at the nearest tables. No one was reacting to our little conversation, which strongly suggested Willie's gun was still tucked away out of sight in its holster. It was a small window of opportunity, but it was better than nothing.

"Don't worry about it, smart guy," he said sarcastically. "Maybe you'll get lucky and they'll have some of that slop in hell. Move it."

"If you insist." I wiped the worst of the sauce on my napkin, then dipped my hands into the finger bowl, swishing my fingertips around for a final cleaning. I started to stand up, giving my fingers one last wiggle—

And half turning toward Willie, I held up the lemon wedge I'd surreptitiously plucked from the edge of the bowl with my left hand and squeezed the juice straight into his eyes.

His first reaction to the jolt of citric acid suddenly burning into his face was to snap up his right arm to protect it. A fraction of a second later his brain caught up with his reflexes and he reversed direction, aiming for his gun.

But he was too late. I'd already dropped the lemon and locked my left hand solidly around his holstered weapon before his own hand could reach it. At the same time, I got a grip on my plasmic.

He froze in place. "Hell," he muttered.

"Not necessarily," I soothed quietly. "I assume you're here because you think I killed your boss. I didn't. Nor am I really interested in killing you. Not unless you insist."

His eyes flicked around the room as if gauging the response if he shouted for help. Whatever he saw brought his eyes grudgingly back to mine. "What do you want?"

"Let's start with both of us walking out of here alive," I said. "If you're feeling generous, I'm also in the market for information."

"What kind?"

"The kind that points us to Ms. Parsons' real killer," I said. "Enemies, business rivals, random people she's pissed off. Any thoughts?"

"Right," he growled. "Like I'm going to grease your way while you take over her territory? Forget it."

"Let's start over," I said, resisting the urge to roll my eyes. As my father used to say, *When the only tool you have is a hammer, every problem looks like a nail. That logic also applies to criminal paranoia.* "I had no interest in Ms. Parsons' business, I have no interest in your business, and I have no interest in Alainn in general or Bilswift in particular."

I glanced down at my plate. "Well, except maybe this sauce recipe. More important from your point of view, I'm very high on Detective-Sergeant Kreega's radar, and there's a good chance one of her badgemen is waiting outside in the rain to tail me home. Killing someone in full view of witnesses is usually considered a bad idea." I nodded sideways toward my table's other chair. "So is having a confrontation while standing in the middle of a crowded room. Shall we sit?"

He gave a snort. "Sure. See you around, Roarke." He spun around, the movement breaking my grip on his gun, and stalked toward the back of the room. I watched as he reached the bar and turned right, exiting out the café's rear door. I sat down, craning my neck that direction for another minute to make sure he wasn't going to pull a double-reverse on me, then turned back to my meal and the booth I was watching.

My meal was still there. The three people in the booth weren't.

I swore under my breath, doing a quick scan of the room. There was no sign of them. Best guess was that my confrontation with Willie had caught their attention and encouraged them to slip out.

That, or else Willie's arrival and distraction had been a deliberate part of someone's plan to ruin my surveillance.

In which case there might still be a chance.

I stood up, dropped enough money on the table to cover my bill, and headed for the door Willie had disappeared through. If he was working with the two Patth, he might even now be heading for a quick rendezvous with them for further instructions or for all of them to congratulate themselves on a job well done. If they weren't careless enough to have such a meeting out in the open, I could at least tail Willie back to his lair and see where he and Braun had set up shop since their boss's recent passing. Closing and sealing the front of my long coat, I wedged my rain hat firmly onto my head and ducked out into the evening gloom.

The rain had been steady but light when I arrived at Panza's. Since then, it had turned into an equally steady but much heavier shower. I peered out from beneath the dripping edge of my hat, looking around at the hurrying pedestrians and trying to pick Willie's bulk out of the crowd. His coat had been damp, I remembered, but he'd come and gone so quickly that I hadn't had a chance to check out his trousers and shoes to be able to estimate how long he'd been out in the weather before slipping in Panza's back door. If he'd come by car, and was already back in that vehicle, my chances of catching him or even just spotting him dropped pretty close to zero.

There was a muted double flash at the edge of my peripheral vision. I turned that direction, peering into the gloom and passing vehicles, wondering what it was I'd seen. A car came around the nearest corner, its headlights briefly pointing at me as it completed its turn, but that didn't look right. None of the streetlights were out, nor was I seeing flickers from any of them.

And the fact that there'd been *two* flashes . . .

Damn.

With a sigh, I opened my coat far enough to dig out my plasmic. Holding it against my chest where it would be ready but unobtrusive, I headed off to find the body.

CHAPTER EIGHT

Whatever other deficiencies the Bilswift badgemen might have, lack of promptness wasn't among them. The first car was on the scene barely three minutes after I made the call.

Of course, the cynic in me suspected that could have been because they were the ones who'd been detailed to follow and report on my movements. I thought about asking one of them if that was the case, decided staying quiet would be the better part of valor, and found a partially protected spot to watch while they first did a positive identification on Willie's body and then began sealing off the crime scene.

Kreega arrived five minutes later in a second car. Naturally, she spotted me practically before she was completely out of her vehicle. She held a brief consultation with the first two badgemen, then stalked over to where I was sheltering. "Roarke," she greeted me darkly. "Imagine my surprise at seeing you here."

"Well, I *was* the one who called it in," I reminded her. "I didn't think I should leave without at least saying hello."

"And we appreciate it," she said. "Phoned it in with the victim's phone, I understand."

I nodded. "I left mine back in the *Ruth*."

"Really." Her eyebrows went up a fraction. "You do that often?"

"Not on purpose," I said, resisting the urge to add that such things tended to happen when I suspected busybodies would try to trace it. "Don't you ever forget things?"

"No," she said shortly. "You leave your weapon there, too?"

"I'm a licensed bounty hunter," I reminded her. "That entitles me—"

"Yes, I know," she cut me off. "You have it with you, or don't you?"

I grimaced. "I have it. And it hasn't been recently fired."

"Good to know," she said. "We'll check that, of course."

"Not without a warrant," I said. "Nothing to hide, but I'm always leery of badgemen who fall into the habit of cutting legal corners."

"Sometimes cutting corners gets you to the truth faster."

"Sometimes," I acknowledged. "But as my father used to say, *Cut enough corners and pretty soon there's nothing left of the cake.* Not accusing you of trying that, Detective-Sergeant, but I like to do things by the book."

"I'm a big believer in the book, too," she said, giving me a measuring look. "Okay, look. It's wet and miserable out here, and I have a dead body to process, so let's just cut past the first few pages, shall we? Let's pretend you told me your presence here is pure coincidence, that I laughed in your face and threatened to haul you in on suspicion and probable cause, and that you offered me useful information to bargain for your freedom." She raised her eyebrows. "You *do* have useful information, don't you?"

"Well, *I* think it's useful," I said. "Let's start back at the fish shop. You'll remember that we concluded that only Tirano could sniff out which buttons the Javersins pushed to open the safe. What we *didn't* explore was the possibility that someone else might have set up a concealed camera to record the combination while one of the brothers was punching it in."

"I guess I didn't make myself clear." Kreega waved behind her toward Willie's body. "I want useful information on *this* crime."

"What if the two incidents are related?"

"*Are* they?"

I scowled. It had always seemed obvious to me that incidents involving overlapping groups of participants were almost certainly connected. Unfortunately, in this case, I didn't have any solid evidence to back that up. "I don't know," I had to admit.

"Glad we got that cleared up," she said with a hint of sarcasm. "How about we start with how the current deceased ended up here?"

"I don't know the ending," I said. "But I can tell you some of what led up to it."

I recounted the events of the evening, from the time I walked into Panza's Café and ordered dinner to the moment when I followed Willie out into the rain. Kreega listened in silence, occasionally checking over her shoulder to see how the bag-and-tag was going. "But he was fine when he walked out," I finished. "You can ask anyone who was in there."

"Trust me, we will." She held out her hand. "That bounty hunter license of yours—let me see it."

"My license?" I asked, frowning as I opened my coat and got out my wallet. I started to pull out the license, but she simply reached over and plucked the wallet from my hands. "Sure, help yourself," I growled.

"You'd be surprised how many people run around with more than one set of IDs," she said calmly, leafing through the cards and pulling out the bounty hunter license. Taking a step toward the nearest streetlight, she angled it up for a better view. "Says here that you're supposed to identify yourself to Planetary Control when you first call for a landing slot."

"That's if you're on a hunt," I said. "I'm not." I raised my eyebrows as a sudden thought struck me. "Are you saying I *should* be?"

"No idea what you're talking about," she said, sliding the card back into the wallet and handing it back.

"Really?" I asked. "A self-described dealer in exotics is murdered, then one of her chief goons also gets himself dead, and you're saying that neither of them was worth the attention of a professional?"

"What makes you think either killing was by a professional?"

"One shot for Lukki, who supposedly doesn't carry a weapon," I said. "Two shots for Willie, who does. Both from plasmics, which are harder to anchor to particular shootings than firearms. Professionalism is all about the details."

"*Or* the shooter doesn't have a pattern, *or* doesn't know how well a plasmic shot might penetrate a heavy rainfall, *or* figured our late friend over there was big enough to require a double tap," Kreega said. "*Or* the two killings were by two entirely different shooters. I've been in this business long enough to know that one pair of data points doesn't make for much of a chart."

"I suppose," I conceded.

"Besides, if it was a hunter, how come no one's come by to claim Ms. Parsons' body? Don't you have to have a body to collect your money?"

"Most of the time, yes," I said. "Occasionally the client is willing to accept photographic evidence."

"Mm," Kreega said, eyeing me. "Still waiting for that useful information you promised."

"During the hypothetical part of our conversation?"

"Yes, the part right after I hypothetically decided to run you in," Kreega said pointedly.

"For what?" I asked. "I haven't done anything except visit your town, eat some barbequed ribs, and take a day trip into the mountains."

"*And* show up at the scene of two crimes, and have a public scrap with the victim of a third."

"And I already told you everything I know," I said stubbornly. "You want speculation, hey, I can do that, too."

"Thanks, but I already get enough untenable theories from Zilor and Grazimink," she said. "If you want to—"

She broke off, her eyes shifting over my shoulder. "Well, well," she said thoughtfully. "She carries a plasmic, too, doesn't she?"

I turned to look. Selene was hurrying toward us, her wet raincoat glistening under the streetlights, a couple tufts of her white hair peeking out around the edges of her hood. "Are you all right?" she called as Kreega and I both turned to face her. "I saw all the flashing lights."

"I'm fine," I assured her, peering at her pupils. Between the gloom and the shadows from her hood her pupils were too hard to see for me to get anything. "What are you doing here?"

She nodded upward. "The rain was getting worse, so I came to see if you wanted a ride."

"Thanks, I appreciate it," I said. She'd told me she would come by in three hours; I'd told her to make it four; it had now been less than one. Clearly, something was up besides those rain clouds. "Where are you parked?"

"On the other side of Panza's," she said, craning her neck toward the badgeman activity. "What happened?"

"The latest edition of Bilswift's Traveling Murder Scene," Kreega said.

"My old sparring partner Willie," I added.

"Oh," Selene said, sounding suddenly stricken. "What happened?"

"We don't really know," I told her. "He and I had a little chat inside Panza's, and then he came out here and got himself killed. You getting anything?"

For a moment Selene worked the air with nostrils and eyelashes. "I'm sorry," she said. "Rain this heavy clears out everything."

"And sends it into the storm drains," I said, nodding heavily. Even Kadolian magic had its limits. "But what about his—?"

"Are you finished with Gregory, Detective-Sergeant Kreega?" Selene cut me off. "It's very wet out here, and I'd like to get back to the *Ruth*."

"I think I'm finished," Kreega said, looking back and forth between us. "For now. Just keep yourselves available."

"No problem," I said, taking Selene's arm. "This town's beginning to grow on me."

"Wish I could say the same about you." With a final thoughtful look, Kreega turned and headed back toward the other badgemen.

"We need to go," Selene murmured as she led the way back toward Panza's.

"Yeah, I figured that out when you didn't offer to smell Willie's inside clothing, the stuff protected by his raincoat," I said. "And then stopped *me* from suggesting it. What's up?"

She gave the area a quick look. "Tirano's gone," she murmured.

"Terrific," I growled. "When?"

"At least a couple of hours ago."

"And then the rains started," I said. "So that's it?"

"Not completely," she said. "It wasn't this heavy right away, and there were enough sheltered places along the way that still held his scent."

"That's more like it," I said approvingly. "So you found him?"

She glanced at me and I saw frustration in her pupils. "No, I lost his trail," she said. "But before that I was able to follow him to the fish shop."

"And?"

She hunched her shoulders. "I'm afraid," she said quietly, "that Detective-Sergeant Kreega is going to have a very long night."

❖   ❖   ❖

The fish shop's side door was unlocked. Plasmic in hand, I eased it open and slipped silently into the dimness inside.

I needn't have bothered with either the weapon or the stealth. No one inside was in any position to care.

"Single plasmic shot each," I said, my stomach churning painfully as I eyed the Javersin brothers. They'd died only a few meters apart: Darnell by a prep table loaded with fish scraps and entrails, Bicks midway between that table and the wash tubs. "Fair chance they knew their attacker."

"Because they let him in, but then returned to their work?" Selene suggested. She was walking slowly back and forth across the prep area, leaning down to sniff at the tables or bending lower to sample the scents from the floor.

"That, and the fact that Darnell has half a dozen knives at hand and wasn't holding any of them when he was shot," I said. "So not a random intruder."

"Unless he picked the lock and let himself in."

I scowled. Yes, that was indeed another option.

Still, statistically most murders occurred between friends, family, and acquaintances. "Let's start with the assumption they knew him," I said. "We can always widen the field to the general population of Bilswift if we have to. What else can you tell me?"

"Not very much, I'm afraid," Selene said. "The overall smell is overwhelming most everything else."

"Yeah, I noticed." The reek was in fact doing its best to curl my own nostrils. I could only imagine what it was doing to Selene's. "Never seen fish guts decay so quickly. Maybe this is the reverse of the mari-mari ripening schedule."

"It's not just decaying fish," Selene said. "Most of it is the smell of charring."

I frowned. Now that she mentioned it, and now that I was forcing myself to concentrate, I could smell the stench's burned organic component. "Where?" I asked.

She pointed to a compost bin at the end of one of the prep tables whose lid was askew. "That one, I think."

Steeling myself, I walked over to the bin and lifted the lid the rest of the way.

She was right. Smack-dab in the center of the mass of fish waste was a neat grouping of blackened circles. "More plasmic shots," I reported over my shoulder. "About eight of them, deliberately delivered. More than enough charring to contaminate the scent, but not enough to kindle an open flame and possibly burn down the place."

"Unusually considerate of them," Selene said, coming to my side and peering into the bin.

"I doubt respect for the deceased's private property had anything to do with it," I said. "Burning down the shop would have brought the badgemen here in double-quick time. I'm guessing they just didn't want the hue and cry of having two more bodies show up in Kreega's paperwork, at least not tonight. Any sense as to when this happened?"

I saw the hesitation in Selene's eyes. "Probably between one and two hours ago," she said reluctantly.

"So after work hours," I said. I thought about mentioning that that time slot neatly bracketed the time of Tirano's disappearance from the *Ruth*, but it was pretty clear Selene had already connected those particular dots.

Even amid the reek of burned fish she caught the subtle shift in my own scent. "He didn't kill them, Gregory," she said firmly.

"No, of course not," I said, not entirely believing that and knowing she knew I didn't entirely believe it. "But he *was* here tonight, wasn't he?"

Her pupils went dark. "Yes," she admitted. "But the scent's centered on the door we came in. I don't think he came inside any farther."

"Saw the bodies and headed for the tall grass," I said, nodding. "A very reasonable reaction. And as a former employee he would have had his own key, which was why the door was unlocked when we got here."

Selene's pupils took on a wary look. "A minute ago you thought he might have killed them. Now you're saying you *don't* believe that?"

"I never say never," I hedged. "But I'll admit the odds aren't leaning in his favor. The brothers were shot with a plasmic, as were those poor defenseless fish entrails. You don't just pick up a weapon like that at the corner all-goods store."

"Maybe it belonged to one of the Javersin brothers."

"Probably not," I said. "I saw a Packard 3mm in the safe this morning. Most citizens who qualify to use a firearm don't go on to certify with a plasmic, and vice versa."

"Not usually," she murmured agreement.

Though there *were* three spare plasmics hidden aboard the *Ruth*. Odds were good that they were well enough hidden that Tirano wouldn't have found them, and well enough secured that he couldn't get one free even if he did. But those assumptions didn't take into account the Kadolian sense of smell.

Just as the Javersin brothers' murders didn't take into account the mental process of a Kadolian changeling.

"Anything else you can sort out of this mess?" I asked.

"All the scents from this morning are still here," she said. "You, me, Detective-Sergeant Kreega and the other badgemen, and the two Patth. And the Javersin brothers, too, of course. But I can't tell whether any of it is new or left over from earlier. I'm sorry."

"That's okay," I said. "The way this place smells, I'm surprised you haven't already run away screaming." I gazed at the bodies a moment, then turned toward the closed door that led into the office. "What about other visitors? Any scents in here you don't recognize?"

"There are several," she said. "But they're very faint, and could just be from the day's customers."

"Yeah, that makes sense," I said. "You say Tirano didn't come in farther than the door?"

"I don't think so. Why?"

"I was just wondering if we should check the obvious motive." I nodded toward the office. "You think you can open that safe?"

"Do you think that's a good idea?" she asked, her pupils suddenly gone cautious. "The longer we're here, the better chance someone will stumble on us."

"Not to worry," I assured her. "Kreega and her badgemen are tied up right now with Willie's untimely demise."

"I was thinking the murderer might come back."

"Oh. That." I gave her an overly casual shrug. "Well, that would certainly help us identify him. But that's another point for opening the safe. It would tell us whether there's anything in here worth coming back for."

Selene shook her head. "It's not a good idea, Gregory."

"A lot of what we do lately seems to be landing outside the point circles," I said sourly. "Doesn't seem to be much chance of backing out now. Can you open it, or can't you?"

She closed her eyes briefly. "Yes," she said. "It's a six-digit combination, and I know which of the four keys was pressed three times. It shouldn't take long."

"Let's get at it, then," I said, heading toward the office. "The sooner we're out of here, the better."

The office door was a good solid panel, well-sealed and with only a small crack beneath it. We went in fast, closing the door behind us quickly enough that only a little of the stench from the burned fish got in with us.

As expected, the safe was locked. Selene knelt down beside it, sniffed a few times to confirm her earlier button reading, and got busy. "Darnell Javersin opened it recently," she said as she worked the buttons.

"Probably putting in the day's receipts," I said, moving around the room. As I'd told Kreega, there were three good spots where someone could have set up a recorder without the device being obvious. I reconfirmed those three, tagged a possible fourth...

There was a slight creak of hinges as the safe door swung open. "We're in," Selene announced.

"Great." I stepped over to her and pointed to the four suspicious spots I'd found. "There, there, there, and there. Check them out while I look though the safe. I want to know if you can find any scent in particular by any of them."

She nodded, and walked over to the first one. Taking her place in front of the safe, I shined my flashlight inside.

The first thing I spotted were two small piles of commarks, not in nice neat stacks but instead jumbled, as if someone had hastily cleared out the registers and just dumped everything in there to count and organize later. The second thing I spotted was the Packard 3mm I'd seen earlier. Money and a weapon, everything a thief might want, still tucked safely away.

Only sometime in the past few hours, the Packard had been moved.

I looked closer, trying to visualize the steps. One of the brothers had taken the gun out of the safe, showed it to someone— possibly as a strong hint for the person to get lost—and then put it back again.

And if he'd held it close enough to the intruder's face, there might still be some breath or other scent on the end of the barrel. "Selene?" I called softly. "Come here, will you? I need you to check out this gun barrel."

I moved aside as she joined me. I started to pick up the gun, but she waved my hand aside and simply leaned her head into the opening and close to the Packard. For a moment she held position, her eyelashes fluttering. "Yes, there's something there," she confirmed, pulling back again. "The same scent's also in the prep room, but fainter and harder to detect. I don't know who it belongs to."

"Maybe we can eliminate one possibility, anyway," I said, holding out my left hand to her. I'd only been in contact with Willie for a few seconds as I pressed his gun into its holster and he gripped my hand in hopes of pulling it off so he could get to the weapon. "It'll be faint," I warned as she leaned closer to sniff my hand, "but it's the only extra scent I have at the—"

"Yes," she said. "That's him."

I frowned. "Really?"

"Really," she confirmed. "Who is it?"

"Who *was* it," I corrected, still frowning. "Our late, not-really-lamented, Willie. What in the world was he doing here, I wonder?"

"Buying fish?" Selene suggested with a hint of strained humor.

"Let me rephrase," I said. "What in the world was he doing here that would induce one of the Javersin brothers—"

"It was Bicks."

"That would induce Bicks to haul out their gun and shove it in his face?" I finished. "Could he have been looking for Tirano?"

"Or Galfvi?"

"Okay, or Galfvi," I agreed. "Or maybe both. We still don't know which of them robbed the safe." I raised my eyebrows. "Or do we?"

A flicker of frustration crossed her pupils. "I'm getting some of Galfvi's scent at the second spot you marked," she said. "But with everything else in here, I can't tell whether it's specific to that place or just general residue from the office itself."

"Or new or old?"

"*Or* new or old."

"Got it." I huffed out a frustrated sigh. "I don't know, Selene. Tirano, Galfvi, now Willie—the deeper we dig into this thing, the more tangled it gets."

"It *does* seem to be going that way," she agreed. "Do you think there may be two different schemes going on?"

"We already know there are at least two," I pointed out.

"Whatever's happening here with Tirano, plus the portal out there that we're supposed to be investigating. Add in the murders, and we may have three different wheels in motion."

"Unless two of those wheels are connected."

"That would be handy," I agreed as I closed the safe. "But so far I can't see how."

On the other hand, two schemes didn't need to be connected if one was a deliberate diversion. We were here to look for a wayward portal, after all, and nothing closed down avenues of inquiry and freedom of movement like badgeman scrutiny. If whoever was running the Patth portal hunt had found out we were here and decided he wanted to be subtle about taking us out of the game, this would definitely be one way to go about it. Or possibly we were simply dealing with a psychotic.

Or a changeling.

I got to my feet and gave the office one final look. Distantly, I wondered who would inherit the place now that the owners were dead. "Come on, let's get out of here."

"Where are we going?" Selene asked as we headed to the door.

"I thought we'd try Tirano's house," I said. "I'm guessing that even in this rain his doorknob will hold enough of his scent for you to spot it."

"But we don't know where he lives," Selene said, her pupils frowning.

"Sure we do," I said. "He said he lived in a house nearby, remember?"

"And you want me to search all hundred or more of them?"

I shook my head. "He's a Kadolian who works in a fish shop," I said. "A place that buys fish every day from the night boats that come into port. If I was in the Javersin brothers' position...?"

"You'd want him near the docks," Selene said, her pupils showing understanding, "Close enough to smell the catch before the boats even land and tell you whether it's worth buying."

"Exactly," I said. "Come on. Let's go see if our boy went home."

CHAPTER NINE

Bilswift's port and docks were located in a natural cove at the northwest part of the city, a couple of hundred meters east of where the river met the ocean and butting up against the eastern edge of the spaceport that itself jutted out into the sea. Anywhere else, having ocean and river craft crossing paths with each other and then throwing in space and suborbital planetary vessels could have made for a traffic nightmare. Here in the backwoods, with mostly fishing craft on the water and a couple of suborbitals a day, it was hardly even noticeable.

Most of the area around the docks was taken up by warehouses, service and refurbishing centers, and maritime supply stores. But just upriver from all that was a row of five tiny cottages with a nice view of the river and the forest beyond. My guess was that they'd once been homes to some of the fishing captains or crews, or maybe tourist rentals, but now seemed to be occupied by ordinary townsfolk who liked looking at moving water and weren't worried about flood tides.

The middle of those five houses turned out to be Tirano's.

Oddly enough, and unlike the other four cottages, his place had windows only on the north, east, and west sides, with an unbroken wall facing south. Selene speculated that seasonal storm-force winds might come from that direction; my more cynical theory was that the person who built or refurbished that particular cottage had been figuratively turning his back on the rest of the city. It wasn't until we got inside and got a look at the cottage's interior that we discovered the real reason.

The south wall, as it happened, was about half a meter too thick.

"Where do we begin?" Selene asked, shining her flashlight around.

"I'll start with the wardrobe and dresser." I pointed to the south wall. "You find the hidden compartment and figure out how to open it."

"All right."

"And keep your light away from the windows," I warned as we headed to different parts of the cottage's single room. The heavy rain and shadows had hopefully obscured our furtive entrance into the house, but a single careless flicker of light peeking around the window shades could very quickly unravel all that caution.

"I know," she called, already sniffing methodically along the wall.

The stand-up wardrobe nestled against the east wall contained a pair of jackets of different weights, probably for Bilswift's different seasons, three pairs of trousers, a raincoat, and a set of reasonably nice dress shoes. I was sifting through the modest selection of shirts in the dresser when I heard a muffled *click* from across the room.

"Found it," Selene announced. I turned around as she swung back a two-meter-wide section of the wall. "*Well.*"

"You find his phone?" I asked, heading over to her. In the backwash of her light I could see the hidden compartment had a rack of some kind of clothing, along with two pairs of boots. On the other side of the compartment, the area where her light was focused, were half a dozen shallow shelves. "I never believed that nonsense about him losing it."

"More likely he threw it away," Selene said, pointing her light at one of the shelves. "If he was worried about being tracked, I can see why."

I stopped behind her and looked over her shoulder.

At the six-centimeter-high stack of commarks.

"And there used to be more," Selene continued, pointing at the empty space beside the stack. "There was another stack here.

I can smell the spots where his fingers brushed the wood as he picked them up."

"How long ago was he here?" I asked, wanting to see how much there was but knowing better than to contaminate the scene with my touch.

She hesitated. "Two hours or less."

"Two hours or less," I repeated, frowning as I tried to reconstruct the evening's events. "So he leaves the *Ruth*, goes to the fish shop, sees the Javersin brothers have been murdered, comes here and grabs a stack of cash and... what?"

"The obvious answer would be that he's preparing to run," Selene said, her pupils doubtful.

"*Would* be?"

"Yes," Selene said. "Because I'm confused." She shifted her light to the clothing in the other half of the hideaway. "Those clothes look like they're designed for hiking or rock climbing, don't they?"

"I'd say so, yes," I agreed shining my own light on the footwear below the clothing. "Especially the boots. But if he was planning to run for the hills—in this case, literally... ?"

"Why didn't he take time to change?" Selene finished our common thought. "The clothing he was wearing when he came to the *Ruth* was barely even suitable for a rainy night. It wouldn't hold up two minutes in the kind of terrain we drove through today."

"He could have switched shoes," I pointed out. "There's room down there for another pair of boots."

"But not for any other outfits."

"So he didn't head out of town unless he had access to a vehicle," I said thoughtfully. "Okay, odd thought: Remember what Darnell said about Tirano once being some kind of tracker?"

"I remember," Selene said slowly as she pulled up the conversation from her memory. "He said there used to be natives living up the mountain near Seven Strands, and that Tirano used to find abandoned artifacts up there."

"He also told us the natives had all disappeared," I said. "What if they haven't?"

"Are you saying Tirano might have gone to them?"

"It's a thought," I said. "If he's the only one around who can sniff them out, and if he made some friends on his other trips, it might be a good place to go to ground."

"But that's still up in the mountains," Selene pointed out. "If he went there, why didn't he change clothing first?"

I scowled. That was a good point. "Maybe he's just planning on traveling through their territory to Cavindoss and thought hiking gear would be too conspicuous in the middle of a city?"

"Maybe," Selene said, her pupils going suddenly thoughtful. "Gregory, you said Lukki called herself a dealer in exotics. Correct?"

"Yes," I said, nodding. "Yes, I see where you're going. Artifacts from a vanished people would also fit that category. And I doubt Tirano has the contacts and business skills to set up that kind of dealership alone." I gestured toward the stack of commarks. "Especially one that pays this well."

"And if he was working for Lukki, maybe he knew about a safe house she had for emergencies," Selene suggested.

"Maybe," I said, staring at the commarks. "So if he was running, why didn't he grab *all* the cash? Also, Lukki didn't strike me as the sort who would share safe-house information with anyone else."

"Not even her most valuable employees?"

"She *might* tell them about one or two of her hideouts," I conceded. "Maybe. But she'd have at least one that *no* one else knew about. She also wasn't the sort to put information like that on her phone or info pad where it could be tracked or hacked. Did any of the badgeman reports you looked at mention Lukki's address?"

"Yes," she said. "But I'm sure the badgemen have already been through everything."

"That's okay," I said, motioning her to close the secret door. "As my father used to say, *Just because you look at something doesn't mean you see it.* Let's go find out what they missed."

The outer door of Lukki's apartment building was locked, and I hadn't thought to bring a set of lockpicks with me. Fortunately, we only had to wait a few minutes before one of the other residents came along, hurrying through the rain with his head down, and keyed it open. Most people knew enough not to let strangers crowd through a security door behind them, but most people also didn't pay attention to whether or not the door actually sealed once they were inside. This tenant proved to be one of the most, and kept going despite the door hanging up on the small stick I lobbed onto the threshold as it was closing. Twenty seconds later, Selene and I were also out of the rain.

Unlike the tenant, I made sure the door sealed behind us.

"I don't suppose you know which apartment is hers," I muttered to Selene as we dripped our way toward the elevator.

"No, but—" She broke off, lurching to a sudden stop, her eyelashes going like crazy.

"What is it?" I asked quietly, opening my coat and getting a grip on my plasmic.

"They were here," she murmured. "All of them. Willie, Kiolven and Venikel, Detective-Sergeant Kreega"—she braced herself—"and Tirano."

I gripped my plasmic a little tighter. "Well, Kreega having been here makes sense," I muttered. "Badgeman and all that. Any of them here now?"

She gave a quiet sigh. "Tirano."

So he'd had the same thought I had about finding a clue to Lukki's safe house. "Okay," I said, glancing around at the deserted hallway and drawing my plasmic. "Let's find him."

Selene hadn't been able to dig Lukki's apartment number out of the badgeman files. Not surprising, given that sensitive information like that was typically buried under thicker layers of hackproofing than Selene had had time to tackle.

But for a Kadolian, that wasn't a problem. Now that we knew Tirano had been here, and had presumably gone to Lukki's place, all Selene had to do was sniff at each elevator button until she found the floor he'd gone to, and then sniff at each door on that floor until she found his scent on the knob.

In this case, we ended up at one of the fancier corner apartments, sealed away behind a safe-style digital lock. "Well?" I asked as she sniffed at the keypad.

"Six digits; six different numbers," she said.

"So, no," I concluded. "Is he in there?"

She stooped down and sniffed at the wisps of air coming out from under the door. "Yes, he's—" She broke off, her body going rigid as she straightened up. "The two Patth," she said, twitching aside her coat and drawing her plasmic. "They're in there with him."

"Damn," I muttered. Tirano and two Patth on the inside, Selene and me on the outside, and a locked security door between us.

I frowned down at the keypad as a sudden thought struck me. Unless... "Selene, was there any Patth scent on the keypad?"

"No," she bit out. Her pupils were blazing with fear and

helpless anger, her hand tense where she gripped her weapon. "What does—?" She broke off, the emotion in her pupils shifting as she saw where I was going.

Because if Kiolven and Venikel were high enough in the Patth hierarchy to have a set of those handy little security back-door protocols, and if they'd been just a little careless... "Let's find out," I said. Getting a grip on the doorknob, mentally crossing my fingers, I gently turned it.

Careless it was. The knob turned, the latch bolt slid back, and the door was open. Glancing at Selene to make sure she was ready, I gave the door a gentle shove and slipped through into the apartment's common room.

And walked in on what could have been the anteroom of a medieval torture chamber.

Tirano was sitting on an upright chair facing us, his thin wrists tied to the chair's arms, his face rigid. Standing facing him with their backs to us were the two Patth. An end table laden with a selection of kitchen knives and skewers sat between them. The Patth on the left was holding a long and particularly nasty-looking serrated carving knife, its tip hovering bare centimeters above the first joint of Tirano's right forefinger. The Patth on the right was murmuring something in a low voice, his tone somehow managing to be both soothing and menacing. I opened my mouth to announce our arrival—

"Drop it or die," Selene said quietly, gliding toward the Patth with the knife.

"If you're smart you'll listen to the lady," I advised, angling toward my right.

People were never smart. The words were barely out of my mouth when the Patth holding the knife—it was Venikel, I saw as he swung far enough for me to see into his hood—twisted around and hurled the knife at Selene.

Rather, he hurled it at the spot where Selene had been when she delivered her threat. As my father used to say, *They're welcome to know where you* were *as long as they don't know where you* are. Selene had been a bounty hunter far too long to make that kind of mistake, and had angled off to her left as soon as the words were out of her mouth. The knife whistled past her and bounced off the door. Venikel continued his spin, grabbing blindly for one of the knives on the end table—

And snarled something in the Patth language as Selene's shot burned into the edge of his hood and my one-two shots turned the remaining knives into an artistic selection of branding irons.

"I don't know why you people can never just do as you're told," I complained, striding around behind Kiolven. He, at least, had taken note of our willingness to make a mess and was standing motionless with his open hands outstretched to the sides. "You really think you can outrun one of these things?"

"You people, as in the Patthaaunuth?" Kiolven asked, a shimmering of threat in his voice.

"You people, as in everyone who thinks we don't really mean it," I corrected. "Nothing against you or the Patth personally. You want to raise your hands, step away from the young lad there, and tell us what the bloody hell is going on?"

"They want to know where Galfvi is," Tirano said as the two Patth complied. The boy's face was outwardly composed, as Kadolian faces nearly always were, but his trembling voice showed the fear and horror lying beneath the façade.

"Where is he?" Venikel demanded, anger simmering in his face even as he winced at the embers still floating around the charred hole Selene had burned in his hood. "If you know his whereabouts, tell us. Now!"

"Take it easy," I soothed, my eyes on Kiolven. He had also turned to face me, but unlike his partner he was standing quietly, his face and outward attitude calm and cool.

And he was watching me. Very closely.

"So," I said, addressing him. "You're not just the *cold badge* half of the classic hot badge/cold badge game. You're the head of this little search party."

For a moment I thought he was going to deny it. Then, a touch of a smile crossed his face and he inclined his head slightly. "You are indeed as we were told," he said. "Tell me, Mr. Roarke, how well do you know Galfvi and his family?"

"Never met him, and absolutely nothing," I said. "What do you want with him? Escaped criminal? Run out on his wife?"

Out of the corner of my eye I saw a brief reaction cross Venikel's face. Kiolven's expression didn't even twitch. "Not at all," he assured me. "He's been out of contact with his family for a significant time, and they're concerned for his safety."

"Concerned enough to sanction torture?"

"The safety of the Patthaaunuth always takes precedence over the comfort of lesser beings," Kiolven said. "Did Galfvi never express that reality to you?"

"I already said we never met him."

"And you?" Kiolven asked, turning his head back toward Tirano. "He said nothing of his family to you?"

"He cut fish and cleaned tools," Tirano said. His voice was still tense, but some of the quavering had faded. "That's all I know about him."

"I see." Kiolven turned back to me. "Then our duty here has been discharged, and we will be on our way."

"You think so?" Selene asked.

I felt something hard settle into my stomach. Selene was usually the calm half of our team, seldom getting angry, always observing and assessing and waiting for my lead or taking advantage of a promising opening I'd missed.

But here she'd drawn her plasmic before I did. She'd warned or threatened the bad guys without waiting for me to do so. And she'd fired a warning shot far closer to her target's face than I ever would have.

And now, with a peaceable disentanglement strategy laid out in front of us, she was not just rocking the boat but possibly hoping to capsize it.

"You're threatening an innocent boy," Selene continued. "Such actions carry consequences."

"Innocent?" Kiolven sent a sideways look at Tirano. "Perhaps. Perhaps not. But let us pass on that. Do these consequences you speak of entail you summoning the badgemen? Or do you intend to shoot us and be done with it?"

I held my breath...because from what I could see in her pupils it sure as hell looked like she was ready to go with option two.

"I should point out that there are serious difficulties intrinsic to the disposal of murdered bodies," Kiolven continued, his manner still glacially calm. "As for calling the badgemen, I believe Detective-Sergeant Kreega still wishes to question your kinsman Tirano concerning Galfvi's disappearance, the theft of money from the seafood shop, and Ms. Lukki Parsons' murder. Do you really wish to give the authorities that opportunity?"

The unthinking anger in Selene's pupils began to fade. "If we let you leave, what happens then?" she asked.

"We have questioned your kinsman and learned the depth of his knowledge," Kiolven said. Without asking permission, he lowered his arms to his sides. "There is nothing more we can do here tonight."

For another few seconds Selene continued to point her plasmic at the two of them. Then, she twitched the weapon's muzzle toward the door. "Go," she said. "If you bother any of us again, you will sorely regret it."

"Understood." Kiolven gestured to Venikel and started toward the door. Venikel took another moment to send glares at Selene and me before following. Kiolven opened the door, ushered Venikel out, and left, closing the door gently behind him.

"Well, that was fun," I said, holstering my plasmic and drawing my knife as I walked over to Tirano. Behind me, Selene crossed to the door, locked it, and engaged the deadbolt. "You all right, Tirano?" I asked the boy as I cut him free from the chair.

His only answer was to leap to his feet, take four running steps across the room, and fling himself into a clearly surprised Selene's arms. For a moment they hung together, faces pressed into each other's necks, communing silently by touch and scent. Then, Selene gently pulled away. "Are you all right?" I asked again.

"He's fine," Selene answered for him. "Frightened, but unhurt."

"Good." I'd have preferred to hear it from Tirano himself, but the Selene who was only now returning her plasmic to its holster wasn't one I wanted to raise petty complaints to. "So what did they want, Tirano?"

"You heard him speak," Tirano said. With Selene having ended their hug, he was now standing in the middle of the room, looking a bit uncertain. "They wanted to know about Galfvi."

"What did you tell them?"

Tirano looked at Selene. "I told them I don't know where he is," he said. "I told them the last time I saw him he was afraid."

"And the money?" I asked. "Did you tell them about the money in Galfvi's robe?"

"I didn't steal it," Tirano insisted. He lowered his gaze to the floor. "Galfvi stole it," he continued, almost too softly now for me to hear. "I didn't know it was in there. That was why I—" He broke off. "Over there." He pointed to a small duffel bag on the couch.

I looked at Selene, wondering if she would want to look first.

She stayed where she was, so after a couple of seconds I went over to the couch and opened the duffel.

Inside were two shirts, a pair of slacks, a couple of changes of undergarments, and a stack of commarks.

"Good rule of thumb: when you go on a trip, stick with the essentials," I commented, holding up the open bag so Selene could see inside. "So if you're running, why didn't you take the rest of the money?"

"I'm not running," Tirano said, showing no surprise at the implication that we'd been in his home. Probably smelled it on Selene while they were hugging. I'd noted over the years that having Selene as a partner saved a lot of time and conversation. Clearly, being a fellow Kadolian saved even more of both. "I was going to give it to Mr. Darnell and Mr. Bicks to pay them back for what Galfvi stole. Only..." He trailed off, closing his eyes.

"Only you got there and saw they'd been murdered," I said grimly. I again looked at Selene, but could see no suspicion or doubt in her pupils. Apparently, Tirano was telling the truth. "I guess our timeline was a little off."

Tirano raised his head and gave me an odd look. "The timeline?"

"We assumed you'd been to the fish shop first, then gone to your house to get running money," I explained. "I see now it was the other way around. So why did you come here after the fish shop?"

"I thought I could hide," he said. "I knew Ms. Lukki had been killed—"

"Don't lie," Selene said quietly.

Tirano twitched. "What?"

"I said don't lie," Selene repeated. "You didn't come here to hide. Why did you come here?"

Tirano looked at me, then back at her. "I'm tired," he said. "I'm afraid. I need to sleep."

It was obvious Selene wanted to keep the conversation going. It was equally obvious that she couldn't force Tirano to talk if he didn't want to. "All right," she said. "I assume there's a bedroom back there. Find it, clean up if you want, and go to sleep. Are you hungry?"

"No," he said, moving toward a door at the back of the common room. "Thank you. And thank you for—" He looked at the row of knives. "For saving me."

"Sleep well," Selene called as he passed through the doorway, closing the door behind him.

"Well, that was interesting," I commented as I went over to the knives and gave one of them a careful tap. It was still hot where my plasmic shot had superheated it. "I thought you couldn't tell if he was lying."

"You mean by smell?" She shook her head. "No, I can't. Not the way I could with another Kadolian whom I knew well."

"So calling him on his lie was a bluff?"

"No. I mean, not completely." She hesitated. "It's . . . You've seen his expressions and gestures, Gregory. He seems to have adopted them from the humans and other non-Kadolians he's been living and working with these past few years. I don't think he ever fully learned how to express his thoughts and emotions through his pupils."

"You've also been living with *me* all this time," I pointed out. "You've picked up a few human gestures, but your pupils are still your main indicators."

"But I grew up fully with other Kadolians," she said. "Tirano didn't."

"Which is part of the whole changeling thing?"

"*If* he's a changeling."

"Of course," I said. The words were firm enough, but her pupils didn't hold the same conviction that I'd seen there before. She wanted to believe he was fully and properly Kadolian, but I could tell that conviction was starting to erode. "So if he didn't come here to hide, what *did* he come for?"

"I presume he was looking for something." She looked around the room, then headed toward an antique rolltop desk in the back corner. Its cover was open, revealing several short stacks of paper on the writing surface. "Maybe we can figure out what it was."

"Maybe," I said, following her toward the desk. "And if Tirano didn't find it, maybe we can."

CHAPTER TEN

I'd seen Selene do her magic many times over the years, but it never ceased to amaze me. She started at the left end of the desk, going through each stack of paper, sniffing at each page. She continued to the right, methodically checking the papers, the wood and brass of the desk proper, and even a picture frame perched on top of the desk that showed a seascape framed by three half-lit moons. I stayed well back out of her way, half of my attention on her and the rest on the closed door Tirano had disappeared behind. If *I'd* been hunting for something, and if that search had been rudely interrupted by a couple of unhappy Patth, I'd find an excuse to wander out here and see if my rescuers had come up with the grand prize.

But the door remained closed. Selene finished with the papers and desktop, then stooped down and sniffed at each of the drawers. A quick tug on the handles to confirm they were all locked, and she straightened up. "Well?" I prompted.

"Tirano started here," she said, pointing to the right edge of the desk. "Going through all the papers. He reached this spot before stopping."

She shifted her finger to a stack of papers near the center of the desktop, a stack that was noticeably less neat than all the others. "Interrupted by the door slamming open behind him, I assume?" I suggested.

"I think so, yes," Selene said. "Up to this point his touch had been very orderly, holding down the left edge of each stack and rifling through the papers from the right-hand side."

I nodded. It was a standard way of looking at each page while leaving the stack in the same position and with mostly the same neatness as it started with. "But being startled that way threw off his precision."

"Exactly," Selene said. "He tried each of the drawers, too, but doesn't seem to have gotten into them."

"That probably would have been the next step after checking the desktop," I said. "What about Kiolven and Venikel?"

"That's one of the curious points," Selene said. "As far as I can tell, they never came over here."

"Really," I said, frowning at the desk. "They came all the way to Lukki's place and broke in and didn't even look?"

"If they did, I can't find any indication," Selene said. "There's no smell of gloves, either."

"Curious, indeed," I said. "You implied there were other such points?"

"Only one, but a very big one," she said. "Galfvi was also here, before Tirano, and was also searching the desk."

"Was he interrupted by Tirano?"

"I don't think so." Selene traced out an arc through the air that went from the left-hand side of the desk to about a third of the way to the right. "He started at the left side and stopped right here. In fact"—she picked up that stack of paper and pulled off the top three sheets—"this is as far down as he got."

I took the three pages, frowning as I looked over them. They were real estate tax invoices: two of them for buildings inside Bilswift, the third for a parcel of land in the forested area south of town. I peered at the top sheet of the stack Selene was still holding and saw that it was another invoice. "So he was looking for some building or land Lukki owned," I said. "Should be straightforward enough. We take all of them to the local tax office and see which one is missing."

"I'm afraid it won't be that easy," Selene warned. "Each invoice has a different owner name on it."

I took another look. She was right. "Well, isn't *that* convenient," I growled. "So Lukki used multiple names and multiple accounts to keep her assets hidden, and in general to be a pain in the butt."

"Yes," Selene said. "Still, it's nice to see someone still using the classics."

"I suppose," I said. Back in our bounty hunter days we'd spent many a tedious hour digging through targets' assets, accounts, and holdings in search of the bedrock that would finally give us a lead on where they were holed up. "But hey, if it works, it works. So: Bottom line is we don't know where this chunk of real estate is, we don't know what name it's under, and we don't know why everyone wants it."

"Not *everyone*," Selene corrected. "Just Galfvi and Tirano."

"*Just* Galfvi and Tirano?" I asked, frowning at the papers. "There aren't any other scents here?"

"There are a few in the room," Selene said. "Detective-Sergeant Kreega and Badgeman Zilor were here within the past couple of days."

"Checking for clues at the victim's home," I said, nodding. Standard practice, and you didn't need a warrant to look through the victim's home and effects. "Anyone else?"

"Your late friend Willie was here, as were three others," Selene said. "One was probably Ms. Parsons herself—there was the same scent in the badgeman office where they took her body when we went to examine the knife that had cut Galfvi. The other two were probably either associates or clients. But the latter scents are at least a week old, and none of them are on these papers."

My phone vibed. "Hold that thought," I said, pulling out the phone and looking at the ID display. The number wasn't one I recognized, but with the kind of life Selene and I led unidentified numbers were hardly uncommon. I keyed it on and held it to my ear. "Roarke."

"Detective-Sergeant Kreega," an all-too familiar voice came back. "I trust I'm not interrupting anything important?"

"No, not at all," I assured her, wincing. Not quite the last person in the Spiral I wanted to talk to right now, but pretty high on that list. "We were just out sampling the Bilswift nightlife."

"Were you, now," Kreega said, her tone one of polite disbelief. "Where are you right now?"

"Just wandering the streets," I said evasively, trying to visualize the city maps I'd looked at earlier. My phone was gimmicked to show its location as half a kilometer northeast of where it really was, which could come in handy if someone with hostile intentions toward me hacked into it.

On the other hand, if Kreega had obtained a warrant to track my phone, and if that track currently showed us standing in the middle of the river, there were likely to be a few awkward questions.

There was a movement at the corner of my eye, and I looked over as Selene swiveled her info pad around to face me, its display showing a map of Bilswift. In the center of the map was a glowing spot where she had marked my phone's ostensible position at the eastern edge of the Wellington district. A little far out, but still within city limits. "I can see a little park across the street," I added, noting the listing on Selene's map. "Don't know which one."

"Not important," she said. "You wouldn't happen to have dropped by Javersin Brothers Seafood this evening, would you?"

I squeezed the phone a little harder. Had someone seen us go into the place? "We drove past it," I said, picking my words carefully, "but it was already boarded up for the night. Why? Did Tirano or Galfvi come back?"

"Interesting question," Kreega said, her voice going grim. "If one of them did, I'd very much like to talk to him. Darnell and Bicks Javersin have both been shot."

"*Shot?*" I echoed, lacing my tone with surprise and disbelief. "How did—? Are they all right?"

"Hardly," Kreega said, and I thought I could hear a hint of disappointment in her voice. Probably hoping I'd be focused so much on my dramatics that I'd make the rookie mistake of forgetting which details I wasn't supposed to know. "They're dead."

"Damn," I breathed. "What happened? Another robbery?"

"We don't know," she said. "We've got a call in to the Poconos Barline dealer in Tranlisoa to get the factory override combination for the shop's safe, but until we hear back from them we're basically stuck. Unless you think your partner could open it for us?"

"I don't know," I said, pretending I was thinking through a brand-new idea. "I remember she said it was doable, but that it would take time to run all the possible combinations. You want me to ask her if she wants to try?"

"No, we'll hold off on that for now," Kreega said, again a bit reluctantly. Wanting to watch Selene in action, I guessed, but with the side concern about inviting a potential suspect into a crime scene. "If the dealer hasn't gotten back to us by tomorrow morning, maybe we'll give it a go. I just wanted to know if it was an option."

"We're happy to help in any way we can," I assured her. "Let me know if you change your mind. You obviously already have my number."

"Does that bother you?"

"Not at all," I said. "I assume you got it from the spaceport maintenance people. I was just surprised at your call, that's all. But I do appreciate you letting us know about the Javersin brothers."

"Well, you *do* seem interested in what's happening in that part of town," Kreega said pointedly. "I looked up your record, Mr. Roarke. You have a habit of leaving messes in your wake."

"Correlation doesn't necessarily imply causality," I pointed out. "It's usually more a matter of trouble gathering around me than it is of me generating it."

"Either way, Bilswift has enough problems of its own without you adding to them," she said. "I suggest you finish whatever business you have in our town as quickly as possible and then leave."

"We're doing our best," I promised, resisting the urge to point out that she'd also told us not to leave the planet and ask her to make up her mind. "Anything else?"

"Not at the moment," she said. "Enjoy your walk."

"We will. Good night, Detective-Sergeant."

"Good night, Mr. Roarke."

I keyed off and put the phone away. "You heard?" I asked Selene.

She nodded. "She's in over her head," she said quietly.

"Multiple murders will do that," I agreed. "Especially when you have no idea who or what in Bilswift is worth killing this many people over." I stared at the desk again as I put my phone away. "Maybe it's time we met that someone."

Her pupils frowned. "What do you mean?"

"I mean there's someone whose scent ought to be on those papers besides Galfvi's and Tirano's," I said. "Why don't you head to the bedroom area and find someplace to sleep? Preferably where you can also keep an eye on Tirano."

Her pupils shifted from uncertain to suspicious. "Or I could just stay out here with you."

"I'd rather make sure Tirano doesn't go missing again," I said. "Don't worry, I'm not expecting any trouble. At least, nothing I can't handle."

"All right," she said reluctantly. She clearly didn't like where this conversation was going, but also knew it would be useless to continue arguing the point. "You'll be staying here?"

"Yes," I confirmed. Or at least I'd be staying if the person I was expecting to show up decided instead to go to bed early. But there was no point worrying Selene with such details.

"All right." She pointed at my phone. "Do let me know what's happening when you go out later."

I huffed out a sigh, wondering why I even bothered trying. "Sure," I said. "Just get some rest, okay? And keep an eye on Tirano."

"I will," she said. "Be careful."

"Always."

She headed through the doorway to the rear of the apartment, closing the door behind her. I crossed over to the main door, unfastened the deadbolt, and turned out all the lights. Finding a comfortable spot behind the couch where I could watch both the door and the desk, I wadded my raincoat into a slightly damp pillow and settled down to wait. It had been a long day, and I should at least be able to get some rest before the evening got interesting.

But before I could do so, there were a couple of modifications I had to make to my phone.

Selene had asked me to keep in touch if I went out tonight. But as my father used to say, *Promise them whatever they want, give them whatever they think they want, then go ahead and do whatever you want. Odds are they won't even notice.*

I'd been resting for about an hour, and was starting to doze off, when I was snapped back to alertness by the sound of the door across the room being stealthily opened. I sat up, staying out of sight while the wedge of light spilling in from the hallway disappeared and was replaced by the smaller glow of a flashlight.

I moved to the other end of the couch as the glow crossed the common room. If he started to open the door leading to the bedroom area, I needed to have a warning shot set up and ready to fire.

I lined up my plasmic on the door. Actually, given that there were already four murders connected to this case, I might not even bother with a warning.

Fortunately for him, the light stopped at the desk. I heard the sound of rustling papers and cautiously eased my head around the side of the couch.

Standing framed in the backwash glow, his expression one of intense concentration as he leafed rapidly through the stack of real estate invoices, was my old human pinball buddy Braun.

I smiled tightly. Exactly as I'd hoped and expected. Of all the people who should be interested in this unknown chunk of the late Lukki Parsons' property, her close associate Braun should be at the top of the list. The fact that his scent hadn't already been on the papers offered two possibilities: one, that he already knew all he needed to about the location, in which case he'd probably already cleared out whatever made it interesting in the first place; or two, that he'd been lying low but would eventually join the parade of people digging through his boss's desk.

I'd told Selene earlier that evening that Lukki didn't strike me as the trusting sort. Apparently, that lack of trust had extended even to her two bodyguards.

I watched as Braun leafed his way through that first stack of papers and then moved on to the next, and the next, and the next. From the quickness of his scan it was clear he knew what he was looking for, but wasn't finding it. He went through everything on the desk and then stopped, playing his light on the locked drawers. He tried each in turn, then paused a moment. Possibly wondering if he could force them quietly enough and deciding against it.

Abruptly, he spun around and headed back across the room. Again, as I'd expected. He'd hoped to find the missing paper on Lukki's desk, had looked through the stack it should have been in, had gone through all the others where it might have been misfiled, and had come up dry. Stashing away a single paper by itself in a locked drawer might seem like a good option, but he clearly knew that it was instead the perfect way to draw unwanted attention to it.

He reached the door, opened it to another flood of hallway light, and slipped out. I waited thirty seconds after the door closed behind him, then grabbed my raincoat and hat and followed.

The heavy rain Selene and I had slogged through earlier had slowed to a light and intermittent drizzle. The sun had long since set, but the night was still young and the Bilswift citizenry had resurfaced to patronize the shops, restaurants, and tavernos, filling the streets and walkways with a comfortable sprinkling of people and vehicles.

Which, from my point of view, was about as good as it ever got. Trying to follow someone along a deserted street was as obvious as carrying a sign to that effect, while attempting the same in a pressing crowd offered a wary target an abundance of opportunities to slip their leash. Bilswift's traffic was the perfect medium, allowing me to stay anonymous while easily keeping Braun's imposing bulk in sight. I stayed a cautious half block behind him, watching his confident stride and hoping he wasn't headed for a car. If that happened, my evening was over, because our rental was parked too far away for me to get to it in time to continue the chase.

Still, the urgency I'd sensed in his search of Lukki's desk, not to mention the risk involved in sneaking into a place he clearly suspected was occupied, suggested that he was running a tight schedule. Given Lukki's untimely death, plus her self-adopted title as a dealer in exotics, that in turn pointed to a meeting with one or more of her clients.

And if Galfvi had indeed helped himself to the golden ticket, as Selene's analysis seemed to indicate, there was a better than average chance the young Patth would also be at the meeting, invited or otherwise. If so, I ought to be able to grab him and finally get some answers.

My initial encounter with Lukki had been at Panza's Café, which seemed to be her primary spot for meeting new clients and doing business with established ones. But I'd dealt with enough underworld figures to know that they always had another, more anonymous place for the truly dark transactions. I was expecting Braun to be heading to such a place, and I wasn't disappointed. Barely three minutes after leaving Lukki's apartment he arrived at what looked to be a low-class taverno with a faded sign identifying it as THE BLACK ROSE. Bypassing the main entrance, he headed down the alley along the building's western wall to an unmarked and unlit side door. He tapped twice, someone inside opened the door, and he disappeared inside.

I'd known a few bounty hunters who would have responded to a situation like this by boldly walking up to the side door, knocking, and politely asking for the person they were tailing. But as my father used to say, *Bluffing is your emergency fund. Don't spend it unless you've run out of all your other cash.* Ignoring the side door, I went instead to the main entrance and walked in.

The taverno was smaller and considerably darker than Panza's, with an overall sense of furtive edginess. Not just low-class, but probably a watering hole for some of Bilswift's criminal element. Probably didn't have decent barbeque, either. Out of the corners of my eyes I could see the patrons at the various tables and booths watching me as I made my way toward the bar at the back. Most of the clientele were human, but I spotted one table occupied by four Saffi and another hosting a pair of Narchners.

And near the back, at a table beside a door that probably connected to the room Braun had disappeared into, were two Ylps.

I gave them that single glance, then deliberately turned my eyes away. Perrifil had said a Ylpea ship was supposed to come in later this week. Was this that group, having decided to land elsewhere and come to Bilswift via aircar or shuttle? Or was the incoming ship some kind of backup?

Either way, Ylps being on Alainn at all was definitely a curiosity. The Ylpea homeworld was at the other end of the Spiral, and its people spent the majority of their time in that general region. I'd only dealt with a couple of them over the years, but each time I'd come away from the encounter wishing they spent *more* of their time at home. They tended to be arrogant, condescending, quick to anger, and generally unpleasant to deal with. More so even than the Patth.

I'd heard other nonhumans speculate that the main reason humans and Ylps didn't get along was that Ylps simply out-humaned us. I wasn't sure I agreed with that, and was definitely sure I didn't care.

On the other hand, there *was* that Narchner song about some ancient Ylp dynasty skinning its enemies. It would probably be a good idea to avoid them.

The bartender had spotted my approach and positioned himself at the spot where I would reach the bar, his face neutral but watchful. I started a mental run-down through my opening spiel—

"Roarke, isn't it?" a quiet voice came from behind me, the

question punctuated by the gentle pressure of a gun muzzle against my back.

So much for my spiel. "Hello, Braun," I said. "I was hoping I'd run into you."

"Yeah, I figured that when I saw you following me," Braun growled. "What do you want with me?"

I sighed to myself. *Unless you've run out of all your other cash...* "What do you think?" I replied. "I'm here for the meeting."

CHAPTER ELEVEN

Given there were two Ylps in obvious sentry positions by the back-room door, and given my general impression that Ylps didn't trust anyone except themselves, my tentative conclusion was that the others at Braun's meeting would be more Ylps.

I was right. Braun ushered me through the door to a cozy back room where two more of the spindly aliens sat stiffly at a small table, their serrated white eyes staring with unfriendly intensity out of their gray-furred faces. Both were dressed in the same drab brown clothing as the two outside, but the taller one also sported a wide scarf in muted shades of maroon and burnt orange wrapped a couple of times around his neck and shoulders. "Who is this?" the latter demanded in a singsong voice as Braun closed the door behind us, cutting off both the conversational hum and the air of suspicion that had been directed at me out there.

As my father used to say, *When everyone around you is against you, at least you can say your social standing is consistent.*

"Name's Roarke," Braun told him, guiding me to one of the empty chairs at the table and encouraging me to sit with a heavy hand pressed down on my shoulder. "He came and talked to Lukki at Panza's a couple of nights ago. Right before she was killed." He pressed the muzzle of his gun—a Blackman 4mm, I saw now—against the side of my neck and flipped open my raincoat.

"Is he the one who killed her?" Scarf asked.

"No," I said.

"He says no," Braun said. "Me, not so sure. Don't think he killed Willie, though." He pulled my plasmic from its holster and stuck it into his waistband. "He followed me from Ms. Parsons' place and seems to think we want him here."

"You should disabuse him of that notion," Scarf said.

"Hey, I'm with you on that one," I told him agreeably. "Unfortunately, it's not up to me. You see—"

"Hold it," Braun cut me off. Once again his Blackman delivered its silent warning to my neck as he reached into my coat and found my phone. He pulled it out—

"Thought so," he rumbled as he saw the tiny indicator light. He hit the power switch, and the light went off. "Private conversation, you know." He sat down on the empty chair beside me, pointedly setting my phone on the table in front of him where he could keep an eye on it. "Don't want it to accidently go on again or something."

"Purely unintentional, I assure you," I said. "That model does that sometimes. Anyway, as I was starting to say, I don't especially want to be here, either. But when you get a personal invitation and accept a stack of commarks, you're sort of obligated."

"Really," Scarf said, the pitch of his singsong rising into sarcasm territory. "Which of us, pray tell, do your fantasy thoughts envision having done that?"

"It wasn't any of you," I said. "It was Lukki Parsons."

"What?" Braun demanded.

"You heard me," I said. "Lukki hired me as her backup."

For a single heartbeat no one spoke. Braun broke the silence first, though with more of a snort than an actual word. "Right," he said. "Her backup. And somehow she forgot to tell Willie and me?"

"Backups are supposed to be secret," I pointed out. "To be fair—to be fair," I added quickly, holding up a cautioning finger as his eyes narrowed, "Lukki never said she suspected either of you two of anything. But she was convinced she was being watched and monitored, and you never know when and where someone might be listening."

"We were *always* monitored," Braun growled.

"Oh, I don't doubt it," I said. "All I know is that Lukki contacted me and asked me to come keep an eye on this transaction." I nodded back over my shoulder in the direction of Lukki's place. "In retrospect, I wish she'd called us in a couple of weeks earlier."

Another short silence descended on the room. "You said he didn't kill your colleague," Scarf said. "Why do you think that?"

"I saw him get shot," Braun said, a brief shadow of anger and loss flashing across his face. "Couldn't get to him in time, and the killer got away. But he was wearing one of those fancy hooded Patth robes."

"It was a *Patth*?" I asked, hoping my look of surprise would mask my sudden uneasiness. Had Tirano left Galfvi's robe back on the *Ruth*? Or had he been wearing it when he went to the fish shop, back to his house, and then to Lukki's? I hadn't seen it in the common room, but he might easily have stashed it in back before Selene and I got there.

Selene would probably have smelled it if he had. But she hadn't mentioned it, and I hadn't asked.

Fortunately, everyone else's thoughts were already charging off in a different direction. "Why would a Patth wish him dead?" Scarf asked.

"No idea," Braun said. "But I know there are at least two of them in town." His face darkened. "Three if you count Galfvi." He turned his glare on me. "I don't suppose Ms. Parsons mentioned *him* to you?"

"Actually, she did," I said. "And for good reason. That paper you were looking for on her desk? I'm pretty sure Galfvi has it."

It was like I'd run a high-voltage current up their chairs. All three of them gave violent twitches. "What the *hell*?" Braun snarled. "You didn't *stop* him?"

"I wasn't there when he did it," I explained patiently. "That's why I said *I'm pretty sure*. But it's all right."

"How can it be all right?" Scarf demanded, his tone now dropped to violent threat level. "If he knows where the package is—?"

"It's all right," I repeated, loudly enough to talk over him, "because I also know where it is."

The rising tension hit a plateau. "What are you talking about?" Braun asked suspiciously. "Lukki said she wasn't going to tell anyone."

"Anyone except her backup," I said. "She wanted this deal

to go through even if she got sidelined." I glowered at the table. "Obviously, she was expecting to be detained, not killed. The point, Braun, is that she wanted you and Willie to make it work whether she was able to have a direct hand in it or not."

"Fine," Braun said. "Let's assume you're not building a three-layer bull sandwich. Where's the package?"

I shook my head. "Lukki specifically told me not to tell anyone," I said. "If I was needed, I was just supposed to take you there."

"Yeah." Earlier in the conversation Braun had set his Blackman on the table with his hand resting ready on top of the weapon. Now, he closed his fingers around the grip and picked it up, gazing thoughtfully at it. "Yeah, I don't think so."

"I have my orders," I said, feeling a knot form in my stomach. This bluff had already taken me farther than I'd expected it to. And as my father used to say, *The deeper the bluff, the more stuff there is to fall on top of you if it's called.*

"Orders from a woman who's dead."

"And whose murder you still might have been involved with," Scarf added.

"In that case, why am I here?" I countered. "If I was after the package myself, why didn't I just leave you three here to argue about it while I quietly loaded it aboard my ship and took off?"

"It's not nearly that easy," Braun rumbled, still fingering his Blackman as he stared at me.

"It's easy enough," I assured him. "Well? Waiting for an answer here. You want my help, or not?"

The three of them looked at each other, and I caught the slight tingle of ultrasonics as the two Ylps held a brief discussion between themselves in their own language. Braun was still holding his gun, but his attention was on the Ylps. His role here was apparently that of facilitator, ready to act on whatever they decided.

And if they decided I needed to be killed...

Scarf turned to me. "Where and when?"

Silently, I let out the breath I'd been holding. "Tomorrow morning we head up the mountain to a place called Seven Strands," I said. "As early as is convenient for you."

"Seven *Strands*?" Braun echoed, his frown deepening. "Lukki said the package was in town."

"Of course she did," I said. "People eavesdropping on you, remember?"

"Yeah, but—" Braun broke off.

"I know," I said, bracing myself. Abandoning the vagueness I'd been carefully playing so far was risky, but if the Javersin brothers' offhand comment about native artifacts was correct, coming out with a more definitive statement could cement my role as Lukki's backup and confidant. Alternatively, it could also get me killed. "But as my father used to say, *Only an idiot hides a needle in a haystack. The place to hide a needle is in a tub of other needles.*"

Again, I held my breath, watching Braun closely. But if that comment was way off the mark, it didn't show in his face or body language. "Yeah, fine," he said. He looked questioningly at the Ylps. "Nine tomorrow morning? Eight?"

"Six," Scarf said. "We leave at six."

"Six it is," I said, nodding. "Okay. I'll meet you there and we'll—"

"Whoa," Braun cut me off. "You're not meeting us anywhere. You're riding with us."

"After you spend your sleep time within our lodging," Scarf added.

"I'd really rather not," I said, an unpleasant tingle running up my back. If I couldn't get back to Selene to work some overnight setup, this whole soap-bubble house could blow straight off the tub. "I don't sleep well except in my own bed."

"None of the rest of us are going to sleep well, either," Braun said. "Why should you be different?"

"You also, Braun, will not be permitted to leave our lodging," Scarf added.

"Wouldn't think of it," Braun assured him. "Like they say, I can sleep when I'm dead." He gestured at me with his Blackman. "On your feet, Roarke. I think we're done here."

"I think we are," I said, standing up. The stage had been set, but from this point on everything was completely out of my hands. Whether this worked or it didn't, whether I lived or died, was all up to Selene.

The Ylps had set up shop in a small hotel a couple of blocks away from both Lukki's apartment and the Black Rose. Apparently, Lukki had liked keeping things within easy walking distance.

Unfortunately, with such a short walk, and with Braun and all four Ylps watching me like a nest of baby hawks, there was no opportunity for me to slip away into the night.

The Ylps' suite consisted of a single bedroom plus a common room that featured a foldout couch like the one in the *Ruth*'s dayroom. Unfortunately, it was only big enough for one, and Braun laid claim to it. I had to make do with some couch cushions and spare blankets on the floor.

As I'd predicted, I didn't sleep very well, with a restlessness that consisted of three parts concern over the coming day, one part Braun's snoring, and one part the presence of the two Ylpea guards sitting in back-to-back sleeping positions in front of the room's door barely three meters away from my impromptu bed. I had no idea how soundly Ylps slept, and with both of them heavily armed I worried a bit that an unintended noise on my part might startle them into doing something we would all regret.

The Ylpea sleep cycle included times when their mouths opened and shut in time with their breathing, and for a while I toyed with the idea of getting a couple of knockout pills from their hidden compartment and seeing if I could feed one to each of the guards without getting caught. Braun was sleeping with my plasmic and phone under his pillow, but if I could get hold of the Ylps' weapons we'd at least be back to a level playing field.

But again, not knowing how deeply the aliens slept—and knowing full well the consequences should the trick fail—ultimately dissuaded me from the idea.

Eventually, fatigue overwhelmed my concerns and I fell into a restless sleep.

I was jolted awake four hours later by a nudge from Braun's boot. "On your feet, Roarke," he ordered. "Time to put up."

"Or be shut up?" I suggested. Untangling myself from my blankets, I rolled up into a sitting position, wincing at the general complaint from my muscles.

"Something like that."

"Yeah," I said, snagging my shoes and starting to put them on. "By the way, when you get to that sleeping-when-you're-dead thing, be sure to warn them that you snore."

He grunted. "Funny. Come on—I've got some meal bars. You can eat on the way."

The Ylps had acquired a nice twelve-passenger van for our trip up the mountain. The two guards hustled me all the way to the rear and into the right-hand corner seat. One of them settled in beside me, with the other taking the left-hand end seat in the next row forward. Unless I could dematerialize and flow out through one of the van's side windows, it was clear that I was here for the duration. Scarf and the other Ylp took seats in the front row, Braun climbed into the driver's seat, and we were off.

"Going to be a bumpy ride," I warned Braun as he maneuvered us through the morning Bilswift traffic. "That mountain road is pretty rough. You couldn't get us an aircar?"

"What, so that everyone for fifty kilometers around could watch us?" he called back. He reached to the van's control board, and I heard the snick as my side window unlocked. "If you feel sick, do it out the window."

"Thanks," I said, eyeing the window. It was big enough to be sick out of; not nearly big enough to escape through. "I'll keep that in mind."

The trip up the mountain was every bit as unpleasant as the one from the previous day. I mostly watched out the left-side windows as best I could, hoping to spot a gap or other weakness in the Patth fence that Selene and I might have missed on our recon. But with the Ylp beside me blocking most of the view, and seated all the way across the van from the relevant windows, I didn't see anything useful.

We'd been traveling about an hour, and had passed the jeep trail Selene and I had used to get to the river, when Braun turned off onto another rough trail, this one heading to the right and continuing upslope. We bumped along for about half a kilometer, the top of the van scraping against the low overhang of tree branches, until we came to a small L-shaped clearing.

And there, towering over us, was Seven Strands.

I'd never gotten around to researching what exactly the Strands were, but I'd sort of vaguely assumed they were part of an odd rock formation, or maybe some distinctive plant with seven tendrils or fronds or something. Instead, it was a series of suspension footbridges, seven of them, radiating outward from a platform five meters above the ground built around a thick tree at the edge of the clearing.

The bridges were about as simple as such things could get. The framework was a rope mesh holding wooden planks that served as the walkway's floor. Chest-high ropes connected to the support mesh on either side of the walkway provided stability and a token effort at keeping travelers from falling. The bridges headed off in different directions: four toward various points farther up the mountain, one north toward the river, one south in the direction of a lush valley, and one to the west in the general direction of Bilswift.

No. Not toward the city itself, I saw now, but angling a little north of it. Specifically, straight toward the area the Patth had cordoned off with their fence.

The area where our hypothetical portal was supposed to be.

And if the bridge remained five or more meters above the ground its entire length, it might just get us over the Patth fence without triggering the sensor buds.

"Who the hell is *that*?" Braun growled as he rolled the van to a halt near the base of the Strands' tree.

I lowered my gaze, pushing back the flurry of possibilities tumbling over themselves in my mind. At the far end of the clearing, unseen from the spot where we'd entered, was our rental car.

Leaning against its side, her arms folded casually across her chest in the embodiment of casual nonchalance, was Selene.

I let out a silent sigh of relief. Gimmicking my phone so that the indicator light showed it to be on when it was off and vice versa had been easy enough, and Braun had played into the gambit exactly as I'd anticipated. But there had been no guarantee that Selene would be listening in when the phone went active in the Black Rose's back room, and there'd been even poorer odds that she could come up with something on the fly in the next few hours that didn't involve calling in the badgemen for what could easily have degenerated into a bloodbath.

I still didn't have a clue as to what she had planned. But in her stance, and in her pupils, I could see the anxiety-edged confidence that she had things as much under control as she could.

Of course, as my father used to say, *Thinking you have a situation under control simply means you haven't yet figured out all the ways it could go sideways.*

In the meantime, Braun had asked a question. "That's my partner, Selene," I called to him. "She's here to help."

"Since when do we need help?" Braun retorted. "And since when did we add another person? You said Lukki hired *you* as backup. *You*, not *we*."

"*You, we*—what's the difference?" I countered. "It's a pronoun, not an ancient prophecy carved in stone."

"Whatever," Braun bit out. "So what do we need a Kadolian for?"

"What is a Kadolian?" Scarf demanded. "I do not know this species."

"She's a tracker," I told him. "Lukki used to use a local Kadolian named Tirano to dig up some of her other packages. He's not available right now, so Selene will work for us in his place."

"What do we need a tracker for?" Braun asked, his eyes on Selene as she walked toward us, his hand resting on the grip of his Blackman. "You said you knew where the package was."

"I knew where it was as of a couple of days ago," I corrected. "But packages can be moved." I looked at Selene, caught her microscopic upward nod. "And we're wasting time," I added, gesturing toward the platform and its radiating footbridges. "Shall we?"

Braun turned to Scarf. "Your call," he said. "We believe him and we go, or we decide he's lying, kill both of them, and go back and start searching the city."

Scarf looked back and forth between Selene and me. "We believe him a little," he decided. "We trust him not at all."

"Works for me." Braun drew his Blackman and gestured to a rough-hewn and rickety-looking ladder leading up to the platform. "Ladies first?"

"Ladies first," I agreed. "Selene?"

She nodded her thanks and climbed to the platform. There she waited until we were all assembled with her. "As Mr. Braun knows, these bridges can be treacherous," she warned. "I'll lead; perhaps Mr. Braun should take the rear position."

"Sure," Braun said. "Roarke, you're in front of me. The rest of you fill in wherever you want."

A moment later we set off, Selene in front, Scarf and his companion behind her, the two Ylp guards behind them, and Braun and me bringing up the rear.

The bridge was actually less nerve-racking than I'd expected. It swayed back and forth pretty seriously as we started our walk, but once we left the clearing and were back into the forest proper the movement lessened considerably. I wondered about that until I spotted the guy lines from the underside of the rope mesh anchoring us to some of the tree trunks on both sides.

It was an impressive bit of engineering, I had to admit. But I couldn't help wondering what would happen if there was a windstorm strong enough to affect even the bigger trees the bridge was connected to. I hadn't noticed any wind during Bilswift's evening rainstorms, but higher up the mountain the weather patterns could be different.

"The ropes stretch," Braun said from behind me.

"Come again?" I asked.

"I said the ropes stretch," he repeated. "When they're wet. When the big winds come they always bring rain with them. The trees sway, the ropes stretch, and nothing breaks or comes apart."

"Ah." I frowned over my shoulder at him. "And you brought this up why?"

"Saw you looking at the guy lines," he said smugly. "Figured you were wondering about that."

"Actually, I was," I confirmed. "You've got a good eye."

"Lukki didn't keep me around for my looks," he said, his voice going dark. "So if you didn't kill her, who did?"

"I don't know yet," I said. "One of her competitors, maybe."

"She doesn't have any," Braun said flatly. "Not here. Not for this particular kind of package. No one but Tirano could find that for us." Out of the corner of my eye, I saw him gesture toward Selene. "And your Kadolian. We hope."

"Yes we do," I murmured, a small piece of this mystery suddenly solidifying. This was apparently the route Lukki and the others had used to get to whatever this package was that everyone wanted, with Tirano leading the way. Even since we'd climbed up to the Strands I'd wondered how Selene knew the route or how she even knew what the package smelled like.

The answer, I realized now, was that she didn't. She wasn't following the package.

She was following Tirano.

"Well, if it wasn't a competitor, maybe a dissatisfied customer," I suggested. "Was all your work local, or did you just stage from Alainn and get most of your acquisitions from off-world?"

There was a short pause. "Yeah," he said slowly. "Don't think this is a subject we ought to get into."

"Suit yourself," I said with a shrug. "Personally, *I'd* like to know why she and Willie were killed, if only to make sure Selene and I don't meet whatever criteria the killer is using to pick his targets. How many times have you been up here?"

Braun snorted. "None of your business."

"Fine," I said offhandedly. "I was just looking for patterns. That was always the first step in a hunt: Find the target's patterns and try to anticipate their next move."

He was silent another few steps. I watched the Ylps in front of me, making a private bet as to when one of the branches we were passing under would snag the tall Ylp's scarf. "Eight other times," Braun said. "You wondering if Galfvi might come here?"

"He will if he wants the package," I said.

Which was a complete lie, of course. There was no way Lukki would have left the package up here, especially if this was where she'd picked it up in the first place.

No, the package was somewhere in Bilswift, and Galfvi was probably making plans right now to grab it and get it off Alainn. Our only chance to stop him was to get this little side trip out of the way and get back to town.

I could only hope Selene had gotten Tirano to tell her what the package was and had figured out how to put together a replacement that was close enough to fool Braun and the Ylps. If not, there was a good chance Galfvi would get away with his scheme.

And an equally good chance that Selene and I wouldn't leave here alive.

CHAPTER TWELVE

We'd been walking for about fifteen minutes when the footbridge dead-ended at a wide ledge jutting out from the side of a curved cliff face. Selene led us along the ledge, all of us ducking or brushing past the nearby trees and the small bushes and grasses that always somehow managed to hang onto sheer rock this way. Fifty meters later we arrived at a tunnel in the rock with a clearly artificial rain-guard overhang. She looked back to make sure we were all still following, then ducked under the overhang and disappeared inside.

Behind me, Braun muttered something under his breath. "Trouble?" I asked quietly.

"This isn't where we usually went in," he said, his voice heavy with suspicion. "We always went to the next tunnel. Where is she taking us?"

"I don't know," I said. Only Selene wasn't taking us anywhere, at least not directly. The real question was where was *Tirano* taking us? "Maybe Lukki wanted to shake things up a bit. If she thought someone was watching her, she might have put the package where they wouldn't think to look."

"Yeah. Maybe."

The tunnel's walls and ceiling were bare rock, with no padding of any sort, but there was enough light seeping in from behind us to warn us of the various protrusions in time to keep from whacking heads or shoulders. But that light was fading steadily as we continued into the darkness. Ten or fifteen more meters, I decided, and I'd need to pull out my flashlight.

"Why are you here?" Braun asked. "Not *here* here. Here in Bilswift."

"I was hired by Lukki," I said. "Remember?"

"Bull," he said flatly. "I know a con story when I hear it. Plus you weren't checking in with her about some private job when you barged in on her at Panza's. You were trying to get Tirano out of his indenture."

"How do you know?" I countered. "You weren't close enough to hear anything. Whatever Lukki told you afterward—"

"You think Lukki was stupid?" Braun interrupted. "You think *I'm* stupid? We had that booth bugged so we could keep tabs and records on everyone who talked to her. Willie and I were listening in the whole time."

I winced. With my thoughts fully focused on Tirano's situation, that obvious security arrangement hadn't even occurred to me. "It's not what you think," I said carefully, my back tingling unpleasantly. Braun probably already had his Blackman out and pointed at the internal organ of his choice.

"No, I think it's exactly what I think." He was silent a few steps. "Okay, here's the deal. I told you I know a con story when I hear it. I also know what it sounds like when someone's stepped off the deep end and is just trying to claw his way back to the surface. I'll give you one chance to tell me the truth."

There was no way I could tell him everything, of course. The portals were a deep, dark secret, and the admiral would have my hide if I said anything about them.

But walking down a narrow tunnel with my back to my opponent, there was no chance of dodging or fighting my way out of this. I didn't know if part of the truth would be acceptable, but right now it was all I had. "Selene and I are in Bilswift on a completely unrelated job," I told him. "Nothing to do with you or Lukki."

"What job?" he pressed. "You on a hunt?"

"We got a tip there were some artifacts hidden in the area," I said. "We had some time on our hands, and Alainn was close, so we thought we'd drop in and poke around a little."

Braun grunted. "If you're talking about the village near Seven

Strands, that was picked clean years ago. So why did you follow me to the Black Rose? No, back up a step. Tell me why you were at Lukki's apartment."

"Tirano had disappeared," I said. "We were hunting him, and thought he might have gone to the apartment to hide." I frowned, peering ahead down the tunnel. As the morning sunlight from behind us was fading, a new and fainter glow was now coming from in front of us. The tunnel was evidently coming to an end. "Or maybe not to hide but to look for the same paper you came there looking for."

"The one Galfvi already made off with?"

"That's the one."

He digested that for a couple more steps. "So the package isn't really here?"

"I really don't know," I had to admit. "But you had a gun on me, and your friends didn't seem the sort to believe I just happened to stumble into your meeting. I had to say *something*."

"Yeah," Braun said. "Figured as much. So why are we here? What's your woman looking for?"

"You know how Kadolian senses work," I said obliquely. "You saw it often enough with Tirano. Selene's using the same technique."

"Even though she's never been here before?" Braun asked. "Tirano said he had to have smelled something to find it again."

"Tirano is young and inexperienced," I said as confidently as I could. If Tirano didn't come through, we were going to be in deep trouble. "Selene will get there."

"Maybe." Braun hissed out a breath. "Not that it matters. If the package isn't here, we'll just grab a different one. It's not like the Ylps will know the difference."

"Not at all," I agreed, wishing I knew what exactly I was agreeing to.

We'd gone two more steps when something hard prodded against my right side. "Here," Braun said. "Take it."

"What?" I asked, frowning as I reached a hand up to the object.

And found myself holding the muzzle of my plasmic. "You sure?" I asked, taking it from him.

"Not really," Braun said frankly. "But this place can be dangerous, and something doesn't feel right. I think we're being set up."

"I'm starting to get that feeling myself," I said, my throat tightening as I shifted my grip on the weapon and slid it back into its holster. "For the record, if we *have* been set up Selene isn't part of the game."

"I guess we'll find out." He touched my shoulder. "Everyone?" he called, raising his voice to a stage whisper. "Hold up here. We need to talk."

Selene and the Ylps stopped and turned to face us. "Are these words necessary?" Scarf asked impatiently.

"Yeah, they are," Braun said. "Up ahead we're going to come to some caverns, more tunnels, and more caverns. Maybe some ladders leading up or down. There are people living here called the Loporri. Whatever you do, *don't* touch them. Got it?"

"Why not?" Scarf asked.

"Because touching a Loporr releases a chemical scent into the air that alerts all the other Loporri in sniffing range," Braun said. "Different touches make them give off different scents."

"Such as?" I asked.

"Such as touches from other Loporri don't bother them," Braun said. "Touches from moss or game animals tell them someone's tending the plants or that it'll be meal time soon." I saw his throat work. "Touches from intruders like us...let's just say it'll draw more attention than we want. Got it?"

"Got it," I said. I looked past the Ylps and saw the sudden apprehension in Selene's pupils. Apparently, Tirano had forgotten to mention that part to her.

Or maybe had skipped the warning on purpose. He knew she would be leading our little expedition, after all. If he wanted to ditch us, or worse, this was a perfect way to do it. Especially since Selene still couldn't tell if and when he was lying.

Crime. Sociopathy.

Changeling.

"What about the package?" Scarf asked.

"Don't worry about the package," Braun said. "I've got that covered. Just don't touch anyone else along the way." He gestured to Selene. "All right, let's go."

She nodded and continued down the corridor into the ever-increasing light. The tunnel curved, revealing an opening into a larger space.

And as we all filed through onto another ledge I saw we were inside a large cavern, probably a hundred meters across and thirty high.

A cavern, and an entirely new world.

The tunnel behind us had been bare rock. Here, there was no such thing. The walls and floor were covered in a wild patchwork of vividly colored plants. Some were green, especially those near the two openings across the cavern and to our left where the midmorning sunlight was spilling in. Most of those plants looked familiar, matching the grasses and shrubs Selene and I had seen earlier during our drive around the Patth enclosure. But the majority of the plant life was decked out in shades of red and purple, or in the dirty white of mushrooms and other fungi. The ceiling had its own color pattern, mostly consisting of mosses or lichens, and there were strands that seemed to be luminous. Nightlights, possibly, for the long hours of darkness.

Moving unhurriedly around the cavern, picking the plants or ladling water on them, were the Loporri.

My first impression of them was that someone had stacked patterned gray-and-white car tires of varying sizes on top of each other, added spindly arms, short thick legs, and a head and called it a day. Their widest region was at their midsection, with their bulk tapering somewhat in both directions. Their heads were flat on top, maintaining my reflexive tire-stack image, with long hair-like tendrils flowing back from their foreheads to the midsection bulge. Their four splayfooted toes were surprisingly thin, given the rest of their bulk, and appeared to be somewhat prehensile. Size was always hard to judge without a known frame of reference, but I guessed their average height to be about a meter and a half or a bit more.

"Yeah, they look cuddly," Braun muttered in my ear. "Don't buy it for a second. And *don't* touch them."

"Don't worry," I muttered back. "*Cuddly* is the last adjective I would have used."

"Good," he said. "Where now?"

Selene had paused and was sniffing the plants clustered around the tunnel exit, first the ones to our right and then those to our left. "That way," she decided at last, pointing behind me toward the right. "And I see a ladder that'll take us down to the cavern floor. That's probably the way."

She started to pass us, stopped as Braun caught her arm. "Where after that?" he asked. "I don't want to just stand around down there while you figure it out."

"I'm sorry, but you may have to," Selene said. "The mix of aromas from the plants is limiting the distance I can read the scent."

"Don't worry, she'll get us there," I said. A movement by the nearest of the cavern openings caught my eye—

I stiffened. Two of the Loporri had appeared, striding into the cavern from a wide, grassy area just outside, walking with a purposeful tread that was in stark contrast to the leisurely movements of everyone else in sight. A carrying pole rested on their shoulders, on which was suspended the carcass of what looked to be a freshly killed animal. In their free hands, each of them carried a simple but very effective looking crossbow.

And as they paused in the cavern opening, and the animal bounced against their skin, a sudden wave of interest swept over the rest of the Loporri, those nearest the opening pausing first in their work to look at the hunters, the same curiosity spreading rapidly to the whole group. "Selene?" I murmured.

"Yes," she said, and I saw wonderment in her pupils. "Yes, I can smell it."

"Good for you," Braun said tightly. "Come on—we need to get moving before the rest of the colony piles in here."

Selene nodded and started along the ledge, the Ylps right behind her. "Why haven't we ever heard about these people before?" I murmured to Braun as we joined them.

"Probably not intelligent enough to be registered," he said. "And there are other reasons."

"Such as?"

"Such as you mind your own business and don't rock any boats," he growled. "Come on, keep moving."

"Hold it," I said, coming to a sudden halt. Two more Loporri hunters had appeared in the cavern opening from the grassy area. But instead of carrying dinner on a pole, this pair had gripped their hands together to make a seat and were carrying a companion.

But this one wasn't like the other Loporri down there. He had the same coloring and head tendrils that they did, but was taller and noticeably thinner. Even more striking were the scattering of odd bulges across his arms, legs, and torso that looked like giant blisters.

Trailing from each of the blisters were strands of silvery

thread that glinted in the sunlight, each of them three to forty centimeters long.

"What's that?" I asked Braun, fending off his efforts to hurry me along.

"He's called a *Vrink*," he said. "Loporr subgroup. Come *on*."

"Braun, look there," Scarf said. He and the other Ylps had also stopped and were gazing across the cavern at the Vrink, who was now being lowered by his carriers to a sitting position at the side of the opening. "That one. Is it part of our package?"

I stared at him, my blood running suddenly cold. Darnell Javersin had said there were alien artifacts up here. Bicks had said that Tirano sometimes went hunting for them. Lukki had called herself a dealer in exotics.

Somehow, it had never occurred to me that all of that together was going to translate into illegal trafficking. "Braun...?"

"Just can't leave well enough alone, can you?" he bit out angrily. Grabbing my arm, he physically turned me around and gave me a shove back along the ledge. "No, that's not one of yours," he added to Scarf. "Those'll be down below, in one of the adaptation chambers."

"Then let us continue," Scarf said, gesturing to Selene. "Take us there."

Selene gave a sort of jerky nod and resumed her walk along the ledge.

But not before I saw the surprise and horror in her pupils. Apparently, Tirano hadn't let her in on this aspect of our hunt, either.

"I don't get it," I said as Braun and I hurried to catch up to the others. "Why them? What are they good for?"

For a moment I thought he wasn't going to answer. Then, he huffed out a sound that was a mix of frustration and resignation. "Yeah, what the hell," he said. "You've already seen them. Those thread things coming out of the spin beetles they've got under their skin? That's silver-silk."

"You're kidding," I said, throwing another look over my shoulder. Silver-silk was a permanent item on the buy-and-boast apparel list of the Spiral's super-snobbish. I'd never bothered to learn much about the stuff, but I vaguely remembered it being harvested from specialized insects on a single island in the Northern Crescent Sea on Jondervais.

"You think any of us would bother with this nonsense if I was *kidding*?" Braun retorted.

"Okay," I said, frowning some more. "So why isn't the Spiral beating a path up here?"

"Because nobody knows about it," Braun said. "Everyone knows about the Jondervais silver-silk, but this little offshoot factory is a complete secret."

"Ah," I said, still trying to wrap my mind around this revelation.

But as the initial shock faded I could see the horrific logic behind it. Kilo for kilo, silver-silk was one of the most expensive substances in the Spiral. If what the Loporri and Vrinks were producing was genuinely identical to the Jondervais version, anyone who knew Alainn's secret stood to make an incredible stack of money.

As did anyone who happened to have a few Vrinks of his own hidden away in the basement. No wonder Lukki, dealer in exotics, hung around a backwoods place like Bilswift. "So how and why?" I asked.

"The *how* is pretty disgusting," Braun warned. "The spin beetles dig into a Vrink's skin and settle there as parasites. They tap into his bloodstream for food and just live there. Far as they're concerned, the silver-silk is just an accidental part of life. Maybe even a waste product."

"And the Vrinks just put up with this?"

"Yeah, because the silver-silk has a weird side effect," Braun said. "Watch it!"

Ahead, a Loporr unexpectedly emerged from another tunnel onto our ledge and headed toward us. Selene moved instantly, shrinking against the plant-covered wall to our right and giving the rotund creature room to get past her. The Ylps were a little slower on the uptake, but managed to also get out of the way in time to avoid contact.

Braun was already pressed flat against the wall. I followed suit, wincing a little as the ragged edges of the fronds behind me poked into the back of my neck. The Loporr passed Braun.

And stopped directly in front of me, the double concentric circles of his eyes boring into mine.

I froze, my hand reflexively gripping my plasmic. For a moment he just stared at me. Then, almost delicately, he reached a four-fingered hand out toward my face.

"Down!" Braun bit out.

I bent my knees, dropping into a crouch. The Loporr's hand continued forward, now reaching past over my head—

And plucked a short branch holding a cluster of red berries from the vines crisscrossing the wall. He put the branch and berries into a pouch slung over his shoulder and continued his stroll along the ledge.

"Close," Braun muttered as I straightened upright again. "Too damn close. Come on—let's get moving. The sooner we're out of this damned place, the better."

We reached the ladder Selene had spotted without further trouble. The Loporri below us were moving toward the farther opening in the wall, where from our new position I could see a stone-lined firepit a couple of meters outside the cavern in the grassy area. Two of the aliens were stoking the fire, while the two hunters who'd brought in the kill had now handed the carcass off to three more Loporri who were starting to dress it. The grassy area itself was larger than I'd realized, probably stretching twenty meters before it disappeared into rocky cuts on one side and what looked to be a sheer drop on the other.

"Now—go now," Braun ordered, gesturing urgently to Selene. "This is the clearest shot at those other tunnels that we're going to get."

Selene nodded and started down the ladder, keeping an eye below her to make sure none of the Loporri wandered into touching range. She was halfway down when Scarf started his own descent, with the remaining Ylps on the ladder by the time she reached the bottom.

I looked again at the firepit as I waited for enough buffer space to begin my turn on the ladder. Crossbows, group hunting skills, flint knives for cleaning their kill, and now fire. Like hell they weren't intelligent enough to be registered.

But registered sapients automatically had rights, one of which included not getting bought and sold across the Spiral. Everything about this situation reeked of the superrich and superpowerful tweaking the law for their own profit and to the detriment of the Loporri.

"One more thing," Braun muttered as I got a grip on the ladder's uprights and started down. "You and Selene just being here today means you're aiding and abetting. Remember that if you're tempted to go to the badgemen when this is over."

"Don't worry," I assured him. "I know how the game is played."

Still, as my father used to say, *When you go up against someone who's changing the rules, they'll naturally assume you'll try to change them back. They won't be expecting you to change them to something else entirely.*

We reached the cavern floor, and after a bit of careful sniffing Selene pointed us to another tunnel mouth thirty meters away. Fortunately, the general motion of the Loporri was still toward the firepit and we were able to slip past them without touching or being touched. We reached the tunnel and headed in.

Unlike the passageway from the footbridge, this one had the same covering of moss and other plant life that we'd seen in the cavern. Here, though, without any sunlight to mask the glow, I was able to confirm that the lines of lichens in the ceiling were indeed luminescent, giving us enough light to guide our steps. We walked past a pair of side tunnels, which a quick glance showed led to smaller chambers filled with white fungi walls and flooring. Farm plots, apparently, sown with crops that didn't require sunlight.

We were halfway down the corridor when Selene abruptly stopped. "What's the matter?" I called softly.

"The scent," she said. "Gregory, it's different. It's suddenly gone different."

"Like back in the cavern?" I asked. "Maybe it just circulated around through here."

"Oh, hell," Braun muttered. "Listen."

I frowned, straining my ears. There was a low murmur and a sort of swishing sound coming from somewhere behind us. "What's that?" I asked.

"Trouble," Braun bit out. "I need to know what's going on, and I need to know *now*. How is she hunting for the package? What's she keying on?"

As my father used to say, *Be wary of anyone who wants to know something* right now *and won't give you time to think about it.* But the rustling sound behind us was getting louder, and there was growing fear in Selene's pupils, and the odds were increasingly good this wasn't just some clever gambit on Braun's part. "She sent Tirano in ahead of us to track down the package," I told him. "Or, like you said, a different group of Vrinks. You think he brushed against one of them?"

"I think he gave one of them a solid right hook," Braun said bitterly. "He played you, you idiot. This whole thing was a setup and a trap to get us killed. And we walked right into it."

"Do you seek our deaths?" Scarf demanded. He twitched two of his fingers.

And suddenly his three companions sprouted compact Kreznir 2mm pistols. "Betrayal is punishable by death."

"Yeah, let's hang onto the threats for later," Braun said, peering behind us as he waved Selene forward. "Keep going. They take a while to get up to speed—if we hurry, we might be able to stay ahead of them. And put those damn things away," he added, jabbing a finger at the Kreznirs. "You draw blood and there won't even be enough DNA left of you for anyone to analyze."

"Yet she has betrayed us," Scarf said, gesturing at Selene. "She must pay with death."

"You shoot her now and you'll never get out of here alive," I warned as all three Kreznirs leveled at Selene's back. "Anyway, she didn't betray us, Tirano did. Selene, any idea how much farther?"

"Not very," she said over her shoulder, her nose and eyelashes going at double time now as she broke into a fast jog. "I can smell some of the bushes and trees from the forest outside."

"We anywhere near where you usually go in?" I asked Braun.

"I don't know," he said. "I don't think we're far enough, but maybe."

"What if we're not?" I asked. "You know how fast they can move. Will they catch us before we get past this next cavern?"

Braun winced. "Yeah. I think so."

"And they're following this new Vrink scent, right?"

"Weren't you listening?" he retorted. "Yeah."

"Just confirming," I said, looking at the Ylps. "You—head Ylp—give me your scarf."

Scarf half turned. "What do you say?"

"I said give me your scarf," I repeated. "We need to confuse them."

"How?" Scarf demanded, his tone dropping into threatening range.

"By overwhelming the Vrink scent," I said, pulling out my knife. "And we don't have time to argue."

"Just *give him the damn scarf*," Braun snarled.

It was probably the first time one of Lukki's people had talked to him that way. Or maybe he'd figured out what I was doing. Either way, he quickly unwrapped the scarf and tossed it to me. "You will still address me with proper respect," he warned.

"Sure," I promised, flipping the scarf open and cutting it in half. I thrust one half into Braun's hands and laid the other lengthwise along the bare rock of the tunnel floor. Then, mentally crossing my fingers, I pulled out my plasmic and fired three shots into the cloth.

I hadn't had any idea what burning Ylpea scarf would smell like. For that matter, I hadn't even been certain it *would* burn. But burn it did, smolder it did, and the stench that cloud of smoke carried with it was all I could have hoped for. "Now go," I ordered, holstering my plasmic and snatching the remaining piece of scarf back from Braun. "Before one of them figures out they can just walk past it and pick up the scent again."

Selene was already on the move, hurrying down the tunnel. The smell of burning scarf would eventually reach her and probably bury the fainter scent she was following, but with a little luck by the time that happened she'd have figured out Tirano's exit strategy.

Regardless, the smoldering scarf was doing its intended job. The swishing of mass Loporri movement behind us seemed to be slowing or fading, or at least wasn't getting any closer. If the Loporri lost the scent and their reason for attacking us and went back to their lunch preparation, we should be able to get away.

Getting out of this maze, of course, could turn out to be an entirely different challenge.

Fifty meters later the tunnel opened into a smaller version of the one we'd just left, with a scattering of the usual fungi and an opening into the sunlit mountainside.

Unfortunately, the opening was far too small for any of us to get through. "No way out there," Braun muttered.

"Not without explosives," I agreed, looking around the cavern. The mossy plants on the floor were much scarcer than we'd seen elsewhere, but there were three much heavier concentrations near the opening. More puzzling were the indentations in each of those collections, as if the plants had been squashed by Loporri who'd been recently sitting or lying there. "What is this place, anyway?"

"Probably a bird trap," he said. "Lots of bird nests in holes on cliffs like this one. You put a couple of Vrinks by the opening, a bird flies in, and one of the hunters spears or nets it."

"Why would a bird fly in here?" Selene asked. She was still out in the tunnel, sniffing for signs of Tirano.

And right on cue, a red-and-purple-plumed bird flew straight into the room. It circled around twice as if looking for something, or possibly wondering what it was doing there, then flew out again.

"Because Vrinks and silver-silk," Braun said, heading back across the cavern. "Probably some of the scent lingered after the Vrink left. Come on, we need to keep moving."

"What do Vrinks and silver-silk have to do with it?" I asked. I started to follow.

And paused as something caught my eye. Something on the wall beside one of the indented spots, done up in a muted version of the same shades I'd just seen on the passing bird.

"Silver-silk," Braun repeated, a bit more emphatically this time. "You coming?"

"Sure," I said, taking one last look and hurrying to catch up with him. "You say *silver-silk* as if it's supposed to mean something."

He shot me a funny look. "Oh. Right. I never got around to telling you, did I? The thing is, silver-silk attracts prey and repels predators. That's why the Loporri go to all this trouble, and why the Vrinks are willing to sacrifice half their lives hosting giant bugs for the colony."

I stared at him. "You're kidding."

"Do I *look* like I'm kidding?" he growled. "Come on, pick it up. Where to next?"

CHAPTER THIRTEEN

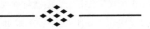

Five minutes later, Selene located the spot where Tirano had left our current route and headed into a side tunnel back toward the outside world. Two minutes after that, we emerged onto a ledge through an opening that Braun confirmed was the one he, Lukki, and Willie had normally used when sneaking into the Loporr tunnel system on earlier missions to snatch Vrinks.

"Only one problem," Braun said. "This ledge leads around the side of the mountain and back to our footbridge."

"That is a problem?" Scarf demanded. He'd taken back the piece of his scarf that I hadn't burned and tried to wrap it back around his neck in its original knot pattern. But with only half the length left for him to work with, it looked rather shabby. One more reason, probably, that I got the stink-eye every time he looked at me.

"It's a problem," Braun told him with strained patience, "because it also passes through the grassy area where the colony is currently preparing their meal."

"And getting through all those milling Loporri without touching any of them will be well-nigh impossible," I concluded. "Terrific."

"It's not as bad as it sounds," Braun said. "The Vrink scent should have faded enough by now to put us in the clear. Once they finish eating and go back inside, we'll have a straight shot."

"How long?" Scarf asked.

Braun shrugged. "No idea. We've never hit them in the middle of a meal before."

"And we're more at the beginning of a meal than the middle," I pointed out. "They were just starting to dress the kill."

"I suppose," Braun said. "Still, it shouldn't be more than a few hours."

Scarf turned to his fellow Ylps, and even with the wind sweeping past us I could hear the ultrasonics as they discussed the situation. "Very well," Scarf said when they finished. "While we wait, you will obtain our package for us."

"Afraid that's not going to work," Braun said. "I've got a way to get hold of them without triggering the kind of riot we just saw, but we can't just hold onto them that way for long. An hour, maybe an hour and a half, and that hold will be gone."

"Then you must estimate when we can leave and plan accordingly," Scarf said.

"While we work out the logistics, how about we wait back in the tunnel?" I suggested, shivering as a gust of cold breeze blew past me. "At least we can get out of the wind."

"I'd prefer to wait out here," Selene said. "Some of the airflow is coming from the meal area, so I'll know when the cooking fire is out."

"Well, you're not staying out here all alone," I said, throwing some resignation into my voice as I studied her pupils. The campfire smoke wasn't the real reason she wanted to stay, I could see. But whatever was going on, she clearly wanted to talk to me about it in private. "You know what happens when you do that." I gestured to Braun. "You four go get warm. We'll join you in a bit."

"Yeah," Braun said, eyeing me suspiciously. "Because you wouldn't make a break for it and leave us here alone, would you?"

"Where would we go?" I countered, pointing to my left. "That way runs us into Loporri"—I pointed to my right—"that way takes us deeper into the wilderness"—I pointed down—"that way is a sheer drop"—I pointed up—"that way—"

I paused, peering at the scraggly bushes and grasses above the tunnel mouth. Half concealed behind them was an additional, narrower ledge. "Actually, that way might be doable," I said thoughtfully. "At least for a short distance. Though it looks like it peters out just around the bend, and I don't see anything above it that would take us any higher."

"There isn't," Braun said, looking up briefly, and then peering down at the drop-off below us. Probably studying the plants down there and wondering if they would support human weight. "We checked out everything about this place before our first score."

He straightened up and once more gave me a threatening look. "Just remember that Bilswift isn't very big, and vengeance lasts forever."

"I'll add that to my list of aphorisms," I said. "It's just like something my father might have said. If you want to freeze out here, you're welcome to join us. Personally, if I were you I'd be more worried that Scarf and his minions might do something stupid than that Selene and I might make a desperate run for it."

"There's that," he said sourly. "All right, fine. But stay here at the tunnel mouth where I can keep an eye on you."

"Fine." I looked over his shoulder at the Ylps. "Meanwhile, your charges look like they're thinking about doing some exploring."

"Serve 'em right if they get themselves killed," he growled. "Don't wander off."

I waited until he'd joined the Ylps, had a brief and inaudible conversation with them, then headed back farther into the Loporr warren. "Well, here we are," I said as I sat down on the ledge in front of the tunnel. "Shall we talk?"

"Yes," Selene said, sitting gingerly down beside me and pointing off into the distance. "You see that over there? I think it's another footbridge."

I looked in the direction she was pointing. Sure enough, I could make out a short section of footbridge planks through the trees. "Yes, I see it," I confirmed. "Probably one of the others from Seven Strands."

"I agree," Selene said. "But it started me thinking. Darnell Javersin said there used to be a Loporr village around the Strands, didn't he?"

"Yes, I remember."

"But the Loporri live *here,* in this mountain warren," she said. "Why would they also have a village out in the open?"

"The usual reason for setting up that sort of thing is if you want a trading post for dealing with other locals," I said. "But you hardly need a whole village for that. You think the village was someone else's?"

"I do." She turned to me, a quiet dread in her pupils. "Gregory, I think it was owned by the Icari."

I looked across the forest at the footbridge. That suspicion had also been poking at the edges of my mind, but up to now I'd had more immediate things to worry about. But now that Selene had said the magic word... "Okay," I said. "Why?"

Her pupils took on a bit of puzzlement. "What do you mean?"

"I mean why would the Icari come here?" I amplified. "Granted that Alainn might have been more impressive ten thousand years ago before they all disappeared, why would they have come here to the Bilswift forests?"

"Perhaps for the silver-silk."

"Could be," I agreed. "Could very well be, actually. But there are *seven* footbridges radiating from the once-upon-a-time village down there. Why the other six?"

Selene turned back to the distant footbridge. "There must be other things they wanted here," she said slowly. "The one over there—maybe it goes to another Loporr colony. The one that leads southward down into the valley... I don't know. Fruits? Vegetables?"

"Could be crops of some sort, yes," I agreed. "What about the others?"

"The one pointing to the river would be for water," she said, the words starting to flow faster as she got into the rhythm of the logic. "Two other bridges into the mountains for more Loporri or other resources. And then—"

She looked back at me, her pupils startled as she hit the critical point. "One to the *portal*?"

"That's my guess," I said, nodding. "More interesting from our immediate point of view, if it runs high enough above the ground—and if it's still there—it may be our best way to sneak past the Patth fence."

"Yes," she breathed. "Yes." Her eyes went wary. "How long have you known?"

"Not very," I assured her. "Maybe ten or fifteen seconds longer than you. We were mostly working through the logic here together." I nodded in the direction of the Seven Strands. "Except that I don't think it was the Icari themselves who were camped here. I think it more likely it was another of their client species like—" I broke off, suddenly realizing I was charging headlong toward a touchy subject.

Too late. "Like the Kadolians?" Selene asked softly.

I winced. As my father used to say, *Better to keep your mouth* shut and be thought a fool than to say the wrong thing and have someone shut it for you. "Or someone else," I said. "I just don't see the Icari sitting around in a primitive village. And it *was* primitive—we know the kind of ruins a proper Icari community leaves behind. And footbridges to resources and water are the sort of things you'd set up for a more primitive society."

"So the Icari moved in here," Selene said, her pupils going thoughtful as she picked up the logic trail again. "They found the Loporri and silver-silk, set up a client species to harvest it for them, and then . . . what? Just left?"

"Or were destroyed, or whatever the hell happened to all the rest of them," I said. "Their clients here may have held on a little longer, but eventually they must have died off or left, too."

"You two are awfully chatty out here," Braun's voice came from somewhere behind me.

I turned to see him walking toward us along the tunnel. "I thought you were watching Scarf and his buddies," I said.

"I thought *you* were supposed to be sniffing for wood smoke," he countered.

"Smelling is air coming in; talking is air going out," I said. "They're really quite compatible together. Seriously, what did you do with the Ylps?"

"Don't worry, I found a side chamber where the Loporri are storing some of their mushrooms," he said. "They're still nagging me to find some Vrinks for them, so I told them to stay put while I went hunting."

"Sounds dangerous," I warned.

"Not as much as you think," he said. "There should be some adaptation chambers nearby."

"Do you really have a way to prevent kidnapped Vrinks from warning the rest of their people?" Selene asked, her pupils going a little ominous. There were a lot of things in the Spiral she didn't like, and slavery and kidnapping were pretty high on that list.

"Yeah," Braun said. "It's kind of iffy, but yeah. A chemist Lukki knew put together a plant-based spray-on patch we can put on sections of a Vrink's arms and legs. Sort of like a transparent bandage. It gives us spots where we can pick them up or lead them along. Since the stuff registers as if the Vrink bumped into some plants, it doesn't trigger any of the warning scents."

"I hear an *unless* in there," I said.

He scowled. "Unless we try to leave the stuff on too long and it rubs off, or if it gets rained on, or if we miss the patch and grab some section that isn't covered up, or if the Vrink squirms and we drop him."

"I'm guessing hitting the ground sends out a call for the medics?" I suggested.

"Something like that," he said. "And like I said, if *you* bump them, it brings the boys with the crossbows. Neither of those has happened yet, but it only takes once."

"Let's try not to make today that once," I said. "Assuming you still want to go through with it."

"You want to get shot by the Ylps?" Braun asked bluntly. "*I* don't. Our buddy Scarf came all the way across the Spiral to get some Vrinks, and I don't think he's ready to call it quits and go home. Even if he was, I doubt his boss would be."

"His boss? Oh, right," I said as a memory clicked. "The Ylpea ship Perrifil said was on its way. I was wondering what was going on there. So Scarf came here to pick up the package, and the incoming ship has some major honcho aboard who's supposed to take delivery?"

"Yeah, and he's either high up in the Ylpea government or in their industrial network," Braun said. "Either way, not someone you want to mess with."

I grimaced. "I seem to run into a lot of people like that."

"I don't doubt it." Braun raised his eyebrows a little. "Don't forget that I'm one of them."

"Not likely to do so," I assured him. "So how many Vrinks have you and Lukki kidnapped?"

"What, you writing a book?" he demanded. "Or just trying to figure out what kind of bounty to ask on me?"

"I'm retired from hunting," I reminded him. "Besides, you already said we were up for aiding and abetting. What's a little kidnapping history between fellow conspirators?"

"They're *thefts*, not kidnappings," he corrected stiffly. "Kidnappings are for sapients. Vrinks aren't sapients."

"Even better," I said. "Especially since no one actually owns them. Almost impossible to prosecute someone when there's no one around to claim loss."

"You sound like Lukki," he growled. "She was always spouting legal jarg like that."

"A good entrepreneur knows all the ins and outs of the business," I said, nodding. "So how many thefts did you and Lukki do?"

"Why do you care?"

"Because we're interested in getting Tirano out of the indenture you and the Javersin brothers had him in," I said. "It would help if we knew how deep he was into your operation."

For a couple of seconds Braun just looked at me, maybe working through his responses and the associated consequences, maybe wondering if he could get away with dropping us both off the ledge. "This last one, the one with the missing package, was our sixth with him," he said. "Don't know if you want to count today as his seventh or not. And after pulling this crud, he's not going to get an eighth. Not with us or whoever he's working for now."

"What makes you think he's working for anyone?" Selene asked, an edge to her pupils. "Maybe this *crud,* as you call it, is him bringing you and the Ylps here so the Loporri can exact justice."

"Maybe you've got a big mouth," Braun warned. "Maybe we really don't need you." His eyes shifted to me. "Either of you," he added. "It's a long way down, and there's nothing at the bottom except predators and scavengers."

"Lucky for us, you *do* still need us," I told him, watching his gun hand out of the corner of my eye. So far he wasn't making a move toward the weapon, but if I waited until he did he'd definitely get there before I could stop him. Under some circumstances, my best move would be to preemptively go for my own plasmic and hope I won the race.

Deliberately, I raised my right hand and scratched idly at my cheek. Braun didn't strike me as the type who would kill two people in cold blood, not even to cover his tracks. But he *did* strike me as someone with a very healthy survival instinct, and if he thought I was going to try to beat him to the punch he might well overreact. Best I not do anything to encourage such thoughts. "So tell me how it used to work," I continued. "How did you get the Vrinks to market? So to speak."

Again, Braun seemed to turn the question over in his mind. "By boat," he said. "Lukki has a boat she would take up the river to an old dock no one uses anymore."

I nodded. "I think we may have seen it."

"Yeah? Anyway, Willie, Tirano, and I would come in here and

find a couple of Vrinks, walk 'em out and back to the Strands, shove 'em in the van, and drive 'em down to the boat."

"Why didn't you use the footbridges the whole way?" I asked. "It looks like there's one that goes straight to the river."

"Yeah, *you* try to get a Vrink to move along a footbridge when he doesn't want to," Braun said sourly. "Wasn't worth the effort, and the van was faster. We usually timed it so that it would be dark by then, and we'd just float 'em back to Bilswift."

"Where you put them aboard the buyer's ship?"

"If the ship was already there, yeah," he said. "Usually there was enough slosh in the timing that we had a day or two to wait. In that case, we locked them up near the river, either in Tirano's place or another house Lukki owns farther upstream. When the buyer's ship got in, we'd put the package back on the boat, run them over to the spaceport, and put it aboard."

"And collect your money."

"The back half, yes," Braun said. "Lukki already had the front half."

"Nice and efficient," I complimented him. "I assume you've already checked Lukki's other place to make sure the original package isn't there?"

"'Course we did," Braun growled. "Also looked at Tirano's. The package wasn't either place."

"So let's assume this is just another score," I said. "You seem sure that Tirano isn't working alone, but from your description it sounds like he could bring a Vrink or maybe even two out by himself, without any help from anyone."

"He couldn't have any help," Selene said before Braun could answer. "I told you he came in here with me, and we came alone."

"Who says he didn't send someone in ahead of him?" Braun countered. "You saw that anthill—lots of places someone could wait in there for him to show up. The only thing anyone needs him for is to find the Vrinks."

"And how would they get the Vrinks out through the crowd?" Selene shot back. "If we're stuck here, they should be, too."

"They could have gone back into hiding."

"Tirano can't hide from *me*."

"Then he got out before the hunters came back."

"Then how did he hit the Vrink that started everyone running toward us?"

"Let's all calm down a little, shall we?" I put in quickly. This whole conversation was still mostly speculation, and as my father used to say, *If you're going to speculate out loud, speculate in the direction that gets you into the least trouble.* "Selene's right, Braun. If Tirano was still in here she'd be able to smell him. She's also right that someone had to hit the Vrink to pin us down until the party out there got into full swing."

I raised a finger for emphasis. "Which means *you're* right about him having an accomplice in this operation. Any idea who it might be?"

"Not a clue," Braun said, glaring at Selene. "We don't have any competitors. No one else knows about the Vrinks and silver-silk."

"No one that you know of," I pointed out. "In that case, maybe another buyer—"

I broke off as the pieces suddenly fell into place. Tirano—Galfvi—Lukki's murder—

"What is it?" Selene asked, her pupils gone uneasy. She'd picked up my sudden change in scent, and knew what it meant. "You have something?"

"I have everything," I ground out. "*Damn* it. We've got the whole thing backward, Braun. Tirano's got allies, all right, but he didn't bring any of them in here. He didn't need to. All he needed was to get us trapped for a few hours, and all he needed to accomplish that was to whap a Vrink on the arm and then nip out along the ledge before the lunchroom back there got too full of Loporri for him to get out."

"What does he need us trapped for?" Braun asked, puzzlement and anger vying for top spot in his voice.

"Because he's working with Galfvi," I said. "And Galfvi knows where Lukki stashed your original set of Vrinks."

"The missing paper from Lukki's apartment," Selene said suddenly. "The other property she owns."

"So what's he going to do with them?" Braun asked, still clearly trying to keep up.

"You already pointed to the answer," I said. "You said Scarf is the Ylpea advance team, with the pickup ship coming in after the Vrinks are secured. Only there's another ship about due to land at Bilswift."

"The *Patth*?" Selene asked, her pupils looking suddenly stricken.

"The Patth," I confirmed. "With Galfvi as their inside man, and Kiolven and Venikel as their advance team."

"What the *hell*?" Braun snarled. "You saying those Patth are the ones who killed Lukki and Willie?"

"I don't know," I said. "But you said Willie's killer was wearing a Patth robe. Those two and Galfvi are the only Patth I'm aware of in Bilswift."

Selene's pupils went suddenly grim. Maybe those three were the only Patth in the city proper, but we knew there was another group of them beating the bushes out in the forest east of town.

More significantly, at least to Selene and me, there was one non-Patth in town who also had a Patth robe available to him.

Once again, a speculative road had led us straight to Tirano.

"Son of a—" Braun clamped his mouth shut. "Let me see if I've got this straight. Tirano gets in here, waits until we're too deep to get out, hits a Vrink and gets us trapped." He threw a black look at Selene. "*Or* he gets us killed. He slips out before he gets stuck in here with us, hightails it back to Bilswift...maybe steals your car—"

"I still have the keys," Selene said, tapping one of her inside pockets as she pulled out her info pad.

Braun grunted. "So Galfvi followed us in another car and waited for him at Seven Strands. Or maybe he brought Lukki's boat up the river and Tirano was supposed to meet him there. Either way, they get back to town, collect the package, and take it to the spaceport."

"And do they then load the Vrinks aboard the Patth ship?" I asked Selene.

"Not yet they don't." Her pupils winced as she peered at the info pad display. "But soon. Perrifil was apparently able to get two of the other parked ships to leave. The Ylpea ship is already on the ground, and the Patth is scheduled to land in three hours."

Braun breathed a curse. "We have to get out of here," he said. "We have to get back and stop them."

"The Loporri are still out there," Selene warned.

"We have to risk it," Braun said. "If the Ylps lose their package they'll have our skins on a drying rack."

I felt my stomach tighten. Maybe that Narchner song wasn't as out-of-date as we'd all hoped. "I thought you said we could just grab more for them."

"You don't think the Ylps at the spaceport won't see the package—a package whose characteristics they were *very* specific about—being trotted over to another ship?" Braun snarled. "You don't think they'll see that and figure we're pulling a fast one on them?"

"Can't we have Scarf call and tell them the new plan?" I asked.

"Quote: *Three Vrinks, no older than two years, no fewer than fifteen implanted silk beetles each,*" Braun said. "Like I said, *very* specific. Most Vrinks have between eight and twelve beetles—it took us four hours of searching before we found three with fifteen, and then it was a nightmare pulling them from their different adaptation chambers and getting them out of here. Like I said, the Ylps on that ship will think we took a better offer for their merchandise, and there's nothing anyone can say that'll convince them otherwise."

"I guess we'll just have to stop the Patth, then," I said. "Okay. Bring the Ylps back here and all of you get on that ledge above the tunnel mouth. Selene and I will join you in a few minutes. Got it?"

"Yeah," Braun said, his voice heavy with suspicion. "What are you going to do?"

"See if I can clear out the lunchroom," I said, starting back down the tunnel. "Come on, come on—time's wasting."

"What if Scarf doesn't want to cooperate?" Braun asked as he and Selene caught up with me.

"Then he gets left behind," I said. "I don't much care either way. Selene, you're with me."

We reached the main tunnel and Braun turned off toward wherever he'd stashed the Ylps. "Where are we going?" Selene asked.

"To find the nearest Vrink," I said. "Keep your fingers crossed that this works."

"So this is one of *those* plans?"

I grimaced. As my father used to say, *A clever operator always has a Plan A, B, and C. A wise operator knows he'll probably end up needing a Plan D.* "Yes," I conceded. "It's one of those."

CHAPTER FOURTEEN

The nearest Vrinks, fortunately, were only a couple of minutes' walk away. They were nestled together in a clump of seven, apparently still undergoing the spin-beetle implantation process. All seven had some lumps under their skin, but unlike the Vrinks we'd already seen some of the bulges were the same gray-white as their skin, others an angry red, while still others ran a range of coloration between those two extremes. The Vrinks themselves were also wider and heavier than the more mature ones, a couple of them approaching the rotundity of the regular Loporri. Apparently, inviting that many beetles aboard caused a serious drain on the host's metabolism and physiology.

"It's horrible," Selene murmured as we eased gingerly into the chamber.

"No argument here," I said, studying the Vrinks as they lounged around, oblivious to our presence, busy getting eaten alive from the inside. *That one,* I decided, zeroing in on one of the larger and therefore probably newer models. "Or else the Vrinks like it for some reason. There are certainly humans and aliens crazier than this."

"I suppose," Selene said. "It's still horrible."

"I agree," I said. "Ready to run?"

She nodded. "Please don't hurt them."

Any more than they already are? "I won't," I promised, drawing my plasmic.

It was a gamble, I knew. Braun had said that contact with non-Loporr animals triggered the danger reaction that brought the hunters running, and I had no idea just how sensitive Vrink skin was. If a few molecules was enough, this plan could go sideways very quickly.

But we had no choice but to risk it. If Tirano and Galfvi got to the spaceport with Lukki's last group of Vrinks, a semi-oblivious Loporr attack would be the least of our problems. *Out-humaning humans;* and humans as a species were very bad at tolerating bald-faced theft of our stuff.

Bracing myself, I stepped over to my chosen target and tapped the plasmic's muzzle gently against his shoulder. "Selene?" I prompted.

Selene fluttered her eyelashes a moment, then nodded. "His scent has changed," she confirmed. "And it's not the same one I smelled before."

"Good, I said, backing away from the target. A nonanimal, non-vegetable, non-Loporr contact. Hopefully, that would be interpreted as one of their proto-Vrinks having fallen or otherwise gotten a boo-boo. "Fingers crossed that it's the one that brings the medics and other concerned citizens and not the hunters. Let's go."

I could hear the rustling of Loporri movement in the distance as we got to the side tunnel where we'd sent Braun and the Ylps. I didn't know if the approaching crowd would stick to the tunnels or also utilize the ledge outside as they hurried to the supposedly stricken Vrink's aid, but my guess was they'd use every route available to them. If Braun hadn't persuaded Scarf to my plan, it was going to get ugly out there. Selene and I reached the tunnel mouth and stepped out onto the ledge.

To see a solid mass of Loporri waddling along the ledge, barely thirty meters away and coming straight toward us. I grabbed for my plasmic—

"Here!"

I looked up. The rest of our group were there, spread out along the short overhead ledge where I'd told them to be. Braun was standing beside two of the Ylp bodyguards, all three of them crouching down and extending their hands urgently toward us. "Hurry!" Braun snapped.

"Take her!" I snapped back, pushing Selene underneath Braun as I stepped into position beneath the Ylps. Selene was lighter than I was, easier for a single person to lift. More importantly, if Scarf had decided to get a head start on some vengeance, better if Selene was in the hands of a human I still trusted not to kill in cold blood.

Fortunately, no one was interested in dealing out death, at least not here and now. Five seconds later Selene and I were standing with the others, all of us holding as still as we could while the Loporri filed by beneath us.

Braun had drawn his Blackman 4mm as soon as he'd gotten Selene steadied beside him and was pointing it warily down at the parade. But again, none of the aliens seemed to even notice us, let alone attach any suspicion to our presence. I guessed that Loporr hunters alerted to an imminent threat would have more global awareness, but my carefully designed attack had given them no reason to suspect danger.

And so they passed us by, disappearing into the tunnel. As my father used to say, *Every person and species has blind spots filled with hidden dangers and missed opportunities ripe for exploitation. Figure out theirs; don't let them figure out yours.*

"Now we go?" Braun asked as the last of the Loporri disappeared into the tunnel.

"Now we go," I confirmed. "I doubt everyone has left the lunchroom, but it should be clear enough for us to get through without bumping anyone."

"I hope you're right." Carefully, Braun dropped onto the lower ledge, holstered his Blackman, and offered his hand to Selene. With only a slight hesitation she took it and let him help her down.

The Ylps didn't offer me any such assistance, and I didn't ask.

Three minutes later, we reached the lunch area. The cooks were still at their jobs, and there were still a fair number of Loporri and Vrinks standing or sitting around watching them. But as I'd hoped, there was plenty of room for us to weave our way safely through them.

And now that I knew to look for it, I spotted the glint of silver-silk threads wrapped around the hunters' wrists and crossbows.

The terminally fashion-conscious of the Spiral probably considered silver-silk to be a vital part of their lives. They didn't have a clue as to how vital it could genuinely be.

"You know the way better than I do," Selene said to Braun as we headed along the ledge section on the lunchroom's far side. "You should probably take point."

"Good idea," he said, though I suspected his agreement was less a matter of him being a better trail guide and more a matter of him hoping there was still a chance of catching up with Tirano and Galfvi. He slipped past her, drawing his Blackman as he did so. Scarf was right behind him, clearly not interested in letting someone who might be a thief and traitor get too far ahead. His three minions were likewise not going to let their boss get too far out of *their* reach. Thirty seconds and a lot of line-shuffling later, Selene and I found ourselves at the back of the row.

Which I was pretty sure was the formation Selene had been trying for in the first place.

"Well?" I asked quietly as we followed the others.

"The scent I noticed when we first left the *Ruth*," she murmured back. "Remember? I thought it was some kind of cooking, but I didn't recognize it."

"I remember," I said. "So: Loporr cuisine?"

"I think so," she said. "The spice and fungi mixture they're using back there is a little different from what I smelled, as if some ingredient was missing from the Bilswift version. But the spices that both scents have in common are in the same proportions."

"And proportion, as every great chef knows, is the key to true professionalism," I said with grim satisfaction. "You think you can track down this scent?"

"Yes," Selene said. "If they start cooking again, I can find them."

"Great." The hunt and subsequent mass gathering that had blocked our way out of the Loporr colony had nearly torpedoed the whole day. But as my father used to say, *Every defeat has the germ of a different victory buried inside it. Just make sure you get to that victory before the other guy does.* "Let's keep this little tidbit to ourselves until we find an opportune moment to trot it out."

"Understood." Selene hesitated. "Gregory...you don't really think Tirano is working with Galfvi to give the Vrinks to the Patth, do you? That was just to keep Braun and Scarf from blaming us, right?"

I sighed to myself. As my father used to say, *Seeing is believing, unless the other guy doesn't* want *to believe.* "I don't see how it works any other way," I said. "Tirano clearly is connected with someone here, and Galfvi's the only one I can fit into that role."

"You don't believe Tirano could have been trying to deliver justice?"

"Do you and I deserve any of that justice?" I countered. "Because he knew full well we were going to be in there, too."

She looked away, but not before I saw the reluctant agreement in her pupils. "No, you're right," she said quietly. "You're right."

"Besides, Lukki and Willie were shot with plasmics," I reminded her. "If Tirano has access to one, and if he was out for justice, he could have shot Braun and the Ylps anywhere along the way. There were at least a dozen places where the footbridge was wide open to ambush. Did Tirano bring Galfvi's robe to Lukki's, by the way? I never got around to searching the whole apartment, and I forgot to ask you about it."

"Yes," she said, almost too softly for me to hear. "He'd hung it up in the shower to dry." She shook her head. "I'm sorry, Gregory. I...I'm supposed to be better at reading people. Especially other Kadolians. But I can't get a feel for Tirano at all."

I shrugged uncomfortably. "Changeling."

The last time I'd attached that name to Tirano out loud, Selene had gone out of her way to remind me that that question was still up for debate. This time, she remained silent. "But that doesn't mean all is lost," I went on. "If he was coerced into working for Galfvi and the others, that could be a mitigating factor. If he was threatened or blackmailed into it, even better. If he's willing to testify, we've got ourselves a hat trick."

"But only if there's someone here he can testify against," she said. "If they all get on that ship..." She took a shuddering breath. "I don't know, Gregory. Between the walk back to Seven Strands and then the drive to the spaceport, we don't have much of a buffer. Maybe no buffer at all. If that Patth ship is truly here for the Vrinks, and if Galfvi is ready to deliver them, we may not be able to get there in time to stop them."

"And you think Galfvi and the others will walk aboard behind them?"

"*I* would," Selene said. "Kadolian changelings are damaged and broken, Gregory, but that doesn't mean they're stupid."

"I never said they were," I soothed. "And you're right, we

might not be able to beat them to the spaceport. But you know what?" I smiled tightly. "For once, I don't think we need to."

Braun didn't want Selene and me driving off on our own. I was equally adamant that Selene wasn't going to drive our rental alone, not with Tirano and three armed and possibly murderous Patth on the loose. We compromised by letting Selene and me drive the rental, with one of the Ylpea bodyguards taking the seat behind us. A Ylp, Scarf took great pains to point out, who would have his Kreznir 2mm close at hand.

Braun also took our phones, lest we secretly call Detective-Sergeant Kreega along the way and bring the wrath of her badge-men down on all of us.

And then, argument over and logistics sorted out, Braun and Selene took control of their respective vehicles and drove like maniacs down the twisty mountain road, toying with an even more certain death than any Ylp could ever threaten us with.

It was going to be close, I knew. If Selene's numbers earlier were right, and if all the numbers worked in Galfvi's favor and against ours, we would miss the Patth liftoff by a good twenty minutes, and its slice into hyperspace by at least two. A call to the badgemen might buy us some time, but even Patth civilians carried a lot of political clout, and without any evidence to back up our charges Kreega might not have any choice but to let them go.

And even if we found the ship still on the ground, if the Vrinks were already aboard and out of sight we would still have lost. Kreega almost certainly wouldn't be able to get a search warrant for their ship, certainly not on our unsubstantiated word.

I sympathized with Selene's anxiety, and was justifiably wary of our resident Ylp's impotent fuming. But my hope was just that, a hope, and I didn't want to raise any expectations that might end up having that much farther to fall if and when they were dashed.

Finally, with everyone's nerves no doubt cranked to full breaking point, we skidded to a halt at the spaceport entrance. I opened my door and was climbing out of the car when Braun, sprinting up from the van now parked behind us, grabbed my arm. "Come on—snap it up!" he barked. "They could take off any second."

"How are you going to get aboard?" I asked, fighting to keep my balance as he all but hauled me bodily out onto the pavement. "We don't have a warrant."

"Don't talk stupid," he snarled. "If the package is aboard—"

"Relax," I interrupted. "It isn't."

"How the hell do *you* know?"

"Because of him." I pointed at the dark blue ground car parked twenty meters from the *Ruth*'s zigzag ramp. "The gentleman in that vehicle is Badgeman Zilor, mandated by Detective-Sergeant Kreega herself to watch our ship and report on all comings and goings and anything suspicious he might happen to see."

I watched as understanding and a degree of cautious hope filtered through the anger and apprehension in Braun's face. "But he's watching *your* ship, not the Patth."

"I get the impression that Badgeman Zilor is very good at his job," I said. "And with four murders in town in the space of a week, I'm guessing Kreega made it clear that her badgemen are to watch everything." I shrugged. "And seriously, now—even if he was half asleep, I doubt you could march three Vrinks past him without him noticing."

"So the package *isn't* aboard?"

"Not unless Galfvi's a magician," I said. "Unless he and his accomplices are complete idiots they'll have checked out the area before moving the package, spotted Zilor, and called a quick abort. They're all probably sitting around somewhere right now trying to figure out a Plan B."

"Yeah." Braun's eyes flicked to Selene as she got out of the car. "And she can find them?"

"In theory, yes," I said. "As a practical matter, she'll probably need to go door to door until she finds the right scent."

"So we start her at the most likely doors," Braun said. "And we need to get moving on this before the evening rain gets here."

I looked to the west. Sure enough, there were already dark clouds forming on the horizon. "We won't have time to get very far," I warned. "But we can at least make a start. Let us park the car and get a couple of things from the ship, and we'll be right with you."

"Fine," Braun said, his voice going a little darker. "Just remember there's one fast and sure way of getting that badgeman away from your ship."

I felt a knot form in my stomach. "Killing him?"

Braun snorted. "Don't be stupid," he said. "Badgemen are like killer ants. Stomp on one and you have the whole hill climbing up your legs. I was talking about someone killing *you*."

"I was afraid that was where you were going with this," I said heavily. "We'll just have to hope that they don't want to risk spreading any more carnage than they already have."

"I wouldn't count on that."

"Yeah. Neither would I."

We parked our rental in its usual spot by the runaround stand, sent Zilor a cheery wave as we passed him—getting a neutral stare in return—and climbed the zigzag to the ship.

"What's the plan?" Selene asked when the entryway was closed and deadbolted behind us.

"For now, we go along with Braun's walking tour of greater Bilswift," I said. "A waste of time, but it could be instructive to see which places he thinks are worth checking out."

"Plus there's safety in numbers?"

I winced. I'd hoped she hadn't heard that last exchange between Braun and me. "It can't hurt," I said. "Lukki and Willie were alone when they were killed, and the Javersin brothers were out of public view in a closed shop when they were taken down. That tells me the killer is at least not reckless, maybe even edging over toward cautious. Even with stacks of commarks doing their best Lorelei impression, I'm guessing he'll think twice before taking on a group that includes six armed people."

"So he'll wait for you and me to be alone?"

"If he's smart," I said, frowning across the dayroom. Something had been nagging at the back of my mind all day, and all this talk about murder had roiled it up to the surface. "Selene, help me run through this, will you? Start with the assumption that someone wants Lukki out of the Vrink and silver-silk business, either because they hate slavery or because they want to move in on her operation."

There'd been a flicker of something across her pupils when I mentioned slavery, but she merely nodded. "All right," she said.

"So the people in the way are Lukki, Willie, Braun, and maybe Tirano," I said. "Those are the ones who need to be eliminated. Right?"

"Right."

"So why kill the Javersin brothers?"

I watched as thoughtful puzzlement come into her pupils. "Maybe they were involved with Lukki and the others?" she suggested doubtfully.

"Maybe," I said. "But I'm having a hard time seeing how. Lukki didn't need them for tracking, transport, or muscle. What else is there?"

"Cover for Tirano?" she suggested. "A proper job for him so no one would be suspicious?"

"Okay, but Lukki could give him that cover without having to let the Javersins in on the gag."

Selene shook her head. "I don't know. But you're right, it doesn't make sense."

"Yeah," I said. If my bounty hunter instincts were fading, at least Selene's were fading, too. "Scenario two: Kiolven and Venikel aren't here to find Galfvi's alleged killer, but to find Galfvi and bring him back to his family, like in the Narchner song Zilor mentioned. In that case, they might have gone to the Javersins to interrogate them, decided for whatever reason they couldn't let anyone know they'd been asking questions, and ended up killing them."

A shiver of revulsion ran through Selene's pupils. "What could they possibly have been asking that they thought required murder?"

"Some leading question, maybe," I said. "Or maybe they didn't want Galfvi hearing about the conversation and didn't have enough imagination to come up with a better plan."

"It's horrible," Selene said, her pupils again going thoughtful. "But if they're looking for Galfvi, why kill Lukki and Willie?"

"Exactly," I said. "We've got four solid murders—five if Galfvi is actually dead—and I can't come up with a theory that fits them all together."

"Could there be two different killers, then?" Selene suggested. "The Javersins killed by one and Lukki and Willie by the other?"

"And both killers decided to surface in Bilswift during the same week?"

"That *does* seem unlikely," she agreed. "We must be missing something."

"I have the feeling there are a lot of somethings we're missing,"

I said sourly. "But right now, Braun and the Ylps are probably missing *us*, and we don't want them to get nervous. Grab some spare meal bars—we told Braun we were picking up a few things, and we need something to show him."

"Yes," Selene said, heading toward the dayroom. "What about you?"

"I'll be exercising my fingers," I said, heading the other way to the *Ruth*'s engine room.

After way too many run-ins with people who insisted on taking our weapons and phones, I'd started stashing spares of both items around the ship. The engine room, specifically, was home to a four-shot DubTrub 2mm derringer and two phones. I grabbed one of the latter and started punching in numbers.

When Admiral Graym-Barker first sent us here he'd assured us he was also sending backup, which would be accessible by phone as soon as they were in Alainn's communications system.

Time to see what that backup consisted of.

Graym-Barker had given us six emergency phone numbers. Connecting with any of them required the receiver to be on the same planet with us, of course, as a StarrComm connection was needed for any interstellar communication. I punched in the numbers for Jordan McKell, his partner Ixil, and the four general alert numbers that would theoretically connect to any of the Icarus Group's limited collection of operatives who happened to be nearby. I even punched in Tera C's number, which I wasn't supposed to have but did anyway.

None of them connected. None of them prompted me to authorize a relay to an orbiting station or incoming ship. Wherever the admiral's backup was, it hadn't yet reached Alainn.

Selene was waiting at the entryway when returned. "Did you get through to them?"

"No," I said, trying to filter out my uneasiness. Graym-Barker could be a pain in the neck, and there was a lot about my methods he loudly disapproved of. But when he said he was going to do something, he always followed through.

"Yes," Selene murmured, her nose picking up the changes in my scent, her own pupils responding with an echo of my own uneasiness. "Hopefully, they're just late."

"Hopefully." Bracing myself, I hit the entryway release. "Okay. Time to take the Braun and Ylp show on the road."

CHAPTER FIFTEEN

◆◆◆

We piled back into the two vehicles, the Ylp I'd heard Scarf call Guard Three again riding backstop behind us, and headed out.

As I'd anticipated, Braun's tour of Bilswift's hotspots came up dry.

The same couldn't be said about the weather. The wind seemed a little gustier tonight than it had been during previous evening rains, and even with the protection of raincoats and hats enough water got blown sideways to thoroughly soak everything from midshin on down. We put up with it for nearly two hours, until the rain was starting to subside, when Selene finally called it quits.

"There's nothing here," she told Braun. "All the scents have faded."

"I don't believe you," Braun said flatly. "Tirano said he could pick up scents even a week later."

"He was talking about inside scents or those on protected surfaces," I told him. "Out here, with rain gushing down on everything, trace molecules get washed away pretty fast."

"What then is your next plan?" Scarf demanded.

"Well, as long as Badgeman Zilor is blocking access to the spaceport, Tirano and Galfvi are effectively stalemated," I said. I paused, pretending a new thought had suddenly occurred to me. "Unless...Braun, you said Lukki had a boat. Would Tirano or Galfvi have access to it?"

"They're not supposed to," Braun said, his voice deepening as he saw where I was headed with this. "But with those two, who knows? You thinking they might bypass Zilor and bring the package in from the river or ocean sides of the spaceport?"

"Theoretically, they still need to come out in the open to get to the Patth ship," I said. "But if it has a back door that's out of Zilor's sight they might be able to pull it off."

"Or they merely kill the badgeman and are done with it," Scarf said impatiently. "That is the simplest solution to their problem. They have already killed Lukki and her servant. What prevents them from killing again?"

"The fact that they're not stupid," Braun said grimly. "Killing a badgeman is the one thing guaranteed to bring the whole Alainn legal system down on top of you."

"It's actually worse than that," I said. "Right now, Zilor's sitting at the edge of a spaceport, which puts it within Commonwealth jurisdiction. Among other things, that means expedited search warrants for everything in the immediate vicinity. I don't know off the top of my head what the legal radius is, but it might include all or part of the Patth ship."

"Your people could then search it without a warrant?" Scarf asked.

"No, they'd still need a warrant," I told him. "But they could get it pretty much automatically and in a matter of minutes."

Scarf made a sort of grinding sound. "They are Patth. They would merely appeal to their embassy, and the badgemen would be ordered away."

"They could try," I said. "But I doubt they'd get anywhere. Economic clout or no economic clout, Braun's right. *No* one likes a badgeman killer. And I'm guessing that also includes the Patth."

"So what's the plan?" Braun asked.

"You scoot over to wherever Lukki's boat is berthed and see if it's still there," I said. "If it is, great. Though even if it is I suppose they could grab someone else's boat," I added in a more subdued tone as if that, too, had just occurred to me. "Okay...let me think."

"We waste time," Scarf said impatiently.

"Thinking is never a waste of time," I told him. "As my father used to say, *Never deliberately play around with a blind alley unless there's a nice café at the end of it.* Braun, are the nighttime fishers already out to sea?"

"They should be, yeah."

"So Galfvi probably wouldn't want to draw attention to himself by heading down the river now. When do the morning fishers head out?"

"How should I know?" Braun said irritably. "Five, six in the morning, probably."

"Good," I said. "Then you and one of the Ylps need to be out on the river by then, watching the traffic and seeing if you can spot our wayward youths. While you do that, the other Ylps need to be in position to watch the spaceport in general and Badgeman Zilor in particular." I made a face. "Just in case Tirano and Galfvi *are* stupid enough to take him out."

"What about you?" Scarf asked suspiciously. "Do you mean to search the city without an escort?"

"No, we'll save that search for evening," I said. "And don't worry, I wouldn't dream of doing it without you. No, Selene and I are going to head back to the Loporr colony and search—"

"To the *colony*?" Scarf interrupted.

"Yes, to look for a substitute package in case Galfvi and Tirano manage to sneak the original past you," I said. "We'll stay in touch so that if you intercept the original one, you can let us know and we can come back."

"You think us fools?" Scarf demanded. "You think we will simply allow you to leave our sight?"

"Don't worry, they'll still be staying with us tonight," Braun said. "Tomorrow... well, we'll see about this field trip of theirs."

I cleared my throat. "About that," I said. "The staying with you tonight part. If Selene and I continue to stay away from the *Ruth*, eventually Kreega's going to pull Zilor off stakeout duty and assign him elsewhere. Until you can set up to block the spaceport yourselves, I'm pretty sure we don't want Zilor to leave."

"What do you say?" Scarf asked.

"He says he wants to go back to his ship instead of your suite," Braun said, his eyes boring into me.

"No," Scarf said flatly.

"You're not thinking this through," I said. "Or else you're forgetting our track record of being helpful and not running off. Remember that Selene and I got you into the Loporr colony, we got you *out* of the Loporr colony, and we went into the *Ruth* and came back out without calling the badgemen down on you."

"Perhaps even now they watch at wait," Scarf said.

"Or maybe we're actually on your side," I countered. "Willingly or otherwise. Aiding and abetting, remember?"

"We don't want to see the Vrinks taken aboard the Patth ship," Selene added quietly. Quietly, and very sincerely.

Of course, she was just as sincere about not wanting to see the Vrinks taken aboard a Ylpea ship, either. But I doubted Scarf would think that direction.

"Should you not instead concentrate your efforts on finding the package here in Bilswift?" Scarf asked.

"The scent is gone, remember?" I said. "At this point your best bet is to catch Galfvi trying to move it and take it away from him. If he instead decides to sit on it, or if you miss him, you'll need the backup package we're heading to the colony to get for you."

"Very well," Scarf said. "But you, Braun, will stand for their behavior. If there is betrayal, you will be first to die."

"Yeah, yeah," Braun said. Apparently, he was getting as sick of Scarf's high-handedness as I was. "Don't worry, I want you and your package off the planet as much as you do."

"And Guard Three will accompany you," Scarf said.

"Not a good idea," I said, thinking fast. The plan—the *real* plan—was for Selene and me to get clear of Braun and the Ylps long enough to see if that other footbridge would lead us to the hidden portal. Having one of them tagging along would give us exactly zero chance of doing that. "There's nothing you can do to help our search, and the more people we have up there the higher the chance someone will bump into one of the Loporri and end the day right then and there."

"Nevertheless, he will accompany you," Scarf said firmly. "Braun and Guard Two can watch the river alone."

"Ah," I said. "Actually, now that I think about it, that makes sense. The more people you've got loitering on watch, the more likely they'll be spotted. In fact, Braun should probably watch the river alone. In fact, he'd probably prefer it."

"What do you say?"

"I'm not saying anything," I protested, looking sideways at Braun in a significant way that I hoped Scarf was smart enough to pick up on. "I'm just pointing out that we humans sometimes like to do stakeouts alone."

For a moment Scarf looked silently back and forth between Braun and me. I held my breath, hoping he'd do the math that I'd tried to present to him: that Braun plus one Ylp could quickly become Braun plus no Ylp. If Galfvi and the Vrinks came into Braun's possession, and with an alternate buyer already in town...

Scarf turned away to face the other Ylps, and once again started blasting away with the ultrasonics. My teeth were beginning to hurt by the time the conversation ended. "You speak correctly," Scarf said, turning back to me. "Guard Three will be better positioned to assist at the river. You and the Kadolian may go to the Loporr colony alone." He pointed at me in a very human gesture. "But you will continue to leave your phones with us."

"All right," I said reluctantly, as if I wasn't the one who'd maneuvered him into that decision in the first place. *Out-humaning humans*... and suspicion and paranoia were two of our most durable attributes. "I'll just point out that if we don't have phones we won't be able to keep in touch with you. But if that's what you want, it's fine with us."

"It is."

"Okay," I said. "One last point and warning. In the past I've found Patth to be very bad losers. If it comes down to you getting the package or neither of you getting it, they may well go with the latter option."

"You speak of them destroying the package?" Scarf asked in clear disbelief. "That is barbaric."

"Barbaric, selfish, and completely wasteful," I agreed. "But that's Patth for you. And when you say *destroying the package* you're being more literal than you realize. One of their client species has a very nasty corona weapon they like to use on everything in sight. A couple of shots with one of those, and even a Vrink's remains will be hard to identify. If they take the time to collect and bag the bones and ashes and toss them into the river, even Zilor's enthusiasm might be hard-pressed to get enough evidence for a conviction."

"A conviction would not be needed," Scarf said coldly. "They would all die in agony for their destruction of our property."

"Just as long as they don't die in agony or anywhere else until we have a replacement package ready," I warned. "Our best bet right now is to draw them out into the open. As my father used to say, *Matching the bait to the fish takes thought and effort, but it saves you a lot of wasted time sitting in the boat.* I'm thinking that in this case, the proper bait for Galfvi is a whole new set of Vrinks."

"Which you are preparing to obtain for us," Scarf said.

"Exactly," I said, nodding. "As you see, we've got several options to play with. But they all start with Selene and me going up to the colony tomorrow."

"Fine," Braun growled. "You've sold us, all right? Get some sleep, then get us some Vrinks."

"That's the plan," I said, taking Selene's arm and heading us back toward our rental. "Good night, all. And trust me, this is going to work."

We were a block away before Selene spoke. "You really think this plan is going to work?"

"Well, not the plan I spun for them," I admitted. "The real plan is for us to try the skyway from Seven Strands leading toward the portal. If the bridge is still functional, it ought to get us over the Patth fence without getting caught."

"Yes." She was silent a moment. "What about the Vrinks?"

"First priority is to find the portal," I said. "No arguments allowed. But after that, yes, next priority is to find a way to sink this triple-cursed slave trade."

"*Slave* trade?" she repeated, all but pouncing on the word. "You believe the Loporri are sapients?"

"Oh, they're sapients, all right," I said grimly. "You didn't see the drawing of the bird in the bird-trap chamber. Luckily for the Loporri, I did."

"There was a drawing of a *bird*?"

"Yep," I said. "Same colors as the one that took a turn around the room, too. On top of that, on our final sneak through the lunchroom I saw one of the hunters busy slicing up one of the carcass's legs, and it sure looked like he was trying to get a long tendon out in one piece. I'm guessing it was for a replacement crossbow string."

"But that's not how non-sapient hives work," Selene said. "Each member has a rigid and well-defined job."

"Hunters hunt, cooks carve up the kill, artisans turn the scraps and other parts into useful stuff," I agreed. "And people like the Vrinks who are there to lure in useful prey usually don't have the artistic bent to draw pictures."

"Unless it was the hunter who would have been there with him who drew it," Selene pointed out. "But either way, it breaks the normal hive pattern."

"Yeah," I said, feeling stomach acid churning in my gut. "And we got both of those tidbits with a single visit. There have to have been other studies, and those studies *have* to have found more evidence than we did."

Over the sound of the car's tires on wet pavement, I heard Selene's sigh. "The silver-silk."

"The silver-silk," I confirmed, some of the acid burbling up the base of my esophagus. "There's mountains of money to be made, and someone in Alainn's upper echelons is getting paid a foothill or two for suppressing all this."

"Sometimes I hate humans," Selene murmured. "What can we do to stop it?"

"We start by blasting it with sunlight," I told her. "We expose Lukki's operation, haul Galfvi and Scarf and their respective gangs out into the open, and make so much noise that somebody who isn't in cahoots with the cover-up will *have* to take notice."

"Somebody like the admiral?"

"I doubt he'd be happy about getting dragged into the spotlight," I warned. "Just on general principles, not even adding in his position with the Icarus Group. But he *is* the top name on my list. But like I said, first things first. I don't suppose you were able to smell portal metal from Seven Strands or the Loporr colony, were you?"

"No," she said. "But at both places we were a considerable distance from the fenced-off area. Once we're inside I'll have a better chance."

"I hope so," I said. "Braun and Scarf are already unhappy with us. We don't want to have to stall to the point where they're even less happy."

The rain had stopped by the time we reached the spaceport. I thought about skipping the runaround stand where Selene usually parked and instead taking someplace closer to the spaceport. But there was always the chance for more rain or hail later in the night, and anyway Zilor was used to seeing our rental sitting there.

I also noted that the *Ruth*'s stern had sprouted scaffolding and that both the starboard and portside thruster casings had been partially opened. After two days of dithering over the status report I'd given them, the port repair team was finally on the job.

Though of course there was no rush on their part anymore, given that the port official had managed to find spots for the Ylpea and Patth ships that she'd wanted to boot us out for. The question now was whether *we* might find ourselves wanting to get clear of Alainn in a hurry. At the moment, with the ship wrapped in scaffolding, that would have to be our absolutely last-ditch option.

I pulled close to the curb and we got out. "Now comes the big decision," I commented, easing muscles that were starting to stiffen from a day that had included way too much exercise. "Whether I'm too tired to eat, or too hungry to sleep."

"Both will have to wait," Selene said. She was standing by the runaround stand's price board, her back unnaturally stiff, her eyelashes fluttering at high speed. "Tirano was here."

"When?" I asked, hunger and fatigue abruptly forgotten.

"Within the past hour," she said, leaning a little closer to the board. "And he left a message."

I nodded. It was a technique Selene and I had employed on numerous occasions: trace out the letters of a message with a finger, and Selene could smell the pattern and read the message.

It was a good and useful trick, the most satisfying part being that even if someone else tumbled to it that knowledge would do them no good. There were no other known sapients or sufficiently sensitive mechanical devices that could duplicate the Kadolian sense of smell. The message would remain solely between Selene and me, and about all a spoilsport could do was cover it over with some other smell in hopes of burying the message.

Against someone with Selene's skills, even that might not be effective.

"He says he's by the dock at the northern edge of the space-port," Selene said. "He wants to know if we'll let him back aboard the *Ruth.*" She turned to me. "He's cold and frightened, Gregory."

"Did he *say* that?"

"No. But he is."

"Yeah," I said, passing over the fact that by her own admission she wasn't doing very well at reading the boy. Still, I could see overall misery creating a pretty significant tweak in anyone's scent. "He's one of yours. What do you want to do?"

She looked at me as if she thought I was joking. "Bring him aboard, of course," she said.

"After he tried to get us killed?"

Her pupils flared with a rapid succession of barely readable emotions. "We bring him aboard," she repeated more firmly. "I don't believe he did that on purpose."

"Okay," I said hastily. I'd never seen Selene in this kind of mood, but it clearly wasn't one I wanted to challenge without solid evidence.

And she might be right. The Loporr attack in the colony might have been an accident.

Though I was damn well going to get a plausible explanation before we served up any more chowder.

"I'll go get him," she said, poised to take off toward the north. "Can you make sure the back door is ready?"

"Sure," I said. "So you're going to head north to the river, then west to the spaceport, then south to the *Ruth*?"

"Yes," she said, clearly anxious to get moving.

But also clearly waiting for my agreement. Motherly instincts or no motherly instincts—or whatever Kadolians had for strange children—she still recognized there were risks in what she proposed to do. If I told her no, she would abide by my wishes.

Me, I didn't have a shred of nurturing instincts, Kadolian *or* human. What I had was an appreciation for the bird-in-the-hand scenario. As my father used to add, *And when someone has figured out which bait to use on you, bear in mind that a clever mouse can sometimes steal the cheese out of the trap.*

"All right," I said. "Do you want to take the car? You could take it as far as you can and then continue on foot."

She shook her head. "It's not that far. And we don't want Zilor to wonder what's going on. Fruit and bird?"

"Fruit and bird," I confirmed. Maternal pressures or not, at least she was still rational enough to set up one of our all's-well codes. "Be careful, all right?"

"I will." The urgency and apprehension in her pupils faded just far enough to allow in a little dark amusement. "You may have noticed that I'm difficult to sneak up on."

"That you are," I agreed. "Okay. Get moving before the sky decides to rain on you some more."

She nodded, slipped around the far side of the runaround stand and disappeared into the night.

I took a slightly ragged breath and turned back toward the *Ruth*. Under most circumstances I'd have insisted on going after Tirano myself. But with another Kadolian involved—and with me far easier to sneak up on—it made sense for her to take point. *And* for her to do it all on foot.

And speaking of Badgeman Zilor...

As usual, he was sitting in his unmarked ground car, facing toward me, probably in anticipation of our return. Once we were aboard, he would probably bring his car around and settle in behind our rental so he could watch both it and the *Ruth*'s entryway. I walked up to the car, gave him a casual nod, and started to pass—

And then broke stride, pausing as if he'd said something that I'd heard faintly through his closed window. I turned back to face him, leaning toward the window and frowning.

His window slid down. "Something?" he asked.

"Just wanted to say good night," I said. I had no idea whether or not Braun had tailed us back to the spaceport, but if he was watching I didn't want to look like I'd initiated this conversation, but rather that Zilor had wanted a chat. "How are things running?"

"Smoothly," he said, his forehead creased slightly in bemusement. "Why do you ask?"

"No reason," I said. "I was just thinking about that Patth ship over there. Wondering what they're doing here."

"You'd have to ask the port director."

"Yes, I might do that," I said. "I was just thinking. Patth ship, Patth fugitive—or Patth corpse, depending—and the ship crew just sitting there aboard." I raised my eyebrows slightly. "They *are* just sitting aboard, aren't they? Not out sightseeing or working lumber contracts or something?"

For a moment he studied me. "Let's cut through the weeds," he said. "What do you know?"

"I don't *know* anything," I said. "I'm just commenting on the coincidence of having Galfvi, Kiolven and Venikel, and now a Patth ship. Seems to me that Bilswift is getting awfully crowded with Patth."

"They own the Spiral, or so they say," Zilor said woodenly. "What are you suggesting?"

"Not suggesting anything," I assured him. "Just thinking of

the pattern I've seen sometimes in under-the-table businesses. Like, say, someone procures a valuable item, someone else comes in to verify the item and make payment, then someone else takes delivery."

"No one follows the whole length of the transaction, so it's harder to pin it on any of them," Zilor said, nodding. "Just happened to be thinking about that?"

"Just happened," I assured him. "Too bad you don't have a StarrComm facility here or I could check the bounty listings."

"Nearest is in Tranlisoa," he said. "Only one suborbital from there to Bilswift—out at six in the morning, back at six at night."

"Not terribly convenient," I said. "But we can probably make it do."

"If you want convenience, there are twelve daily shuttles from Cavindoss to various other cities," Zilor offered. "Cavindoss is kind of a long haul—four hours by ground car—but you get more options. I don't know which flights go to StarrComm cities, but you could look that up."

"I'll be sure to do that," I said. "Thanks."

"No problem. Where'd Selene go?"

So he'd spotted Selene's departure. I'd assumed he would, and figured he'd want to know about it. Fortunately, I already had a story ready. "She was wondering if someone could use the river to transport our theoretical package," I said. "She wanted to see what the docks, ships, and general terrain looked like over there."

"She couldn't wait until morning?"

I snorted. "Really, Badgeman Zilor. Whoever heard of people skulking around being nefarious at eleven o'clock in the morning?"

He shrugged. "The smart ones might," he said. "If only because people like you don't expect them to."

"Fair point," I conceded. "Well, enough of the theoreticals. On to the practicals, namely food and sleep. See you around, Badgeman Zilor."

He nodded, a new or at least rekindled fire in his eyes. "That I will, Bounty Hunter Roarke," he said.

I continued on my way, and as I approached the ramp I glanced over my shoulder to see that he had indeed repositioned so as to face the *Ruth*. He'd been ordered to watch our ship, and he would do so until that order was rescinded.

But I'd bet large sums of money that while he watched he

would also be having an interesting conversation with Detective-Sergeant Kreega.

Meanwhile, I had a ship to prepare for our wayward Kadolian's homecoming. Best to be ready when Selene brought him home.

It would probably also be a good idea to make sure I was armed.

CHAPTER SIXTEEN

I was in the subdeck crawlway beneath the *Ruth*'s main deck and had removed the Number Two equipment bay's inner plate when I heard the sound of the catches on the outer hull plate being opened. I got the DubTrub derringer ready, holding it below the edge of the opening where it would be just out of sight of anyone looking in from the other side, and waited. The last catch popped and the hull plate was lifted away—

"Everything all right?" Selene asked softly, crouching down to peer into the opening.

"Everything's just peachy," I said, trying to look past her shoulder. I could see someone back there, but it was too dark outside for a positive identification. "You find him?"

"Like chickens coming home to roost," she said.

I nodded, breathing a little easier as I slipped the DubTrub into my pocket. Sign, countersign, all in order. "Zilor saw you leave, by the way, so you'll need to come back in through the regular entryway."

"I was planning to anyway," she said, half turning. "Over here, Tirano."

Selene and I, experienced as we were with the necessary techniques, could unfasten the plate, make the transition either in or out, and have everything buttoned up again in ninety seconds flat. Tirano, without a clue as to what he was doing, took a full two minutes just to get through the equipment bay and onto the mechanic creeper I'd prepared for him in the crawlway.

The heavy Patth robe he was still wearing didn't help matters at all.

"I'll close everything," Selene said. "You concentrate on getting him upstairs."

"Got it," I said. "Tirano, I'm going to roll backward to the entrance to this little rabbit hole. Think you can stay with me?"

"I'll try," he said, his voice shaking a little. "Are you . . . ?" He broke off.

"Am I what?" I prompted. "Come on, we don't have all night."

"Are you going to shoot me in the back?"

I blinked. "No, of course not," I assured him. "Did you think I was going to?"

"You're carrying a firearm," he said, still sounding nervous. "I can smell it."

"That was in case you and Selene were intercepted by Braun or the Ylps." I hesitated, but I couldn't resist. "You know, the people you were trying to steal the Vrinks from."

"I wasn't trying to steal from them," he protested. "I *wasn't*."

"Sure," I said, feeling ashamed of myself. As my father used to say, *Never stand behind or tower over someone you're questioning. It's rude and patronizing, and anyway you need to be able to watch his expression and body language.* "Sorry—I shouldn't have said that. Come on, let's go. I'll tell you when to stop, and after I climb up I'll help you out."

"Okay." He sniffed. "Is that more of the crab chowder?"

I rolled my eyes. All I'd done was get the quick-cook package out of the pantry and set it beside the cooker. I hadn't even opened the damn thing. "Yes, it's more chowder," I said. "The faster we get up there, the faster I can get it started."

He was on his second helping when I heard the entryway open. "Gregory?" Selene called. "Who's here?"

"Just the pair of us in the dayroom," I called back. "Everything good?"

"Just ducky," she said. "I'll be right there."

"Okay." I listened, my hand wrapped around the DubTrub, as she shut the hatch and double-locked it. Twenty seconds later she joined us.

Looking like she'd just taken a swim through a swamp. "What in the *world*?" I asked, goggling a little.

"It's not as bad as it looks," she assured me, looking at her arms with distaste. "Most of it's just water, though there's some oil and fuel mixed in."

"And garbage?"

"And dead sea life," she said. "I suppose that qualifies. It's not too bad. Tirano, are you all right?"

"Whoa," I protested. "We're not moving on to Tirano until we finish with you. You fall in the river or something?"

"It's not important," she said, resolve and warning in her pupils. "We need to hear from Tirano now."

"You don't get to tell me what to do," I said, putting some irritation into my tone. I didn't know if she was trying to avoid talking about something in Tirano's presence or was setting up a hot badge/cold badge routine. If it was the latter, I might as well lay a bit of pseudoantagonistic groundwork for it. "But fine, let's hear from Tirano. Starting with why you tried to kill all of us in the Loporr colony today."

"I didn't," Tirano insisted nervously. "It was...no, I can't tell you. He said I can't tell anyone."

"We're not just anyone, Tirano," Selene said earnestly. "We're your friends. I'm one of your people. You can tell us."

Tirano shook his head. "I can't."

"Suit yourself," I said nonchalantly, standing up from my fold-down seat. "Badgeman Zilor still out there, Selene?"

"Yes," she said. "I'm sorry, Tirano."

"It was Galfvi," Tirano said quickly, the words tumbling out of his mouth. "He said we were in big trouble, and that he was the only one who could get us out of it. He said this was the only way."

"Okay, now we're getting somewhere," I said, sitting back down. I glanced at Selene, hoping for a clue as to whether our bluff had actually broken Tirano down to the truth or if he was just gearing up for more lies.

But there was nothing I could see either way in her pupils. Clearly, she was still having trouble reading the boy.

"Let's start from the beginning," Selene said. "Tell us what kind of trouble Galfvi says you're in."

"He said"—Tirano swallowed visibly—"that me helping Lukki

collect Vrinks from the Loporr colony is a big crime. He says that if the badgemen catch us we'll go to prison for the rest of our lives."

"I think he's exaggerating," Selene said gently. "There are extenuating circumstances and mercy protocols that would certainly be invoked."

"Was he exaggerating when he said that was why Lukki and Willie were killed?" Tirano asked bluntly.

I saw a wince flash across Selene's pupils. "We don't know why they were killed," she said. "It could have been about the Vrinks, but it could have been about something else entirely."

"We still have to get off Alainn," Tirano said. "He said we need to buy passage on some ship."

"Not too many to choose from around here," I pointed out, watching his pupils closely. Something unreadable flicked across them, but too quickly for me to try to read. "So why did Galfvi think that siccing the Loporri on us would get you out of all this trouble?"

Tirano flashed a look at me, then went back to looking at Selene. "He told me we needed enough money to run," he said. "I told him we were going up to the colony"—his face contorted—"and he said I should cut off the strands from the Vrinks. All the strands, from all the Vrinks."

"How many did you get?" I asked.

"Thirty-six," he said. "He told me we needed fifty, but . . . I bumped one of the Vrinks." His face went all tormented and pleading. "I didn't touch him on purpose. I didn't mean for the hunters to come after you."

"It's all right," Selene soothed. "We all got out without getting hurt. Where are the strands now? Did you give them to Galfvi?"

He shook his head. "I haven't seen Galfvi since the night he disappeared. The night he gave me this." He plucked at his Patth robe. "We just talked by phone."

"I thought you said you lost your phone," I reminded him.

He dropped his gaze to the deck. "I know," he muttered. "I didn't."

"Where are the strands now?" Selene asked.

"Here." Tirano dug into an inside pocket.

And drew out a fistful of thirty-centimeter threads of silver-silk.

I didn't care a spoiled fig for the world of fashion, or the bank accounts of the rich and snobby, or whatever passed for esthetics or bragging rights at that stratospheric level. But here and now, watching the ordinary lights of the *Ruth*'s dayroom turn them into shimmering, glistening, *living* strands of solid light took my breath away.

As my father used to say, *The rich spend a lot of their wealth on stupid, wasteful, and prestige-signaling garbage. But every now and again, they get it right.*

With silver-silk, they'd definitely gotten it right.

Carefully, I stood up and walked over to Tirano. Just as carefully, I eased the collection of strands out of his grip. "Selene?" I asked quietly, still staring at them.

"The official market value of a thirty-centimeter strand of silver-silk is six thousand commarks," I heard her voice through the sudden pounding of my heart.

"The *official* value?" I asked.

"There's also a black market," she confirmed. I looked at her, to find that while I'd been letting myself be dazzled she'd been working her info pad. "There, a thirty-centimeter strand can bring seven or eight thousand."

Which meant I was holding somewhere between two hundred and three hundred thousand commarks in my hand. An odd thought crossed my mind: that this made the sixteen thousand Galfvi had lifted from the fish shop look pretty shabby in comparison.

"What were you supposed to do with them?" Selene asked.

"He said he'd call me about getting on a ship," Tirano said. "But I only got thirty-six."

"Don't worry, we'd be more than happy to settle for that," I assured him. "Do you have a schedule worked out with him? I assume you're not supposed to just call whenever you feel like it."

"He said he'd call me," Tirano said.

"Have you tried calling him?" Selene asked.

"Four times," Tirano said. "But he didn't answer."

Selene looked at me. "Or he can't."

I nodded. Standard bad guy paranoia dictated you used one phone per call, dumping the old model and grabbing a new one the minute the conversation was over. "No problem," I said. "Tell you what: Finish your meal and then head back to my cabin and get some sleep. You look like your day's been almost as long as ours."

"Possibly even longer," Selene added. "Can I get you more chowder?"

"No, thank you." Tirano quickly scooped the last two spoonfuls into his mouth. "I'm done."

"Okay," Selene said. "Use the bathroom—take a shower if you want—then get some sleep. And don't worry. By morning we'll have a plan ready to go."

"All right." Tirano's eyes drifted to the strands of living light in my hand. "Can I...?"

"We'll hold onto these," I told him firmly. "We'll keep them safe."

He looked at me, looked at Selene, then gave a tired-looking nod. "Okay. Good night."

He stumbled through the dayroom hatchway and headed aft. Selene stepped to the hatch, leaning her head against the inside wall. I waited, not moving, watching her in silence.

Two minutes later she nodded and turned back toward me. "He's been to the bathroom, and is in your cabin," she reported, walking over to the foldout and sinking wearily onto it. "Another two minutes and he'll be asleep."

"As long as he's behind a closed door," I said, resisting the urge to go down the corridor and double-check for myself. Selene generally knew what she was doing, and now wasn't the time to make her think I had doubts about her skills or her judgment.

Whether I did or not, it wasn't time for her to think that. "Let's hear about your midnight swim. How did you find which boat was Lukki's?"

"You suggested to Braun that he check it out," she said, looking puzzled that I was even asking.

"Of course I did," I said, also wondering why I was asking. All she'd had to do was walk along the docks until she caught Braun's scent, then go to whichever boat he stopped at. "Sorry. Brain glitch. I'm guessing the dock was locked?"

"Locked and fenced off," she said. "I had to swim around it." She looked down at herself. "It wasn't particularly pleasant."

"I can imagine," I said. Though of course I couldn't, not really. All I was getting was a faint whiff of the watery mix. She'd gotten the stink full blast. "Anything useful aboard?"

"They definitely used it to move Vrinks," she said. "Probably this latest package. Their scent was strong, no more than seven to ten days old."

"Any sign of Galfvi?"

"His scent was there," she said. "The boat's a cabin cruiser style, the hull a fiberline composite, with a covered cockpit and galley. There was also room for four bunks, but all but one of them had been removed."

"Probably to make more space for the Vrinks while they were being moved."

"Yes, that's where most of the Vrink scent was," Selene confirmed. "And Galfvi's, too."

"Could you tell if he'd slept there recently?" I asked. "It would be nice to know where he disappeared to."

She shook her head. "His scent wasn't on the remaining bunk. It was concentrated at the fore section of the cabin, with a bit on the deck between the cabin and the dock." Her pupils took on a look of wry humor. "Most of it, actually, was on the starter module."

"*Only* on the starter? Not on the wheel or throttle?"

"No, and not on the driver's seat or docking controls," she said. "He tried to start it, and when he couldn't he left."

I nodded. That still left the question of where he was, but it made sense that Lukki would have made sure her boat was properly secured. "Interesting. Okay. Timeline?"

Selene's eyes unfocused, her pupils settling into a look of concentration. "The night we visit the Javersin brothers' shop he steals money from the safe, puts it into his robe, and gives the robe to Tirano for safekeeping."

"For safekeeping, or because he doesn't want to get caught with it."

"Or both," Selene said. "He then goes to Lukki's apartment to find where she hid the Vrinks. Maybe Lukki sees him coming out of her building, so he kills her—"

"Whoa," I said. "*He* kills her? You sure?"

"Who else could it have been?"

"Well..." I paused, running through the possibilities. An ambitious Braun? A suspicious Scarf? One of the Patth currently beating the bushes looking for a portal, killing her for some unknown reason? The Javersin brothers, or Kiolven and Venikel, or some semi-random Bilswift resident, for even more obscure reasons?

Selene herself?

I watched the reaction in her pupils as she spotted the sudden change in my scent. Lukki was the one who'd enslaved Tirano and drawn him into this tangle of kidnapping and sapient trafficking. If Selene thought killing Lukki would somehow free him, would she actually take such a drastic step?

I had no idea. I'd seen Selene in many situations, but never in full mama bear mode. But this wasn't the time to confront her with such suspicions. "I wouldn't put it past Badgeman Zilor," I improvised. "You've seen his single-minded obsession with Galfvi. If he tried to get to him through Lukki, and if the threats went sideways, he might have overreacted."

Selene shook her head. "I don't really see him doing something like that."

"You never know what someone's capable of until push comes to poke," I pointed out. "Anyway, that's Kreega's problem. So Galfvi gets a location and heads out. What then?"

"He heads to one of the places Braun showed us, the house near the river with the blue-and-white picket fence outside—"

"Wait a second," I again interrupted. She'd seemed to show some heightened interest in that particular house during Braun's tour of greater Bilswift, but she hadn't said a word to me about it, not then and not later. "The Vrinks were *there*?"

"They *were* there," she said. "Not now. They were gone at least a day before we arrived."

"Ah," I said, watching some of the pieces come together. "Okay, let's recap. Lukki meets with me at Panza's, decides for whatever reason that there's trouble afoot and she needs to move the package. She hustles—alone—to where she and the others stashed the Vrinks, moves them elsewhere, and heads back home just in time to get shot down in the street."

"Galfvi finds the listing for Lukki's hidden lair," Selene picked up the narrative. "It's close enough to the river to use the boat, so he goes to the dock to get it and go pick them up."

"Only it's locked down," I said. "So...what? He finds a van to steal?"

"There was no scent of vehicle emissions beneath the car overhang," Selene said. "My sense is that he would want to make sure the Vrinks were in fact there before doing something that could attract the badgemen."

"Lucky for him he did it in that order," I said. "Because the

Vrinks *weren't* there, and he'd have been stuck with a hot van. So what does he do then?"

Her pupils clouded over. "He calls Tirano."

"And tries to work out a Plan B," I said. "Because the sixteen thousand commarks he stole from the fish shop isn't nearly enough to get them off Alainn, at least not fast enough."

"Yes," Selene said, her pupils going puzzled. "But why now? Why did Lukki suddenly think she had a problem?"

"No idea," I admitted. "Maybe she had a conversation with Tirano that didn't feel right. Maybe she had one with Galfvi."

"Or maybe," Selene added quietly, "she had one with you."

I stared at her, my world turning suddenly sideways. I'd been so busy wondering if she'd killed Lukki during the time we were apart that it had never occurred to me that she might have the same question about me.

And if she was wondering if I'd had a hand in Lukki's death, it was for damn sure Detective-Sergeant Kreega was, too.

"You know I would never kill anyone in cold blood," I said, forcing my voice to stay calm.

"I know." She looked me straight in the eye, her pupils taking on an edge of hurt. "Just as you know neither would I."

I hesitated. But since she'd started this conversation... "And if there *was* a good reason?" I asked, forcing myself to meet that gaze. "One that would make it self-defense or defense of someone else?"

"Do you think I killed her?" Selene demanded.

"I don't know," I shot back. "Do you think *I* did?"

The frustration and betrayal faded from her eyes. "No," she said tiredly. "Not if you say you didn't."

I took a deep breath, feeling my own spark of anger subsiding. "Likewise," I said. "I'm sorry, Selene. I didn't expect to walk into a murder on this job, let alone a bunch of them."

"I know," she said, lowering her gaze. "We need to get out there and find the portal. The rest... it's really none of our business, is it?"

"No, it's not," I agreed. "But we'll still see what we can do for him."

"Thank you," she said. "I assume we're leaving him here tomorrow?"

"I don't see what else we can do," I said. "There are way too many people out there looking for him. You'll need to impress on him that he should not, under any circumstances, talk to Galfvi or anyone else without one of us here with him."

"I'll try," she said. "If I can find his phone, we'll take it with us."

"Good idea," I said, though I privately doubted she'd succeed. Tirano had clearly been taking skullduggery lessons from Galfvi. "Meanwhile, we should get some sleep."

"Yes." Selene hesitated. "Do you want to sleep in my cabin?"

"No need," I assured her. "Galfvi's convinced him they need to get off Alainn, and I'm pretty sure Tirano caught my offhand reminder that right now the *Ruth*'s their best bet. It's generally considered bad form to kill the pilot of the ship you're hoping to hitch a ride on."

"Yes, he noticed," she confirmed. "So you'll sleep here?"

"It's more comfortable than the engine room," I said. "Besides, here I'll be able to hear if he pops the entryway and heads out for a walk."

"You think he might do that?"

"Not really," I said, eyeing my partner of all these years, a partner I'd always thought I knew.

But then, I'd been wrong before.

CHAPTER SEVENTEEN

We woke up early, gathered our gear, and were out of the *Ruth* about half an hour before sunrise. Badgeman Zilor wasn't at his usual post, but the same unmarked car was there with two different badgemen inside holding silent vigil. Whatever Zilor had told Kreega about possible Patth activity in the port, she'd apparently taken it seriously.

The mountain road was even more nerve-racking in the dark, and the rising sun blazing into the windshield just made it worse. But finally, we were there.

"Okay," I said as we climbed up the ladder to the platform. "Dealer's choice. You want to go directly to the fenced-off area, or look around a little first?"

"Look around where?" Selene asked, doing a slow three-sixty as she sampled the air.

"I thought we might check out the area we spotted yesterday," I said, pointing along the footbridge angling off to a different part of the mountains. "I'm curious as to whether there's another Loporr colony at the end or if it's something else of interest."

"Do we really care?"

"I think we do," I said. "Remember that the only reason we think the portal is downslope is that the Patth have fenced off that area. They could be wrong."

"Or deliberately trying to decoy us," Selene said thoughtfully. "Though I don't remember seeing any spot at the end of the other bridge where even one of the smaller Gemini portals would fit."

"Neither did I," I said. "But the bridge could end in a trail or ravine that leads farther in."

"Possibly to a field or gap that *would* hold a portal," Selene said. "Yes, that could be the case. Shall we try that one first?"

"Sounds good to me." I took hold of the two rope handrails, stepped out onto the bridge—

And dropped like a rock as the wooden slats disintegrated under my weight and the right-hand handhold snapped.

"Gregory!" Selene gasped, grabbing my backpack's strap as I dangled over the five-meter drop. So far the left-hand rope was holding, but I didn't expect that to last much longer.

Fortunately, Selene was already on it. Still gripping my backpack, she swiveled my body toward her, pivoting me around my lone handhold until my right could reach the edge of the platform. The rough wood provided only marginal purchase, but adding a second anchor point eased some of the strain off the rope.

But not enough. Even as I tried to figure out my next move, the rope snapped, and an instant later I found myself once again hanging by one hand and Selene's grip.

And with the platform offering no options, and Selene's strength diminishing toward its own breaking point, there was only one thing left to try.

"Let go," I ordered, stretching out my left hand and getting a grip on a section of the right-hand rope lattice that had been holding up the slats, the lattice that from my new viewpoint I could see was as frayed and untrustworthy as the slats themselves. "Let go *now.*"

With a worried and frustrated hiss, Selene did so. As my backpack came free, I let go of my right-hand grip on the platform and grabbed the section of lattice I was already holding onto with my left.

And as my full weight came onto the rope, the lattice began to unravel.

Unravel, but not disintegrate. As my brief close-up of the interwoven ropes had hinted, the mesh came apart in sections, cross-straps breaking in sequence while the longer side rope I was holding mostly together. Each cross-strap held a fraction of a second after the one beside it broke, as did the one after that and the one after that, turning an otherwise catastrophic fall into a marginally but adequately zipline-style controlled descent.

Five seconds later I was on the ground, landing harder than a civilized step off a ladder but way more lightly than an unhindered five-meter drop would have cost me. All in all, I could definitely call this one a win.

"Gregory?"

I looked up to find Selene looking anxiously down at me. "I'm all right," I assured her, taking another look at the underside of the footbridge. "Wish I could say the same about the bridge."

The thing was a mess. Without the strain of my weight, the cascading unraveling had stopped, but the first six meters of the bridge were a complete shambles. The lattice was gone, the slats broken by the stress or hanging intact but limply onto one of the side ropes. The far lengthwise rope was still more or less solid, but at this point I guessed even a slightly overweight squirrel would hesitate to try his luck with it.

"I assume we're not going that direction anymore?" Selene suggested, a hint of relieved humor replacing the brief surge of tension and fear.

"I think that's a safe assumption," I agreed in kind as I returned to the ladder and started up. "Let's hope the other bridges have weathered the years a little better."

"Yes," she said. "Let's."

She was sniffing carefully along the single rope still connecting the demolished footbridge to the platform when I reached her. "Does it smell as rotten as it looks?" I asked.

"The broken ones are very distinctive," she said. "Interestingly, the intact boards don't reveal the decay as strongly as the ropes do. The outer shell must contain most of the scent."

"But you *can* tell the difference between those and the good ones, right?"

"I think so," she said. "So far, the bridge we need seems safe."

So far. Meaning that somewhere along the line we might unexpectedly find ourselves dangling over rocks, streams, or dense forest. And as Braun had pointed out so elegantly, there was nothing down there but predators and scavengers.

And both our phones were back on the *Ruth*.

But the only other options were to tackle the Patth encampment head-on or go back to the admiral and tell him we'd failed to find his precious portal. We'd have better odds with the predators and scavengers. "I don't know why the Icari even bothered with these things," I groused as I walked to the edge of the platform. "Ridiculous concept, ridiculous design. Were these clients of theirs too stupid to fly aircars or something?"

"They couldn't use aircars up at the Loporr colony," Selene said, her pupils looking puzzled. "There's nowhere for them to land."

"What about that big grassy area?" I asked. "The place where they all got together for lunch."

"The rock there is frangible," she said. "I saw that when we went through. Land too much weight there or run thrusters too close and the whole structure will collapse down the mountain."

"Really," I said, trying to pull up the memories of our hurried passage through the area. But it was no use. Focused on the Loporri and getting us out of there, I hadn't picked up on any of the physical parameters she'd clearly been paying attention to. "And I suppose the cavern openings onto the ledges or the sheer cliffs where their bird-trap holes are have too much wind for anyone to safely hover?"

"Probably," Selene said. "Actually, I think the footbridges are an excellent solution."

"Provided you properly maintain the things," I growled. Bracing myself, I got a grip on the side ropes and stepped gingerly onto the first slat. It didn't offer even a protesting creak in return. At least the Icari had kept some of their squirrel trails in working order. "Let's go."

Estimating distances when driving on twisty mountain roads was always tricky, and for some reason Seven Strands didn't show up on the official Bilswift maps. But our best estimate had put the eastern edge of the Path fence to be about three kilometers away, with the farther, western edge another eight.

A minimum of three kilometers on a rickety, swaying collection of old rope and old boards. Just as a nice bonus, the footbridge was currently on a ten-degree downward slope, which meant the return walk would be the same ten degrees upward.

More than once the grumpy thought occurred to me that people who had the genius to create Icarus portals surely could have figured out something easier to use.

The first kilometer was the hardest. I was fully and painfully aware of my every step, watched the slight wind-driven swaying of the bridge with trepidation, and winced at each squeak from whichever board I was currently standing on. But the bridge held, and the occasional creaking remained at an almost pleasant cricket level, and after about twenty minutes I finally started to relax.

Of course, as my father used to say, *Sometimes the only reason the universe eases up its choke hold on you is so that it can get a better grip.* But for once even his cynicism was overly pessimistic. The second kilometer took us down past the treetops into the forest, where the builders had set up the same sideways tethering system we'd seen on our trip to the Loporr colony. But aside from a new set of sounds as guy lines stretched or contracted, and less overall swaying of the bridge, everything remained the same.

We were nearing our estimate of three kilometers when I spotted the jeep trail we'd driven from the main road through the trees to the river.

"We're here," I muttered a warning over my shoulder. "Time to make like little field mice."

A minute later, we were over the Patth fence.

I strained my ears as we continued on, a fairly useless effort as the Patth were hardly likely to have set the fence to blare a loud and obvious alarm centered at the source of the intrusion. We kept going, moving as quietly as possible, until the fence and the jeep trail were lost to view behind us. "Anything?" I murmured again to Selene.

"There are definitely Patth somewhere in here," she said, as if we needed that confirmation. "Not nearby, though. At least a couple of kilometers farther west. And..."

"And?" I prompted.

"I'm not sure," she said. "I need to get closer."

"Okay," I said, touching the butt of my plasmic just to reassure myself that it was still there. "I guess we get you closer, then."

We'd walked another fifteen minutes when she suddenly moved up right behind me. "It's here," she breathed. "I can smell it. It's here."

I stopped and looked around, an eerie sense trickling through me. So Graym-Barker's information had been right. There was indeed a portal hidden in the wilds of Alainn.

Distantly, I wondered if I'd ever get used to close encounters with these things. Probably I wouldn't. "Where?"

"I think it's straight ahead."

Again, exactly as our theory predicted. The Icari had craved silver-silk as much as the Spiral's current crop of rich and powerful, and had spent one of their precious portals in order to get access to it. "Okay," I said, picking up my pace.

And then, quite suddenly, we were there.

Or at least we were *somewhere*. The bridge came to an end, not at another platform like at Seven Strands, but fastened to a thick-trunked tree. "End of the line," I announced, looking down the trunk. It was a good seven meters to the ground, but the tree had a branch pattern that looked reasonably straightforward to climb. "I'll go first," I added, ducking under the rope handrail and getting a grip on the two nearest branches. "Wait until I'm on the ground before you start." Trying to simultaneously watch handholds and footholds, I started down.

The route had looked straightforward. It turned out to be not only straightforward but actually pretty easy. The bark on the branches was just rough enough to provide good traction for hands and feet, and both the horizontal and vertical spacing was nearly perfect for an average-sized human. Maybe the Icari engineers who designed these things hadn't been *completely* incompetent.

I reached the bottom and made a short inspection tour of the immediate area, watching in particular for signs of predators. The area was patterned with thick tufts of tall grass—or possibly strangely built bushes—that could hide an average cat, but I didn't see any movement that might suggest any of them was currently occupied. Other trees were surrounded by leafy bushes or saplings. It wouldn't be a Sunday stroll, but the area looked reasonably passable.

Selene reached the ground and joined me. "Anything?" I asked.

"Patth, as I said before," she said, sampling the air. "And portal metal. And something else. Something familiar, but it's too faint for me to identify."

"Well, when it gets closer you can take another shot at it," I said. "In the meantime, let's find the portal."

"Yes." She pointed to an empty space between two trees. "This way."

Looking ahead from the footbridge, I hadn't spotted any real break in the tree cover. It was therefore something of a shock when we passed around a wide bush and found ourselves at the edge of an actual, real-life clearing. "Whoa," I said, stopping and looking around. "Where did *this* come from?"

"Not from logging," Selene said, sniffing. "All of Bilswift's logging operations are to the north and south of the city. You'd also need an air grappler to take anything out of here. Maybe it was a lightning strike that burned and sterilized the ground too much to support trees or other large plant life."

"Yeah," I said, my stomach tightening. "Or maybe it was cleared out by a crash-landing portal."

"That can't be," Selene pointed out. "The Icari vanished thousands of years ago. How can the forest not have come back by now?"

"Maybe this one was in orbit like the Alpha portal and didn't crash until more recently." On the other hand, there was no sign of the widespread shock-wave damage that usually accompanied crashed space objects. "Or maybe portal metal is nastier to plant life than we know. Or at least *this* plant life."

She shivered. "Yes," she murmured. "Maybe. It's this way."

She set off across the clearing, sniffing as she went. I stayed at the tree line, not wanting my scent to interfere with her search, and took another look around. The short viny ground cover we'd seen during our hike seemed to be doing just fine, and there were occasional tufts of the tall cat-sanctuary grasses. But there weren't any plants larger than that. Maybe Selene was right about the lightning strike, and the local flora was simply taking its time growing back.

"Gregory?"

She was standing halfway across the clearing beside one of the tall tufts, her back stiff. "You find it?" I asked, walking over to her.

"Yes," she said, pointing to her feet. "Here." A flicker of emotion crossed her pupils. "I know who it is, Gregory. The person I'm smelling." She shifted her finger to point west. "It's Huginn."

My stomach instantly formed itself into a double knot. "Oh, hell," I muttered, peering in that direction as if the short, wiry man might suddenly spring into view. Huginn was an Expediter, one of the cadre of elite, high-ranking operatives who served the Patth with the kind of training, skill, and devotion that would impress even an EarthGuard commando or Commonwealth special agent.

And the last time we'd encountered Huginn, he was attached to Sub-Director Nask.

In hindsight, of *course* Huginn would show up here. Nask himself was probably sitting in distant orbit aboard the *Odinn*, keeping long-distance watch over the team searching the Bilswift forest. "How close?"

"At least three kilometers away," Selene said. "Probably more. There was a gust of wind—"

"Yes, yes, got it," I cut her off, taking off my backpack and pulling out the collapsible shovel. "Let's get this done before they get any closer."

Given that Selene had smelled the stray molecules of metal that had managed to sift their way through the dirt told me the portal wasn't buried too deeply. Sure enough, I'd dug down barely fifteen centimeters when I heard the unmistakable clink of metal on metal. I dug my way around to one side until I found the mark of one of the hatches, then cleared out the square meter of ground around it.

Finally, we were ready. "Here goes," I said. I reached for the hatch control—

"Wait," Selene said suddenly.

I frowned up at her. There was a fresh kaleidoscope of emotions flicking across her pupils. "Gregory, there's something wrong," she said. "Something..."

I looked back at the portal. It looked like every other Icari portal I'd ever seen. Not that that was a huge list. "You mean like a booby trap?" I asked.

"No, it's..." She inhaled deeply. "You can open it. You can try."

I frowned. I could *try*?

Sitting around wondering what she meant would get us nowhere. Carefully, ready to throw myself flat on the ground, I keyed the control.

For a few seconds nothing happened. Then, almost reluctantly, that section of metal unfastened itself from the surrounding hull and swung downward.

But instead of folding itself up and melding with the inner hull like portal hatches usually did, it just hung there.

For a long minute I stared at it. Then, with a sense of dread, I lowered my arm through the opening.

Both the receiver module and launch module of an Icari

portal had artificial gravity fields, pointed radially outward from the center of each sphere toward their respective hulls. Reaching through the hatch I'd just opened should have immediately given that part of my arm a sense of gravitational pressure pushing back at me.

But there was nothing. No pressure at all. With my other hand I brushed some loose dirt into the opening and watched it drop freely into the darkness.

I looked up at Selene. "Selene?" I asked carefully.

She nodded, her pupils brimming with disbelief and misery. "Yes," she whispered.

"It's dead."

CHAPTER EIGHTEEN

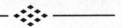

Dead.

I rolled the word through my mind a few times as I stared into the emptiness, listening to the sound, tasting the meaning. *Dead.*

Not *powered down.* Not *damaged.* Not even *broken.*

Dead.

Why had Selene used that word? Did she know something about the portals that I didn't?

I pulled my arm back out and stood up. It felt strange and disrespectful, maybe even a little irreverent, as if I was just dismissing it. But I couldn't think of anything else to do. "So what now?" I asked.

Selene was still staring into the opening. "I don't know," she said. "I suppose we have to tell the admiral."

"Yeah," I said. Briefly, I thought of Expediter Huginn, toiling away in the distance, wondering what *he* was going to tell *his* boss.

But that was his problem. I had a big enough collection of my own. "Well, unless his backup force has arrived we'll need to get to a StarrComm center. It's probably too late to do that today, but we can head out tomorrow."

"In the *Ruth*?"

I chewed at my lip. With Graym-Barker's hoped-for prize

having turned into the Spiral's biggest paperweight there was no need for us to stick around Alainn in general or Bilswift in particular. The sooner we got out of here, the better. That Ihmisit port official, Perrifil, would certainly appreciate having her landing pad back.

But at the moment the *Ruth* was still partially disassembled while the repair crews chased down the phantom problems I'd presented to them. Until they buttoned everything back up even atmospheric flight would be problematic. "We'll have to take a shuttle," I said. "Zilor rattled off a list of when and where they went, but I wasn't really paying much attention. We can look up the schedules once we're back aboard and have sorted through our options."

I gestured behind us. "In the meantime, I guess we should throw some branches on top of the hole and head back to Seven Strands."

"Yes." For another moment Selene gazed at the portal. Then, she straightened up and nodded. "Yes. I'm ready."

As anticipated, the uphill slope of the footbridge made the return trip tougher and feel longer.

But more oppressive, at least to Selene, was the forest scene we'd just left.

Me, I was more confused than dejected. As far as I'd ever heard— as far as I'd ever seen—the Icari portals were purely mechanical devices: physical mechanisms and electronics. Machines.

So how could one be *dead*?

Had Selene known something none of the rest of us did? Had she been speaking purely figuratively? Or was it simply that her English had momentarily failed her?

They were questions I needed to ask, wrapped inside a conversation we needed to have. But that was for later. Right now, we needed to concentrate on our uphill climb, get back to Bilswift and the *Ruth,* and figure out what to do about Tirano, Galfvi, and the rest of the rogues' gallery we'd fallen in with. Time enough to talk once we were securely inside our ship.

We were a block away from the *Ruth,* the evening rain had started, and I was mulling over what I wanted for dinner when I spotted the group of dark cars clustered silently around the spaceport entrance.

As casually as possible I pulled over, bringing the car to the side of the road a hundred meters short of the runaround stand where we usually parked. "What is it?" Selene asked.

"We've got company," I said, nodding toward the silent watchers. "Don't know if they're waiting for us, or for a warrant—"

I broke off, twitching reflexively to my right as something suddenly entered my left-hand peripheral vision. I turned to see Detective-Sergeant Kreega looking at me through the side window, her face stony. Huffing out a sigh, I slid the window down. "Evening, Detective-Sergeant," I greeted her cheerfully. "What brings you out in the rain at this hour?"

"Like you don't know," Kreega ground out, gesturing at the back door. "Open up."

I did so, and she climbed in behind me. "Not going to be much of a ride," I warned. "We're just going up there to the—"

"Not yet you're not," she cut me off. "Badgeman Station. I trust you remember the way?"

"Of course," I said, giving Selene a sideways look. But her face was turned away, her pupils out of my view. "Do I get to ask what this is all about?" I asked as I pulled back onto the street and did a U-turn. The waiting cars, I noted, had now come to life and were forming themselves into a conga line behind us.

"You can ask yours after we've asked ours," Kreega said. "And I suggest you watch your answers. Unless you want to end up sleeping in a couple of my cells tonight."

Fifteen minutes later we were at the station. Kreega escorted us inside and to a compact meeting room that was nevertheless probably the largest one in the place. She seated us at the far end of the oval table and took up position beside the door.

A minute later, the rest of the crowd filed in.

I'd expected Zilor and another pair of Bilswift badgemen to join us. I wasn't really expecting Detective-Lieutenant Sovelli to have flown in from Cavindoss for whatever mysterious occasion this was, but it hadn't been out of the realm of possibility.

But the formal-suited Commonwealth official and her two aides were a complete surprise.

The seven of them sorted themselves out around the table, ending up with Zilor and Sovelli sitting on either side of Selene and me, the Commonwealth official at the far end directly across from us, and the rest filling in the other chairs. Kreega remained standing by the door, as if concerned that I might try to make a break for it through all the other people.

"State your name, please," the official said.

"I'm pretty sure you already know it," I said. "Why don't we start instead with you stating yours?"

An uncomfortable ripple ran around the table. But the official merely gave me a frosty smile. "Third Consul Rebekah Townsend, Department of Human-Sapient Relations." She raised her eyebrows slightly. "And I wasn't talking to *you*, Mr. Roarke."

I frowned at Selene. She was sitting quietly, but there was a fire in her pupils that I'd rarely seen before. "I am called Selene," she said. "Do you wish my full name?"

"Yes."

Selene rattled it off, all eighteen syllables of it. No one bothered to write it down; presumably, they already knew that one, too. "I assume you're here about my petition?" she continued.

"We are," Townsend confirmed. "You claim to have evidence that runs contrary to all established data."

"I have evidence that runs contrary to all official *policy*," Selene corrected. "In this case, I submit that the data and policy are misaligned."

"And you, Mr. Roarke?" Townsend asked. "What do *you* say?"

"I fully support Ms. Selene," I said, wondering what in the Spiral I was supporting her in. What the hell was this petition she'd filed, and when the hell had she filed it?

"So you also claim the Loporri are sapient beings?"

With a supreme effort I kept my mouth from dropping open. So *that* was the stick Selene had poked into the hornet's nest currently buzzing around us. "Selene?" I murmured.

"Last night," she murmured back. "While you were asleep."

I nodded. Now that I thought about it, I *had* half woken up in the middle of the night with the sense that someone was moving around the ship. But no one came into the dayroom, and I didn't hear any follow-up noises, and I'd drifted back to sleep.

I wished she'd at least talked to me first. I could have told her this wasn't a smart move, especially not with the rich and powerful of the Spiral obsessing over silver-silk. I'd have told her there were better ways of going about it.

And she would have reminded me right back that if the rich

and powerful were doing something evil, they deserved to have a stick poked in their nest, hornets or not.

"Mr. Roarke?" Townsend prompted impatiently.

But whether or not I agreed with her methods and timing, Selene was my partner, and I was absolutely not going to leave her twisting in the wind alone. "I do indeed, Consul," I said. "More than that, I believe Ms. Selene and I can prove it."

"I would be most interested in seeing this evidence," Townsend said. "Tell me where it is, and I'll send my people to bring it to me."

"Yes," I murmured, a sudden uncertainty creeping into my gut. The rich and powerful... and clichéd though it might be, government officials were all too often the epitome of both.

Did Townsend want the proof so she could send it up the ladder to the Alainn government and the Commonwealth's Chief Representative? Or did she want it so that she could make it quietly disappear?

"Yes," I repeated. "About that. The proof is in the Loporr colony a few kilometers up the mountains from here. It's obviously too late to go there tonight, but we'd be happy to show it to you first thing in the morning."

For a moment Townsend didn't reply, her eyes flicking back and forth between us, a measuring look on her face. "Yes," she said. "Well, here's the problem. Ms. Selene strongly implied in her petition that her evidence was in fact in Bilswift, not some cave warren halfway to Cavindoss. I flew all the way from Quisivoa specifically to review her claim, and I'm not at all pleased at being strung along this way. Do you have any evidence here, or don't you?"

"The evidence is in the Loporr colony," Selene said. "Surely after coming all this way, Consul Townsend, you can wait a few more hours to see it."

"I'm afraid you overestimate the strength of citizen petitions." Townsend pushed back her chair and stood up, her two aides hastily following suit. "As well as underestimating the number of demands on a Commonwealth official's time. Good evening." She turned toward the door—

"Fine," I said. "You want evidence? We'll show you."

Townsend paused and looked back. "Here?"

"Here and now," I promised, my mind racing. All we had were the three Vrinks that Lukki had hidden somewhere in Bilswift, and we didn't really have them.

Or did we?

"But we'll need an hour or two to prepare," I added. "Surely you can give us that much more of your time."

Again, she gave us that measuring look. "Let me guess," she said. "You don't actually have this evidence in hand?"

"It's close," I assured her. "We just need some equipment from our ship, and in a couple of hours we'll hand it over to you. While you wait, may I suggest Panza's Café? They do a very serviceable Earth barbeque."

"We'll wait here," Townsend said, her face going a little stonier. "Detective-Sergeant Kreega, you'll assign one of your people to accompany them."

"I'll go myself," Kreega said, her face and voice grim.

"Good," I said briskly, standing up and gesturing Selene to do likewise. Out of the corner of my eye I saw Sovelli start to stand as well, then subside. "We'll let you know when we're ready."

"One hour," Townsend warned. "After that I leave, and Ms. Selene's petition leaves with me."

We were back in the car, with Kreega once again sitting behind me, before the detective-sergeant spoke. "You want to tell me what's going on here?" she asked.

"Selene filed a petition, and we're going to offer supporting evidence," I said. "Weren't you listening?"

"I was listening just fine," Kreega growled. "I also know a con game when I smell it."

First Braun, now Kreega. Con-game smelling must be a local hobby. "It's not a con game," I assured her. "Well, maybe a little. What do you know about what's going on in your city?"

"I *know* everything," Kreega said, a hint of bitterness creeping into her voice. "I can't *prove* any of it."

I looked sideways at Selene. She kept her eyes on the road ahead of us, but gave a small confirming nod. "Would you like to?" I asked Kreega.

For a few seconds she was silent. "It can't be done illegally," she warned. "I can't make it stick if I get the evidence illegally."

"Don't worry, I've got you covered," I said. "What do you know about Consul Townsend?"

"Not a thing," Kreega said. "You really think the Loporri are sapient?"

"We've seen evidence of it," I told her. "Whether we can

get the Commonwealth to agree is an entirely different story."

Kreega snorted. "Don't know why. They throw around decisions like that all the time."

"This one might be a little different," I said. "But let's cross that footbridge when we get to it. Selene and I will need a few minutes in the *Ruth*, then we'll be ready to go."

"Just don't call in another petition," Kreega warned. "You created enough of a rat's nest with this one."

"No more petitions," I promised. "As for the rest..." I smiled tightly. "I think we can persuade Consul Townsend to handle that herself."

I'd told Townsend that we needed to pick up some equipment. Fortunately, we mostly just needed to get to our phones.

The first call was quick, though not without requiring some fancy verbal footwork. The second, to Graym-Barker's backup agent—a man named Maijo—who'd finally arrived in Tranlisoa took more time and considerably more persuasion. For that one I needed to pull out every talking point in my repertoire, add in several invocations of the admiral's name, and slather on a layer of pure unadulterated bluff. But in the end, he reluctantly agreed to cooperate.

At least, I was pretty sure he agreed. There was probably still a thirty percent chance he would reconsider as soon as my dulcet tones were out of his ear.

But it was the best I had. If he reneged... well, I still might be able to make this work.

Explaining the plan to Selene and convincing her to give it a shot fell somewhere between those two extremes.

The evening rain had started by the time we rejoined Kreega. "I was starting to wonder if you'd gotten lost," she growled as we dripped our way into the car. "Where are we going?"

"Not sure," I said. "Selene?"

"We'll start in the northeast part of town and work our way south," she said. Outwardly, her voice and demeanor were calm, but I could see the tension in her pupils. "With the wind coming from the west, that gives us the best chance of finding them."

I nodded and turned the car that direction. Consul Townsend had given us an hour, and we'd already used up a third of that. If she was a stickler this whole thing might still go sideways.

But if I was right about her I was pretty sure she would wait as long as it took.

I still didn't have a full grip on the timeline surrounding Lukki's murder, but it hadn't sounded like she'd had a lot of time to move the Vrinks from the blue-and-white-fenced house to their final hideaway. With that in mind, I set up the first part of our grid search in the neighborhoods near that area. Under normal circumstances, this kind of search would be the proverbial slice of quiche, but with the rain doing its best to wash all relevant aromas out of the air we needed to get closer to the source than we otherwise would have.

We'd covered a fifteen-block area and were dangerously close to Townsend's deadline when we found them.

"Are you sure?" Kreega asked, frowning out the window at the dilapidated house I'd now parked in front of. "This place looks like it's been abandoned for years."

"Probably exactly what Lukki hoped everyone would think," I told her, eyeing the house and assessing my entry options. Straight through the front door, I decided. "Note that what Selene is smelling is cooking odors. The Vrinks are *cooking*."

Kreega muttered something under her breath. "Unless someone is in there with them."

"No," Selene said. "They're alone. They're also using the same mix of spices and fungi I smelled at the colony."

"Something else to add to our sapient attributes list," I said, opening the door. "I'm going to check things out. You give Townsend a call and give her the address."

"Wait a minute," Kreega called after me as I got out of the car. "You can't go in there. Interfering with the scene will give Townsend grounds for dismissing the petition."

"Trust me," I said, giving her my best confident smile before heading across the small lawn to the front door. It was locked, but under the circumstances I figured that Lukki hadn't had time to be clever.

I was right. Two minutes later I found the key in an artificial rock slab partially shielded from the neighbors' view by a ragged bush. I opened the door to a familiar whiff of pungent cooking aroma, and slipped inside.

They were back in the kitchen, just as I'd envisioned: three Vrinks, seated facing each other in an equilateral triangle formation, eating with their fingers from a steaming pile of spiced mushrooms on a flat board on the floor between them. They looked up as I entered, then returned to their meal. The room was dark—the building's power had probably been cut off years ago—but there was enough light coming in through the dusty windows for me to see the glints from the threads of silver-silk hanging from the lumps in their arms and torsos.

Time to get to work.

I had finished my task and was waiting by the front door, watching through the peephole, when a car rolled up behind ours and Townsend and Sovelli climbed out. Kreega and Selene were waiting for them, and the three humans held a brief discussion before Kreega led the way through the matted ground cover to the house.

I waited until they were under the roof overhang, then opened the door. "Greetings," I said, backing up to let them in. "Thank you, Consul, for giving us the few extra minutes we needed."

"The wait had better be worth it," she warned. "Where are they?"

"Kitchen," I said, gesturing down the hallway. "Afraid there's no light in here."

"Not a problem," Sovelli said, producing a flashlight. He flicked it to lantern mode, bathing the entryway in soft light. "Down there?"

"Yes, sir," I said, again pointing the way. "They're eating, so try not to disturb them. *Cooked* food, you'll note," I added.

"Which you could easily have prepared for them," Townsend said tartly as she followed Sovelli down the hall. "I know procedure out here isn't exactly professional, Detective-Sergeant Kreega, but you should at least have known better than to let him come in alone."

Kreega didn't answer, but flashed me a dark look as she passed. I gestured to Selene, and we joined the procession.

We entered the kitchen to find things exactly as I'd left them, except that the three Vrinks were now surrounded by Townsend, Sovelli, and Kreega. For a moment the three of them just stood there, staring at the aliens. "These are them?" Townsend asked. "These are the Loporri?"

"Vrinks, actually," I corrected. "An important subset of the Loporr species." I braced myself. "Selene?"

"Consul Townsend," she murmured. "And Detective-Lieutenant Sovelli. Not Detective-Sergeant Kreega."

I nodded. That was pretty much what I'd expected.

"Consul Townsend and Detective-Lieutenant Sovelli what?" Townsend asked, frowning at Selene.

"I asked Selene earlier to tell me which of you were surprised by the Vrinks' appearance," I told her. "From the changes in your scent, she concluded it was the two of you."

"What are you talking about?" Sovelli demanded, dropping his hand to his holstered GovSev 6mm.

"I'm talking about the Vrinks," I said, feeling a flood of revulsion as I looked at both him and Townsend. An official supposedly dedicated to the Spiral's sapients, and a badgeman supposedly dedicated to serving all in his community. "I'm talking about the beetle parasites that should have threads of silver-silk dangling from them, and your surprise that those threads aren't there. I'm talking about the reason very bad people like Lukki kidnap Vrinks and sell them all across the Spiral, and why some of the people at the very top of the food chain have been making sure the Loporri and Vrinks remain classified as non-sapient so that the quiet trade remains only moderately illegal."

"You say there should be silver-silk threads," Kreega said, still clearly trying to catch up. "What happened to them?"

"Simplest thing in the world," I said, producing the small set of scissors I'd brought from the *Ruth*. "I cut them off."

"What?" Kreega asked, still clearly confused. "Why?"

"Because each of them is worth thousands of commarks," Townsend said, glaring at me.

"Which I don't actually care about," I told her. "What I cared about was catching you and Sovelli knowing something you weren't supposed to know. Weren't you listening?"

"Oh, we were listening," Sovelli assured me darkly. "Unfortunately for you. Because your little trick is going to cost you."

"Maybe," I said. "Maybe not."

"No, it definitely is," Sovelli said, drawing his GovSev. "Sorry, Detective-Sergeant Kreega. You were just at the wrong place at the wrong time."

"You really think you can get away with murdering three people, one of them a badgeman?" I asked, watching Selene out of the corner of my eye. So far, nothing. "I don't care how high the rot goes, the people making money from the silver-silk trade are going to stick their necks out only so far for you."

"You might be surprised," Sovelli said. He gestured back toward the front door. "No, actually, you probably won't. Not going to live long enough. Okay. Back in the car, all of you. Time to take a little drive up the mountain."

"Where we'll come upon the perfect place for a tragic accident, I assume?" I said, not moving. Where the hell were they? "I don't think you understand just how hard a sell that's going to be. Experienced drivers like Detective-Sergeant Kreega don't just drive off the road, you know."

"She won't be driving," Sovelli said. "You will. And when she tries to get you to pull over—well, things like that happen sometimes."

"Yes," Selene murmured.

Finally. "I suppose." I cleared my throat. "Speaking of being surprised...Braun?"

"Yeah, we're here," Braun growled as he and the four Ylps appeared in the doorway leading from the kitchen to the house's garage.

Their weapons pointed squarely at us.

CHAPTER NINETEEN

———— ❖❖❖ ————

"Who the hell are *you*?" Sovelli demanded.

"The official owners," I told him, gesturing at the Vrinks. "Well, as official as these things get. You cut it a little close, there."

"Wanted to scout the area first," Braun said, gesturing a silent order at Sovelli. The detective-lieutenant hesitated; then, with clear reluctance, leaned over and put his GovSev on the floor. "Needed to make sure it wasn't a trap. Couldn't believe they would come here without backup."

"They knew they'd need to dispose of us and didn't want any awkward witnesses," I said. "Which is good news, actually. It means Sovelli's the only one of his force who's in on the graft."

I gestured to the Vrinks, still working on their meal. "Anyway. Here's the package, as promised. I suggest you get it aboard the Ylpea ship and off Alainn as quickly as possible."

"Sounds like a plan." Braun hefted his gun. "First, how about all of you put your weapons and phones on the floor?"

We complied, Kreega reluctantly, Townsend icily, Sovelli borderline apoplectically. The three Ylp guards collected our abandoned hardware and then herded us into a corner of the kitchen while Braun carefully sprayed a sort of liquid plastic onto the Vrinks' upper arms. "You don't really think you have to worry about Loporr hunters here, do you?" I asked as he and Scarf eased their prizes onto their feet.

"Never hurts to be careful," Braun said. "Here's how it's going to work. We go out that door and seal it behind us. You stay inside and behave yourselves, and no one has to get shot."

"And you load the Vrinks aboard that Ylpea ship out there?" Kreega asked.

"You catch on fast," Braun said approvingly. "If the badge-men watching the port are smart and don't interfere, they won't get shot, either."

"I don't think you'll have to worry about the Bilswift badge-men," I said. "I'm betting Consul Townsend has them all back at the station helping her aides with some nonsense paperwork." I raised my eyebrows at Townsend. "Or am I wrong?"

"Some of them are also at Panza's," Kreega said, glaring bitterly at Townsend. "Zilor checked in with me while we were waiting outside, said they'd gotten a tip that a big contraband deal was about to go down in there."

"So, no badgemen at the port," I said, nodding. "Looks like clear sailing, Braun."

"Yeah," he said. "One more thing." Silently, he held out his hand.

"Oh. Right." I dug the silver-silk strands I'd clipped from the Vrinks out of my pocket. "I'd have thought we'd at least get a finder's fee," I pointed out as I handed them over.

"Your finder's fee is to end this day with your life intact," Scarf said tartly as he reached over and plucked the strands from Braun's hand. "It is more than you deserve."

"Normally, I'd be inclined to dispute that," I told him as the three Ylpea guards started easing the Vrinks down the hallway toward the door. "But as my father used to say, *Arguing against people can be productive. Arguing against leveled guns usually isn't.*"

"Smart man, your father," Braun said. He waited until Scarf and the others had disappeared down the hallway, then followed, keeping his Blackman trained on us. "Nice and quiet, now, and no one has to get hurt."

"For an hour?" I suggested.

"Better make it two." Braun gave Townsend a speculative look. "On second thought, sit tight until sunrise. Little Miss Fancy here could use a lesson in how the lesser people live." With a sardonic smile, he disappeared into the hallway. Straining my ears, I heard the front door open and close, followed by the unmistakable hiss of a thermite seal-strip being applied.

"Garage," Kreega said, heading the direction Braun and the Ylps had first appeared from.

"No point," Selene said. "They already sealed the door. I can smell it."

"And the windows were already sealed when we got here," I added. "Also unbreakable by anything we've got with us."

Kreega ignored us, disappearing down the hall. She was back a minute later, looking just as angry but with a resigned edge to the expression. "So that's it?" she demanded, loading all her frustration into the glare she leveled at me.

"Not even close," I assured her. Crossing to the stove, I opened the oven door and retrieved the spare phone I'd brought from the *Ruth*. "To quote Braun, here's how it's going to work," I said, stepping over to Townsend. "A small contingent of EarthGuard Marines should have landed a few minutes ago at the Bilswift spaceport. At the moment—"

"EarthGuard *Marines*?" Kreega echoed, goggling at me. "What the *hell*—?"

"At the moment," I continued raising my voice to talk over her, "all they can do is detain the Ylps for unregistered animal cargo. A small fine, they can pay it instantly, and they can basically be on their way." I raised my eyebrows at Townsend. "*Or...*" I paused.

For a second she didn't seem to get it. Then, abruptly, her expression went from confused to horrified. "No," she breathed. "No. Not a chance. I can't."

"It's the only way to stop them," I said, holding out the phone. "If you call in a preliminary declaration of Loporr sapience, the Marines can hold them on kidnapping and sapient-trafficking charges. And *those* don't just go away with the wave of a commark-laden hand."

"I can't," Townsend repeated, a hint of dismay creeping into her defiance. "I'd be..."

"You'd be what?" I pressed. "Dumped on by the handful of people currently making money off the illegal silver-silk trade?"

"It wouldn't work anyway," Kreega said. "A declaration like that requires a full Commonwealth review and confirmation."

"But the preliminary assessment would be in force during that process," I pointed out. "Meanwhile, the Ylps and every other smuggling operation either goes frozen or unravels."

Townsend shook her head. "No."

"As you wish," I said with a shrug. "You still should call your friends. Only now you should warn them that the Bilswift connection is done. No more Vrinks, no more silver-silk. Ever."

"What are you talking about?" Sovelli demanded. "If you're thinking about slaughtering all of them—?"

"Is *that* your first thought?" I cut him off, feeling my eyes widen. "Mass murder?"

"Don't be squeamish," he growled. "They're just animals. And it's the only way to permanently stop the trade."

"No, they're sapients," I corrected him. "And you *really* need to work on developing some imagination. The footbridge from Seven Spirals is the only way to the Loporr colony. A few satchel charges, and the bridge goes poof."

"Aircars—"

"Can't land there," I said. "You know it, I know it, and I'm pretty sure your overlords know it."

I turned back to Townsend. "Your choice, Consul. Declare the Loporri sapient and continue with a controlled distribution of their silver-silk, or sit there and watch it dry up before your eyes."

"They'll kill you," Townsend said softly. "One of them will order your death in reprisal."

"They might succeed," I acknowledged, forcing my voice to remain calm. "They might not. Either way, the silver-silk trade will still be gone."

For a long minute no one moved. Then, with clear reluctance, Townsend reached out and took the proffered phone. "They're going to hate you," she warned. "They're going to hate us both."

"I've been hated by worse," I said. "And really, I wouldn't worry about your career. There are a lot of people out there, many of them influential movers and shakers, who stand ready to loudly celebrate visionaries like you who can see past physical limitations and find the shining souls that lie beneath the surface."

She gave me a disbelieving and rather scornful look. "You aren't serious."

"Trust me," I assured her. "That is *exactly* how they talk."

Taking a deep breath, Townsend punched in a number.

❖   ❖   ❖

By the time Zilor and the other badgemen responded to Kreega's call to get us out of Lukki's hideout, the brief spaceport battle was over.

For Scarf and his three Ylpea guards, so were their lives.

"I hope you're happy," Kreega said, glaring at me across her desk, "with the mess you've made of my city."

"Sorry," I said. I wasn't particularly sorry right now—I was too tired for that much emotion. But then, her glare didn't have much genuine anger behind it, either. It had been a very long day, and an even longer night.

But fatigue apart, emotion or not, she was right. Bilswift and Alainn would never again be quite the same.

"Maybe you should focus on the silver-silk lining," I said. "Your founders hoped this place would draw in tourism. Now, with a brand-new group of sapients, that might happen. Native village, lectures on customs—the whole works. It's happened before."

"Except that in those places tourists could go right in and see the sapients up close," Kreega said. "They can't do that here."

"They can get close enough," I assured her. "Just because aircars can't land doesn't mean they can't hover off the side of the mountain and let people look inside."

Kreega snorted. "Yeah. Big thrill."

I shrugged. "Whale watching on Earth and Urgil sighting tours on Hopstead are very popular. But those details will be up to you and the city fathers." I stood up. "If that's all, Selene and I need to get back to work."

"That's *not* all," Kreega said, pointing me emphatically back into my seat. "There's still a little matter of four murders, remember?"

I sighed to myself. I'd hoped she'd forget about those long enough for Selene and me to get out of Bilswift and over to the Tranlisoa StarrComm center. "I'd assumed the Ylps were responsible."

"That would be convenient," Kreega said. "Especially since they're all dead and can't be questioned. Problem is, the Ylps were armed with firearms and the victims were killed with plasmics."

"Have you checked out Kiolven and Venikel?" I asked. "I know Patth sometimes carry plasmics, and Braun said he saw Willie's killer in a Patth robe."

"Of course I checked them out," Kreega said. "They were in Tranlisoa on business when Lukki was killed."

"Kiolven might have been," I said. "But not Venikel. He was the one who jumped me our first night in town."

Kreega frowned. "Are you sure? The Tranlisoa badgemen confirmed their alibi."

"You assume human badgemen can tell one Patth from another."

"Well, there *is* some very good computer ID software available," she pointed out. "But fine, let's assume you're right. What's their motive for the murder?"

"They might be working with Galfvi," I said. "We know now that Galfvi was going behind Lukki's back to get those Vrinks to the Patth ship that's sitting out there in your spaceport."

"*Formerly* sitting out there in my spaceport," Kreega corrected. "They left about an hour after the battle."

I sighed. Stuck here giving statements and being debriefed, I hadn't heard that particular bit of news. "Which pretty much proves they were Galfvi's buyers."

"Or it proves they get nervous around EarthGuard Marines and gunfire," Kreega said. "Can't really nail it down."

"Especially now that they're gone," I said. Yet another group unavailable for questioning. "So where are Kiolven and Venikel now? Are they still in Bilswift, or have they also faded into the sunset?"

"I assume they're still around," she said. "We've been a bit busy here, you know." She raised her eyebrows. "Speaking of alibis, I should point out that you and Selene *were* here in town at the time of Parsons' murder. Actually, come to think of it, you were in town for all four murders."

And here we were, back where I'd always known we would end up. "Motive?" I asked.

"Tirano, of course," Kreega said. "You were looking to free him from his slavery—excuse me, his *indenture*—and so methodically took out Parsons and everyone else who might have a claim on him."

"There are easier ways to break an indenture than murder."

"Maybe," Kreega said. "But not any more profitable ones. Badgeman Zilor told me you suggested he file bounties on Parsons and her people."

"Whoa," I protested. "I never *suggested* he do that. He asked how the bounty hunting business worked, and I told him."

"Still suggests you were thinking about the possibility," Kreega said. "You aren't planning to leave town anytime soon, are you?"

"As a matter of fact, we are," I said stiffly. "Selene and I need to go to Tranlisoa to make a StarrComm call."

"Are you taking your ship?"

"Have you seen our ship lately?" I countered. "No, we'll take a shuttle. Probably drive to Cavindoss and take one of the ones from there."

"Mm." For a moment Kreega studied my face. "You're smart, Roarke. I'll give you that. Smart, resourceful, and I get the feeling you're okay with skating over the line if you think it necessary. Not to mention being able to whistle up a squad of Marines on short notice. In my experience, all of that makes for a bad combination."

"Sometimes the job requires that kind of footwork," I conceded. "But I always try to arrange things so that it doesn't."

"And you're glib on top of it," she said. "Your father's influence, no doubt. All those aphorisms of yours . . . but that's beside the point. The point is that you're a suspect in four murders, and I'm going to keep at you until I know for sure one way or the other where you fall."

"Fair enough," I said. "Can I get back to my work now?"

"As long as you don't leave Alainn," she said. "Is Tirano still aboard your ship?"

It was a question I'd been expecting in one form or another ever since the interview began, and I was ready for it. "Not unless he dematerialized and sneaked in through the *Ruth*'s cutter array," I said. "Which you already know, of course, since you've had your badgemen watching it practically since we landed."

"Minus one or two gaps," Kreega said, watching me closely. "You're saying you wouldn't give him refuge if he asked for it?"

"That's an entirely different question," I pointed out. "But I'd probably go along with the Commonwealth legal standard of innocent until proven guilty. Unless you have evidence that he's involved with the murders?"

Kreega shook her head. "You misunderstand my interest. I simply note that he's one of the few remaining people connected to Lukki Parsons who's still alive. I'd like to keep it that way, at least until we've had a chance to talk to him."

"A noble goal," I said. "Are you extending the same consideration to Braun?"

"I'd be more than happy to do so," she growled. "Unfortunately,

Mr. Braun managed to slip away from the port confrontation just before all the shooting started. We haven't seen him since."

"Can't really blame him," I said. "Good luck tracking him down. If Tirano comes knocking at the *Ruth*'s entryway, I'll be sure to let you know." I frowned as a sudden thought struck me. "One more thing. Was Lukki armed when you found her?"

"She was never armed," Kreega said, frowning. "She always said she had people for that."

"Yes, she told me that, too," I said. "Good morning, Detective-Sergeant. And do get some rest."

Once again, I turned to the door. This time, Kreega didn't call me back.

Selene was waiting in the outer office. "You finished?" I asked as she stood up.

"Yes, a few minutes ago," she said. "You?"

I nodded. "Let's get back to the ship. I need a couple of hours of sleep before we do anything else, and I'm pretty sure you do, too."

"We could still make the six o'clock shuttle from Bilswift," she said as we walked outside to our car. "It would save us the drive to Cavindoss, and we could sleep on the way."

"Actually, I've reconsidered," I said, peering to the east where the glow of dawn was silhouetting the Loporr mountain. Somehow, the view made me even more tired. "I think we'll have you go to Tranlisoa alone while I go back to the portal."

Selene looked at me, her pupils showing surprise. "What for?"

"You said the thing was dead," I reminded her. "I want to figure out what exactly that means."

"It means it doesn't work anymore," she said, her pupils going oddly cautious. "It's broken."

"Exactly," I said. "And sometimes things that are broken can be fixed."

She remained silent until we were in the car and heading back toward the spaceport. "You want me to call the admiral," she said slowly. "You'll be talking to me on your phone from the portal, and I'm going to ask him how to fix it?"

"Exactly," I said. "From what I could see it looked like a Gemini, and by now they must surely have done some work on the set they picked up from Popanilla and Fidelio. If I can describe what I see, maybe send you some pictures to pass on to him, maybe they can tell me what's wrong."

"It's been sitting there for at least ten thousand years," she reminded me. "We assume working portals have some kind of housekeeping protocols that keep everything running. But without those..." She shook her head.

"I agree it's a long shot," I said. "But we might as well be as complete about it as we can. Especially since the admiral will yell at us if we don't."

"There's that," Selene agreed, all emotion fading from her pupils. She was as tired as I was, maybe more so. "How much sleep were you thinking?"

"At least four hours," I said. "That would still leave us enough time for you to drop me at Seven Strands and continue on to Cavindoss to catch one of their Tranlisoa shuttles. By the time you're on StarrComm with the admiral I should be inside the portal and ready to describe what I see."

"All right," Selene said. "But wouldn't it be better if we did it the other way? You go to Tranlisoa and I go to the portal?"

I shook my head. "No."

"There might be something inside the portal I would smell that you would miss."

"It's better the other way."

"Why?" she demanded, a flash of annoyance momentarily crowding out the fatigue in her pupils. "Because you think going to the portal will be dangerous?"

"No," I lied, knowing she would know it was a lie but too tired to care. "Because Graym-Barker is less likely to yell at you than he is at me."

She turned away, gazing out the windshield as I maneuvered us through the still sparse morning traffic. She knew the truth about my reasoning, or at least suspected it. But I didn't have the energy to argue.

Besides, I was also right about the admiral. Selene and her Kadolian senses were far more valuable to him and the Icarus Group than I was. That required him to at least make an effort to be civil to her. Me, not so much.

I skipped our usual parking place by the runaround stand in favor of something closer to the *Ruth*. We would theoretically be heading out again well before the evening rains and possible hail, and right now I didn't want to walk any farther than I had to.

Zilor had already put in a full night's work, but one of Kreega's other badgemen was back on duty. I didn't bother to wave at him as we drove past.

We got out, Selene still giving me the silent treatment, and headed the last twenty meters to the ship. I had one foot on the end of the zigzag when Selene suddenly jerked to a halt. "Selene—" I began crossly, looking back at her.

The rest of my complaint died in my throat. The look in her pupils... "What is it?" I asked.

She closed her eyes and pointed toward the river. "There."

I braced myself and stepped off the zigzag. "Show me."

Braun was bobbing gently in the water, tangled in a group of reedlike plants at the mouth of a small stream that trickled into the main river just west of the docks where Lukki's boat was berthed. From what I could see from the riverbank, it appeared that he'd been killed right there, probably while getting away from the spaceport firefight and heading for the boat.

It was also clear he'd been killed by a double plasmic shot to the chest.

I huffed out a sigh. Like Selene and I weren't tired enough. "Okay," I said. "You want to stay here on watch, or go back and tell the badgeman?"

"I'll go," she said, backing away from the body.

I didn't blame her. Even this soon after death, dead bodies started taking on a disturbing scent. Distantly, I wondered if Graym-Barker fully understood the full cost of our service to his organization. "Okay," I said. "Just tell him, and then go home. A shower, food if you need it, and sleep."

"What if he doesn't let me?"

"Plead excessive fatigue," I said. "Wave vague Kadolian physiology concerns in his face, maybe invoke life-threatening exhaustion. You know all the right trigger words—use as many of them as you have to."

"Okay," she said, still backing away. "What about you?"

"I'll be in when I can," I told her. "Just go."

A minute later, she was gone.

I took a deep breath, wondering vaguely how much sharper the mix of odors was for Selene, and huffed out a sigh. A long day, a long night, and another long day ahead.

With my hoped-for portal investigation work now pushed yet

farther into the distant future. I tried to imagine what the admiral would say about that, but my brain really wasn't up to the effort.

Gazing at the body, the last known member of Lukki's gang, I settled down to wait for the badgemen.

I'd been hoping Kreega would decide that Selene and I had done our part in this investigation, that we were too exhausted to be coherent, and that anyway she and her badgemen knew more about Braun than we did.

But this was Kreega, and she now had *five* murders on her hands. She brushed aside all of Selene's protests and warnings and hauled us both back to the station, apparently under the assumption that we had crucial facts about Braun's last day that she needed to know.

Which, in all fairness, we probably did.

She kept us there until nearly noon, when the preliminary autopsy was done. As I'd already concluded, he'd died from two plasmic shots to the chest.

"But what's interesting is that he doesn't seem to have gone for his own weapon," Kreega said. "That suggests he knew his attacker."

"Or that he was focused so hard on getting to the boat that he was caught off-guard," I said.

"Maybe," Kreega said. "Either way, you'll note that he was killed crossing Bosmo Creek, right at the moment he needed to concentrate on his footing. The perfect time for an attack."

"You can also add in the spaceport battle going on that would cover both the sound and the flash," I pointed out.

"*And* that the killer knew the best spot to intercept him," Kreega continued doggedly. Clearly, she was still pushing for either Galfvi or Tirano to be guest of honor on the hot seat. "That suggests intimate knowledge of Bilswift and environs."

"Not necessarily," I said. "Selene and I have only been here a few days, and she at least knew about both the boat and that section of the river bank."

"Really?" Kreega asked, frowning suspiciously. "Took a stroll along the river, did she?"

"Just checking out the area," I said. "Hunters don't like blind spots in their operational zones."

"I thought you were retired."

"Force of habit," I said. "Can we go now? We've told you everything we know, and from this point everything will just be fatigue hallucinations."

"Or maybe you'll just be too tired to lie," she said pointedly. "Fine. Go get some sleep. We'll let you know if we need you again."

"Just don't need us for at least a few hours," I warned.

Once again, Selene had finished her part of the debriefing ahead of me. She was waiting in a chair in the station foyer, her eyelids squeezed shut. "Wakey, wakey," I called softly as I came up to her. "Time to go to bed."

With a visible effort, she opened her eyes. "I thought we were going to Cavindoss," she muttered.

"Not yet," I said, taking her arm and easing her up out of the chair. "Probably not at all, actually. At this point we might as well call it a day and try to catch up on our sleep. If we hit the sack midafternoon we should be able to get up in time for you to take the six a.m. Bilswift shuttle. That'll leave me with the car, which means we won't have to coordinate a pickup when you get back."

"All right," she said as she stumbled toward the door. "You want me to drive back to the *Ruth*?"

I peered at her face. Normally, her eyelashes did a sort of slow, rhythmic beat, similar to how a snake periodically flicked out its tongue, and for the same air-sampling reason. Now, her eyes half closed, the eyelids and lashes were stopped dead. "That's okay," I assured her. "I've got it."

With the somewhat heavier midday traffic, the drive to the spaceport took an additional ten minutes. In my current state, it didn't feel like more than two or three years. I got us to the ship, parking even closer this time, then got us going on the ordeal of climbing the Alpine mountain that the *Ruth*'s zigzag had become.

Lurking among the cobwebs in the back of my mind was the thought that Tirano might have deadlocked the hatch. If he had, we were just going to sack out at the top of the zigzag, because there was no way I was going to try to negotiate our way back down.

Fortunately, Tirano had missed that particular aspect of the day's string of heavy ironies. I got the entryway open, maneuvered Selene through it, and closed it behind me. "Okay," I said, turning aft toward Selene's cabin. "Let's get you to bed—"

Abruptly, she stiffened in my arms. "He's gone," she breathed. "Gregory, he's gone."

It says a lot about my state of mind that I didn't even make the connection with my thoughts of two minutes prior. "Who?"

"Tirano."

I looked back toward the two cabins. The hatch into Selene's was closed. The one into mine, the one Tirano had been sleeping in, was open.

"Must have gone out the back door," I said, starting to walk again. "Or maybe out the front during the firefight."

"We have to go after him," Selene said, her voice flat and mechanical. "We have to find him."

"No, we don't," I said. "Not until we've had some sleep. Come on."

"But he's all alone out there," Selene said, clearly trying to work up some emotion for the situation and just as clearly failing completely.

"No, he's not," I said again. "He's got Galfvi, remember?"

Either she didn't remember, didn't care, or was too tired to argue the point. I got her into her cabin and onto her bed, and before I even got her shoes off she was dead to the world. I covered her with one of her blankets as best I could and went out, closing the hatch behind me. Backtracking to the entryway, I made sure it was locked and deadbolted.

And then, just to be on the safe side, I locked the hatch into the crawlway that led to the *Ruth*'s Number Two equipment bay's back door.

If Tirano wanted to take off without discussing it with us first, there was nothing I could do about it. But I could damn well make sure he didn't just waltz back in again whenever he wanted to.

I kicked off my own shoes on the way across my cabin. I had a vague memory of pulling up my blanket when the long-craved unconsciousness took me.

CHAPTER TWENTY

I slept nearly around the clock, awaking just after midnight with a growling stomach. I got up, went to the dayroom, and grabbed the nearest quick-cook meal in the pantry—ravioli, as it turned out—and tossed it into the cooker. I was just pulling out the steaming bowl when a bleary-eyed Selene joined me, her drawn face and pure white hair making her look more like the Ghost of Christmas Future than any living person. I sat her down, gave her my ravioli, and cooked up a second package for myself.

We ate mostly in silence, both of us still too tired for conversation. We finished, and I sent her back to her cabin while I did a fast and cursory cleanup. Then, after double-checking the *Ruth*'s various locks, I headed back to bed.

I awoke the second time at three-thirty, finally feeling human again. I had a shower, changed clothes, then went to the dayroom for a quick breakfast. While I ate I put together a pouch with a few meal bars and a couple bottles of water for my upcoming day trip to the dead portal, then went back to the engine room to snag a couple coils of rope and all the rest of our limited selection of climbing gear.

Years ago, with most of our bounty hunting centered in cities and other more or less civilized areas, I would have scoffed at the idea of lugging around outdoor survival gear. Our experiences on Popanilla with Easton Dent had persuaded me otherwise.

On the way back from the engine room, I heard Selene in the shower.

By the time I had everything packed away she had again joined me in the dayroom. "How are you feeling?" I asked as she selected a meal bar and breakfast cola and sat down across the table from me.

"Much more rested," she said. "I really didn't want to take all that time, but I'm glad you insisted."

"Me, too," I said. "Hard enough to hold your own with the admiral when you're awake enough to think straight."

"Yes," she murmured. "Gregory...I was wondering if we might want to hold off on that another day and instead go find Tirano."

"And if Huginn and the Patth find the portal while we're doing that?" I countered. "Rights of first possession is a nice theoretical idea, and planting a flag in virgin territory has a definite historic flair to it. But Huginn has the numbers on his side, and I don't think the admiral would be impressed by even the most philanthropic of excuses."

"Why do we care if Huginn finds it?" Selene asked, her pupils going a little frustrated. "It's *dead*, remember?"

"Unless we can fix it," I said. "Which is why this day is crucial. If it's permanently dead, then you're right, Huginn and Sub-Director Nask are welcome to it. But if it isn't, we need to find out as soon as possible."

She closed her eyes and nodded. "I understand," she said reluctantly.

"Good." I looked at my watch. "I got you passage on the shuttle this morning while I was eating. The landing pad is just south of the spaceport proper, not too far, but we should probably leave in half an hour or so."

"All right." She finished her bar and stood up. "I'll be ready."

My own preparations took only a few minutes, mostly loading the equipment I'd already picked out into my backpack.

And before we left, I made sure to unlock the hatch into the crawlway. Tirano might come back, and I was certainly willing for him to do so if it didn't involve me being murdered in my bed. More to the point, if Selene or I needed to use the *Ruth*'s back door I wanted it to be available.

The shuttle lifted precisely on time, the quarter-sized grav-beam towers raising it from the pad to where it was safe to kick in its thrusters. I watched it head toward the stratosphere, both to make sure it was properly on its way and also to make sure Selene didn't sneak off at the last minute to go Tirano hunting. Then, with my gear already stowed in the rental's trunk, I headed east into the mountains.

It was obviously necessary this time for me to have my phone with me, and I worried once or twice that Kreega would get a warrant for its location and become suspicious about where the gimmicked reading showed me to be. But right now I didn't really care what she thought. Besides, if she hadn't already figured out Selene and I weren't exactly what we seemed, she couldn't be very good at her job.

I'd told Selene I'd head up to Seven Strands to start my trek back to the portal. But between then and now I'd come up with a slightly different plan. On the walk back from our first visit I'd noted a few more of the easy-climb trees along our route, one of them on the far side of the Patth fence and not far from the jeep trail that seemed to offer reasonable access to the footbridge. If I could get up that tree and onto the bridge, it would save me a whole lot of walking.

It turned out to be harder to spot the target tree from the jeep trail than it had from the bridge. But after a couple of false starts and double-backs I finally found it. Strapping on my backpack with my main collection of tools and supplies and looping the rope coils bandolier-style over my shoulder, I worked through the underbrush to the tree and started up.

Climbing this particular type of tree, as I'd already discovered, was pretty easy. Working my way across to the footbridge through the tangle of other tree branches was less so. But with a little persistence and only a couple of scratches I made it.

I kept careful watch on my progress along the bridge, painfully aware that falling through a broken slat while I was alone would be far worse than doing so with Selene there to come to my immediate aid. But the structure remained secure, and after a few minutes I arrived at the end.

The portal, like the bridge, was just as we'd left it. I'd brought a more powerful light with me this time, and by its focused glow I could see that the hatchway I'd opened up was maybe thirty degrees around the hull from a straight-line connection with the smaller launch module section of the portal's double sphere. That meant that instead of my immediate drop taking me straight through to the launch module I was going to end up inside the receiver module, near the cusp where the two spheres met. Slightly less than ideal for initial transit purposes, but it would mean I would have a resting spot when it came time for the climb back up.

I tied my rope securely around the trunk of the nearest tall tree, double-checked the knot, and dropped the other end down the hatchway I'd opened. I'd brought a signal booster, just in case the portal metal interfered with my phone transmissions, and wrapped it around the rope right at the opening. From that position it should be able to pick up my transmissions and kick them out into the planetary phone system and vice versa.

I attached my ascenders to the rope and my boots, took one last look around at the clearing and the thick forest beyond, and started down.

I'd set my light to lantern mode and fastened it to my belt, and as I climbed down I could faintly see the distant curve of the receiver module's inner hull. There was a slightly musty odor, though possibly it had been worse before we popped the hatch and let it have a day open to the outside air. Fortunately, the rain didn't seem to have made it this far up the mountain, so hopefully I wouldn't have to wade through a fresh puddle at the bottom of the module.

The silence didn't bother me. All the other portals I'd traveled through had been equally noiseless. But the rest of the atmosphere was totally new and more than a little eerie. Other portals were fully lit, the glow coming from an unseen and untraceable source, and had been filled with breathable air that smelled like all impurities had been freshly scrubbed out of it. This place felt less like a portal than a tomb.

Halfway down, I finally understood why Selene had declared the place to be dead.

I reached the lowest point of the receiver module and unfastened the ascenders. The interface opening into the launch module was about three meters up the curved wall. I pulled one of my grappling hooks from my backpack, attached it to the other rope looped around my shoulder, and lobbed it over the cusp. It caught and I pulled and walked my way up to the opening.

I'd secretly held onto the hope that, even if the receiver

module's gravitational field was off, the one in the launch module might still be functioning. But it wasn't. I got up on the cusp and straddled it while I peered inside the smaller sphere.

My plan had been to turn the grappling hook around and flip the rope to the other side of the opening so that I could walk down the launch module the way I'd just climbed up the receiver module. But that turned out to be unnecessary. As with other portals I'd seen, the interior of the launch module was covered in a mesh designed to cover the controls, displays, and associated power and control cables. The mesh at the top of the sphere had sagged considerably in Alainn's gravity, as had the cables it was supposed to be holding in place, but in the lower section the mesh was still in place and offered a sort of broad rope ladder down. A quick test showed that the mesh would still take my weight just fine.

Still, with the memory of the near disastrous failure of the Seven Strands footbridge fresh in my mind, I decided at the last moment to go ahead and reconfigure the grappling hook and the rope to that side. It would be highly embarrassing for the mesh to fail somewhere along the line and leave me stranded with the means of escape sitting tantalizing a couple of meters above my head.

I worked my way to the bottom of the module, where I spent a few minutes studying the cables and unlit displays beneath me and the sagging cables and equally dark displays above me. Shifting my light back to spotlight mode, I methodically took pictures of every section of the module's inner surface, including close-ups of everything within easy reach. I made them into a file and fired it off to Selene, where she could access the pictures whenever she was ready to do so. Then, pulling out one of my water bottles and taking a sip, I turned off my light and lay down on the curved surface to wait.

Our timing had been based on the assumption that I would be walking all the way from Seven Strands, which put me somewhat ahead of schedule. On the other hand, we'd also assumed Selene would pass my photos on to the Icarus Group and let them do a quick analysis and gather some questions before she contacted me. The necessary time frame for all that was a lot harder to anticipate.

It was just over two hours after I'd sent the file and settled down when my phone vibed with her call. Sitting up straight, shaking off the light doze I'd fallen into, I keyed it on. "Selene?"

"I'm here, Gregory," she said. "Happy happy. You?"

"Dancing with joy," I gave the countersign we'd arranged. "You at StarrComm?"

"Is that him?" Graym-Barker's familiar growl came somewhat distantly from the other end. "Roarke?"

"I'm here," I called, hearing the subtle shift in the background as Selene switched her phone from private to speaker. "Nice to hear your voice, Admiral."

"I wish I could say the same," he said stiffly. "What in the name of God's green Earth did you think you were *doing*?"

I frowned. "Excuse me?"

"This political satchel charge you just dropped on the Commonwealth," he bit out. "Your big Loporr sapience claim. Do you have any *idea* the kind of uproar this is causing?"

"It seems to me that the only people who would be worried are the ones benefiting from the illegal Vrink trafficking," I said stiffly. With the opportunity of yet another Icari portal hanging in the balance, this was not the topic I'd expected him to lead off with.

"*And* the investigators and scholars over the past thirty years who concluded the Loporri weren't sapient and now look like idiots," he shot back. "*And* their universities and research establishments who rubber-stamped their findings and look like even bigger idiots. *And* the passionate and deceptively loud self-appointed defenders of public morals who have pounced on all of the above."

"Admiral—"

"Not to mention the quiet and highly secretive governmental sponsors who provide our funding and do not like seeing the name of one of their supposedly secret operatives splashed across every news feed and social grid in the Spiral," he finished darkly. "One has to wonder if you have a firm grip on our priorities."

As my father used to say, *Poking a helpless bear is some people's way of showing their superiority and dominance.* I'd seen that in superiors and clients before, and I was more than willing to sacrifice a little pride to keep things running smoothly. In this case, I'd been fully prepared to shift into humble mode, to explain that we'd been caught up in the moment and that it furthermore had been an important connection to our mission.

But that last one was just one jab too many. Because as my father also used to say, *Sadly, those people often forget that if they hit a particularly soft spot, it may not matter how well they think they have the bear tied down.*

"I have a firm grip on *my* priorities," I told him coolly. "Not sure about yours or the government pipers you've got calling the Icarus Group's tune. I *can* tell you I'm sitting in the middle of their biggest one. Do we want to get down to business, or shall we call it a day and go home?"

"We get down to business," the admiral said briskly. "From your photos it looks like there are two large access panels near the current bottom of the launch module. I assume you brought tools; I'm sending you pictures on how to open them."

"Okay," I said, frowning. There'd been a subtle change in his tone there, from angry bureaucrat to the perennially cantankerous mood I was more used to from him.

Was a quick switch like that really in his repertoire, and I just hadn't seen it yet? Or had the angry bureaucrat part been a rebuke he'd been ordered to give me despite a personal disagreement with either the substance or the philosophy behind it?

Not that it made any real difference. Whether Graym-Barker himself was mad at me or it was the people above him, it was still someone who held the *Ruth*'s finances in hand.

I'd always assumed the admiral was more or less in charge of the Icarus Group, with the money people shoveling over the necessary funding with no questions asked. I was now getting the sense that he was maybe just another employee like Selene and me. Higher up the food chain, but still subject to the whims of someone else.

If so, I really ought to make it my business to find out who that someone else was.

The pictures Selene sent popped up on my info pad. I turned my light back on, looked around, and found the two panels the admiral had specified. The bolts holding them in place didn't fit any of the Commonwealth standards, but my fancy midsized Proteus driver conformed neatly to the shape of the holes. The captions on the admiral's pictures had already warned me that the threads were backward from what I was used to, and a minute later I had the first panel open. "Got it," I announced.

"Here's a picture of the interior," he said. Right on cue,

another picture came up on my info pad. "Note particularly the blue glow coming from the long cylindrical tube—"

"Not glowing," I interjected.

"—and the"—he stumbled a bit at my interruption—"and the two pale yellow bulbs that look like melted hens' eggs."

"Also not glowing," I said, taking a picture of my own and sending it to Selene. "Aside from that, everything looks intact. No broken tubes or wires. No rust or scorch marks that might indicate a burned-out circuit."

There were a few seconds of silence as the admiral digested that. "All right," he said. "Seal it back up, and then—"

"Why?" I asked. "Why seal it, I mean? Are we trying to pretend to Huginn and Nask that we were never here?"

"Roarke—" He broke off. "Fine. Don't seal it, but do set the cover back on top of the equipment bay. At some point we might need to know which cover goes with which bay."

"Right," I said. That one actually *did* make sense—I'd seen systems where the cover or fastenings were integral parts of the mechanism, usually involved in safety interlocks. I slid the cover under the mesh and laid it on the bay, then moved on to the next panel. Another minute's work with my driver, and I had it open. "Ready with bay number two."

"Here's a picture," he said as another shot opened up on my info pad. "The glow on the central tube in this one should be a pinkish red—"

"Whoa," I said, frowning at the maze of equipment. "There's no tube."

"What?"

"I said the glowing red tube isn't there," I repeated, taking a photo of my own and then looking back at his. "In fact . . . let's see. Two of the three thick connector cables in your picture aren't there, either."

There was a brief silence. "What about the third one?" the admiral asked.

"The third one's there," I confirmed. The cable in question was a millimeter or so in diameter and bridged the space between a pair of connectors like the ones the missing set had apparently fit into. I looked back and forth between the bay and Graym-Barker's photo, feeling rather like eight-year-old me doing a *spot-the-differences* puzzle. "Everything else I can see looks like your picture."

"But nothing's running?"

"Nothing's glowing or chugging or making thruster noises," I said, trying hard not to be too sarcastic. As my father used to say, *The only known system that still functions with half its components missing is a government bureaucracy.* "Were you expecting them to?"

"A meter to the left is another access plate about the same width but half again its length," the admiral said, ignoring my question. "Do that one next."

I ended up opening ten more access panels for him. Nine of the underlying equipment caches looked just like the pictures he sent, though nothing in any of them seemed to be running.

The tenth equipment bay, like the second one I'd opened, was missing components. Four of them, to be exact.

"So," the admiral summarized as I lowered the last panel back on top of its bay. "Twelve panels, seven missing components. And those are just the ones you can reach. Who knows how many more are missing from equipment bays in the upper part of the module?"

I shined my light up at the sagging mesh and cables above my head. Actually, my guess would be that all of those were intact. Digging into them would be fine when the sphere's radial gravity field was up and running, but as soon as it went off—possibly when the first component was pulled—everyone involved would find themselves performing a fifteen-meter free fall. A maintenance person with even the slightest experience would know enough to start at the bottom.

Though the fact that the components hadn't been replaced strongly suggested this hadn't been normal maintenance.

On Meima we'd seen evidence of a battle. Had whoever was responsible for killing this Alainn portal gone the more subtle sabotage route?

But there was no point in bringing any of this up right now. The admiral was envisioning wholesale damage, and as my father used to say, *When someone already knows what answer he wants, it's usually best not to argue.* "That's a good question," I said dutifully. "But I'd need a full scaffold or repulsor-and-grav setup to look into that."

"I suppose you would," he said regretfully. "Another day, perhaps."

Even given my less than enthusiastic attitude toward the man, his manner, and his methods, I couldn't help but feel a flicker of empathy. Whatever Admiral Sir Graym-Barker's career path had been like before Jordan McKell and his team found the original Icarus portal, I had no doubt the device and the project had consumed his entire life for the seven and a half years since then. And up until this moment, he and the Icarus Group had had a mostly unbroken streak of success.

Though to be fair, a lot of the most recent successes were due to Selene and me. Not that the admiral seemed to notice.

"All right," he said, the regret fading into his business-as-usual mode. "That's it, then. Pack up and get out of there. Selene will return to Bilswift on the evening shuttle. Once she's back, you two will be free to return to your crockett hunting duties until and unless something else arises that requires your attention."

"Wait a minute," I said, frowning. "That's it? We're just quitting?"

"What more do you suggest we do?"

"I don't know," I said, floundering a little. "We know which components are missing. What if we take replacements from one of our own Gemini portals and plug them in here?"

"To what end?"

"To the end of seeing if the damn thing works," I said with a sudden flash of anger. After all Selene and I had been through, the Icarus Group was just going to abandon any further efforts to salvage something from the mess?

"Again, to what end?" the admiral persisted. "We would be trading one working portal for another. I see no real gain in that. Do you?"

"Well, there *is* the whole science thing," I said. "You remember science, don't you?"

"Calm down, Roarke," he warned. "Didn't you learn not to get emotionally involved in your work when you were a bounty hunter? Think it through. Best-case scenario is that we swap out one working portal for another. A portal, you'll note, that's buried up to the top of its receiver module in a backwoods planet like Alainn. A portal, moreover, being sniffed at by the Patth. Agreed?"

I clenched my teeth. "I suppose. But this is a Gemini portal. Aren't you curious to see where it links?"

"That's the best-case scenario," Graym-Barker continued, ignoring the question. "Worst case is that the reason those components are missing is that they burned out or otherwise failed. Absolute worst case is that something elsewhere in the system caused those failures, and would cause similar failure in any replacements. At that point we would have lost one working portal and gained absolutely nothing."

"I think that scenario rather unlikely," I said stubbornly.

"When you're gambling with irreplaceable alien artifacts, you learn to avoid the soothing siren song of the word *unlikely*," the admiral said. "As for your question, after ten thousand years I don't expect there to be anything of real interest at the other end of this particular Gemini. Odds are also very good the linked portal will be underground, necessitating a long and laborious process of digging it out."

"It would still be another portal."

"Which we would then need to transport back to one of our locales if we wanted to study it," he countered. "Unless it happened to already be in a location that would be useful for us. Dare I invoke the word *unlikely* on that possibility?"

I glared at the open equipment bay, wanting to unload a salvo of choice language squarely into the admiral's smugness.

But I couldn't. I'd seen the book of portal addresses—rather, the book that listed half of each of those address—and the Icari had apparently sprinkled a *lot* of portals around. He was right; the odds of this one linking to someplace we would actually want to travel were pretty damn low.

"If that's what you think, fine," I growled, trying for some obscure reason to hold onto at least a shred of dignity. "Thanks for your time. Selene, I'll be waiting for you at the shuttle landing pad when you get in."

There was no answer. Mouthing a curse, I keyed off my phone, shut down my info pad, and packed them both away. I looked around, making sure all the access panels were on their proper equipment bays, and turned toward the opening to the receiver module.

And paused, a petty and very unprofessional thought popping into my head. The Icarus Group was just going to wave away all the effort Selene and I had put into this and abandon the portal to the Patth?

Fine. Their job, their money, their decision. But in that case, I was at least going to grab myself a souvenir.

The connectors holding the remaining cable in that second bay took a little ingenuity to loosen. But once I figured out the proper technique, they were easy enough to unscrew. I'd originally thought of taking only the cable, but the cable plus one connector turned out to be a perfect fit for the larger of the two hidden compartments in my artificial left arm. The other connector would fit in the smaller compartment if I dumped my collection of knockout pills, and for a moment I was tempted to walk out with a complete set.

But those pills had proved awfully useful in the past, and even in my current state of snit I had enough brain power to organize my priorities. The cable and one connector would have to do.

I replaced the tools in their case and stuffed everything into my backpack. With the spare rope again coiled over my shoulder I headed back up the inside of the launch module, allocating my weight equally between the mesh and the rope-and-grappling-hook setup I'd left anchored to the cusp. It would be a long climb back to ground level, but with the ascenders doing most of the work it would be more tedious than tiring. I reached the cusp, once again balancing myself there, unhooked the grappling hook and turned it around—

And felt my breath freeze in my throat.

The rope I'd left hanging from the tree at the edge of the clearing, the rope that was my only way out of here, was gone.

CHAPTER TWENTY-ONE

$$\diamond\diamond\diamond$$

As my father used to say, *Panicking in a crisis is the worst thing you can do. Doing absolutely nothing is second worst.*

I had my phone out again almost before my stunned brain fully grasped the situation I was in. I punched in Selene's number and held the phone to my ear, mentally crossing every finger I had.

A waste of effort. No signal, no connection, no Selene. The booster had been attached to the rope, and whoever had made off with the rope had obviously taken the booster along with it.

Either the portal metal was completely blocking my attempt, or the metal plus my distance from Bilswift plus Bilswift's semirural status was doing so.

But right now none of that mattered. What mattered was finding a way out of here, and finding that way fast.

Because the rope hadn't just pulled itself out of the receiver module. Someone was out there, someone who didn't want anyone poking around the portal, and I doubted that person would be satisfied with just cutting off my escape. If he wasn't still up there preparing to shoot at me, it was because he'd headed out to find allies or maybe a couple of sticks of explosives.

Or else he'd simply gone for something to cover the hatchway with so he could shovel on enough dirt to make the portal my tomb.

Selene might be able to rescue me. She certainly knew where I'd been, and when I failed to show up at the shuttle she would know something was wrong and come straight here.

But if my playmate knew about me, he surely also knew about her. I had to get out of here before he turned his attention in that direction.

The full-range Icarus-type portals that could connect to any other similar portal had receiver modules that were forty meters across. The receivers for the smaller, dyad-linked Gemini types like the one I was currently stuck in were only twenty meters across. A small favor, but at this point I would take all of those I could get.

I gazed up at the distant rectangle of muted light, running through the list of my assets. A reasonably well-stocked tool kit, at least for small, close-in work; a length of rope more than long enough to reach up to the hatch; a pair of ascenders if I ever got that rope anchored somewhere; three collapsible grappling hooks of different sizes; a collapsible shovel; a light; an info pad; a set of night-scope goggles; a plasmic; a knife; a currently useless phone; and the clothes on my back. Not exactly a sterling selection.

On the other hand, the portal also had a few resources of its own. There were the equipment bay access covers, which while thin seemed pretty sturdy, plus all of the equipment itself. I hadn't yet seen anything that might be useful in this situation, but there were still a few bays I hadn't looked into yet. And, of course, there was the mesh and the cables that the mesh was securing.

I shifted my gaze to the smooth curve of the sphere. There were access hatches like the one at the top of my prison all around the receiver module, each of which could go inward or outward on command. The controls for switching back and forth between inside and outside were probably as dead as everything else, but I'd already seen that I could still pop the releases and let gravity pull the hatches the rest of the way open. Normally, an open hatch would meld itself to the rest of the hull on the side it had been opened to, either inside or outside, flowing into it somehow and leaving no trace of itself until it was keyed to reclose.

But I'd also already seen that that melding wasn't working. So the question was, how much of a lip would an open but unmelded hatch create between itself and the dirt outside?

Easy enough to find out. I looked around, located one of the hatches a little ways up the module's curve, and went over and keyed it.

Unfortunately, unlike the hatch high above me, Alainn's gravity was merely holding this one in place. It took several minutes, some creative use of my Proteus driver between the cracked hatch and the hull, and a good part of my repertoire of curses before I finally got it all the way open.

The dirt behind it had a pungent odor to it, the kind of aroma that tourist brochures called *exotic* and most visitors probably blocked out of their consciousness after the first half hour. Selene could probably have told me which nutrients were in the soil, their relative proportions, and possibly even which local creatures had died to enrich the dirt for its role in the great circle of life.

I didn't care about any of that. What I cared about was that the open hatch and hull created a lip nearly twenty centimeters wide.

I had found my stairway.

I looked up again. Or rather, I corrected myself somberly, I'd found a stairway to the sphere's midpoint. The rest of the trip upward would require me to hang from some kind of rope-and-grappling-hook gizmo that I was going to have to invent on the spot.

But at least now I had a plan. Climbing onto the hatch lip, I reached up to the next hatch in line and keyed it open.

The first few were relatively easy. But as the hull's curve started to shift more toward vertical I discovered that the hatch lip alone didn't give me sufficient standing room to let me safely reach the next one up the line. Working my way back down to the bottom of the sphere, I returned to the launch module and picked out half a dozen equipment bay covers. If I could jam one of them into the soil behind each successive lip—and if it was strong enough to carry my weight—it would provide a more secure platform for me to work from.

And as long as I was in there anyway, I cut out a few sections of mesh and folded them into my backpack. If I could jam two of the grappling hooks into the dirt behind a close pair of the soon-to-be overhead hatchways, maybe I could string the mesh between them in a sort of work hammock while I leaned over and did the same with the third grappler or possibly the shovel.

Of course, that would leave me sitting or kneeling on a mesh whose tensile strength I didn't know, connected to grappling hooks stuck into dirt of questionable density and sturdiness, leaning out over ten or more meters of open space. I could only hope that I would come up with a better plan by the time I needed it.

Forty minutes later, I'd reached the vertical section of the sphere. From this point on I would be working above my head.

And I hadn't come up with a better plan.

I opened the midpoint hatchway, leaning out of the way as it flopped inward to land with a muffled clang along the inner hull. From this point on, the hatches wouldn't lie flat, but would instead hang vertically: small angles at first, then increasingly larger ones as I went up the hull. Could I use that fact to help with my climb? Maybe wrap the mesh around it instead of one of the grappling hooks?

Idly, I poked at the dirt behind the opening, trying to envision the engineering that would be required. Maybe I could push the hatch closed again after I'd wrapped the mesh around it, making a much more secure anchor than a grapple in dirt.

It would at least be worth experimenting with. I would work an access panel into the dirt in this hatchway, I decided, then stand on it and see what I could do with the next one up. Bracing myself, I set the edge of the panel against the top of the lip and started wiggling it into the dirt.

I'd gotten the metal maybe eight centimeters in when all resistance suddenly disappeared, sending me slamming chest-first into the side of the sphere, a cascade of dirt exploding through the opening and pouring down my chest and legs. I grabbed at the lip for balance, squeezing my eyes shut against the accompanying cloud of dust, my fingers digging easily into the dirt outside the portal. I waited until the dirt flow had finished and the dust was starting to settle, then carefully opened my eyes.

The dirt wall that had been behind every other hatch I'd opened today was gone. In its place—

In its place was open air. Musty, dusty air, but air.

Still gripping the hatchway lip, I fumbled my light from its belt anchor and held it up to the opening. No mistake; the dirt that had been resting against the hatch was now lying at the bottom of the sphere. In fact, the nearest wall of dirt was now nearly a meter away from me.

I stared into the gap for a few seconds, my brain trying to

make sense of it all. It was erosion, clearly, some kind of strange process that had leached the soil away from the portal and left this gap.

Only I couldn't think of what that process could possibly have been.

Water? But why here and not farther down the portal's curve? Had there once been a subterranean river through here that had dissolved the dirt but only to this depth? I leaned into the hole and pointed my light upward.

Whatever kind of river had done this, it had clearly been very good at its job. As far as I could tell the empty section ran all the way up to ground level.

I still had no idea what combination of environmental factors could have done this. But right now, that didn't matter. What mattered was that I could climb through the hatchway into the open void and continue my climbing on the *outside* of the sphere. All the fancy meshwork I'd envisioned, all the anchoring questions, especially all the risk of falling to my death—all of that was gone.

At least until I reached the point where the erosion zone terminated and the ground once again closed over the portal. But I was more than happy to save that bridge until I reached it. Easing myself through the hatchway, making sure my rope coil and backpack didn't get caught on the edge, I climbed into the musty air and started up.

I'd hoped the gap would run at least halfway up the side of the receiver module. I'd assumed it would end far sooner than that, maybe only after two or three hatchways.

Either Alainn had the Spiral's strangest erosion patterns, or the universe was just in a playful mood today. I was nearly to the top of the sphere, within a few meters of ground level, when I finally hit the end of the open area.

For a moment I toyed with the idea of opening the highest hatchway I could reach and trying to swing a grappler through my original hatchway and hook it on something solid. But that was an iffy proposition at best, especially with the opening in the middle of a clearing with nothing nearby but a few tall bushes. More important, at this point I was ready to trade in a fast uncertainty for a long, tiring, dirty certainty.

Hooking one leg over the nearest open hatchway, I put on

my night-scope goggles to shield my eyes. Then, unfolding my shovel, I started digging.

My first job was to get through a network of tiny root strands that seemed to underlie the thick layer of dirt, probably the reason that part of the surface had stayed suspended over the emptiness all these centuries instead of simply collapsing into the void beneath me. As I continued upward I found that the same tiny threads permeated the whole mass. There wasn't any connection I could see with the ground cover roots, and the threads didn't seem clustered beneath any of the bushes I remembered being near the portal opening. My best guess was that they were some kind of subroot system coming from some or all of the trees grouped around the clearing's edges.

I'd never dug upward before, and it turned out to be a rather mixed experience. On the plus side, I didn't have to lift each shovelful a meter or more up a gravity well to wherever was convenient for dumping it. On the minus side, all the dirt I wasn't having to lift was pouring squarely on top of my head and shoulders, sifting down my collar and occasionally into my nose and mouth. Still, my progress was much faster than it would have been digging down from the other side.

And with my unknown opponent lurking somewhere out there, time was way more important than cleanliness.

I'd estimated the layer of dirt to be about three meters. In the end, it turned out to be only about two.

The worst part of the experience, as it turned out, was having to worm my way out the narrow hole I'd dug. Not only was the dirt smelly and filled with slimy maggot-like creatures, but all my fears about falling to the bottom of the receiver module were now rushing back full force. It was only an assumption that the root network that had held up the soil this long would do the same for me, especially after I'd poked a human-sized hole through it. It wouldn't be a straight-line fall like an interior one would have been, but I still would hit the outer surface of the sphere pretty hard on my way down.

Unless, of course, my sliding path somehow diverted me through one of the hatchways I'd opened, which would then lead directly to that more bone-crushing fall I'd originally worried about.

But once again, the universe seemed to be on my side. I clawed my way to the surface, pushing through the ground cover—the little vines were actually rather fragrant where my shovel had cut through them—and pulled myself onto open ground.

I'd made it.

My muscles wanted to rest. My lungs wanted to enjoy the feeling of dust-free air. But my brain was in charge, and it knew I needed to get the hell out of here before my rope-stealing opponent came back to wreak whatever mischief he had planned.

My breakthrough into the open air had created a few reasonably sized pieces of sod with the viny ground cover still attached. I took a few minutes to pull the portal mesh pieces I'd cut out of my backpack, weave the ends into the vines at the edges of the hole, and arrange the sod pieces on top as best as possible. If I ever had to get out of the portal a second time, there was no point in showing potential enemies how I'd done it the first time.

The rope and booster were nowhere in sight. I spent a couple of minutes searching through the nearby woods for them without success before deciding I had better things to do right now. Brushing off the worst of the dirt as I went, I headed for the tree and the bridge.

After the ordeal I'd just been through getting out of the portal, the trip back to the car was almost literally a walk in the park. I climbed up the anchor tree, walked the short distance along the footbridge, then climbed back down to where I'd parked the rental. I paused there to partially undress and shake out the worst of the dirt that had collected in my shirt during the dig. I got my clothes settled again and headed back to Bilswift.

My ordeal in the portal had ended up eating up most of the day, leaving it too late for me to go back to the *Ruth* and shower before Selene was due to arrive. I drove instead directly to the shuttle area, and was sitting in the car watching as the craft came in for an impressively smooth landing. I waited until she emerged, then got out of the car and waved her over.

She was still too far away for me to read her pupils when the sudden twitch in her step showed that she'd spotted the dirt stains on my face and clothing. "Gregory?" she called.

"I'm okay," I assured her, opening the door for her. "Come on, let's get back to the ship. I'm dying to tell you about my day."

It wasn't very far back to our usual spaceport parking spot, but with the evening traffic the drive was long enough for me to run through the highlights. "It's a shame he didn't just cut the rope," she commented after I'd finished. "You'd have heard the impact as it fell into the portal, and might have gotten a glimpse of him."

"Not exactly the top possible silver lining on my list," I said.

"I also might have been able to get his scent off of it."

"Oh," I said. I hadn't thought about that possibility. "Yes. Though given how often the suspects around here wear gloves that might or might not have done us much good."

"True."

She was silent as I eased the car into its space. "Gregory... have you noticed how our list of suspects keeps shrinking?"

"Not just shrinking, but dying," I agreed sourly. "Lukki, Willie, the Javersin brothers, and now Braun. Looks like the only ones left are Galfvi, Kiolven and Venikel, Detective-Sergeant Kreega, and Detective-Lieutenant Sovelli."

"And Badgeman Zilor." Selene hesitated. "And Tirano."

I winced at the sudden sadness in her pupils. "He could still be mostly innocent," I reminded her. "We know from Zilor what a manipulative SOB Galfvi is. Someone with Tirano's naïveté could easily have been talked into one of his schemes."

Selene shook her head. "I know you're trying to make me feel better," she said. "And I do appreciate it. But no. I'd hoped we could stand in for his parents, at least a little. Teach him ethics and morals, give him guidance. But that didn't happen."

I sighed, the acid taste of guilt in my mouth. "Because we've been too busy with the portal."

"No," Selene said, the sadness in her pupils deepening. "Because he didn't *want* us to. Morals are *hard,* Gregory. Hard to maintain, hard to follow, sometimes hard even to justify. Without them, life looks so much easier."

"But is generally a lot more self-destructive."

"Because it only *looks* easier," Selene agreed. "In the long run, it isn't. But Tirano's too young to realize that." She closed her eyes briefly. "And he's a changeling."

"Maybe, but I'm not ready to give up on him just yet," I said firmly as I opened my door. I had no idea what we could do for him, but I wasn't about to give up on something that was this important to Selene. "Come on. I need a shower, we both need food, and I want to know what else the admiral had to say."

"It wasn't good," she warned as she joined me on the walkway. "We'll talk about it when we're inside."

"I can hardly wait," I muttered, looking around as we walked. The unmarked badgeman car I'd grown accustomed to wasn't anywhere in sight. Had Kreega pulled it off duty now that the Vrink trafficking thing had been resolved?

Or was it gone because she'd found Tirano?

I thought about mentioning that possibility to Selene. But it would only distress her, and anyway she'd probably already thought of it. We reached the zigzag and I started up—

"Wait," Selene said suddenly, leaning down to sniff the handrail. "Gregory, he was here. Tirano was here."

"When?" I asked, taking a couple more steps up the zigzag to get some extra height and giving the area a quick scan. The spaceport itself was mostly empty, but outside its boundaries Bilswift's usual mix of cars and pedestrians was going strong. I could see no sign of Tirano.

"Not long ago," Selene said, her eyelashes going like mad as she moved to one side. "He came from..."

She trailed off. "What is it?" I asked, coming back down.

"He came from over here," she said slowly, gesturing toward the *Ruth*'s stern and the river in the near distance beyond. "But then he left in *this* direction," she continued, pointing toward the spaceport exit and the city beyond.

"So he was planning to go into the ship, but changed his mind?"

"I don't think so," Selene said, her pupils registering confusion. "Venikel was with him."

"When he left?" I asked. If Venikel had been watching the *Ruth* and had been able to intercept Tirano—

"No, he was with him both ways," Selene said. "When he left, *and* when he arrived." She looked at me, apprehension now mixing with her puzzlement. "Do you think...?"

I felt my stomach tighten. Venikel walking Tirano to the *Ruth*, pausing there to make sure he left his scent, then heading the two of them off into the city.

"Yes," I confirmed, drawing my plasmic and double-checking the charge. "Tirano's the bait. You and I are the fish."

I slid the weapon back into its holster. "Come on. Let's not keep them waiting."

CHAPTER TWENTY-TWO

A cab would have been a nuisance for us to track down, requiring calls and time checks. A private car might have lost us the trail completely.

But then, this was *supposed* to be easy for us. As I'd already anticipated, Venikel and Tirano stayed on foot.

We'd been following their trail for about twenty minutes, and had entered a compact warehouse district, when Selene abruptly stopped. "No," she breathed. "Oh, no."

"What is it?" I asked, my eyes darting everywhere. Like the spaceport, this part of the city seemed largely deserted at the moment. Perfect place for an ambush.

"Burned flesh," she murmured. "I smell burned flesh."

I huffed out a sigh. And there was only one weapon I knew of that could do enough of that kind of damage for Selene to pick it up from this distance. "Where?" I asked.

She pointed to a small warehouse. "That one, or the one behind it."

"Okay," I said, taking her arm and pulling her gently away. "Go back to the *Ruth* and do whatever cleansing you need to. Kreega and I can handle this."

"Are you sure?" Selene asked, her pupils making it clear that she very much wanted me to be sure.

"Yes," I assured her. "Go on. I'll be there soon."

"All right." She looked at me with a mix of pain, revulsion, and guilt. "I'm sorry."

"It's all right," I said. "Just go."

I watched until she was out of sight. Then, turning back toward the suspect building, I pulled out my phone and keyed in the emergency number.

Kreega and her badgemen had been through a lot already this week. With five murders and a minor cultural upheaval on their hands, they probably thought things were as bad as they could get.

They were about to find out that things could always get worse.

Kreega and about half her force came in response to my call. Only Zilor and the detective-sergeant herself were able to make it all the way to the crime scene without having to drop out from the horrific stench.

"You might have warned us," Kreega muttered as we gazed at the charred remains of what had once been a living being. The tone of her voice made it clear she was breathing through her mouth.

"I *did* tell you it was probably a corona weapon," I reminded her. "But I'll admit that the reality far outstrips the theory." I waved at the warehouse's high windows. "And the closed windows don't help."

"Any idea who it is?" Zilor managed. Obviously holding onto his lunch with everything he had; also obviously determined to stick it out as long as his chief did.

I took a few steps closer to the corpse, noting the wisps of smoke still drifting off it. I wasn't any less affected by the sight and smell than Kreega and Zilor, but I had the dubious advantage of at least having smelled it before. "It's not Tirano," I said, a small piece of my brain making a note to call Selene with that news as soon as I could. "Too tall and not thin enough. From what I can see of the skeleton and joints, I'd say we're looking at what's left of a Patth."

"A *Patth*?" Kreega echoed.

"Is it Galfvi?" Zilor asked.

"Could be," I said. "I only saw Galfvi the one time, and didn't get a clear estimate of height or build. More likely it's either Kiolven or Venikel. Or possibly someone from that Patth ship might have come ashore before it left."

"If not that particular ship, maybe someone from one of the

two cargo ships that landed in Quisivoa last night," Kreega said. "Or the one that landed in Porsto this morning." She gave me a wan smile. "What, you don't think I keep an eye on what's happening on my world?"

"I should have known you would," I said, inclining my head to her. "Thanks for the reminder not to underestimate you."

"You're welcome." She nodded toward the corpse. "So what do we do now? Not much left for an autopsy."

"Which I gather is the reason the Patth like having their Iykam friends use them," I said. "Makes the victim much harder to identify, not to mention destroying most of the usual evidence markers."

"But it *could* be Galfvi?" Zilor persisted.

"I already said I can't tell," I said, frowning as I took a few more steps. The center of the corpse's chest...

"Something?" Kreega prodded.

"Not sure," I said. "There's an area in the center of the chest that looks..." I hesitated, but there really was no tactful way to say it. "That looks sort of twice-baked."

"Yes, I noticed that," Kreega said. "Like he'd first been shot with a plasmic?"

"Or possibly with a firearm at close range," I said. "Though those would have to be very impressive propellant burns to show up against a corona blast."

"So the killer took the second shot just to destroy the evidence?"

"I can't think of any other reason," I said. In point of fact, there were at least two other explanations I could think of for wanting to finish off the victim with a corona weapon. But that wasn't something I wanted to get into right now. "Regardless, an autopsy should at least be able to tell whether he was killed with a plasmic or a slug weapon."

"We'll get that started right away," Kreega said, pulling out her phone. "Anything else you want to tell me?"

"You mean about the crime scene?"

"Or about where you and Selene have been all day."

I turned back to her. Most of her face was occupied with not being sick, but there was enough left over to hold some dark suspicion. "You're joking," I said.

"Am I?" she countered. "You seem to know a lot about these corona weapons and the people who use them. More than anyone else around here knows."

Briefly, I considered informing her about Expediter Huginn and his gang of portal-hunters out in the forest. Huginn knew way more about corona weapons than I ever would, not to mention being able to commandeer the Iykam guards from those three Patth ships Kreega had mentioned.

But unless I could trot Huginn out in front of her as Exhibit One, bringing up his name would just sound like more convenient excuses.

"I need to get back to the *Ruth*," I said. "I need to see if Selene's all right. Can we talk about our day later?"

"I suppose," Kreega said, that look still on her face. "But let's not make it *too* much later. Say, in an hour?"

It would take them longer than that to process the crime scene, I knew. But Kreega didn't seem in the mood for logical arguments. "I'll try," I said.

"Make it a really good try," Kreega said. "Badgeman Zilor will drive you back to the spaceport."

"That's okay," I said, waving Zilor back. "You might need him here. I can walk."

"I said Badgeman Zilor will drive you."

I wanted to glare at her, but it just wasn't worth the effort. "Fine. If you insist."

"I insist," Kreega said. "Badgeman?"

"Yes, Detective-Sergeant," Zilor said. "This way, Mr. Roarke."

"In an hour," Kreega reminded me as we headed toward the warehouse door.

I nodded tiredly. "In an hour. Or as soon afterward as I can."

Selene was waiting for me in the *Ruth*'s dayroom, having dumped her clothing, showered off the scent of the burned Patth, and cleared out her lungs in the ship's clean room. "How are you doing?" I asked from just outside the hatchway. "Do I need to shower this smell off?"

"You're all right for now," she said. "The rain you came through washed enough of it off."

"Okay," I said, entering the dayroom and crossing to the pantry. I'd never gotten around to eating any of the provisions I'd brought to the portal, and was suddenly ravenous. "Let me know if that changes."

"I'm all right," she said. "Did you find out...?"

"One of the Patth," I told her. "From what I could see of the facial bone structure I'm guessing it was Venikel."

"The *hot badge* half of their hot badge/cold badge routine."

"Right, though if those were just the roles they were playing it might not mean anything about their personalities," I pointed out as I selected a package of cheese pasta and put it in the cooker.

"My point was that even if Venikel was playing a part, he might have overplayed it, or played it to the wrong person."

"That's certainly possible," I agreed. "You'd think he'd have learned to read his audience well enough to modify his act when necessary, but we've both seen people essentially talk themselves into getting shot."

"Which leads to the question of who shot him."

"Well, for starters it was someone with access to a corona weapon," I pointed out. "That drastically limits our list of suspects."

"Unless the killer took it from Venikel."

"Oh," I said, feeling stupid. Or maybe just tired. With me, that tended to go hand in hand. "Yes, that's probably it. I don't remember seeing him carrying one, but those robes of theirs could hide a small arsenal. It would certainly be the handiest corona weapon for the killer to get to. Oh, and before he was charred he was shot with a plasmic."

"Interesting," Selene said, disgust in her pupils. "So the follow-up shot was simply to destroy evidence?"

"Or to delay identification of the victim," I said. The cooker pinged, and I pulled out my meal. "But probably to wipe the evidence. Sorry—did you want something?"

"No, thank you," she said. "I ate on the shuttle."

"Okay," I said, pulling off the cover and digging in. "Speaking of the shuttle, Kreega wants us down at the station in an hour to tell her all about our day." I waved at her with my spoon. "So the admiral's not happy?"

"The admiral's quietly furious," Selene admitted, her pupils wincing. "I think it's mostly because of my petition."

I stared at her. "Seriously? I assumed that was just him delivering someone else's grump at us."

"If it was, it was a grump he mostly agreed with," she said. "He's already ordered Maijo off Alainn, and said we were—"

"Wait—he pulled our *backup*?" I interrupted. "What if we need help?"

"I asked him that," she said, her pupils going a little bitter. "He told me we wouldn't need any, because as soon as the *Ruth* was back together we're to leave Alainn."

"What if someone from the Commonwealth needs us to testify about the Loporri?"

"I assume he doesn't care."

Or he did care, but in the exact opposite direction. If Selene's petition got bogged down in the process or the bureaucracy, the Loporri and Vrinks could slip back into their former non-sapient status. Apparently, none of the shadowy figures above the admiral would be upset if that happened. "Well, luckily, the mechanics out there seem to be taking their time," I said. "Besides, we have five murders to solve."

"Six."

"Oh. Right," I agreed, scowling into my pasta. I really *was* tired. "The admiral have anything else to say?"

"No," Selene said. "But I had the impression that if we'd found a working portal he might have been more willing to support us on the Loporr situation."

"I wouldn't be surprised," I said. The portal was probably worth a lot more than the illicit silver-silk trade to whoever was above Graym-Barker in the food chain. But without the portal to balance their books, all they saw was the crater Selene's petition had made in their overall profit margins.

And suddenly, working for Graym-Barker and the Icarus Group looked less like a noble task and more like we were a minor footnote on someone's personal accounting sheet.

My phone vibed. I pulled it out, wincing at the ID. "It's Kreega," I told Selene as I keyed it on. "Good evening, Detective-Sergeant," I said. "Sorry, I'm running a little late."

"Don't worry about it," she said, her voice tight. "I'm calling to tell you not to bother coming in until tomorrow."

I frowned. "Trouble?"

"You could say that," she said, her voice taking on a hint of bitterness. "Bureaucrats from the Commonwealth office in Quisivoa have dropped in to interview all of us about our part in the space-port fracas where your Ylpea friends got themselves slaughtered."

"Not really my friends," I said. "I also understood the slaughter only happened because they ignored the Marines' order to surrender."

"It did, they did, and we have recordings," Kreega said sourly. "Doesn't mean the bureaucrats are just going to accept that. I'll let you know when you can come and talk to me about where you and Selene went today. Try to keep those memories fresh."

"Don't worry," I promised. "We'll be ready when you are."

I keyed off. "You heard?" I asked Selene.

She nodded, her pupils troubled. "Do you suppose they'll want me to testify, too?"

"They might," I said. "Not about the shoot-out—we weren't there—but possibly about the evidence I assume you listed in your petition."

"Yes," she murmured. "Do you suppose...?"

"I never suppose anything when it comes to bureaucrats," I said. "Double that if they're government bureaucrats. Depends on whether the Commonwealth reps here are for your petition or against it."

"From the way the admiral was talking, I assume most are against it."

"Possibly," I conceded. "But in this game that's less important than you might think. As my father used to say, *When it comes to political battles, the only numbers that matter are those of the rungs everyone's standing on.* Someone who wants their name in the Visionaries List in the history books might well be willing to buck an overall trend, especially if he or she doesn't have a financial stake in the outcome. We'll just have to wait and see which way the people with the heavy-duty lungs decide to make the wind blow."

Selene lowered her eyes. "I'm sorry, Gregory. I just wanted justice for the Loporri. I didn't mean to cause so much trouble."

"Don't worry about it," I assured her. "I don't mind making trouble if it's the right kind of trouble."

"But this is trouble with the Commonwealth," Selene said. "We know how to deal with criminals and badgemen. But bureaucrats don't make any sense to me."

"Oh, they're easy enough," I assured her. "Really. It's just a matter of playing along and finding out which answers they want. After that, all you have to do is make your answers sound enough like those until they're too deep in agreement with you to get out without looking foolish. As my father used to say, *Give a man enough rope, and he'll waste hours trying to untangle it.*"

I frowned suddenly. *Rope.* Hadn't Selene had some point about rope earlier?

She had. She'd wondered aloud why the intruder at the portal had pulled up the rope instead of just cutting it and letting it fall mockingly at my feet.

I hadn't had an answer then, and I still didn't. Pulling up twenty meters of rope didn't require huge amounts of physical prowess, but it still took more time and effort than a simple slash with a knife. Not to mention he'd had to deal with the knot I'd put in at the tree end.

The obvious answer was that he wanted the rope for something. But what? What made this rope so special that it wouldn't be easier to just go to the store and buy one for himself?

I smiled tightly. "Because he *couldn't* go to the store," I said under my breath.

"What?" Selene asked.

"I said because he couldn't go to the store and get a rope of his own," I said. Suddenly, all the pieces seemed to be falling together in my head.

"I need you to do a search for me," I said, standing up and crossing to the pantry, my dinner suddenly forgotten. Most of our limited collection of office supplies were in one of the drawers in my cabin, but I was pretty sure I'd seen a pen and pad of paper in here.

"What do you need?" she asked, pulling out her info pad.

There they were. "Remember us talking with Zilor about Narchner songs?" I asked as I scooped up the pen and pad and headed back to the table. "There's one in particular I need to track down. Just start with some kind of list, and we'll narrow it down from there."

"Got it," she said, eyeing the paper and pen curiously. "What are you going to do?"

"Write a note," I said. "A very long, very detailed note."

Detective-Sergeant Kreega answered on the fourth vibe. "Roarke?"

"Yes," I confirmed. "Did I wake you?"

"That's all right—I had to get up and answer the phone anyway," she said sarcastically. "This had better be good."

"It is," I said. "How would you like to go someplace interesting tomorrow morning and get away from the bureaucrats?"

"Only if I can sell my absence to them afterward," she said. "Does this interesting place of yours fit that bill?"

"I think it will," I said. "Oh, and we'll need to take your car. That all right?"

"Does this trip qualify as official badgeman business?"

"Very much so," I said. "How does six o'clock sound?"

"Like an hour before my alarm goes off," she said. "Still waiting for the punch line here."

"Punch line enabled," I said. "I'm expecting that Selene and I will be able to hand over a murderer."

There was a brief silence. "If this is a joke, stop waiting for me to laugh," Kreega warned.

"It's no joke," I assured her. "An early morning, a short trip, and we'll deliver you a murderer."

I pursed my lips, running through the logic and my list. *Most* of the pieces were in place, anyway. There were still a couple that I should probably track down. "And if we're lucky," I added, "we might be able to deliver two of them."

"All right, you sold me," Kreega said. "Six o'clock at the *Ruth*. I'll be there."

"*Two* of them?" Selene asked after I keyed off. "There are two different murderers?"

"Actually, I think there are three," I told her. "Though one might have been self-defense." I scowled at the remains of my dinner, long since gone cold while we'd been working. Another minute in the cooker, and I could finish it off and try to get some of that sleep I was so sorely behind on. I had enough of the pieces to make my case. Really I did.

But I didn't have *all* of them. And in this case, those missing pieces could make all the difference in the world. "And much as I hate to say it, we still have one more job this evening," I said as I stood up.

"Do you need me?" Selene asked.

I winced. She was as tired as I was, maybe even more so. "Well..."

"I understand." She stood up and headed for the dayroom hatch. "I'll get my jacket."

CHAPTER TWENTY-THREE

———— ❖ ————

It was still early enough for Panza's Café to be doing a brisk business, both in food and drinks. The noise level didn't change as Selene and I walked in, but I could see some of the patrons pause in their conversations to give us wary or borderline hostile looks. I ignored all of them and led the way back to the bar.

My old acquaintance Lefty was on duty again tonight. He spotted me as we approached, his expression more toward the wary end of the scale. "Evening, Lefty," I said as we took a pair of seats that had been conveniently left open right in the center of the bar. "How's business tonight?"

"Not too good," he said coolly. "Some of our regulars have fallen on hard times."

"Or have fallen, period," I said. "Sorry about Lukki and Willie."

"And Braun."

"And Braun," I agreed, mildly surprised that news of his death had already reached the general public.

Or if not the general public, maybe just the group I was interested in talking to. That could save time. "Speaking of Lukki, I was hoping to have a chat with anyone who might have worked with her," I continued. "I have a small business proposition to offer."

"Sounds like an exciting opportunity," Lefty said, his voice still cool and now edging into sarcasm. "If I see any of them, I'll be sure to let them know."

"Thanks," I said, pulling a folded twenty-commark bill from my pocket. "Just to make sure you don't forget," I added. Reaching to his hand, I pulled it toward me and pressed the bill into his palm. "Don't lose it, now."

He glanced at the bill, a hint of a smirk touching his lips. "Sure," he said. He turned away, fumbling a bit as something fell out of the bill. He stooped to pick it up...

I counted down the seconds, just for my own amusement. There were five of them before he stood upright again, staring at me with wide eyes, his right fist clenched tightly around the coiled-up strand of silver-silk I'd wrapped inside the bill. "To make sure you don't forget," I repeated. "We'll be at that booth over there. The one Lukki used to sit at."

Without waiting for a response I took Selene's arm and led her back toward Lukki's booth. "You think this is a good idea?" she asked quietly as we passed between the occupied tables. "Lukki's booth, I mean?"

"Unfortunately, I think we have to," I said. "It's what a challenger to her business would do to claim right of succession."

"But that area will still hold her scent," Selene warned. "That will make it more difficult to identify her other associates."

"I know," I said. "But again, it's what we have to do. And don't forget that the bug Braun told us about is presumably still active. If Galfvi's been tapping into it, and if he's still monitoring it, this may help flush him out."

"I thought you knew where he was."

"Ninety-five percent sure," I said. "Same ninety-five percent that I know who all the killers are. Clearing that last five percent is why we're here." I looked back at the bar as I ushered her into one side of our new booth. "Speaking of Lukki's associates...?"

Selene shook her head. "Lefty's not one of them. No smell of her, Willie, or Braun on him."

"Okay," I said, taking the seat across from her and keying my info pad for the menu. "I don't know about you, but I'm still hungry."

We'd been there an hour, and I was topping off my rack of ribs with a disappointing slice of Key Lime pie when Selene's pupils suddenly went alert. She gave me a sharp look—

"Mind if we join you?" a wiry man asked as he appeared beside her. Without waiting for an answer, he sat down, nudging Selene half a meter over toward the wall with his hip to clear enough room for himself. "Sometimes hard to find a good seat in here."

"Not really the case tonight," I pointed out. Another figure loomed in my peripheral vision, and I found myself being similarly hip-shoved as someone else moved into my side of the booth. I felt a brush of long hair across my cheek, caught the whiff of what was probably a local perfume— "Ma'am," I greeted my new seat mate. "I'm Roarke; this is Selene. And you are...?"

"Call me Fisher," the man said. He nodded to the woman beside me. "Call her Honey. We understand you have some goods for sale."

"Could be a sale," I agreed. "Could be a trade. Could be part of a larger business transaction."

"Good—glad we got that settled," Fisher said with a sort of brisk sarcasm. "You want to start again, this time with clarity?"

"Actually, let's start with some introductions," I said, watching Selene's pupils. Her reaction had been a good indication that at least one of these two had been in recent close proximity to Lukki or one of her late associates, but I needed to hear it from them. "Starting with how exactly you two fit into Lukki's team."

For a moment they eyed each other across the table. Then, I felt Honey give a small shrug. "We're the owners of her boat," Fisher said. "The *official* owners, the ones with all the legal documents. We ran her packages whenever she wanted to use the river or ocean."

"Excellent," I said. "Now we're getting somewhere. All right. I presume Lefty showed you our little conversation piece?"

"No, but he told us about it." Fisher's mouth twisted. "*After* he put it somewhere no one was likely to trip over it."

"Smart boy," I said, nodding. At six thousand or more commarks each, anyone else in the café would similarly have taken quick steps to protect it from sticky fingers. "The point is there are more where that came from. Twenty, maybe even thirty of them."

Fisher leaned forward a little, his eyes glinting. "Where?"

"Somewhere up the river," I said, mentally crossing my fingers. This was one hundred percent speculation, and if I was wrong it was going to damn us in double-quick time as not being even casual members of Lukki's group. But it was the only handle I had. "I'm pretty sure it was hidden aboard your boat's dinghy."

"The dinghy's *gone*?" Honey demanded.

I let out a quiet breath. So Lukki's boat *had* had a dinghy. That had only been an assumption, albeit a logical one. But now I had proof.

And the fact that there hadn't been any such auxiliary boat when Selene swam aboard—I'd checked that with her earlier—was fairly conclusive evidence that Galfvi had taken it.

More important, I was now almost a hundred percent sure I knew where our rogue Patth was hiding. "You didn't know?" I asked.

"We haven't been to the boat since Lukki was killed," Fisher growled. "The *hell*. So who took it? Wasn't Braun, was it?"

"I don't think so," I told him. "No, we think it was either Tirano or Galfvi. You know them?"

"I've heard of Tirano, I think," Fisher said. "Lukki never let us meet him."

"You sure about that?" I pressed. "It's important."

He shook his head. "Just heard the name."

"Never even heard of anyone named Galfvi," Honey added.

"I see," I murmured thoughtfully, as if weighing their answers.

All for show, of course, since I fully believed them. If either of them had met Tirano, they surely would have mentioned that he was the same species as Selene. But neither of them had, and if Selene's pupils and judgment were any indication neither of them had reacted to that possible connection in any other way, either.

Both had worked for Lukki. Neither knew Galfvi or Tirano.

And both were still alive.

"Well, we'll just have to work around it," I said. "Our only shot now is to find that dinghy. Lucky for us, I know where to start looking. You two up for a late-night cruise?"

Again, they eyed each other silently across the table. "Sure, why not?" Fisher said. "So what exactly are we talking about?"

"You've got the boat; I know where the threads are," I said. "I'd say thirty percent to you."

"Fifty to us."

"Forty."

"Fifty," Fisher said firmly. "You might know where the threads are, but do you know how to get them to a buyer?"

I felt my heart rate pick up. I'd hoped for this opening, but I'd figured I'd have to make it myself. "I have a few contacts," I said evasively. "Why, you have someone better?"

"Lukki's marketer," Fisher said. "Knows everything about everything. He's the one who set up the buyers and the transport."

I looked at Selene, made a show of thoughtful deliberation. "You'd be paying him out of your fifty percent," I warned Fisher. "You think he'd be interested?"

Fisher snorted. "In a share of thirty threads? Damn straight he would."

"Okay," I said. "But I want verbal confirmation. Give him a call and ask."

"I don't know," Fisher said, giving me an appraising look. "He likes to keep to the background."

"Let me clarify," I said. "Call him, or Selene and I find a way to get to the threads without you or your boat."

"It's all right," Honey said as Fisher's eyes narrowed. "I'll do it."

"Yes, you should do it," Selene agreed as Honey pulled out a phone and started punching in a number. "That way your partner doesn't have to adjust his grip on the Jinnger he's pointing at Mr. Roarke under the table."

Fisher's face went rigid. Honey froze with her number only halfway keyed in. "Oh, please," I said, putting a little scorn into my voice and trying hard not to smile at their reaction to what must have seemed to them like a magic trick. But then, as Selene had pointed out to me in the past, the proprietary self-lubricating composites the Jinnger Firearms Corporation used in their slug guns had a very distinctive smell. "You think this is the first time someone's pointed a gun at us? Frankly, I'd be a little worried if Lukki hadn't hammered some caution into you. You can finish that call any time, Honey."

Fisher hesitated, then nodded. She nodded back and finished keying in the number. A moment of silence... "Smitty?" she said. "Honey. Got a guy here with a proposition."

She laid out the general parameters, concentrating on the deal and high reward/risk factor but not mentioning the silver-silk or any of the other specifics. I also noted enough odd words sprinkled through her monologue to show she was adding in confirmation codes. "He wants to know if you're in," she concluded.

She leaned closer to me and turned the phone so that I could hear. "If you think it's legit, go ahead," a lazy-sounding voice came. "Just make damn sure he's not a badgeman or a shill."

"I'm neither," I spoke up. "But thanks for asking. Welcome aboard; she'll call you later with an update."

Honey keyed off. "No one asked you to talk to him," she said irritably.

"No one asked me not to," I said, pulling out a couple of hundred-commark bills and setting them beside my plate. "So that's settled. Good. If the rain's on its usual schedule it should be clearing up just about the time we get to the docks. Shall we go?"

"Sure," Fisher said as he slid out of the booth and stood up. "We'll take our car. You sit up front; Honey and your friend can sit behind us."

"With Honey's Jinnger pointed at me?" I asked as Honey, Selene, and I also got out.

"Or at her," Fisher said casually. "Dealer's choice. Out the door and turn left."

Selene's analysis earlier had been that Galfvi had tried to start the boat and been unable to do so. As it turned out, that failure was due to the owners' setup. As Fisher stood at the helm and put in the key, Honey opened a camouflaged section of the bow railing near where one of the lines tying us to the dock was connected and held down a hidden button. Fisher pressed the starter, and the engines hummed to life, the dual propellers churning into the water and making small waves aft.

"Lukki had us set it up this way," he told us as he guided the boat away from the dock. "Didn't want anyone being able to run off with it by themselves. So where are we going?"

"Upriver," I told him as I put on my night-scope goggles. "Stay as close to the south bank as you can without running us aground."

"How far upriver?"

"A few kilometers," I said, adjusting the goggles' brightness level. "I'll tell you when we're there."

Distances in darkness and on the water were difficult to judge, but from what I'd seen from the jeep trail it had looked like the northern edge of the Patth fence would be close enough to the river bank to be visible. Sure enough, half an hour after we headed out I spotted the fence's nearer corner.

"Move a little ways back toward the middle," I told Fisher. "We don't want to look any more conspicuous than we already are."

"Sure," he said, easing the boat away from the bank. "How much farther?"

I thought about it a moment. So far all the pieces were falling in with my current theory. If that theory was indeed correct... "I'm guessing another seven kilometers," I said. "Maybe seven and a half."

"Got it," he said, eyeing me suspiciously. "What do you know that I don't?"

"Mostly it's just hunches," I said. "The idea is to take what I know about how the other guy thinks—or maybe just what I *think* I know about how he thinks—and overlay it on the situation at hand."

He grunted. "Sounds pretty soggy."

"It can be," I conceded. "Hopefully, this one will bake up a little firmer."

We'd gone another seven and a half kilometers, and I could see the rocky patch where the jeep trail hit the river and the dock in the distance, when we found the gap.

It looked just about the way I'd imagined it. A narrow but deep cut had been dug out of the bank, either from general erosion or some unusually high river level in the past, with a stream flowing through it. The Patth fence bridged the gap, leaving an opening high and wide enough for someone to squeeze through without touching any part of the fence itself. With the sensor buds strung along the top to guard against climbing attempts, there was every chance someone taking the low road would be missed completely.

At the very back of the cut, partially concealed in a tangle of grassy bushes, I could make out the prow of a narrow metal dinghy.

"There," I told Fisher, pointing. "See it?"

"Looks like our dinghy, all right," he said sourly. "Whoever took it better not have holed it. You say the rest of the silver-silk is in there?"

"I've searched everywhere else," I said, beckoning to Selene. "How close can you get us without triggering the sensors on the fence?"

"Bigger question is how close I can get us without hanging up on the bank," he said. "Honey? Time to take over. Me and our new friends are heading ashore."

❖   ❖   ❖

The landing was just as wet as I'd expected, but not nearly as difficult. Honey, who appeared to be the more competent of the pair at close-in work, got us to within a couple of meters of the shoreline and held the boat there while Selene, Fisher, and I waded ashore. The sides of the cut were mostly wet stone instead of wet mud, which caused a few scrapes and bruises as we fought our way through the flowing water and under the fence. Fisher groused under his breath the whole way, but personally I was happier with a few damp bruises than I would have been dragging mud through the streets of Bilswift and into our rental car. We drew enough attention to ourselves as it was.

"Looks okay," Fisher said. He'd gone straight to the dinghy while I helped Selene up the side of the cut and was crouching over it like it was a pet that had been hit by a car. "A little banged up, but nothing too serious. So where's the stuff?"

"Let me look," I said, kneeling beside him and feeling along the boat's underside. "His usual technique... Damn. Not here."

"What do you mean, not here?" Fisher demanded, shooting to his feet and glaring down at me. "What the *hell*?"

"It *was* here," I said, picking a spot on the hull at random and pointing to it. "You can feel the adhesive residue where he stuck the package. He must have taken it with him."

"Taken it where?" Fisher looked around, then pointed west. "There?"

I looked that direction, feeling my stomach tighten. There were lights over there, distant and diffuse, but definitely not just reflected starlight. Presumably Huginn and his team, putting in late hours in their portal hunt. "Actually, the people over there are the last ones we want to meet up with," I told Fisher.

"Not if they've got the package," Fisher countered.

"They don't," I assured him. "That's the last place our thief would have gone."

"If you say so," Fisher said, clearly not entirely convinced. "So what do we do now?"

"We go home," I said throwing some angry regret into my voice. The sole point of this trip had been to find out if Galfvi could have sneaked into the Path area, and how he could have accomplished that feat. Now that both questions had been answered, it was time to disengage with our new companions. "There's no way we're going to find him in the dark. Maybe we can come back tomorrow—"

"Maybe?" Fisher interrupted. *"Maybe?"*

"What exactly do you want me to do?" I demanded. "Go bumbling around in the dark and hope I trip over him?"

Fisher grunted. "I'll tell you what I want," he said.

And suddenly his Jinnger was in his hand and pointed at me. "I want you to get the silver-silk you promised us. I want my half of your thirty threads."

"I said *maybe* thirty."

"You bring me thirty, you keep half," he said, ignoring my correction. "You bring me less, Honey and I keep all of them. Selene stays aboard until you get back with the loot." He glanced at the distant glow, then up at the sky, then back at me. "You've got one hour. Oh, and I'll take that." He pointed at my holstered plasmic. *"And* your phone." He shot a look at Selene, standing silently watching the drama. "You can just put yours on the ground. I'll get 'em in a second."

In the darkness I couldn't see Selene's pupils. But with her out of position to take any action, and with me kneeling on the ground under Fisher's gun, we really didn't have many other options. Silently, I drew my plasmic and handed it to him, butt first, then handed over my phone.

"Good," he said, stuffing both items in his pockets and taking a step back. "Well, don't just sit there. Clock's running. You're not back in an hour, we head to your ship and see if there's something else we can take to make up for tonight's losses." He considered. "Or maybe we start with Selene's fingers. That'll be up to Honey."

"I'd strongly recommend against that," I said, hearing the death in my voice as I rose to my feet. "Bear in mind that you haven't lost anything yet. You can still walk away from this. But if you hurt Selene, that offer ends. And it will cost you. Very, very dearly."

For a moment he seemed taken aback. He looked at Selene, back at me. "Yeah, got it," he said. "Like I said: One hour." He gestured inland with the muzzle of his gun. "Better get going."

I gave Selene what I hoped was a reassuring nod, and hurried off into the darkness. With a desperate and probably armed Galfvi somewhere to the east and a determined and definitely armed Huginn somewhere to the west, the window for Fisher and Honey to get out of this alive could close at any minute.

I needed to make sure that if that window closed it didn't close on Selene.

CHAPTER TWENTY-FOUR

$\diamond\!\!\diamond\!\!\diamond$

Running through an unfamiliar forest in darkness lit only by starlight had always been high on my list of stupid things not to do. The night-scope goggles helped considerably, but they also tended to enhance the shadows at ground-level, making my footing marginally worse than it might otherwise be.

But I didn't have a choice. My best estimate was that the clearing and portal entrance were about half a kilometer east, plus whatever distance to the north or south that I needed to veer in order to line up with it. And that was just the beginning of the next hour's to-do list. I had to travel as quickly as I could while simultaneously not incapacitating myself.

Skill, experience, and dumb luck were with me. I didn't trip, twist my ankle, or blunder into a nest of whatever the local equivalent of hornets were. Even better, I came close enough to the north end of the clearing to spot it through the trees. I turned in that direction, maneuvered through the bordering line of trees, and was soon at the open hatchway leading down into the portal.

It looked just the same as I'd left it, with no indication that anyone else had stumbled on it since then. There was equipment down there in the launch module, equipment that could be useful to have right now. Unfortunately, without a rope and climbing gear there was no way I could get down there and back up again in the time Fisher had allotted me.

But there was still the mesh I'd used to camouflage my exit hole. I pulled off the chunks of sod, unlaced all of the mesh pieces except one, and replaced the sod on top of the remaining one. With no time to do the job properly, I basically just laid the sod pieces in place, without trying to make it look like a solid bit of normal ground. Even in the darkness I could tell the new version wasn't going to fool anyone; in the daylight it was going to be laughable.

But I had what I needed, and that was all I cared about. Stuffing the mesh into my jacket pockets, I hurried from the clearing and headed for the climbing tree and the footbridge beyond.

Nearly half of my hour had elapsed by the time I climbed back down to ground level outside the Patth fence and reached the river end of the jeep trail. Leaning over the water, I could see that Fisher's boat was exactly where I'd left it, holding position in the current a few meters off the back door Galfvi had taken under the fence. I wasn't close enough to see where everyone was, but Fisher and Honey were probably watching for my return and Selene was probably secured inside the cabin.

I spent a moment tying the ends of my pieces of portal mesh together, ending up with a length that was several meters long. Then, taking off my jacket and boots, I wrapped the mesh loosely around my neck, and slipped into the water.

As I'd noted from our earlier dip, the water was cool, but not cold enough for any of us to risk hypothermia. I conserved my energy, staying low and letting the current take me back toward the boat. As I got closer I saw that Fisher was alone on the deck, standing at the starboard rail just aft of the cabin. He was facing south, toward the fence and the forest beyond, naturally expecting me to reappear from that direction. Honey was nowhere to be seen, but she was probably in the cabin where she could maintain the boat's position and also keep an eye on their hostage.

Shifting my direction slightly, I headed toward the bow.

I reached it and brought myself to a halt against the rough fiberline composite of the hull, getting a relatively secure fingertip grip on the edge of the deck. Carefully, I pulled myself up high enough to see.

Not surprisingly, the cabin blocked much of my view of the

aft section of the ship. But for the moment, what was happening back there wasn't important. From my current vantage point I could see through the windshield into the darkened cabin well enough to confirm that Honey and Selene were indeed both there. Honey, as expected, was in the driver's seat, her hands on the wheel and throttle, her eyes on the riverbank as she concentrated on keeping the boat in position. Selene was seated in the passenger seat beside her, her wrists tied together with what looked like marine repair tape, gazing straight ahead.

I held my position, waiting in the chilly breeze, watching Honey closely. Even with the cabin's only entrance behind Selene toward the stern, my scent should eventually sift inside. Until then, the biggest danger was that Honey would decide to give her eyes a change of scenery and spot the shadowy half head interrupting the smooth lines of her boat.

And then, I saw Selene stir in her seat. Slowly, casually, she eased her head around, looking first toward the shore, then working her gaze along the bow area. Her eyes met mine—

She didn't react, but merely continued her scan until she was facing the bulk of the river and the forested area north of it. Then, with the same seeming indifference, she reversed her sweep, ending up with her eyes again facing forward.

The stage was set. Selene was ready.

All I needed to do now was spin up the players.

Lowering myself back out of view, I unwrapped the portal mesh from around my neck. Most propeller-driven boats, I knew, had a set of vanes or baffles designed to deflect any debris away before it could tangle itself in the screws. But that naturally assumed that the debris was just floating along in the current and not being carefully fed out with the deliberate intention of threading the gaps in the baffles and getting sucked directly into the screws.

It took me over a dozen tries to get it right. But finally I felt the steady pull on the mesh that meant the end was sitting right at the intake and ready to make a mess of Fisher's plans. I got my fingertips back on the deck, confirmed that Selene and Honey were still where I'd last seen them, and let go of the mesh.

For a couple of seconds I thought I'd somehow missed. Then, I felt the hull give a sudden quiver, the bow starting to swing starboard toward the bank as the propeller on that side seized up.

In the cabin Honey leaped into action, grabbing at the control panel and shutting down the fouled screw.

Behind them, Fisher appeared in the cabin doorway, calling something that sounded urgent but was too faint for me to make out the words. Honey replied, jabbing an emphatic finger behind her. He said something else and disappeared, and a second later I saw him hurrying along the deck toward the stern.

Lengthening my grip, I hauled myself out of the water, shifting my body sideways and rolling beneath the rail onto the deck.

For the first couple of seconds I thought my entrance had been completely unobserved. But even with most of Honey's attention on her power and steering controls the movement apparently caught her eye. She snapped her head up, and I saw her eyes widen. She opened her mouth—

And let out a sort of whelp as Selene launched herself sideways and slammed into her, sending them both tumbling onto the deck out of my sight.

I scrambled to my feet and charged aft toward where Fisher was lying down just inside the rail, leaning over the stern, his right hand probing the water as he felt around for the obstruction. I was nearly there when either the vibration of my footsteps on the deck or some hint of a reflection warned him of my presence. Instantly, he rolled onto his back, his left hand grabbing the railing for support, his right hand scrambling for his holstered Jinnger.

But he was already too late. He'd barely closed his hand around the grip when I bent my knees and threw myself onto my left hip, sending myself sliding feet-first across the last meter of deck between us. The soles of my shoes connected with his, and with momentum still driving me toward him I straightened my legs convulsively and shoved him straight off the stern and into the river.

I was back on my feet almost before the splash drowned out his startled curse, racing back toward the cabin. Selene was a decent enough fighter, but with her hands tied she couldn't keep Honey down forever.

I needn't have worried. The two of them had landed in the narrow space between the seats and the control console, and with no room to move—and Selene's weight fully on top of her—Honey was completely helpless. "You okay?" I asked as I relieved Honey of her half-drawn and pinned Jinnger and then helped Selene to her feet.

"Yes," Selene said. "Fisher?"

"Went for a late swim," I said, peering aft. There was no sign of him yet. "Keep an eye out," I added, handing Selene the gun. "I'm going to get us a little distance."

I stepped over to the wheel. Honey had managed to get onto her back and was starting to get up. I put my foot warningly on her stomach, and she reluctantly subsided. "What are you going to do with us?" she asked.

"Nothing drastic," I assured her. "Probably just tie you up and leave you aboard. By the time anyone comes to investigate our job here should be finished."

"What if no one gets curious?"

"Then I'll let the badgemen know to come get you," I said. I nudged the throttle, and the boat started moving up the river. "Don't worry, we'll come back and get Fisher," I added. "I just want to go get my jacket and boots."

Fisher was waiting on the riverbank when we returned, Jinnger in hand, looking like he was dearly hoping for a clear shot. Unfortunately for him, we didn't give him one. Reluctantly, and with a lot of muttering, he obeyed my order to toss his weapon into the river before I would let him aboard. With him and Honey trussed up in the cabin glaring at us and each other, I took the boat back to Bilswift.

I didn't bring it to dock nearly as smoothly as either of the others would have, though I was willing to place some of the blame on working with only one propeller. I shut everything down, again promised to deliver them to Detective-Sergeant Kreega if they weren't out of there in a day or so, and we left.

Fisher's car was waiting where we'd parked it, and my plan had been to drive it back to Panza's and swap it out for ours. But it was getting late, Selene and I were both wet and tired, and the *Ruth* was only a fifteen-minute walk away. A quick consult, an equally quick agreement, and we set off on foot.

I hadn't expected Tirano to have returned to the ship in our absence. But it was clear from the disappointment I saw in Selene's pupils as she sniffed the air that she had. "It's all right," I soothed as I closed and deadbolted the entryway. "I'm sure he's all right."

"You can't believe that," she said, her voice dull and tired as she turned aft toward the bathroom and our cabins. "He was with Venikel, and Venikel's dead."

I winced. What could I say?

Probably best that I didn't say anything. "You want the first shower?" I called after her. "Or are you hungry?"

"I'm too tired," she said over her shoulder. "I'll just get these clothes off and go to bed."

"You sure?"

"Yes. Good night, Gregory."

"Good night," I said lamely. "I'll see you in the morning."

"Six o'clock," she said, keying open her cabin's hatch. "I'll be ready."

I watched as she walked inside and closed the hatch behind her, feeling her ache and aching right along with her. Tirano might indeed be all right. I was pretty sure he was.

I was also sure we would never see him again.

CHAPTER TWENTY-FIVE

We left the *Ruth* at five minutes to six the next morning. Kreega was already waiting for us outside, in full uniform in her official patrol car. "I assumed you wanted this car instead of my private vehicle?" she asked, eyeing my backpack and coil of rope as Selene and I climbed in.

"Yes, perfect," I said. "Okay. Out of town, and up the road to Cavindoss."

She eyed me suspiciously. "Are we *going* to Cavindoss?"

"No, only partway."

"Are we going to Seven Strands?" she persisted, her eyes flicking again to our equipment. "Or the Loporr colony?"

"Neither," I said, looking casually around. A few cars were visible at the edge of the spaceport, along with a van I didn't recognize tucked away around a corner just within view. "I could tell you where we're going, but it would be easier just to drive there."

She held the look another second, then shrugged and turned back to the wheel. "All right," she said, pulling away from the curb. "I'll play. It just better be good."

"It will be," I promised, watching in the mirror as the van pulled out and slipped into tailing position behind us. So far, exactly as I'd predicted. "Meanwhile, let's just enjoy the morning air."

"Fine," Kreega said. "As long as that air doesn't smell like burned Patth."

I swallowed hard. "Definitely not the plan."

Which didn't necessarily mean it might not happen. But it definitely wasn't the plan.

No one spoke much during the drive. I gave directions when necessary, but Kreega seemed content to just sit back and wait for whatever performance I had planned.

Selene's thoughts during that time were her own business. But I was pretty sure a lot of those musings were on Tirano. The Kadolian child she'd hoped to save from himself.

The child who was probably lost to us forever.

Changeling.

I had Kreega pull to the side of the jeep trail at the same place I'd parked the day before. "Okay," I said as we all got out. "That way"—I pointed west—"is a quick-set fence a group of Patth put together to wall off about seventy-five square kilometers of forest area. "That way—"

"Since when do the Patth get to put up fences in an Alainn forest preserve?" Kreega interrupted.

"Since they're Patth and figure they can do anything they want," I said. "The point is that they're holding a very important and very private Easter egg hunt in there. *That* way"—I shifted my pointing finger to the east—"is a tree we can climb to a footbridge that will take us over the fence without triggering the alarms and straight to the aforementioned Easter egg." I raised my eyebrows at her. "You game?"

Kreega peered west, then east, then straight up. "Where in all of this do we get to the murderer you mentioned?"

"If we're lucky, at the end of the rainbow," I said. "If not, we may have to shake the bushes a little more. Again, are you game?"

Kreega squared her shoulders. "Lead on."

The climb up the tree, as always, was pretty straightforward. Kreega was a little leery of the footbridge, but she took it in stride without serious argument. A few minutes later we reached the end, and a minute after that we were back on the ground. Resting my hand on the grip of my plasmic, I led the way through the trees and bushes to the clearing.

Only to find there was no rope leading from the trees down into the portal.

I stopped short, staring at the empty hatchway. The rope *had* to be here—it was the only way the pieces of this puzzle fit together, the only way this made sense. Galfvi was here in the Patth enclosure—last night's excursion had all but proved that. The portal was the obvious place for him to take refuge, and if he wasn't here then the three of us would never find him, not with this much wilderness to search.

But then why had he taken my rope? What other use could he have had for it?

I turned to Kreega, wincing at her increasingly dark expression. I looked back at the clearing, shuffling through my stack of theories—

"Burned rope," Selene murmured. "I smell burned rope."

I frowned at her . . . and then, suddenly I had it. Not a puzzle piece I was expecting, but one that in hindsight fit perfectly with all the others. Smiling reassuringly at Kreega, I headed across the clearing to the open hatchway.

There it was, just as Selene had indicated: the burned end of a rope. Burned, moreover, by a distant plasmic shot. The remaining bit of rope, the part lying on the ground, had been woven painstakingly beneath the viny ground cover, and I followed it to where it had been securely tied around one of the trees, the loop and knot concealed by a bush and some carefully positioned branches.

Kreega was right beside me. "So?" she asked.

"So he's in there," I told her, nodding toward the opening.

"In where?" she asked, frowning back at it. "What's down there, a cave or something?"

"More the *or something*," I said. I unlooped my own rope from around my shoulder and tied it to the tree above Galfvi's remnant, again putting in the most solid knot I could. Midway through the final cinching I pulled three pairs of ascenders and three pairs of gloves from my backpack. "Here," I said, handing one of each set to Selene and Kreega. "Might as well put these on now."

A minute later, fully geared up, we crossed to the opening. I squatted down beside it, peering cautiously in. Most of the receiver module was in darkness, but at the bottom I could just make out a faint and diffuse glow. Someone with a light was camped out inside the launch module.

The simplest approach would be to drop the rest of my rope loop down the rabbit hole and slide down after it. But as Selene had pointed out earlier, a length of rope hitting the bottom of the portal would make a distinctive thud, and the last thing I wanted was to alert our quarry. Instead, I fed the rope into the opening, meter by meter, until it was all in.

Now came the tricky part.

"I'll go first," I said quietly to the others. Basic safety protocols dictated that I should lock my ascenders onto the rope and use them to make a controlled descent. But that would take longer, and at the moment I was more interested in surprise than with playing by the rules. "Join me once I'm down."

Maneuvering my legs into the opening, I got a firm grip on the rope with my gloved hands and pushed off.

Proper rappelling involved a climbing harness with a friction-braking descender setup and a whole lot more practice and experience than I had. Unfortunately, we didn't carry the necessary gear aboard the *Ruth*, and taking a few practice runs was clearly out of the question. But I had good gloves, and strong hands, and boots that could squeeze against the rope for extra safety.

The overriding concern was to get down fast enough that no one could take a shot at me and safely enough that I wouldn't be lying helpless at the bottom with a pair of broken ankles while that same someone shot me at his leisure.

Fortunately, neither of those worst-case scenarios played out. I landed at the bottom of the receiver module with ankles intact, and quietly enough that there was a fair chance he hadn't heard my landing. I turned to the opening between the receiver and launch modules, a part of my brain noting the makeshift rope climbing ladder that had been set up between the two spheres—

I had just enough time to see the mesh twitch when a shadowy figure suddenly loomed up in the opening against the muted lighting and the flash of a plasmic shot scorched its way past my left arm.

I flinched away from the heat, trying to get to my own weapon before he could line up his second shot. But the very nature of the sphere's curvature meant I was flinching uphill, with all the limitations inherent in that geometry. I wiggled around, trying to at least make myself a moving target, finally getting my plasmic clear of my holster. A second burst of fire lit up the receiver module.

Only this one wasn't from my attacker. It was from the tiny lighted rectangle above me.

"Gregory!" Selene's anxious shout came faintly as her second shot burst against the portal metal.

"I'm all right," I shouted back, rolling up onto hands and knees as she fired a third time. "Keep him pinned!"

I got to my feet and headed up the slope. "Stop!" I shouted to Selene, and scrambled up the rope ladder. I reached the top, leaning slightly to the side to hopefully throw off my attacker's aim, and brought my plasmic to bear—

Galfvi was standing motionless in the center of the curved floor, his plasmic on the deck in front of him, his empty hands in the air. "I surrender," he said quickly. "Don't shoot. I surrender."

I took a deep breath. "Clear!" I shouted toward Selene and Kreega. "Come on down."

"As for you, Galfvi," I continued, lowering my voice to a more conversational level as I got one leg over the cusp, "it's time we had a long conversation."

"Just make it quick," Galfvi warned with a sort of dark smirk. "As you humans say, *Eat, drink, and be merry, for tomorrow you may die.*"

I had him lying on the deck, his plasmic secured in my belt, when Selene and Kreega arrived. "So *this* is where you've been hiding," Kreega said as she sat him up and looped a set of plastic restraints around his wrists. "Looks like you were planning for the long haul."

"Oh, he was," I agreed, eyeing the bags of food and water bottles, the inflatable mattress, and the chemical toilet he'd set up on the mesh around him. "But this wasn't his original plan. He didn't actually set up shop here until last night or this morning, after he found the entrance Selene and I opened up yesterday. Until then, he was just sort of lurking around, hoping none of the Patth working west of here would run into him."

"Meanwhile, stealing your rope and trying to trap you in here," Selene said, looking at Galfvi with an edge of anger in her pupils.

"He definitely took my rope," I said. "But in all fairness, I don't think he knew anyone was inside. I was here in the launch module at the time, talking quietly with my light focused on the various equipment bays, and I doubt he could see or hear anything. All he knew was that someone had been in here, that they'd left their rope behind for some future visit, and that until they came back the place would be a good hiding spot."

"I thought you said it was the Patth who'd put up the fence in the first place," Kreega said, frowning. "Why would he need to hide from them?"

"Because they're not *his* Patth," I said. "He's not with them, I mean. In fact, I'm pretty sure they'd prefer to have nothing at all to do with him."

"That's a new one," Kreega commented, eyeing Galfvi. "I thought Patth always stuck together. All kin to all the others, like Kiolven said."

"I'm sure they like to think that," I said, straining my ears. Nothing yet. "But there are always exceptions. Galfvi is one of them."

"How so?"

"We could start with Badgeman Zilor's suspicions about him," I said. "He thought our young friend here was running a scam or planning a theft." I considered. "Actually, it was a little of both."

Kreega made a sound deep in her throat. "How about we skip the froth and get to the murder part?"

"Okay," I said. "But I really should add a little context so it makes sense—"

"*Who did he kill?*"

"Lukki Parsons," I said hastily.

"And Parsons' two thugs and the Javersin brothers?"

"Actually, he just killed Lukki," I told her. "You ready to hear the how and why?"

Kreega gave me a look of strained patience. "Sure."

"I don't know how deeply Galfvi was into Lukki's silver-silk-running business," I said. "Probably not very—I can't see her trusting him very much. More likely he found out about it from Tirano, who Lukki hired to help her locate the Vrinks inside the Loporr colony. Anyway, recent events strongly suggested it was time for Galfvi to get off Alainn, and for that he needed a quick infusion of cash. So he—"

"Hold it," Kreega interrupted. "What events?"

"I'm guessing it was the quiet arrival of the current group of Patth into the Bilswift area," I said, waving a hand around me. "The ones hunting for the thing we're currently standing in. Galfvi probably jumped to the conclusion that they were looking for him."

"I never thought they were looking for me," Galfvi protested mildly. "They're my kinsman Patthaaunuth."

"I keep forgetting," I said. "But even if they weren't hunting him—and as it happens, they weren't—one of them still might recognize him and call it in to the Patth authorities."

"Why are the Patth authorities mad at him?"

"Actually, I have no idea," I said, eyeing Galfvi speculatively. "Would you care to enlighten us?"

"I have no idea," Galfvi said. "It's as much a mystery to me as it is to you."

"Sure it is," I said. "Whatever he did, he apparently made his family mad enough that they sent a couple of hired guns to bring him home."

"Kiolven and Venikel," Kreega murmured. "We identified the charred body as Venikel, by the way. So Galfvi killed him, too?"

"I didn't kill anyone," Galfvi protested.

"Well, you're half right," I said. "Like I said, the only one he killed was Lukki."

"So *Kiolven* killed his partner?" Kreega asked, frowning. "That doesn't make any sense."

"You're right, it doesn't," I agreed. "But getting back to the story. As I said, the Patth poking around out here had nothing to do with Galfvi or his family, but he didn't know that. Fortunately for him, he knew that Lukki had just brought in a group of Vrinks from the Loporr colony that she was holding for a Ylpea buyer, and he figured if he could steal them from her he should be able to find a different buyer and sell them for enough cash to get off Alainn and start a new life elsewhere."

"How did he know about the Vrinks?" Kreega again interrupted. "Not being pedantic, but I need an evidence trail to follow if I'm going to make any of this stick."

"There are a couple of possibilities," I said, keeping my voice casual. Odds were very good that she would never need any evidence against Galfvi, but this wasn't the time to mention that. "Possibly from Tirano; more likely by tapping into the monitor system Lukki had set up in her permanent booth at Panza's Café. We already know Galfvi put in his own monitor at the Javersin brothers' fish shop in order to steal the combination to their safe. Once Tirano had tagged Lukki as someone of interest Galfvi would want to keep tabs on what she was doing."

"We'll check on the booth," Kreega said, nodding. "Enough setup. When do we get to Lukki's murder?"

"Right now," I said. "By this time Galfvi probably knew some of the spots where Lukki stashed her kidnapped Vrinks. I'm guessing that after my talk with her that night in the café she mentioned something to Willie or Braun about their location—maybe not a specific address, but just a street or something. Galfvi hoped to get to her apartment ahead of her and get the exact address, but he first had to load his robe with the cash he'd taken from the fish shop, give the robe to Tirano, and send him high-tailing it to the *Ruth*."

"So Tirano *was* with you that night," Kreega growled.

"Well...yes," I admitted. "But until we knew what was going on, we thought it best to hang onto him."

"Which didn't work out very well," Selene said quietly.

Kreega looked at her, and I thought I could see a flicker of almost sympathy cross her face. "So why did Galfvi send him to you?" she asked.

"Two reasons," I said. "First, any Bilswift citizen who saw someone in a Patth robe hurrying through the rain would naturally assume it was Galfvi. Not a great alibi, but better than nothing. Second, if Kiolven or Venikel spotted the robe they would hopefully target Tirano and not him and again give him some breathing space."

"And the stolen cash?"

"An emergency fund," I said. "Not enough to get him off Alainn in the style he preferred, but he would at least have some running money. Getting it back from Tirano wouldn't be a problem—he'd already wormed his way into Tirano's confidence, and figured he could talk him into almost anything."

I looked at Selene, saw the understanding and quiet pain in her pupils as she remembered Tirano's unintended role in our near-disastrous trip into the Loporr colony. "Anyway, so after Galfvi sent Tirano off into the rain, he headed for Lukki's apartment. Unfortunately for her, she got there ahead of him. He still needed that address, and figured he had nothing to lose, so while she was still on the street he hailed her, probably telling her he had a message from Tirano. She knew who he was—she'd seen him at the fish shop with Tirano—and didn't have any reason to be suspicious, so she let him get close."

Kreega muttered something. "And he grabbed the weapon she always said she never carried and killed her with it."

"Right," I said, my stomach knotting with the mental image. I'd seen my share of killings as a bounty hunter, including the handful I'd participated in. But those had always been the result of a gunfight or a case of self-defense. Cold-blooded murder was a different thing entirely, and it always set my teeth on edge. "Her plasmic, the same one he used to cut the rope up there once he and his gear were down."

Kreega looked up, her forehead furrowing suddenly. "Wait a minute. He deliberately sabotaged his only way out?"

"Like you said, he was in for the long haul," I told her. "But he wasn't worried. He knew that Huginn and the Patth out there—Huginn is the Patth Expediter in charge of the hunt for this thing—would eventually find him, and he figured he could talk his way out from under them. The most important part, the only part that really mattered, was to stay clear of Kiolven and Venikel."

Beside me, Selene inhaled sharply. "He's here," she murmured. "And—"

I frowned at her. There was confusion in her pupils, the look of her trying to sort out a group of different scents. "Speaking of whom, I believe our final guest of honor has arrived," I said, drawing my plasmic and turning toward the hatchway. "Kiolven? We're in here. Come on in and join the party."

"Do not shoot," Kiolven's voice came from the other sphere. "I am not armed."

"Understood," I said, frowning at Selene. "Be advised that we are."

"I understand."

And then, suddenly Selene's look of uncertainly turned to one of pure dread. "Gregory!" she gasped. "They're here. *Iykams*."

For a crucial half second I just stared at her in confusion of my own. We'd been in Bilswift nearly a week, and never once had she caught a whiff of Iykam scent. Where in hell—?

And then it was too late. Even as I turned back to the hatchway Kiolven appeared, rolling with gymnast-class dexterity through the opening and sliding down the rope ladder toward us.

And behind him, framed in the opening, three vac-suited Iykams appeared.

Their corona weapons pointed directly at us.

CHAPTER TWENTY-SIX

———— ❖❖❖ ————

"Set down your weapons," Kiolven said, his voice quiet, his manner that of someone fully in control. "There's no need for any of you die today."

"Roarke?" Kreega bit out, her GovSev pointed unwaveringly at Kiolven. "Talk to me."

"Do as he says," I said, an edge of bitterness in my voice as I laid my plasmic on the mesh and added the one I'd taken from Galfvi. "Those are the weapons that turned Venikel into charcoal. You really don't want to get shot with one."

Kreega hissed out a curse, but lowered her weapon to the floor. Selene had already laid down her own plasmic.

"Thank you," Kiolven said as, one by cautious one, the three Iykams climbed over the cusp and came down into the launch sphere. "Arms straight out to your sides."

I did as ordered, feeling uncomfortably like I was being set up for an impromptu crucifixion. Distantly, I wondered if any Narchner songs mentioned that especially nasty part of Earth's history.

Fortunately, all Kiolven had in mind was a search. He handed my backpack to one of the Iykams to paw through, then went through my pockets and clothing *very* thoroughly, even finding and checking the small hidden slots in my jacket. It was just as well, I reflected, that I hadn't followed my original plan of putting the note I'd written into one of those. When he was done, he did the same with Galfvi, Selene, and Kreega. The detective-sergeant glared fire at him and the Iykams the entire time, but endured the search in stoic silence.

I did note with interest that one of the items he confiscated from Galfvi was a small AuVid display of the sort used for remote monitoring of bugs. I wondered if Kreega had ever had time to check out Lukki's booth at Panza's, decided this wasn't the time to ask.

"My apologies," Kiolven said when he'd finished. "But Mr. Roarke is clever enough to have brought along a small transmitter or recorder, and we don't want our conversation today to be made public." He cocked his head at me. "Speaking of cleverness, it appears that you expected me. I gather you weren't equally prepared for my associates?"

"No, the vac suits were a terrific idea," I complimented him, my brain racing furiously to revise my plan. I had expected Kiolven, all right, and I was ready for him. The Iykams, though, were a complete surprise.

Though in hindsight I realized they shouldn't have been. Kreega had told me three Patth freighters were currently on Alainn, and I knew each Talariac-Drive ship had at least three Iykams guarding that ship's pilot. I didn't know where Kiolven stood in the Patth hierarchy, but if he was high enough he'd have the authority to borrow those guards as long as the ship was in port.

And with Venikel having been violently and unexpectedly taken off the game board, it made sense for him to call in whatever backup he could get.

Great for him. Terrible for me. My plan didn't accommodate this many extra opponents, especially ones carrying corona weapons. I would have to improvise.

And as my father used to say, *Improvisation is typically one part inspiration and nine parts desperation. If you hope to pull out anything better than a draw, you need to seriously improve that ratio.*

"Hardly a perfect idea, though," I continued as one of the Iykams collected our weapons and stuffed them into my backpack for safekeeping. "Selene was still able to pick up their scent, either from the exteriors or from you where you'd touched them before they suited up."

"Ah, yes," Kiolven said, eyeing Selene interestedly. "Expediter Huginn warned me about her remarkable abilities."

"I assume that was when you and Venikel met with him at Panza's?" I asked.

He frowned at me. "How did you know about that? I saw you as we entered, but your angle wasn't adequate for you to identify him. And you left before he did."

"Process of elimination," I said. "Though you're right, I would have preferred to confirm it visually. Unfortunately, Willie showed up before I could arrange a walk-by. You have anything to do with his appearance, by the way?"

Kiolven shook his head. "No."

I shifted my attention to Galfvi. "You?"

"No," he said softly, his eyes and face holding a graveyard look. All his efforts to elude Kiolven had come to a screeching halt, and he was fully aware of the consequences of that failure.

"So that was Willie on his own," I said, turning back to Kiolven. "So all you did was follow him out of the café and kill him." I raised my eyebrows. "Or rather, before Venikel killed him. He was the muscle of your little team, wasn't he?"

"You have an amazing imagination, Mr. Roarke," Kiolven said. "But you substitute fantastical theories for reality. Neither I nor my late partner had anything to do with any deaths, either here in Bilswift or anywhere else."

"Really?" I asked. "A witness to Willie's killer told me he was wearing a Patth robe."

"I don't doubt it," Kiolven said, turning a stern gaze on Galfvi. "I'm sure you've already surmised that Galfvi killed Lukki Parsons. It's obvious he wished to eliminate the rest of her organization, as well."

"Maybe," I said. "But he'd already given his robe to Tirano."

"And you believe each Patthaaunuth has only one?"

"Okay, fine," I said. "You suggest he was taking out Lukki's gang. What was his motive?"

"That remains uncertain," Kiolven said. "I would suggest he was driven by the Patthaaunuth attributes of justice and friendship. His Kadolian friend Tirano had been enslaved by these humans. He was merely attempting to right that wrong."

"Murder is a lousy way to go about doing that," I pointed out.

"I didn't say the plan was a good one," Kiolven said. "You merely asked for a motive."

"Well, it's an interesting theory," I said, scratching my head thoughtfully. "But you see, there are a couple of problems with it. I know of at least three members of Lukki's group who are still walking around, people I saw or talked to last night. If Galfvi was so eager to kill everyone, how did he miss them?"

"I presume he merely ran out of time."

I shook my head. "Sorry, but no. Because that's the other problem. The dinghy he used to sneak into the fenced-in enclosure out there was already gone when Braun was killed. Galfvi couldn't have done that one."

"Unless he came back to continue his string of murders," Kiolven said. "There is, of course, a simpler explanation. As I said, the killings were from a desire for justice. Who else but Tirano had an equally strong desire and therefore equally strong motive?"

I looked at Selene, saw the flash of anger in her pupils. "So you're saying Galfvi killed Lukki and Willie, and Tirano killed Braun?"

"That is the likely conclusion."

"I suppose." I paused. "So where did Tirano get the plasmic Braun was killed with?"

Kiolven nodded toward Galfvi. "From him, no doubt."

I shook my head. "Sorry. Your Iykams have the plasmic Galfvi took from Lukki."

"Stolen from your ship, then." Kiolven smiled. "I'm told you keep a store of backup weapons."

"Told by Expediter Huginn, I assume," I said. "One problem: All our backup weapons are still aboard. I checked them last night."

"He could have used it against Braun and then replaced it."

"It would have carried his scent."

Kiolven looked at Selene. "You raise questions for which I unfortunately have no answers," he conceded. "Perhaps when Detective-Sergeant Kreega has completed her investigation those answers will be forthcoming."

"Actually, I think those answers can be forthcoming right now," I offered. "If you're interested in the truth, that is."

For a moment he studied me. "Certainly," he said. "This truth pertains to Galfvi, I presume?"

"Actually, it pertains mostly to you," I told him. "You see, the problem isn't just who shot whom and where everyone was at the time. The problem is also the pattern of the murders. You suggested the killer was trying to wipe out Lukki's organization. But as I already pointed out, that doesn't hold water."

"I also suggested the killer ran out of time."

"No," I said firmly. "Because there's also the hippo in the hamper we haven't yet addressed: Bicks and Darnell Javersin. They weren't connected in any way to Lukki, so why were they killed?"

"Perhaps they *were* connected to her," Kiolven said.

"No," I said. "They weren't connected to Lukki. They didn't have to be." I pointed to Galfvi. "Because all that mattered was that they were connected to Galfvi."

Out of the corner of my eye I saw Kreega turn toward me. "They *what*?" she muttered. "Are you saying—?"

"That Galfvi killed them?" I shook my head, keeping my eyes on Kiolven. "No. Actually, the whole repulsive mess is pretty straightforward once you get through the utter childishness of it."

Kiolven had good command of his face and stance. But like everyone else, he had no way to control his scent. And hearing his people's ancient rituals labeled as repulsive and childish was apparently more than he could take from an upstart alien. "Yes," Selene murmured her confirmation. "There was a reaction."

Kiolven jerked his head around toward her. "You dare—?"

"You invited me to tell the truth," I cut him off. "You want me to spell it out, or don't you?"

He shifted his glare to me. "You merely wish to brag of your cleverness."

"*You're* the one who said I was clever," I reminded him. "Anyway, isn't bragging basically what you were doing when you popped in with your escort? You certainly *looked* like you were gloating."

He stared at me another moment, then gave a small shrug. "Expediter Huginn was right about you. Very well. Enjoy your moment in the sunlight."

"Thank you," I said. "Actually, there were two points that put me on the right trail. The first was a Narchner song that one of Detective-Sergeant Kreega's badgemen told me about."

"Zilor," Kreega muttered. "He told me he'd had a chat with you."

"Right," I said, suppressing a grimace. Under the circumstances, I'd hoped to keep Zilor's name out of this. "He told us about a song that spoke of Patth families sending operatives to find wayward kinsmen and bring them home. The song further claimed that those wayward sons would be tried, exiled, and erased from family records."

"Sounds rather drastic," Kiolven said evenly.

"That's the problem," I said. "It *isn't* drastic. Certainly not drastic enough for a Narchner song about another species. Those are always bloody and nasty and demonstrate how good the Narchners are compared with everyone else. What Zilor missed was that it wasn't just the family memories and records that were purged. The family's goal was to eliminate *all* memory of the troublemaker.

"Which meant killing everyone who knew him."

"What the *hell*?" Kreega said, staring sandbagged at me. "You can't be serious."

"Selene?" I invited.

"No reaction," Selene confirmed quietly. "It's the truth."

Kreega looked at Kiolven, her expression sending a shiver up my back. "You killed all of them because they knew Galfvi?" she asked quietly. "No other reason? Because they knew Galfvi?"

"Our culture is not your culture," Kiolven said calmly. Maybe he wasn't very good at reading human expressions. More likely he saw the death in Kreega's eyes perfectly well and simply didn't care. "Humans have participated in activities others would deem equally horrific. You cannot judge us without inviting judgment upon yourselves."

"We'll see what a court of law has to say about that," Kreega said. "You want to kill your own people, fine, I can't stop you. But not mine. *Not mine.*"

"A Patthaaunuth court of law might deliver equally harsh verdicts over human atrocities," Kiolven said. "But this discussion is pointless. As in all things, strength is always the deciding factor, and the strength lies with me."

"Does it?" I countered. "Because I'm pretty sure Expediter Huginn gave you a direct order to stay away from Selene and me and anything we got involved with." I waved a hand at the Iykams. "Yet here you are."

"Expediter Huginn offered suggestions, not orders," Kiolven countered. "I chose to ignore them."

"In my experience, suggestions from Expediters *are* orders."

"Your experience doesn't include the political power of the—" He broke off, giving me a small smile. "But we aren't here to bore you with the internal workings of Patthaaunuth society."

"Fine by me," I said, gesturing toward Kreega. "But since

you bring up Patth society, it's my understanding that the Patth Director General is as opposed to killing badgemen as everyone else in the Spiral. What makes you think you can get away with that without consequences?"

"That part will perhaps be a challenge," Kiolven conceded, eyeing Kreega. "I didn't expect Mr. Roarke to pull you into this."

"You committed murder in my town," Kreega said coldly. "I was already in. You said there was another point besides the Narchner song, Roarke?"

I nodded. "It was something Kiolven asked me early on, when we interrupted their planned torture interrogation of Tirano. He asked me how well I knew Galfvi and his family."

"So he'd know if he should add you to his list."

"Exactly," I said. "Luckily for us, we'd never met Galfvi and I told them so. Otherwise Selene and I might be in your morgue right now along with Lukki and the others. But let's get back to the question of shooting badgemen. You said, Kiolven, that explaining that would be a challenge. What if I could show you how you could avoid the whole situation?"

"The law of the family is clear," Kiolven said. "So are the requirements of the ancient decrees."

"I'm sure they are," I said. "But what if I were to suggest an alternative?"

"There are no alternatives."

"There are always alternatives," I said firmly. "Let's start with the bottom line. How much is Galfvi's family paying you to bring him home and clean out his backtrack?"

"That information is not to be shared."

"Why not?" I asked. "You've already decided to kill all of us anyway, haven't you? Or at least Selene and me. Why else would you have had Venikel leave such an obvious trail after he caught Tirano and took him to that warehouse? You wanted us to follow them to a nice secluded place where you could kill us."

"A killing that clearly did not take place," Kiolven said, his voice going dark. "How did you escape his trap?"

"We'll talk about that later," I said. "Right now—"

"We will talk about it *now*," Kiolven cut me off. "Tell me what you did."

I raised my eyebrows. "Or what? You'll kill us? But let's not live in the past."

"Roarke—"

"You said before that strength is always the deciding factor," I went on. "But as my father used to say, *Having strength on your side is good. Having economics on your side is better.* So again, how much are they paying you?"

"Four hundred thousand *cesmi*," Galfvi spoke up quietly.

I frowned at him. "Come again?"

"Four hundred thousand *cesmi*," Galfvi repeated. "The equivalent of eight hundred thousand commarks."

"Never heard of them," I said, a sudden shift in Selene's pupils catching my eye. If I hadn't heard of *cesmi*, maybe she had? "Private Patth currency, I assume. Regardless, four hundred thousand of anything is a tidy sum."

"Not at all," Galfvi said contemptuously. "That is the minimum established price for this task. My family is led by misers."

"On that we agree," Kiolven said with some of Galfvi's own disdain. "Sadly for their preferences, while four may be the traditional minimum, *eight* is *my* minimum."

"And they paid it?" Galfvi asked.

"They did."

"See?" I said. "You're more important to your family than you thought. That must warm your heart. But never mind that. A tidy sum, Kiolven, as I said. But what if you could trade that eight hundred thousand *cesmi* for a larger number? Say, a billion?"

Kiolven made a contemptuous sounding noise. "You seek to bribe me from my responsibility?"

"Oh, please," I said scornfully. "Do I *look* like I have two billion commarks on me? No, I'm talking about something far bigger, something far more important to the Patth than one wayward son, no matter what he's done or how annoying he might be. Something for which the Director General will hand over a freighter full of money without a second's hesitation."

I waved my hand around the launch module. "This."

Kiolven made another rude noise. "Again, you spin fantasies."

"Do I?" I countered. "Why do you think Expediter Huginn gave you such strict orders to stay away from us? Because he knew we were looking for this thing, too, and he didn't want you chasing after us and accidentally blundering into it. It's incredibly, *incredibly* valuable, and he has no interest in sharing the acclaim and rewards when it's handed over to the Director General."

I lifted a finger. "But here's the thing. Right now, it's not working. That's because it's missing several key components. Without them, its value drops from a billion *cesmi* to whatever scrap metal goes for on your home planet."

"Then why do you waste my time with this fantasy?"

"Because I can run it straight back up to a billion for you." I gave him a sly smile. "Because I'm the one who has those missing pieces."

For a long moment the launch module was silent. I kept my eyes on Kiolven, carefully avoiding looking at Selene. She knew that was a complete lie, but she also knew not to derail whatever angle I was working.

Finally, Kiolven stirred. "You lie," he said flatly. "You seek merely to bargain back your life with morning dew."

I gave a theatrical sigh. "Fine. You want proof? I'll give you proof." I gestured toward one of the Iykams as I took off my jacket. "You mind asking him to take a step back? I need to get into the equipment bay he's standing on."

His eyes still on me, Kiolven gestured to the Iykam. I waited until the alien was out of the way, then walked over to the bay and knelt down beside it. I pulled off the loosened cover and looked up at Kiolven. "As the magicians say, watch very closely," I said.

I rolled up my left sleeve and opened the compartment at the elbow of my artificial arm. "As you see, we humans are full of surprises," I added as I pulled out my souvenir cable and connector. "Watch closely."

Leaving the elbow compartment door open, I knelt down and fastened the cable and connector back into place. "And as they also say, hey, presto," I finished. Gesturing at the bay, I stood up and got a grip on my elbow compartment's door.

And with everyone's eyes now focused on the equipment bay, I deftly plucked out the folded piece of paper I'd hidden under the cable and shifted it to a concealed position in my right palm. "That was a free sample," I told Kiolven. "You want more, you have to deal."

Slowly, he raised his eyes. "Where are the rest of the components?"

"Locked away in a very secure place," I assured him. "But easily accessible. The key's aboard the *Ruth,* whenever you're ready to go get it."

"Where is it?"

"I'm sorry; I was apparently unclear," I said. "I meant whenever you're ready for *us* to go get it. *All* of us." I looked at Galfvi. "Including him."

"The family wishes him disposed of."

"The family will have to wait their turn," I said. "He killed a human on Alainn, and there are going to be consequences for that. Anyway, right now you have more important things to do. Shall we get the key, or would you rather see if Huginn finds this place first? I can deal with him just as easily as I can deal with you."

"Not if you are dead."

I shrugged as casually as I could. Appealing to greed was all well and good, but accidentally crossing over into wounded pride territory never ended well. "If your professional pride is worth losing a couple billion commarks over, I suppose I can't stop you. Though there would still be the fallout over killing a badgeman to deal with. But it's your call."

From my point of view, the scenario I'd painted for him should have been a no-brainer. But apparently he was the type who had to weigh every decision. For another moment he stared at me and pondered.

But in the end, the lure was too strong to pass up. "You will ascend first," he said, gesturing to the rope bridge leading into the receiver module and the hanging rope beyond. "Then the Kadolian, then the badgeman. Do not linger."

"Don't worry," I said, letting out a silent sigh of relief. The first crucial hurdle had been successfully passed.

Now all I had to worry about was all the rest of them.

I'd wondered why Kiolven would risk sending me up first, ahead of him or any of his Iykams. I found out as soon as I reached the top and found three more of the corona-armed aliens standing guard there. Clearly, Kiolven was the type who didn't want to let his opponents even know how many cards he had in his hand, let alone how he intended to play them.

Fortunately, so was I.

I waited until Selene appeared, her hands fumbling uncertainly at the edge of the hatchway as she made a show of trying to make the transition from a vertical climb back to a horizontal crawl. As she struggled, drawing most of the Iykams' attention, I surreptitiously dropped my note into the collection of sod sections that had once been much better camouflage for yesterday's exit hole. Now, with the area looking less like professional landscaping and more like a child had tossed some dirt clods onto a sand-sifter, it should be more apt to draw attention.

I could only hope it would attract the *right* attention.

We reached Kreega's patrol car to find the van I'd seen following us from the spaceport parked behind it. I offered to stay in the van with Kiolven and the Iykams if he allowed Kreega and Selene to drive back in Kreega's car; Kiolven ignored my suggestion and instead loaded all of us into the van.

The vehicle was a twelve-passenger model like the one Braun had used to take us to Seven Strands. I ended up in the rear right-hand seat, the same one Braun and Scarf had put me in during that earlier trip. The geometry of its position made it the most secure and escape-proof of the twelve seats, and the fact that I was put there instead of Kreega presumably meant Kiolven considered me more of a threat than she was.

I wasn't sure whether or not that was a compliment, but decided I might as well treat it as one.

The midday Bilswift traffic was out in full force, and as Kiolven maneuvered us through the streets I wondered if he would reconsider his plan to go straight to the *Ruth* and instead take us someplace where we could hole up until after dark when things eased up a little. But either he was anxious to get his hands on his billion *cesmi* or he really did believe that Patth could do whatever they wanted without consequences. He drove the van right up to the *Ruth*'s zigzag and piled us out again.

Three minutes later, we were gathered in the dayroom. "We're here," Kiolven said, his eyes steady on me. "Where is the key you spoke of?"

"It's very close," I assured him, looking surreptitiously at Selene. Reflexively, Kiolven followed my gaze.

And with his attention pointed the wrong direction, I popped open the wrist compartment in my left arm and thumbed out one of my knockout pills.

Most of the time, I used those handy little pharmaceuticals against enemies, opponents, or occasionally even badgemen who were inconveniently in my way. This was not one of those times.

"And I'll get it for you," I added, "just as soon as I wake up." Giving him a smug smile, I popped the pill into my own mouth.

He was fast, all right. I'd barely gotten my mouth closed again when he was on top of me, trying to pry my jaws apart. But he was too late. I'd already swallowed the pill, and I'd seen on many occasions just how fast the things were.

His fingers were still digging at my lips when the universe went black.

CHAPTER TWENTY-SEVEN

I'd tried other people's knockout drugs over my career—or more precisely, been unwillingly dosed with them—and speaking purely as a target I had to say that the one I used was a far superior product. Some drugs had left me woozy or nauseous, while others had forced me to wake up in stages, with consciousness returning noticeably sooner than nerve endings or muscle control. My drug, in contrast, brought me fully awake within a few seconds and with none of the more unpleasant side effects.

Of course, I *did* wake up flat on my back on the dayroom deck, a knot on my forehead where Kiolven had apparently let me hit the floor without trying to stop me, and with heavy-duty conduit tape tying my wrists together. But you couldn't have everything.

Carefully, I opened my eyes. I was lying beside the pantry at the starboard side of the dayroom, as far from the open hatchway and any shot at escape as possible. Kreega and Galfvi were sitting together on the dayroom foldout couch, their wrists secured with the hack-proof magnetic shackles and chains that had been pulled from their hidden compartments in the wall behind the two of them. Selene was on one of the fold-down seats, her wrists and ankles trussed up like mine, her torso and legs also taped to the wall for extra security.

Sitting on the fold-down on her far side, my plasmic in his lap and his eyes focused on Galfvi, was Kiolven.

"Finally," he said, turning to face me with an expression I'd never seen on a Patth before. "You should know that over the past five hours I considered killing you."

He stood up and took a step away from Selene. "Considered it many, many times." He lifted the plasmic and pointed it at my face. "I restrained myself because I knew it would be too easy."

"It would also be horribly wasteful," I warned, my heart kicking up to full throttle. I didn't know what emotion was behind that look, but the rest of his body language screamed something from the insane rage category. "The two billion *commarks*, remember?"

"Two billion *commarks*?" He shook his head. "No. I no longer believe that was truth."

"You saw the places where missing components used to be," I persisted. "You saw the one I replaced. Just let me get the key, and you can have the rest of them."

Again, he shook his head. "You truly do not understand the Patthaaunuth, human. For us, personal pride and the thirst for revenge will always win out over money or even power. You have shamed me in my eyes, and in the eyes of these others."

He drew himself up. "If Galfvi's crimes against his family were sufficient for me to erase his memory from the universe, how much more should I be driven to erase yours?"

"It's an interesting dilemma," I agreed, trying to work moisture into a suddenly dry mouth. "But as my father used to say, *When you hold all the cards, curiosity doesn't cost anything.* Wouldn't you like to know why I took the knockout pill?"

For a few of my highly accelerated heartbeats he seemed to consider. "Tell me."

I looked at Selene, saw the tense confirmation in her pupils. "Two reasons," I said. "First, I didn't want your Iykams around for this part of the conversation. Too many extra bodies, too many extra guns, and they'd have wanted a cut of the payoff."

"And you thought they would become bored and leave?"

"Not bored, no," I said. "But leave, yes. Because you'd commandeered them from their freighters, and you could only do that while their ships and pilots were in port. Once the freighters approached their scheduled departure time, you had no choice but to let them go back. I hoped a five-hour nap would do the trick." I made a show of looking around. "Seems I was right."

"I could have held them," Kiolven said. "Galfvi's family is strong, and strength is still the deciding factor."

He shifted his aim, focusing his plasmic now on my right arm. "Perhaps I failed to mention that before they left, they searched this ship. They searched it thoroughly. They found no key."

"That's because it isn't meant to be found," I said. "But there was a second reason."

"I don't care," he said. "All that matters is *my* reason for letting you sleep to the drug's completion." He cocked his head as if doing more pondering. "Perhaps I will begin with your remaining arm."

"That seems way off from your usual style," I said, forcing a puzzled frown onto my face. "When you killed Willie, Braun, and the Javersin brothers you didn't make them suffer."

"I killed only the brothers," he said. "Venikel dealt with the others. And none of them suffered because none of them tried to make a fool of me. Or perhaps I'll begin with one of your eyes." He raised his weapon to point at my right eye.

"Because that's been bothering me," I said, trying not to wince. "This tradition of expunging family members must be pretty ancient. Has anyone tried to modernize it? You know, bring it into the era of space travel?"

"No; the arm," he concluded, again shifting his aim.

"But you really need to hear my second reason for taking the pill," I said quickly. "I dropped a note back by the portal, and I had to give the intended recipient time to find it and read it."

"Whatever its contents, they are meaningless now," Kiolven said calmly. "If indeed there even was such a note. The Iykams searched the ship, the entryway is deadbolted, and we are alone."

"Oh, no, there was a note," I assured him. "Let me quote the first part for you: *I have information that you urgently need and which you cannot obtain without me. The price is that you must first save my life.*"

Kiolven tilted his head slightly, the first hint of uncertainty touching the stony resolve of his expression. "Who was this note for? Tell me his name."

"You know his name," I said, shifting my attention to Kreega as she sat silently beside Galfvi. Out of the corner of my eye I

saw Selene bend forward slightly, easing her bound hands awk-
wardly toward the underside of her fold-down.

It was a subtle enough movement. But Kiolven was a professional, and was thoroughly keyed up, and even as his eyes
automatically started to follow my own gaze he spotted Selene's
movement and spun back to her. "Stop," he ordered, swinging
his plasmic around to point warningly at her.

"The rest of the note," I continued quietly, "had the instructions on how to get into the *Ruth*'s secret back door."

Behind him in the open hatchway a figure slipped silently
into view in the half-lit corridor, a plasmic ready in his hand.
The weapon spat a single, blazing shot, and with a scream of
rage and pain, Kiolven spun halfway around, his weapon flying
out of his ruined hand.

And as he fell to his knees, still burbling in agony, Expediter
Huginn stepped calmly into the dayroom. "That what you had
in mind, Roarke?" he asked.

I took a deep breath. "Pretty much exactly. Thank you."

"You're welcome." Huginn stepped around behind Kiolven,
dropping a compact medkit on the deck in front of him and
kicking away the other's smoldering and useless weapon. "Let's get
these people untied and out of here. I'm sure Detective-Sergeant
Kreega has a couple of hours' worth of paperwork she needs to
get started."

He gave me a cool, measuring look. "And after that," he added
softly, "you and I need to have a long talk."

CHAPTER TWENTY-EIGHT

In the end, it took more than a couple of hours. Kreega was mad as hell and wanted to charge all of us—Selene and me included—with every crime she could think of. The attempted late-night intervention by the Patth ambassador only made her attitude worse. Especially when the ambassador insisted that Galfvi and Kiolven, as Patth citizens, be released into his custody.

Fortunately, by the time the conversation expanded to include the regional authorities, Alainn's overall planetary legal department, and a couple of Commonwealth undersecretaries for offices I was never quite clear on, Kreega had turned us over to Badgeman Zilor. With his eyes and hopes on Galfvi's own list of charges and the clear expectation that Kreega would win the jurisdictional battle, he got through our paperwork in record time. We promised we'd stay in Bilswift for a few more days in case he needed us, and beat a hasty retreat.

But not before Huginn pulled me aside and reminded me of our deal. I confirmed my commitment and told him to call me when he was free to talk.

Four days later, with ill will and resentments still hanging over Bilswift like the evening rain clouds, he finally was.

"Rather surprised you chose this place," he commented, taking a sip of his drink and sending a measuring gaze around Panza's

Café. "I knew you were something of a sentimentalist, but I wouldn't have thought this fit that particular bill."

"It's less sentimental than historical," I told him, sniffing at the barbeque aroma wafting from the kitchen and wishing there'd been time for an order of ribs. But Huginn had made it clear that he had work to do, and that this would therefore be a one-drink conversation.

Though I suspected that what I had to say might take some of the edge off that urgency.

"This was Lukki's booth," I went on, running my fingers across the table between us. "This is where it started—Lukki, Galfvi, Tirano, the Vrinks, and all the rest. It seemed only fitting that we should put the endcap on here."

"As I said, sentimental."

"Besides, I thought you might want one more meal of whatever the Patth dish was you were eating when Selene and I first arrived," I added. "What was it, if I may ask?"

He pursed his lips. "It was basically a spice roast," he said. "Modified slightly for human consumption. One of Sub-Director Nask's favorites that I've developed a taste for."

"Yes, I've heard of spice roasts," I said. "Though I imagine you had to give the kitchen a fair amount of instruction on the correct preparation."

"That I did," he confirmed. "And now you're stalling. Time to pay your part of your deal. Interesting back door you have on your ship, by the way. I don't think I'd have been able to find it or get in without your instructions."

"Glad you like it," I said. "Actually, most bounty hunter ships have either a back door or some kind of camouflage for loading passengers that local authorities want to hang onto."

Huginn grunted. "We could have used something like that," he said. "The Patth and the Commonwealth may have come to an agreement, but that doesn't mean Kreega and her badgemen liked it. I half expected them to have brought in the traditional European torch-and-pitchfork mob to see them off."

"I think European mobs mostly use flashlights now," I said. "But they're gone, and the Patth get to decide on their judgment." I raised my eyebrows. "There *will* be judgment, won't there?"

"Oh, yes," Huginn said darkly. "As well as a long-neglected review of the ancient laws and traditions that are still technically in force. You were right—the old Purge laws only applied to Patth, and they obviously can't be allowed to spill over onto other species in the Spiral."

"Or should be abandoned altogether," I said. "Killing someone who simply knew the offender? No offense, but that's barbaric."

He shrugged. "Different cultures, different rules," he said. "Which isn't to say I disagree with you." He took another sip of his drink. "But we're not here to discuss legal philosophy."

"No, we're not," I agreed, trying to relax. There were several directions this conversation could go, some less pleasant than others, none that would leave me looking particularly good. But I'd made a deal, and Huginn had kept his end of it. "Okay. Let me start by telling you I'm on to your little changeling plan."

Huginn raised his eyebrows fractionally. "Our *what* plan?"

"Your changeling plan," I repeated. "Your idea of letting Selene and me find the nonfunctional portal and confirm to the Icarus Group that it *is* nonfunctional. They then check off Alainn as a failure, and everyone moves on to more promising pastures."

His eyes were steady on me. "And?"

I braced myself. "And then," I said, "after we're gone and the Icarus paperwork has been filed, you sneak in under cover of darkness, pull out the dead portal, and drop one of your own very functional Janus portals in its place."

"And why would we do something that insane?" he asked, his face still not giving anything away.

"Because it's *not* insane," I said. "The hijacking of your Fidelio portal showed that even something that big is still vulnerable to theft. Plus the very nature of a Gemini means that if someone gets hold of one they have instant access to the other. You need a secure place for them to sit while you study them."

"Our portals *are* in secure places."

"I'm sure they are," I agreed. "But most of the time *secure* also means *sensitive,* and as I just pointed out putting a portal in a sensitive spot may not be the best long-term idea. Even hiding it out in deep space isn't a good option, because the supply and personnel traffic back and forth can draw attention and theoretically be traced. I imagine the Patth hierarchy has had long and heated discussions on the subject over the past few months."

I waved a hand around me. "And then, you found Bilswift."

I took a sip from my Dewar's, waiting for Huginn to respond. But he remained silent.

"Bilswift is a backwoods area on a back-woodish planet that nevertheless has a comfortable degree of traffic in and out," I continued. "Equally important, there are enough Patth already established in the major cities that someone seeing a few new ones pop in won't even notice. You could drop your Fidelio portal here, in the exact spot Selene has already certified there's nothing of interest, and study it to your heart's content. No one from the Icarus Group would ever give the place a second look. In fact, it occurs to me that you could set up a Patth birdwatching society or something in Bilswift or Cavindoss and hide your heightened presence in the area even better. Either way, you'd be free and clear."

Huginn shook his head. "You have an amazing imagination, Roarke. I'll give you that."

"I appreciate the compliment," I said. "But we both know better. You see, I got a good look at the underside of that clearing. I saw how you'd already prepped the area by digging the portal mostly clear, leaving only enough sod on top to give visitors something solid to walk on. All you have to do now is scoop off those top two meters, haul the dead portal up with some of your heavy lifters, drop the Fidelio portal in its place, and refill the dirt around it."

"That's *all*, is it?" he asked wryly.

"I've seen Sub-Director Nask in action," I said. "For him, I'm guessing this will just be a typical Tuesday. Incidentally, I want to compliment him on the support mesh you used under the crust. Even while I was digging through it I thought it was some kind of exotic root system that crisscrossed beneath the soil and held it up against whatever strange erosion had taken place. It was only later, after I was out and thinking about it, that I realized what the underground gap really signified."

For a long moment Huginn stared at me, probably deciding whether he should keep up his bluff or admit the truth and move on. "Suppose what you say is true," he said at last. "What then?"

"Two things," I said. "First, obviously, you might as well junk the plan. There's no point in moving the Fidelio portal here now that we know what you're up to."

"Now that *we* know?"

I forced myself to meet his gaze. "The Icarus Group knows the Alainn portal doesn't work. They don't know about the changeling part of the plan."

"And you think it was a smart thing to tell me that *you* knew?"

I took a deep breath. "I'm sure there are a hundred situations where you'd kill me without hesitation," I said, keeping my voice even. "I don't think this is one of them."

Huginn mulled at it a moment. Then, his lip quirked in a tiny smile. "Maybe, maybe not. Luckily for you, Sub-Director Nask still considers you a useful asset."

"I'm honored," I said, breathing a little easier. "Dare I say I feel the same way about him?"

"I wouldn't," he said. "At least, not in his presence. I'm still waiting for you to get to the urgent information you promised."

"Good news, then, because we've arrived," I said. "As far as I can tell, the only thing wrong with the portal is that some of the components are missing. But you have a pair of working Gemini portals, plus maybe one or two more that you might have scrounged up when we weren't looking. I'm thinking you could raid one of them for the missing parts and see if you can get this one up and running."

Huginn shook his head. "I've already suggested that. Sub-Director Nask and the Director General agree that such a move would put the donor portal at unacceptable risk."

"Yes, the Icarus Group reached the same conclusion via the same arguments," I told him. "Especially since they don't expect to find anything useful at whatever portal this one was linked to ten thousand years ago. Did that point also figure into the Director General's decision?"

"It did," Huginn said, his forehead creasing slightly. "Do you know something about the other portal that we don't?"

"Nothing about the other portal, no," I said. "What I *do* know is that the Alainn end wasn't abandoned ten thousand years ago. It was still in operation until at least a hundred years ago. Possibly only fifty."

Huginn sat up a little straighter, the hand gripping his glass suddenly tightening. "Explain," he said quietly.

"The footbridges from Seven Strands," I said. "I'm sure you know Lukki and her people used the one leading up to the Loporr colony to bring out the Vrinks they were trafficking. You probably also know that Selene and I used the bridge leading to the portal to sneak over your fence. I do appreciate the gap you engineered for us in the riverfront section, though. If we hadn't found the bridge we would probably have gone in that way."

"You're welcome," he said. "And?"

"And those two bridges are in good condition. *But.*" I lifted a finger for emphasis. "I tried one of the other bridges, the one that leads into a different part of the mountains, and the thing disintegrated under my feet. *That* was a bridge that's been sitting untended for a few thousand years."

"But the other two hadn't," Huginn murmured, a quiet intensity growing in his face. "Someone was still traveling between the portal and the Loporri."

"Someone who liked silver-silk enough to have kept those bridges maintained," I confirmed. "Whoever that was, they might still be hanging around the other end." I raised my eyebrows. "And *that* might be worth risking one of your other Gemini portals for."

"It might indeed," Huginn said, his eyes focused on something distant.

Abruptly, the eyes came back to my face. "Why?" he demanded.

"Why tell you?" I shrugged. "Three reasons. One, the Icarus Group already said that wasn't a risk they were willing to take."

"So did the Director General."

"So you said," I agreed. "Two, because I'm curious about who or what is at the other end, and Sub-Director Nask strikes me as being more willing to change his mind than the people at Icarus. And three..."

I felt a hard lump form in my stomach. "Because whoever's running Icarus at the moment threw us to the wolves," I said. "We had backup already here on Alainn, but when Selene filed her petition about Loporr sapience that backup was withdrawn. Quickly and immediately withdrawn."

Huginn frowned. "They withdrew your *backup*? Don't they realize how valuable you two are to them?"

"Apparently not," I said, hearing a sudden edge of bitterness in my voice. "Let me make it clear: If he'd been available, I wouldn't have needed to call on you to get us out of Kiolven's trap, and we wouldn't be having this conversation. But he wasn't, and I did, and you did. As far as I'm concerned, you earned this information."

Huginn shook his head, his frown deepening. "That doesn't sound like Admiral Graym-Barker's style."

"I agree," I said. "It makes me wonder if he maybe isn't calling the shots at Icarus anymore."

"Could be," Huginn said. "That would be unfortunate."

"You think that highly of the admiral?"

Huginn smiled. "We know and understand him," he corrected. "A known opponent is always easier to prepare for than an unknown one."

"Sounds like something my father might have said."

"Very likely," he said. "Anything else?"

"Yes," I said. "I know you're the one who killed Venikel."

I'd expected a sharpening of his expression or a quick denial or even a reflexive threat. But he merely cocked an eyebrow. "Really," he said. "Why would I do such a thing?"

"I'm sure you didn't *want* to," I said. "But your plan revolved around you giving Selene and me enough rope and subtle guidance to find the portal and confirm it was dead. I imagine you were annoyed beyond belief when first Galfvi and then Kiolven started tearing through Bilswift threatening to blunder into and derail the whole scheme. That was probably a major part of your talk with Kiolven and Venikel when you met them here: Stay away from Selene and me. Unfortunately, Kiolven decided his mission took precedence and chose to ignore you."

"And that *will* cost him," Huginn said darkly. "But it'll cost him according to Patth law."

"As it should," I agreed. "Because Selene and I were slated to be their next victims. They must have decided there were enough hints that we knew Galfvi, even if only through Tirano, for them to add us to their death list." I cocked my head. "So when exactly did you decide you wanted Tirano for yourselves?"

Huginn hesitated, then gave a small shrug. "Originally? When Admiral Graym-Barker hired you and Selene to hunt portals for him. Sub-Director Nask realized there must be something unique about Kadolians, and started looking for one we could hire. It's something in the scent, isn't it? Some alien residue she can still pick up?"

Briefly, I wondered if Selene's abilities in that area were a state secret. But if Nask didn't already know, he would soon. "It's the hull metal itself," I told him. "Metals don't give off a huge amount of scent, but there's enough that she can pick it up, and it's very distinct. Did you say you *hired* Tirano?"

"Yes," Huginn said. "And to answer your next question, he came with us willingly."

"I'd like to confirm that."

"I'll see what I can do," Huginn said. "But even with such a valuable prize as Tirano we're hardly talking motive for murder."

"I didn't say you murdered him," I reminded him. "I'm guessing he pulled his weapon first. But he was using Tirano as bait in order to kill us, and both parts of that plan were unacceptable to you. When he wouldn't back down and drew on you, you really had no choice."

"Sounds reasonable, I suppose," Huginn said. "Still just speculation, of course."

"Actually, it isn't," I said. "Because you're the only person in the mix who would have then used a corona weapon to burn the body. Not to impede identification, but to keep Selene from getting close enough to the crime scene to pick up your scent. You had to keep the portal and family vengeance parts of this scenario completely separate, which meant you couldn't be seen interacting at all with Kiolven and the others. I assume you used Venikel's own corona weapon on him?"

Huginn pursed his lips. "I'll see what I can do about getting you a meeting with Tirano before we leave," he said. "Are we done?"

"We're done," I confirmed. "When are you taking the portal out?"

"Why?"

"It sounds like an interesting project," I said. "I hoped you'd let me watch."

He smiled. "You really *are* an interesting opponent, Roarke."

"Better the one you know, right?"

"So I've heard." He finished his drink and slid out of the booth. "I'll be in touch about the Tirano meeting."

"I'll be waiting," I said. "One other thing."

He paused at the side of the booth. "Yes?"

"I heard something about Galfvi getting shot while you were escorting him and Kiolven to the shuttle. What's the story on that?"

"Not really a story," he said, shrugging. "Galfvi grabbed my plasmic while we were walking him from the van to the shuttle and tried to make a break for it. Badgeman Zilor took him down with a shot to the upper torso, and Galfvi got to finish his walk in a great deal of pain. Nothing to it."

"Really?" I asked. "He got *your* plasmic, and Zilor just *happened* to be on hand and ready to shoot?"

"Zilor's profile listed him as having a high marksman proficiency,"

Huginn said. "He was also hot to deliver justice to Galfvi for Lukki Parsons' murder, and furious about the Patth pulling diplomatic rank and stealing him away. I figured he should at least get the minor satisfaction of making Galfvi hurt a little."

"And your plasmic was of course unloaded?"

Huginn gave me a small, enigmatic smile. "Like I said. I'll be in touch."

I was not, in fact, invited to watch the portal operation. But Selene had kept track of the traffic flow around Alainn, and I knew when the Patth heavy lifters arrived and could anticipate when they'd be in position.

And even seen from the distance of Seven Strands, the whole thing was pretty impressive.

It started with three heavy lifters dropping out of the sky, the ground and portal presumably already having been prepped. For a couple of minutes they held position, staying just high enough to keep their thrusters from setting fire to the forest. I watched the cradle being lowered, though the cables attached to it were too thin for my binoculars to resolve, and saw the twitch as the lifters took up the slack. The blaze from the thrusters intensified, and they began their slow drive up Alainn's gravity well.

And then, looking eerily like a double moonrise as they were bathed in the glow of the thrusters, the twin spheres of the portal appeared.

I felt a lump in my throat as the portal followed the lifters skyward. That could have been us, I knew. We could have had a new Gemini portal for the Icarus scientists and techs to study, and I might even have been able to talk Graym-Barker into risking one of their others to learn this one's secrets.

But Selene and I had been abandoned and left in the wind. This was the price the Icarus Group had paid for that decision.

There would surely be a price for me to pay as well, I knew as I drove back to Bilswift. The only questions were what that price would be, and when it would be exacted.

Both answers, I suspected, were already waiting for me.

Tera C—I still didn't know her last name—was seated in the *Ruth*'s dayroom when I walked in. "I see you made it," I commented as I walked to the pantry and pulled out a breakfast cola. On the table in front of her, I noted as I passed, was the recorder I'd left for her to listen to. "I wasn't sure the timing would work."

"It was tight," she said. "But the admiral was *very* clear that you needed a talking to."

"So *that* part of Icarus he's still in charge of?" I asked, sitting down across from her.

"What happens inside the Icarus Group is none of your business." She tapped the recorder. "Huginn *really* let you leave with this recording?"

"Not sure he knew Lukki had bugged the booth," I said with a shrug. "Or he knew and didn't care. It's not like he didn't expect me to tell you all about our conversation anyway."

"Gregory, he practically confessed to Venikel's murder!"

"No, he just didn't deny it," I said. "It would never stand up in court. Besides, as we've just seen, the Patth are very much into dealing their own justice to their people, and to hell with any other laws or badgemen who stand in their way."

"Yes," she said, a sour look on her face. "That's fine for Huginn. Not so good for you."

"You heard my reasons," I said, gesturing toward the recorder. "Would the admiral rather Selene and I had died here?"

A muscle in her cheek tightened. "The admiral, no," she said, her anger fading. "Some of the others . . . maybe. All I know is that when I bring this back to them you're going to be in serious trouble. You and Selene both." She paused, her eyes flicking to the dayroom hatchway. "Where *is* Selene, by the way?"

"With Huginn," I told her. "He offered to let her come and say good-bye to Tirano."

"What, in the middle of the night?"

"He said he had to leave Alainn right away, and this was her last chance. He also probably thought I'd come with her and thereby miss the chance to see them take out the portal."

"Ah." She gave me a speculative look. "How was it?"

"Well worth getting up in the middle of the night for," I said. "So let me sweeten the pot a little. First of all, we kept the Patth from pulling their changeling routine on us."

"Though knowing they were doing that would have given us a crack at their working Gemini portal," Tera pointed out.

"You don't seriously think that would have been a good idea, do you?" I asked darkly. "The admiral's new bosses might not remember the doomsday scenarios that were discussed the last time Nask lost a portal, but I do."

"Fair point," Tera conceded. "But if that's what you consider sweetening the pot, you really don't understand that phrase."

"Let's try this, then," I said. "Do you know what currency the Patth use?"

"It's the commark, isn't it?" Tera asked. "Everyone else uses it."

"I mean their local currency, the one they use among themselves on the Patth homeworlds," I clarified. "It's called the *cesmi*, and it comes in at two commarks per."

She shook her head. "Never heard of it."

"Neither had I," I said. "But I noticed a reaction from Selene when Kiolven mentioned it. I asked her about it later, and she said the term was very similar to the *cesmer* currency that her fellow Kadolians use."

"So what?" Tera asked. "There've been a lot of local currencies in the Spiral over the centuries. There are bound to be a few naming coincidences."

"And that may be all it is," I agreed. "But what if it isn't? What if the Patth and Kadolians are connected?"

"You mean like the Kadolians come from one of the Patth planets?" Tera asked. "I suppose that's possible. It's not like we know much of either species' history."

"Or even their home worlds or current bases of operations," I agreed. "Selene says the Kadolian remnant moves around a lot, but that doesn't really tell us anything."

"Certainly not about where they come from."

"True," I said. "But here's the thing. What we *do* know is that sometime in the distant past the Kadolians were a client species to some unknown species. I'm wondering if the similarity in currency names means the Patth were, too." I paused for emphasis. "What if the ones they were clients to were the Icari?"

For a moment Tera just gazed at me. "You have any proof?"

"No," I admitted. "But there are indications."

"Such as?"

"For starters, like you just said, we don't know where either species came from. There are also indications that the Patth knew about the portals before you and Jordan McKell stumbled on the original Icarus."

"They were certainly quick to start chasing us," she agreed, nodding thoughtfully. "Anything else?"

"Just the bombshell," I said. "We all agree these portals are great. But they don't travel on their own. Someone had to have moved them from wherever they were built to wherever they ended up. And to make a trip like that even marginally efficient, that someone must have had a really good, really fast stardrive."

Abruptly, Tera stiffened. "The *Talariac Drive*?"

"Or maybe something even better," I said. "My point is that no one knows how an obscure species like the Patth suddenly came up with this game-changing tech—tech that no one has ever been able to duplicate—and parlayed it into economic dominance of the Spiral."

"Because they didn't invent it at all," Tera said, her eyes glinting as she saw where I was heading. "They reverse engineered it."

"I think that's as logical as anything else," I said. "And now, thanks to the Alainn portal, they may have the chance to find a group of people who've been collecting silver-silk for hundreds or thousands of years."

The glint abruptly went out of Tera's eyes. "Are you saying there may be more Icari tech out there?"

"Maybe even some Icari themselves," I said. "I know, I know— don't look at me like that."

"Why not?" Tera bit out, her earlier anger back in full force. "Damn it, Roarke. *We* could have had that contact. Instead, you gave it to the *Patth*?"

"You gave up your chance to it when you left us to die," I shot back. "Anyway, it's not as bad as you make it sound. You already keep track of what the Patth are doing. Well, now's your chance to look for changes in attitude or travel locations or tech and start connecting brand-new dots."

For a few seconds Tera continued to glare at me. Then she took a deep breath and exhaled it. "They won't be happy about this," she warned. "They *really* won't be happy."

"Hopefully, they'll learn from their mistakes," I said. "So do Selene and I still have a job? Or are you cutting us loose right now?"

"You still have a job," Tera said reluctantly as she stood up. "The idea you floated for us a few months ago is nearly ready, and they'll need you for that. But when that's over...I can't promise anything."

"Understood," I said. "Just let us know. And you might remind them of all the chestnuts Selene and I have pulled out of the fire for them."

"I'll see what I can do." She hesitated. "For whatever it's worth, I don't blame you. Also for whatever it's worth . . ." Her lips compressed. "Maijo's a good man, and a good operative. But he tends to focus on the immediate situation and not the larger view."

"And he follows orders to the letter?"

"We're all supposed to do that," Tera reminded me. "I'm just saying that if your backup had instead been Jordan or Ixil, they'd have been here when you needed them, pull-back order or no."

"I know," I said. Oddly enough, I genuinely did. I'd had my differences with both of them, but when it came to crunch time both of them had always had our backs. "I hope this doesn't get them in hot water, too. *Or* get you there."

"Don't worry, we can handle it." She gave me the ghost of a smile. "Anyway, sometimes being in hot water means you're doing things right."

"We can hope," I said. "Good-bye, Tera."

"Good-bye, Gregory," she said. "Give my best to Selene."

Picking up the recorder, she headed out into the corridor. A minute later, I heard the sound of the entryway being opened and once again sealed.

I'd been sitting there an hour, gazing into my cola and thinking about the future, when Selene returned.

"Did you see him?" I asked as she took the seat across from me that Tera had recently occupied. "How was he?"

"Yes, I saw him," Selene said. "Huginn even let me have a few minutes alone with him."

"And?"

She shrugged, a deep weariness in her pupils. "He said he was fine," she said. "He told me Huginn had rescued him from Venikel and offered him a job with Sub-Director Nask and the Patth, and that he'd accepted."

"Did you warn him that the Patth were just using him?" I asked. "That they didn't care about him personally?"

"Yes," she said. "He said . . . he told me everyone has always used him—Lukki, the Javersin brothers, Galfvi." Her pupils took on an edge of quiet pain. "Us."

"I would argue that last," I said. "But maybe that's how it looked from his point of view. So he's set on going with Huginn?"

"They're already gone," she said. "I watched their shuttle lift. Did you see them take the portal?"

"Yes," I said, feeling an unreasonable surge of guilt. Unreasonable, because Selene had specifically asked me to let her see Tirano alone. Guilt, because I should have made it my business to be there for her afterward anyway. "It was interesting. Not as spectacular as I'd hoped."

"You should have tried to get closer," she said. "Seven Strands *was* a bit far away."

"Next time," I promised. "Brought home the scent of the platform on my shoes, did I?"

"Yes," she said. "How is Tera?"

"Mad at us for letting the portal go," I told her. "Probably not as mad as the admiral and his bosses will be when they get the full report on what happened here."

"Are we fired?"

"Not yet," I said. "Tera says they still need us for at least one more job. After that..." I shrugged. "I guess we'll just have to wait and see."

Selene nodded and fell silent. I went over to the pantry and got one of her favorite meal bars and a breakfast cola. "The *Ruth* looks to be back together," I said as I set them in front of her. "As soon as the maintenance office opens and we get final certification we'll be out of here."

"All right." She hesitated. "What do you think will happen with the portal?"

"No idea," I said. "It could be that the last users deliberately took out a few components and that it'll just be a matter of plugging in replacements to get it to work. It could just as easily be like the admiral warned, that those pieces burned out and the new ones will burn out, too. In that case, the Patth will have lost themselves a portal for nothing."

"And if it *does* work?"

I shook my head. "I don't know, Selene. They may find the other end of the portal abandoned. They might find whoever the client species was the Icari had collecting silver-silk for them. They might even find a remnant of the Icari themselves. Right now, it's a big fat gamble."

"You humans are supposed to be good at gambles like that."

"We used to be, anyway," I said. "Maybe not so much anymore. You worried that they'll find the people who the Kadolians used to work for?"

It was an insensitive question, and I wished instantly that I'd kept my mouth shut. But Selene didn't seem to notice. "I hope not," she said. "There's another possibility, Gregory. The people who disabled the Alainn portal may not have been trying to keep people here from traveling to the other end. They may have been trying to keep those at the other end from coming *here*."

I felt my stomach tighten. That thought hadn't even occurred to me. "In that case, we'd better hope the Path can't get it working," I said. "Or maybe not."

"What do you mean?" she asked, her pupils looking puzzled.

"Remember that the last place the people at the other end saw before they boarded up the portal was Alainn," I reminded her. "Not exactly the height of Spiral civilization or commerce. Definitely not the height of military capability. As my father used to say, *The enemy of my enemy may find himself having bitten off more than he can chew.*"

"I suppose." Selene paused. "But I presume that applies to both sides."

"Unfortunately, yes," I conceded. "And right now, we don't even know what the sides are."

"Or if you and I are part of any of them."

"Or that," I agreed soberly.

And that could be a problem...because as my father also used to say, *Just because no one notices the ant on the battlefield doesn't mean he's safe from getting stomped on along with everyone else.*

Selene and I had to figure out what side we were on, and figure it out fast. Or else we had to make damn sure we stayed off the battlefield.

I just hoped we could figure out what and where that battlefield was before it was too late.

The End